THE LAST STAND

ALSO BY MARION BLACKWOOD

Marion Blackwood has written lots of books across multiple series, and new books are constantly added to her catalogue. To see the most recently updated list of books, please visit: www.marionblackwood.com

CONTENT WARNINGS

The *Court of Elves* series contains violence, morally questionable actions, and later books in the series also contain some more detailed sexual content. If you have specific triggers, you can find the full list of content warnings at: www.marionblackwood.com/content-warnings

THE LAST STAND
COURT OF ELVES: BOOK SEVEN

MARION BLACKWOOD

Copyright © 2022 by Marion Blackwood

All rights reserved. No part of this book may be reproduced in any form or by any electronic or mechanical means, including information storage and retrieval systems, without permission in writing from the publisher, except by reviewers, who may quote brief passages in a review. For more information, contact info@marionblackwood.com

ISBN 978-91-987259-9-5 (hardcover)
ISBN 978-91-987259-3-3 (paperback)
ISBN 978-91-987259-2-6 (ebook)

Editing by Julia Gibbs

This is a work of fiction. Names, characters, places, and incidents either are the product of the author's imagination or are used fictitiously. Any resemblance to actual persons, living or dead, events, or locales is entirely coincidental.

www.marionblackwood.com

For everyone who has been through enough

CHAPTER 1

*H*aving ambition was incredibly dangerous. It had gotten me beaten up, betrayed, and imprisoned. And it had led me right into the middle of a war where I was at the top of the enemy's hit list. But as I looked around the sunlit forest, the only feeling in my chest was gratitude. Warm, sparkling gratitude. If I had been content with my lot in life, if I had stayed an indentured spy in the Court of Stone, I would never have met any of these extraordinary people. But because I hadn't been content, because I had ambition, because I fought and schemed to make my life better, I had met friends. Family. People who I now loved with all my heart. And once this was all over, we would have that wonderful life waiting for us. Together.

"Incoming!" Valerie called.

I scrambled out of the way as a sky whale dove down between the trees and opened its gigantic mouth. A series of loud bangs echoed into the late summer air as three wooden cabins fell from the whale's mouth and landed in a row along the edge of the clearing. The dark-haired elf seated atop the sky whale gave a cheerful wave before they flew back above the treetops.

"I thought I had seen it all, but this…" I shook my head in amazement at the massive sky-colored whales that descended from the heavens and dropped the completely intact buildings they had brought from Poisonwood Forest on the grass. "This is something else."

Mordren came to a halt next to me, his shoulder brushing against mine. "Agreed."

The firebird I had flown here on nudged me in the ribs. I let out a soft chuckle and drew my fingers through its fiery plumage.

"Yeah, you're pretty cool too," I assured it.

A contented rumble went through its red and orange chest. Flames rippled over its body as the firebird shook out its feathers before leaping into the sky. Craning my neck, I watched it as it joined the mass of birds in every shape and color currently descending on the forest.

"Finally," Idra said as she and the two thieves came to stand next to us as well. "Something good is happening in this place."

Theo and Valerie glanced at her, but they didn't ask her to elaborate further. I was still the only one who knew what she had been through here at the hands of Prince André Truthseeker. When she was ready, she would tell them. And if she never was, that was fine too. Valerie and Theo never talked about their past either, and we never pried.

Eilan zigzagged through a cluster of midnight foxes before jogging up to us, while Mendar came striding towards our small group from the other side of the clearing. A blood panther prowled next to him.

"Hadeon, Ellyda, and Vendir?" Mordren asked as Eilan took up position on his left.

Eilan smoothened his windswept hair before replying, "They're approaching on Orma right now."

The Prince of Shadows gave his brother a nod right as Mendar reached us.

"This is incredible," the leader of the Poisonwood elves said as he spread his arms to indicate the area around us while coming to a halt next to Theo. "The forest is huge, and healthy. There are mountains and lakes and streams and glens full of flowers and mushrooms that aren't hallucinogenic." A hint of uncertainty swirled in his brown eyes as he looked at us. "Is it really okay that we make this our home?"

"Yes," Idra said firmly as she held his gaze. "You and your people and all of the animals, make yourselves at home and fill this place with life again. I have one request, though."

"Anything."

A carefully constructed mask that showed no emotions fell across Idra's features as she raised an arm to point towards the far side of the clearing. "There is an old castle that way. Please tear it down and build something new."

Surprise flickered across Mendar's face, but he inclined his head in acknowledgement. Golden light danced over the crown of spiky red branches that still sat firmly around his brow when he straightened.

"We will need to stay here with you for the time being," Mordren said. "At least until we know what has happened to the rest of our lands."

"Of course." Mendar pushed his long black hair back behind his shoulder before motioning towards the swooping sky whales. "As soon as all the buildings are down, we'll find cabins for you all."

"Much obliged. We–"

"I can't handle this anymore," Ellyda's voice cut through the air.

We all turned to see her stalking towards us with Hadeon and Vendir hurrying along behind her. Pain and desperation shone across her entire face.

"I can't handle it," she repeated. "There have been too many people, too many new experiences, too much sensory input, too much *everything*." Her voice cracked on the final word and her violet eyes were wild and panicked as she stopped in front of Mendar. "I need somewhere empty and quiet. I need to recharge. And I can't do that when there are people and things happening all around me all the time. Please."

"Oh, yes, of course." Mendar raised his hand as if to steer her away, but stopped right before touching her and instead motioned towards a row of cabins. "This way."

Blowing a sharp whistle, he flashed a couple of hand signs at Endira. The white-haired elf nodded from across the grass before she left to go carry out whatever order she had been given. Ellyda didn't even look back at us as she disappeared with Mendar, but we all watched her go.

"I'll stay here with her," Hadeon said. Worry swirled in his red eyes. "She's in really bad shape right now and I wanna be here for her when she comes out of it."

"I'll stay too," Idra announced.

"Me too," Vendir added. When the two warriors turned to look at him, he cleared his throat and gestured towards the messy camp. "Someone needs to help the Poisonwood elves set up their camp. Especially since I'm assuming that this will be our base for a while too."

Theo looked after the disappearing Ellyda for another few

seconds before shifting his gaze to us. "We want to stay and help too, of course, but first we need to check in with our gang and make sure they're all okay."

"Yeah." Valerie nodded, and then turned towards Eilan. "Any chance you can help worldwalk us there?"

"Sure," he replied before raising his eyes to Mordren. "Someone needs to contact the other princes, though."

"Kenna and I will handle that."

"Court of Trees?" Idra asked, though it felt like it was more of a statement.

Mordren nodded. "Yes. Iwdael should be the easiest one to find."

Silence fell as we all just looked at one another for a few seconds. This somehow felt like the beginning of the end. As long as we were standing there, hidden in a forest in the Court of Light, the rest of the world seemed very far away. But once we worldwalked out, the battle would begin. The final war to save our people and our courts from having to worship High Commander Anron as our new god. And it would begin as soon as we left here and made the first move.

Drawing in a breath, I gave my friends a decisive nod. "If we're not back by nightfall, assume that we have been taken."

"We'll come for you if that happens," Hadeon said as he looked between me and Mordren.

"Let's hope it doesn't come to that." I shifted my gaze to Eilan and the two thieves. "Good luck."

"You too."

After exchanging one last look, Mordren wrapped a hand around my waist and worldwalked us out.

To the Court of Trees.

The place where we would make our first move in this war.

CHAPTER 2

Another forest appeared around us. I fought down a flash of nausea as the world righted itself and I stepped out of Mordren's embrace.

"You still get nauseous when someone else worldwalks you?" he asked, amusement lacing his voice.

"Yes," I muttered and swallowed again before clearing my throat. "Which is why I prefer to do it myself."

A sly smile spread across his lips. "Well, I was feeling nostalgic."

"Uh-huh." I rolled my eyes at him before turning to study the area around us. Confusion flitted through me. "Where are we?"

The Court of Trees had no logical structure to it. Everything was just spread out randomly over a gigantic forest, which meant that there were very few discernable landmarks that would help with navigation. And out here, there were only trees. For all I knew, Mordren could have dropped us anywhere in the forest.

"A bit northwest of Iwdael's castle," he answered before motioning towards my left. "If we head that way, we should reach the edge of the buildings around the castle soon."

Nodding, I started in the direction he pointed. A second later, Mordren fell in beside me. We walked in silence since we didn't know when we might run into a potential enemy, but I studied the woods around me as I walked.

It had been weeks since we left for Valdanar, and summer would be coming to an end soon. The Court of Trees didn't really follow the natural order of the seasons, but I had learned to recognize the signs. And now, the trees we passed had a gold-tinted hue to them and the bushes were heavy with ripe berries, which I knew meant that we were approaching fall in a few weeks.

The sound of voices up ahead made my gaze snap back to the area in front of us. A couple of buildings were visible there as well, but we should have still been a long way from the castle and any crowded areas. After exchanging a glance, Mordren and I snuck forward on silent feet.

Bronze glinted a few strides away.

Mordren pushed me up against a tree and pressed himself close to me as well. My heart thumped in my chest. Moving slowly, we leaned out and glanced around the thick tree trunk.

Dread raked its icy fingers up my spine.

The forest up ahead was teeming with High Elves. Golden light glinted off their polished breastplates as they moved slowly but systematically in every direction. Swords and bows swung at their sides. It looked like they were searching for something. Or *someone*.

We had known that Anron would make it back before us,

but we hadn't expected him to start making his moves so soon. When we returned to our island, we had approached from the back and landed directly in the Court of Light to evade the air serpents he probably had patrolling the sky. Apparently, he had sent out search parties to find the other princes straight away as well. And he had Princess Syrene on his side.

Mordren placed soft fingers under my chin and turned my face back to him. *"We have to go back,"* he mouthed at me.

I nodded.

If Princess Syrene knew about Iwdael's hiding places in this forest, the Court of Trees might be more compromised than we thought. I flicked my gaze from side to side as we edged backwards and away from the searching soldiers. We couldn't afford to get spotted. But we also couldn't leave because we had to find Prince Iwdael.

A blast of wind hit me in the back.

Pain and shock flashed through me as I was thrown off my feet and flew through the air. How the hell had a High Elf managed to get behind us? We had just come from that direction.

Another bout of pain pulsed through my body as I smacked into a tree and tumbled to the ground.

"We've caught someone!" a voice yelled from terribly close by.

Sucking in a breath, I blinked and tried to clear my head while struggling to my feet and drawing my blades all at the same time. The dark brown tree trunks swam around me. I leaped back just as something whistled through the air.

Thuds echoed into the forest as a rain of arrows hit the tree where I had been standing only seconds ago.

THE LAST STAND

From a short distance away, screams suddenly split the air. My heart pounded in my chest as I tried to keep the archers in view while also figuring out where Mordren was.

Another volley of arrows sped towards me from the left. I raised a fire shield that incinerated them right as I spotted Mordren. Half of the High Elves around him were on their knees screaming. The others were battling his shadows. I took off towards him.

Lightning cut through the air. I threw myself backwards and barely managed to avoid getting struck by the bolt. It cracked into a tree, leaving a black scorch mark on the trunk.

"Careful!" a soldier snapped. "It's the Prince of Shadows and the Lady of Fire. High Commander Anron wants them alive."

Rolling to my feet, I swung my sword in a wide arc as a group of soldiers swarmed me. They leaped back and I managed to straighten in time to meet the blade coming for my neck. Steel clanged into the warm air as I blocked his attack. Shoving his sword away with one hand, I flicked my knife with the other.

A scythe of flame shot towards the High Elves on my right. Screams ripped from their throats as they dove for cover, but a wave of water washed down from the side and extinguished the fire before it could do any real damage. I had a lot more fire power to throw at them, but I couldn't go all out. If I did, I would burn down the whole forest.

The soldier on my left swung his sword at me again. I leaped aside to evade it while shooting another flaming scythe at the enemies on my right. Steam hissed and spread through the trees like mist as another wall of water stopped my attack. Ducking under another sword strike, I rammed my knife into the second soldier. My blade carved a deep rut in his armor but did nothing to actually hurt him.

Panic pulsed through me.

There were too many of them. My one advantage was that they had to be careful not to kill me, while I didn't have to show the same restraint. But I couldn't keep fighting this many people all at the same time. I was good. But I wasn't that good.

Shadows and fire flashed in the corner of my eye as Mordren fought the soldiers who surrounded him. Screams of pain still echoed through the woods. The sound pounded against my eardrums and masked some of the noise from my own attackers.

Dodging another sword strike, I jumped back and raised my knife to cast more fire to keep the rest at bay.

My breath exploded from my chest as a High Elf soldier rammed me from the other side. His massive frame landed on top of me as we crashed down on the thick grass. My lungs screamed for air but I yanked my hand up and stabbed the soldier in the neck before he could get his wits about him again.

Blood sprayed through the air as I pulled out the knife and drew my knees up. The High Elf's hand flew up to his throat as if that would stop the death that now hovered over him. Stunned shock bounced in his pale green eyes. Using my knees and my arms, I heaved him to the side to get his weight off me. Wet gurgling came from his throat as he toppled over. I sucked in a desperate breath.

Crushed flowers clung to my clothes as I rolled out from underneath him and got ready to leap to my feet.

A boot was planted on my chest, shoving me back down. Dull pain spread through my shoulder blades as my back hit the ground once more. I yanked up my knife to stab the foot keeping me pinned, but bronze gleamed from all sides of me.

"Grab her!" the soldier above me snapped.

Dread seared through me as a strong hand shot down and caught my wrist before I could ram my knife through the boot on my chest. I twisted my other hand, trying to get my sword in position, but another soldier grabbed that arm as well.

Blinding panic crackled through me as hands came down on my arms and legs from all sides. I kicked and thrashed against them. The hands around my limbs tightened and the soldier above me shifted more of his weight over to the foot on my chest until I thought my ribs were going to snap like twigs. A gasp slipped my lips as I fought against the soldiers keeping me trapped and the panic that threatened to drown me. But it was useless. There were too many of them. And they were too strong.

The pressure on my body disappeared in a flash, and bloodcurdling screams tore through the forest. Air rushed back into my lungs as I sucked in a deep breath. The hands holding me down were gone so I leaped to my feet to find the soldiers around me doubled over on the ground, screaming their lungs out.

My gaze snapped to the other side.

Mordren stared straight back at me as he continued sending waves of pain magic rolling over my attackers. Bronze flashed behind him.

"Watch out!" I screamed as I leaped away from the soldiers and darted towards Mordren.

An armored fist slammed into his side.

Since he had used his magic to help me, his own attackers had received an opening to take him down. My heart squeezed painfully as Mordren stumbled to the side. The soldiers behind me stopped screaming as his magic faltered and the forest was suddenly eerily silent.

I slashed my blades through the air, sending a barrage of flaming scythes at Mordren's attackers. The ones on the right dove aside while a white-haired soldier on the left raised a wall of water. Steam exploded into the air.

Mordren struggled upright and sent a mass of shadows at the soldier who had punched him, but another attacker wrapped an arm around his neck from behind. I leaped over a fallen tree and shot a concentrated line of fire straight at the enemy behind Mordren. A sizzling noise cut through the forest as the fire burned a hole right through the High Elf's body. He collapsed screaming to the ground.

Running straight for a boulder, I jumped onto it while calling, "Mordren! Pain circle. Now."

He spun in a circle, sending massive waves of intense pain over the soldiers around him. Cries of agony split the air. They fell back and doubled over on the ground, but the High Elves who had attacked me were already racing for us again.

I pushed off from the edge of the boulder.

Wind whipped in my hair as I flew through the air straight at Mordren. He timed his circular movements so that he was facing me right when I reached him. My arms wrapped around his body, and his around mine, as I connected with him. The force sent us toppling over. But it didn't matter.

The moment I had a firm grip on him, I worldwalked us out together before any of the soldiers could grab either of us again.

Thick grass greeted us as we slammed down on the ground. Both Mordren and I let out a huff on impact. Silence so loud that it was deafening rang in my ears.

Lying on Mordren's stomach, I gazed down into his

glittering silver eyes. His lethal muscles pressed into my body as he held me tight, his arms around me. A small smile tugged at my lips.

"Well, that was fun," I said.

He chuckled, making his chest shake against mine. "Hmm. I have to say, though, I prefer our current position to our previous ones."

Shifting underneath me, he sat up while moving me with him until I straddled his lap. Blades of grass clung to his shining black hair. I reached up and plucked them out, letting them flutter back to the ground.

His fingers wrapped around my wrist. Moving my hand away from his hair, he placed my fingers against his jaw and kissed my palm.

"Are you okay?" he asked, his eyes searching my face.

"Yeah," I assured him. "We should probably get going, though. I dropped us in the glen I worldwalk to when I'm going to Stella's hut, so there could be people close by."

After tucking a loose curl behind my ear, he brushed a soft kiss over my lips and then nodded. "Alright. Let's go then."

I climbed off his lap and then pushed to my feet. Next to me, Mordren straightened as well and smoothened down his dark shirt before running his fingers through his slightly messy hair. I shook out the crushed flowers from my hair and clothes too.

Once we looked fairly presentable, we started in the direction that would take us away from Stella's hut and the other buildings farther in.

Sneaking through the trees, we put as much distance between us and the populated areas as we could without making noise. As long as we stayed on this side, we should be able to search the forest without being noticed.

For a while, we only walked through the woods in silence.

"We still need to find Iwdael," I finally said in a soft voice while glancing over at Mordren. "If we–"

A hand slammed across my mouth as I was yanked sideways and shoved into a tree.

CHAPTER 3

Panic flashed through my chest as the arms that had come out of nowhere kept a tight grip on me. I sent a pulse of fire up and down my body. The attacker sucked in a sharp breath and let go before the flames found their mark. Yanking out my blades, I whirled around right as someone let out a muffled groan of pain next to me.

Leaves fluttered down to reveal a gorgeous elf with long silver hair and turquoise eyes as she crumpled to the ground under the weight of Mordren's pain magic. I snapped my gaze back to where my attacker should be.

Nothing.

Only a brown tree trunk stared back at me.

"In hindsight, we should probably have led with a *hello*," a voice said behind us.

I spun around and blinked at the third person who had appeared seemingly out of thin air. Twinkling yellow eyes met me before they shifted to the Prince of Shadows.

"Mordren, if you could stop torturing my lover, I would appreciate that very much." Iwdael Vineweaver, the Prince of

Trees, shot Mordren an amused look before fixing his gaze on the tree next to me. "Augustien, you can come out now."

The waves of pain must have ended because the beautiful elf kneeling on the grass removed the hand she had been biting to stop her cries of pain, and instead blew out a shuddering breath. At the same time, the brown tree trunk next to me shimmered. I stumbled back a step in surprise as Augustien, the golden-haired elf who had been Iwdael's lover when we left, became visible in front of the tree.

"Thank you," Prince Iwdael said when the turquoise-eyed beauty struggled to her feet. "I would introduce you, but we're in a high-risk area so we should probably leave first, don't you think?"

"Lead the way," Mordren said.

Iwdael set off at a brisk pace. Once we had covered a short distance, he glanced back at me and Mordren and said, "Keep walking."

Before we could even reply, he grabbed Augustien and worldwalked away.

"He'll be back," the female elf said, even though I had already guessed as much. "He needs to worldwalk us back to the camp one at a time."

"Thanks, uhm...?" I began.

"Reena," she filled in.

"Reena. How did you know that we were there?"

"Prince Iwdael keeps scouts throughout the forest so that we know when the High Elves are getting too close and we need to move our camp. They saw you when you walked through."

"Ah. How–"

The Prince of Trees materialized a few steps in front of us. "Reena, darling, if you please."

She closed the final distance to him and wrapped an arm around his waist.

"Keep walking," he said to us again before the two of them disappeared.

Leaves rustled in the canopy above as a warm wind whirled through the forest. It made the sunlight flicker against the green foliage like tiny gems. I cast a glance over my shoulder to make sure that we had left the High Elves far behind, before turning back to Mordren.

"Looks like we didn't need to worry about Princess Syrene outsmarting Iwdael and finding his hideout," I commented.

"Indeed." A slight smile tugged at Mordren's lips. "He may be laid back and disorganized, and he lets his feelings get the better of him at times, but Iwdael is a lot smarter than most people give him credit for."

The prince in question appeared in front of me a second later and held out a hand. "Well then, Kenna, shall we?" He shifted his gaze to Mordren. "Ke–"

"Keep walking," Mordren filled in. "I know."

Iwdael chuckled.

Taking his hand, I stepped into his embrace. Then I was worldwalked away by someone else for the second time that day. My stomach rolled as we materialized in a different part of the forest that looked exactly the same as the one we had left behind.

"You okay?" Iwdael asked as I blew out a steadying breath.

"I'm fine."

"Splendid." He swept his long brown hair over his shoulder, making the leaves and twigs that decorated it shift and sway. "One moment, please."

Before I could say anything else, he was gone. Blowing out

a soft chuckle, I shook my head and turned to find Reena standing there alone.

"Where is Augustien?" I asked.

"Prince Iwdael sent him ahead to let the others know."

"Others? Who else is here?"

"The Court of Water."

The air vibrated next to me. A moment later, Iwdael returned with Mordren. The Prince of Shadows straightened his suit before giving him a nod of thanks.

"Rayan is here too?" I asked before Iwdael could say anything.

A bright smile lit up his handsome face. "Yes. And Lilane too."

"We should probably save our story for when we're back at your camp then."

"That sounds reasonable." His yellow eyes glittered as he stole a glance at me while he strode forwards. "But maybe I can get a hint. Was it a successful mission?"

"Yes. And no."

"Ah, so there is a long story attached to it."

"I'm afraid so."

"Well, we'd best get a move on then." Iwdael threw an arm around Reena and leaned down to kiss her cheek as they walked. "Are you alright, darling?"

She flicked a glance at Mordren as he and I fell in beside them.

"Yes, I'm okay," she replied.

I nudged Mordren in the ribs. Raising his brows, he glanced down at me. I just looked back at him expectantly. After discreetly rolling his eyes at me, he cleared his throat.

"My apologies," he said to Reena. "I believed you were an enemy back there."

"It's okay," she repeated, but a small smile blew across her lips.

Prince Iwdael matched it, apparently satisfied that Mordren had apologized to her, and then he kissed her cheek again. I watched them curiously.

"What is it?" Iwdael asked, his voice full of amusement.

A slight blush crept into my cheeks. "Nothing."

"You're wondering what happened to Augustien."

I cleared my throat, embarrassed that he had seen right through me, before admitting, "Yeah."

"Oh, Augustien and I are still a thing. And so are Reena and I." Mischief glittered in his eyes. "I've always said that love was too wonderful a force to limit to only one person."

Reena laughed pleasantly and wrapped an arm around his back. Warmth spread through my chest as I watched them. Iwdael always seemed to spread love and joy around him wherever he went. And I respected him a lot for that. Once this was over, I might even need to take some lessons from him on how to just relax and enjoy life.

Beautiful wooden buildings rose before us. I stared at them. I had called their hideout a camp but it was really more of a village.

"Uhm...?" I said very eloquently.

Iwdael laughed and winked at me. "That's one of the perks of being the Prince of Trees. If I want a house, I just wave my hands and *poof*... a house."

"Wow," I said.

Mordren swept his gaze over the bustling camp before giving Iwdael an appreciative nod. "How convenient."

He grinned. "Isn't it?"

"Mordren!" a voice called from between the buildings. "Kenna. You're back."

A smile spread across my face as Rayan Floodbender, the Prince of Water, strode out in front of us. His long black hair billowed behind him and his purple eyes glittered with excitement. Surprise fluttered through my chest as he drew me into a hug.

"Please tell me that you have good news," he said once he had stepped back again.

Mordren and I exchanged a glance before looking between the two princes.

"It's a long story," I said.

Iwdael nodded since he already knew that. "Let's go sit down."

"Yes, we…" Prince Rayan narrowed his eyes at me as he at last took in the state of me and Mordren. "Why do you look like you've just been in a fight?"

I cleared my throat sheepishly.

"Oh, by all the spirits," Rayan muttered before huffing out a laugh. "Yes, let's go sit down indeed so that I can heal you two while you tell me this long story of yours."

Some ushering and a few brief but enthusiastic greetings later, we found ourselves seated at a table in Iwdael's cabin. Rayan and his wife Lilane Frostsinger sat opposite us while the Prince of Trees had taken the seat at the head of the table. After a few gulps of water, we launched into the tale of what had happened when we went to Valdanar. As we started, Rayan rose and walked around the table to heal both old and new injuries before sitting down next to his wife again.

All of them raised their eyebrows in surprise when we told them about the elves and animals from Poisonwood who had accompanied us here, and they all frowned at the cruel actions of the empress and emperor. Since they didn't know that Eilan was a shapeshifter, we glossed over that part and instead told them about how we had manipulated Lester and Danser into backing us up.

"So unfortunately, the emperor and empress won't kill Anron for us," I finished.

"But we can now kill him ourselves and they will thank us for it instead of sending their whole army to wipe us out?" Prince Rayan asked.

"Yes."

He and Iwdael exchanged a look. "Then I would call that a success."

"Partly a success, I guess."

Lilane laughed, making everyone turn to look at her. Her long brown hair rippled as she shook her head before her glittering brown eyes slid to Mordren. "You know, I have always thought you were quite scary when you schemed. No offense."

"None taken," Mordren assured her while a satisfied smirk tugged at his lips.

She turned to me. "And when you outmaneuvered Volkan and schemed your way onto the throne in the Court of Fire, I thought you were quite scary too." Another pleasant laugh filled the air as she looked between me and Mordren while shaking her head again. "But when the two of you are scheming together, you're downright terrifying. Do you know that?"

"Oh Lilane," Iwdael began, mirth sparkling in his eyes too. "Don't feed their egos like that. We'll never hear the end of it."

Mordren narrowed his eyes at him, which Iwdael only answered with a wink.

"What he means is," Rayan began as he shot an exasperated look at Iwdael, "well done."

I nodded in acknowledgement before lifting a hand to

motion towards the open window. "And it looks like you've been busy too."

"Yes," the Prince of Water confirmed. "We have been sneaking people out of our courts and breaking the bracelets with the sword Ellyda made. It's slow going, but at least it's going."

"And Edric?"

"We take turns guarding the magic inside the temple. Right now, it's Edric's turn."

"We'll need to get word to him that–"

Loud banging cut through the cabin as someone pounded on the door.

"Prince Iwdael," a male voice called. "We've caught Rose wandering through the forest."

Chairs scraped against the floor as the five of us shot to our feet. Striding across the wooden floorboards, Iwdael threw open the door and looked down at an elf with short black hair.

"Who?" Iwdael asked.

"Rose," the scout said. "She's a worldwalker from the Court of Shadows. She used to have a bracelet, but she doesn't have it anymore. But none of us have broken her out." His green eyes were full of confusion. "So how did she get free?"

Iwdael turned to Mordren. "Do you know who she is?"

"Yes. She is Imelda's daughter."

"The healer?"

"Yes."

Imelda had sold us out to Anron earlier because he had been threatening her daughter. And now that daughter was suddenly free and was wandering around the Court of Trees. Worry coursed through my body.

This could not be good.

CHAPTER 4

My stomach was still trying to recover from yet another worldwalking trip when Iwdael materialized with Mordren next to me. The Prince of Shadows took a step forward, completely unbothered, while I drew in a steadying breath and straightened. A pair of piercing blue eyes stared back at us from across the small glen.

"My prince," said the elf I assumed to be Rose.

Two of Iwdael's scouts were holding on to her arms, presumably to stop her from just worldwalking away, but she bowed her head to Mordren. Her long black hair rippled as she straightened again before shifting those breathtaking blue eyes to me and Iwdael, who were the only other people in the clearing since Rayan and Lilane had stayed behind in case this turned out to be a trap.

"Prince Iwdael," she said. "Lady Firesoul."

"Rose," Mordren began, raking his scrutinizing gaze over her. "We were under the impression that you were Anron's captive. How are you here?"

She glanced over her shoulder as if making sure that said High Elf wasn't lurking behind her. "He set me free so that I could deliver a message to you. And as a gesture of good faith."

"Good faith?"

"Yes, my prince. He knows that you know who I am and..." She shifted uncomfortably on her feet and flicked worried eyes between the ground and Mordren's face. "And what my mother... did."

"I see." Mordren's voice was smooth and calm. "And what was the message?"

"Prince Iwdael."

I whirled around at the sound of that very familiar voice. A half-elf with short copper-colored hair had materialized on the thick bed of grass and flowers behind us. Warm light from the afternoon sun filtered down through the fresh green leaves around us and cast golden shapes across his freckled face.

"Felix," I blurted out.

He blinked at me in surprise. "Kenna."

"What are you doing here?"

Felix was a worldwalker who worked for Prince Edric in the Court of Stone. We had been friendly when I lived there, but he had also been madly in love with Monette, and even though she had used him almost as much as she had used me, it hadn't been until I helped them escape from Anron that Felix had at last broken away from her.

"I have a message for Prince Iwdael." Felix's brown eyes drifted to the Prince of Trees and then darted between Mordren, Rose, and the two scouts before finally returning to me. Uncertainty blew across his face. "But it looks like you're, uhm... busy."

"Yes, we are indeed in the middle of something." Amusement tugged at Iwdael's lips. "Would you mind just waiting there for a few minutes?"

Felix smiled sheepishly and moved a little to the side. I gave him a small smile back.

Leaves rustled around us as a late summer wind caressed the trees. Pushing a loose curl back behind my ear, I turned to face Rose again. Mordren and Iwdael did the same.

"Now, the message if you please, Rose," Mordren said.

"Yes, my prince." She flicked her gaze between me and Mordren. "High Commander Anron ordered me to tell you that he wants to talk to you and Lady Firesoul."

I furrowed my brows. Talk? Was there really anything left to say at this point?

"About what?" I asked.

"He wants to offer you a deal, but for what, he didn't say." She rolled her shoulder, and the scout holding on to her arm tightened his grip. "He only told me to worldwalk to the Court of Trees and wander around until someone found me and brought me to you. And then to tell you that he wanted to offer you a deal and that he is waiting for you right now."

"Right now?"

"Yes."

"Where?"

My frown deepened as she described a remote location in the desert in the Court of Fire. What was Anron up to?

"This is a trap." Prince Iwdael studied Rose for another few seconds before shifting his attention to us. "If you go, you will be worldwalking into an ambush."

"Maybe." I ran a hand over my jaw and then turned back to Rose. "Did he say if he was alone?"

She nodded. "Yes, he said that he would be alone. He also

said that you can bring as many people as you want, but he recommends coming alone. There will be no fighting under the flag of parley, that's what he said."

"Oh, this is definitely a trap," Iwdael announced and crossed his arms.

"But what if it isn't?" I looked between him and Mordren. "If Anron truly is alone, this might be our chance to kill him."

Both Mordren and Iwdael opened their mouths, but someone else beat them to it.

"Only one way to find out."

I whipped around. "Felix, wait!"

He only flashed me a mischievous grin and disappeared.

A groan ripped from my throat. I ran a hand over the hilt of my blades and cracked my neck while feeling the magic inside me burn hotter. I had used the weeks it had taken to get back to our lands to train until I had regained control of my now much more powerful fire magic. If Felix wasn't back in exactly one minute, I would worldwalk over there and rain hell down on Anron.

"When the hell did he get this bold?" I muttered.

Prince Iwdael chuckled. "Well, he has been the main line of communication between our courts ever since you got us out of that castle. He has really stepped up. And he has done it well."

Felix materialized in the exact same spot as before, once more filling up the footprints that he had left in the thick grass.

"High Commander Anron is standing there next to that big boulder," he announced. "And he's alone. I worldwalked to a few random spots a bit farther out in every direction, but there's no one else there."

The rest of us exchanged a glance.

"Then this might be our chance to kill him," I said at last.

Mordren gave me a slow nod. "Agreed."

"There's no talking you out of this, is there?" Iwdael huffed.

I flashed him a wicked smile. "I'm afraid not."

Steel sang into the humming forest as I drew my sword and knife. A couple of birds flapped away at the sound, as if they knew that it signaled bloodshed to come. Spinning the blades in my hands, I met Mordren's gaze.

"Well then, let's go kill the High Commander."

CHAPTER 5

Red sand stretched out as far as the eye could see. The air out here was so warm that it vibrated over the sand, but it didn't bother me anymore. Not since I had claimed my fire magic.

As soon as the world righted itself around me, I snuck forward on silent feet. High Commander Anron was standing with his back to me, exactly where Felix had said he would be. Raising my sword, I got ready to stab Anron through the back of the neck the moment that Mordren appeared in front of the commander and created a distraction.

"You should know," Anron began right before Mordren worldwalked in. "My legion will systematically wipe out your whole courts if you kill me here under the flag of parley."

Mordren froze. And so did I. His shadows had already wrapped around Anron's ankles, preventing him from moving, and my blade was hovering a mere breath away from his skin. Repositioning the sword, I placed it against Anron's carotid artery. He didn't even flinch at the cold touch of steel.

"If you do that, there will be no one to draw magic from," I challenged.

"I know. But I would already be dead so what do I care about that?"

"You wouldn't dare."

He let out a vicious laugh. "Oh you have no idea just how spiteful I can be when pushed far enough."

Keeping the blade steady, I shifted my position so that I could meet Mordren's gaze from where I stood behind Anron's back. Most of our courts were still trapped by those magic-blocking bracelets, which meant that they wouldn't be able to fight back if the whole legion decided to start slaughtering civilians. Anron could be bluffing. But there was no way to know for sure. And given our history, I wouldn't put it past him.

Mordren gave me a small shake of his head.

I agreed. We couldn't risk it.

After removing the sword from Anron's neck, I slowly circled him while keeping my blades out until I had reached Mordren. Anron cast an expectant glance at the black tendrils still snaking across the red sand. For a moment, Mordren only stared back at him. Then he pulled back his shadows.

"Prince Mordren," Anron said before he slid his calculating blue eyes to me. "And the Lady of Fire. Or is it *Princess* of Fire?" His voice took on a mocking tone. "I forget."

Since he had been to my coronation, he knew very well that the title of princess was a step down from prince. He was trying to bait me, but I wouldn't give him the satisfaction so I let an equally smug smirk curl my own lips.

"Anron," I said instead, leaving out his title entirely.

"Trying to kill someone during a parley." He tutted and shook his head at us. "How uncivilized."

"Invading our lands and stealing our magic." I flashed him a smile dripping with sweet poison. "How uncivilized."

Anron chuckled before switching topic. "When did you get back, *Princess?*"

"A while ago," I lied smoothly since we couldn't very well tell him that we had only just arrived because we had brought the whole of Poisonwood with us.

"Get to the point," Mordren cut in.

The blazing sun beat down from the pale blue heavens and reflected off Anron's beautifully decorated breastplate as he shifted his weight and cocked his head. Long brown hair slid over his armored shoulder. I flexed my fingers on my hilts.

"You lied about the magic," High Commander Anron announced.

My blood froze. I had suspected that he had figured that out back in Valdanar, but I had still been desperately hoping that I was wrong. Keeping a carefully neutral mask on my face, I only continued looking back at him in silence. I wasn't going to give anything away if I didn't have to. But my heart started up a nervous staccato when a sharp smile stretched his lips.

"I can't believe I didn't put it together sooner." Anron shook his head in a show of regret. "Your king had stone magic. As does Prince Edric. That means that there has to be at least two sources of magic for each element."

The desert said nothing. And neither did we. Anron's smile only widened, as if he was enjoying this.

"So, here is my deal for you." He reached into his armor and pulled out a small stack of black bracelets that he let dangle from his fingers as he held them out in front of himself. "Tell me where the magic is and put on the bracelets. In exchange, I will spare the rest of your people. Everyone else in this land will get their magic back." He wiggled his fingers, making the magic-siphoning jewelry rattle. "I'll take these off everyone. If... you and the other three princes put them on and also give me the rest of the magic."

Silence fell as he waited for our answer. I tightened the grip on my blades and then glanced over at Mordren. His silver eyes held the same answer that pulsed through my whole soul. We looked back at Anron.

"No," we said in unison.

Genuine surprise flashed across his face.

"You're outnumbered here," I said and raised my chin in challenge. "Your army might be stronger but the people of this continent far outnumber your legion. And I think you will find that they like self-proclaimed gods about as much as we do."

Anron recovered from his surprise and instead shot me a mocking smirk. "Big words, Princess. As it always is with you. But the reality is quite different. Yes, the people of these lands might outnumber us." His smirk sharpened. "But more than half of them are human. What are you going to do? Make them stand on each other's shoulders so that they can even reach our necks and swing their tiny blades at us? They're weak, and you know it. And you Low Elves might have your specialized powers, but there are too few of you and even fewer who have magic suited for battle." He drew himself up to his full formidable height and looked down at us like we were children. "Face it. You are outmatched. But if you do as I say, everyone will live a happy life."

Mordren snorted. "Right."

"Well, everyone except for you. The general public will be left alone as long as they accept Queen Syrene as their worldly leader and me as their god. Even the other three princes will be free to do as they please. Though they will still have to wear the bracelets. But you..." Malice gleamed in his eyes. "I told you that I can be incredibly vindictive when pushed too far. And you, you have pushed me too far. Your life would not be easy, I will be honest about that. But at least you can take comfort in knowing that you saved everyone else from being slaughtered in a war you cannot hope to win."

"I don't think you heard us the first time," I said. "The answer is no."

Surprise flickered in his eyes again. "You would truly decline my offer? An offer that guarantees mercy for everyone but you? I thought you were supposed to be the good guys."

A wicked smile spread across Mordren's lips. "Whatever gave you that impression?"

"You will come to regret this decision." He locked his gaze with Mordren for a few seconds before turning his cold blue eyes on me. "When your friends are lying slaughtered around you in droves, you will regret that you spit on my mercy."

"We've already told you," I began. "The people of these lands, human and elves, don't want new gods. They have no interest in worshipping someone who brought war and death to their home. And I have no interest in giving up my power and freedom."

Mordren flashed him a sharp smile. "I think you will find that we can be quite spiteful too."

High Commander Anron snorted and shook his head at us.

Spinning my sword in my hand, I gave him a quick rise and fall of my eyebrows, and called up my worldwalking powers. "We'll see you on the battlefield."

CHAPTER 6

*E*lves hurried back and forth like ants. I jerked back and blinked in surprise as Mordren and I appeared in Iwdael's camp and found it full of people who were packing up their gear.

"Kenna!" Lilane Frostsinger called from a few strides away. Twisting around, she nudged Prince Rayan in the ribs. "Darling, they're back."

The Prince of Water turned to look at us before raising his voice. "Iwdael!"

A moment later, Iwdael stuck his head out of a doorway. After giving us a quick onceover, he briefly disappeared inside again. I stared at the empty doorway while Rayan and Lilane made their way over to us.

"Uhm," I began and flicked my gaze around the busy camp. "What's going on?"

Before they could answer, Iwdael jumped out of the building. I flinched and a spike of ingrained fear flashed up my spine when I noticed the item in his hand. Fire flared to life along my arms as I whipped my head from side to side.

"Are we under attack?" I demanded.

Next to me, Mordren's body had tensed up as well.

"Oh, spirits, no," Iwdael said as he strolled up to us. "Not at all."

My pulse was still thrumming in my ears but I blew out a long breath, snuffing out the fire along my arms, and instead pointed to the wooden weapon in his hand. "Then what's with that?"

"Oh, this?" Iwdael lifted the massive bow he was carrying and held it out in front of himself as if studying it. Mischief glinted in his eyes. "We've always known how to make them. I just figured it was time to use them. Conquering old fears and all that."

"Besides," Lilane added, "we need more long-range weapons. And if the High Elves are using them, we might as well use them too."

"Good call," Mordren said as he gave them an appreciative nod.

"Yes, it is." Iwdael grinned at him. "How did the meeting with our resident megalomaniac go?"

"He offered us a deal," Mordren answered. "If all five of us put on the bracelets and also give him the bowls of magic, he will free all the other citizens as long as they bow to Syrene as their queen and worship Anron as their god."

Rayan raised his dark brows. "And what did you say?"

"We very politely told him to fuck off."

A laugh bubbled from Iwdael's throat as he slapped Mordren on the shoulder. "Good man. What a tedious life that would have been. And life is far too long and far too short to be spent doing anything other than the things that bring you joy."

"I agree," Rayan said. "That you made the right choice, I

mean. The Court of Water would never have bowed to Syrene as their queen after she helped Anron kill King Aldrich."

"And I have a feeling that especially the Court of Stone would never have acknowledged Anron as a god either," Lilane said. "Not when they have had princes such as Aldrich Spiritsinger, and now his pupil Edric. The belief in the spirits is strong in their court." A small smile played over her lips. "In ours too."

"After what Anron and his High Elves have done to the elves of our courts, I doubt any of them would have agreed to worship him willingly." Mordren's eyes took on a scheming glint. "Though, this meeting did reveal one important factor."

"What's that?" Iwdael asked.

"Anron is worried."

All three of them raised their eyebrows. From across the grass, a pair of elves appeared with an armful of bows that they placed into a neat pile. Wood clattered as a third one added a cluster of arrows to the gear.

"Worried?" Rayan said.

"Yes," I answered since I had been thinking the same thing as Mordren. "Otherwise, he would never have called the meeting."

Mordren nodded. "Lester and Danser's Flying Legions have returned to Valdanar, which means that his fighting power has been cut down to a third of its previous size. He wants to finish this without having to risk a war that, at the very least, would end with a portion of his army dead. Since he has been cut off from Valdanar, there will be no more reinforcements. The High Elves he has with him now is all that he will ever have."

"So you're saying that the odds are actually not as bad as we think?" Rayan asked.

"Indeed. If we can free our people, we might stand a chance of winning this."

Before anyone could say anything else, Reena jogged up to Prince Iwdael.

"My prince," she said. "We're ready."

"You're leaving?" I asked, my gaze shifting between the silver-haired beauty and the Prince of Trees.

"Yes," he answered. "That was the message Felix was here to relay. It's our turn to guard the temple and the magic." Turning to Rayan, he waved a hand. "Do you have the sword?"

The Prince of Water nodded. Steel sang into the noise of the busy camp as Rayan unsheathed a sword I recognized very well. It was the intricate blade that Ellyda had forged while she was held in captivity by the High Elves in King Aldrich's castle. The one that could shatter the magic-blocking bracelets.

Adjusting his grip, he held out the sword to Mordren who stood next to him. "We have been taking turns breaking people out of our courts." Embarrassment drifted across Rayan's handsome features. "But I'm afraid that no one has freed people from your courts. So you have some catching up to do."

Mordren's fingers closed around the beautifully forged hilt. "I see."

"My prince," Reena said again.

"Right, yes." Iwdael cleared his throat. "We need to get going. You know how Edric gets when people display a poor sense of punctuality."

Stifling a chuckle, I gave him a nod.

"We'll send Felix to find you when it's your turn to guard the magic." A frown creased his brows. "Where are you staying?"

Mordren and I exchanged a glance.

"Uhm..." I began. "In a forest." I cleared my throat because we still hadn't had time to get into the whole Court of Light revelation. "It's... where the Court of Light used to be."

"Ah," Iwdael said and nodded as if that wasn't the shock of the century.

Raising my eyebrows, I looked from face to face. Neither of them seemed at all surprised by the mention of a court that no one except Idra had known existed.

"Did you know about that?" I asked, befuddled.

"Not until recently," Prince Rayan answered. "Apparently, King Aldrich had told Edric about it as a safety precaution when the High Elves invaded."

"A safety precaution?"

"Yes. The temple holds all the bowls of magic." When I only continued frowning at him, he elaborated. "Including the two bowls that used to belong to the Court of Light."

"Oh."

"Oh, indeed. It's still not common knowledge, though. Only the people who help guard the temple know about it." Rayan narrowed his purple eyes at me. "Which makes me very curious as to how you know about it too."

"It's a long story. And it's not mine to tell."

"Ah, I see."

Iwdael cleared his throat and gave us a decisive nod. "Alrighty, when it's your turn to guard the magic, we'll send Felix to find you in the Court of Light. Until then, give them hell."

Matching smiles spread across my and Mordren's lips.

Oh we would definitely rain down hell right on top of their heads.

It was time to start breaking our people out.

CHAPTER 7

Convincing the others that it was easier if I did this alone had been a lot more difficult than I had expected. Idra in particular had been violently opposed to me going on my own. But as I snuck through the darkened halls of my occupied castle, I knew that I had made the right decision. This was a stealth mission. And who was better suited for it than a spy who could walk through walls?

The red stone walls watched me silently as I snuck down yet another corridor. I knew that I couldn't free everyone in the castle, so I had to focus on the ones who could contribute most in a battle. However, there were some others that I needed to get first.

Silk whispered against my skin as I phased through the wall at the end of the hall. Another dark corridor met me. Doors lined the red stone on my left all the way to the end. I slipped through the first one.

A comfortable bedroom stared back at me on the other side. Silvery moonlight streamed in through the skylight above and fell across the elf sleeping on the bed. The sheets were tangled around his legs as if he had kicked them off in his sleep. His short blond hair was matted to his forehead.

Moving silently, I closed the distance to the bed and then placed a gentle hand over his mouth.

He jerked up, but the noise he made was muffled by my hand. I raised my other one and pressed a finger to my lips. Blue eyes blinked up at me in shock.

"Lady Firesoul?" he mumbled from under my hand.

I removed it and gave him a smile. "Hello, Nicholas."

Nicholas, who had worked for me as a messenger before the High Elves took over the Court of Fire, sat up and straightened his rumpled white shirt. "You're here. You're back."

"Yes." I took a step back from the bed and motioned for him to stand up. "And you're getting out today. But first, I need your help."

He scrambled out of bed. Embarrassment colored his cheeks when he realized that he was standing there barelegged in his underwear. Clearing his throat, he hurried over to a chair by the desk and pulled on a pair of pants.

"Put on some shoes too," I said. "And then give me your hand."

After Nicholas had gotten dressed, he raked a hand through his short messy hair and then approached me. I drew one of the swords I had strapped to my back.

"Uhm…" Nicholas said as he hesitantly held out his hand.

I took it and moved it into position before sliding Ellyda's magical sword under the bracelet that circled his wrist. Holding his hand steady over the bed, I pushed upwards. The black bracelet shattered and shards rained down to bounce across his mattress.

"Wow," he said as he rubbed his wrist.

"Yeah." I smiled and then motioned towards the inner wall. "How many of the other messengers are here?"

"All of them."

I blinked in surprise.

"High Commander Anron moved everyone back to their respective courts after you broke into the castle and freed the princes," Nicholas explained. "Only the people who follow him willingly, like Princess Syrene, are still there. Everyone he took hostage was sent back to their court. Since we don't have any magic, we can't really do anything to oppose the High Elves anyway. And from what I overheard, it sounded like he wanted to make sure that there were no spies up there."

"But High Elves still patrol inside the castle?"

"And the city. And the barracks. We can move around freely, but we're constantly being supervised to see if we have any contact with any of you."

Dragging a hand through my hair, I blew out a sigh. "Well, I guess it would have been too easy if there hadn't been any guards. And why would anything ever be easy?" I rolled back my shoulders and then started towards the door. "Let's get the other messengers first."

The deserted red corridor slowly filled with surprised messengers as I repeated the process and woke them one by one to shatter the bracelets. Once everyone was dressed and ready to leave, I took the lead and waved them forward.

This was the tricky part. I could walk through the walls, but the messengers with me had to use the corridors and doors like normal people. I stayed a few steps ahead of them, scouting out the halls, as we moved towards the part of the castle that I had given to Valerie and Theo and their gang, the Hands.

The common room filled with mismatched furniture and

trinkets that the thieves had stolen from different places lay dark and deserted since Theo and Valerie had gotten their gang out as soon as the Court of Fire fell. Sadness blew through my soul as I studied the empty room.

This used to be ours. Mine. And now strangers walked these halls as if they owned them.

But we would get it back. We would get it all back.

Shaking my head, I motioned for the messengers to climb out the window. A few of them looked back at me as if I was crazy, but then Nicholas blew out a steadying breath and climbed up on the windowsill. I snuck back to the door and glanced through the small crack to make sure that no High Elves were about to walk in on us.

Moonlight fell in through the windows and illuminated the corridor outside, but other than that, nothing moved.

Soft grunts came from a dark-haired messenger as she climbed out the window. I kept my eyes on the corridor while the others followed.

A shadow fell across the floor, blotting out the patch of silvery moonlight.

Alarm pulsed up my spine. *Shit.* I pushed the door closed right before a High Elf soldier rounded the corner.

CHAPTER 8

"Keep going," I hissed at the elves who had turned to look at me with fear on their faces.

Darting across the floor, I positioned myself by the wall on the other side of the door. Then I ran right through it. The rooms on the other side of the wall flashed past me as I raced down the length of the corridor that the soldier was now walking through.

I skidded to a halt as I at last reached the same hallway, except beyond the corner that the soldier had come from. Whipping my head from side to side, I desperately searched for something I could use, but the corridor was bare except for the torches on the walls.

My pulse pounded in my ears. Based on my calculations, the soldier was very close to the door now. Darting over to the closest torch, I yanked it out of its metal holder and dropped it on the floor.

Wood clattered against stone.

The footsteps beyond the corner stopped.

"Lendir?" the soldier called. "That you?"

The sound of boots against stone started up again, but this time they were coming towards me. I let out a silent breath of relief and then leaped into the wall. Running back through the rooms on the other side of the red stone wall, I hoped that this bought us enough time to get everyone out.

When I finally reached the Hands' common room, it was empty. I climbed up on the windowsill to find them all waiting for me on the ground outside. The drop wasn't that steep so I twisted around and grabbed the ledge before lowering myself down.

A small cloud of sand swirled up around my boots as I hit the ground.

"Let's go," I whispered.

My heart continued thumping in my chest as we made our way across the courtyard. Only when we were standing outside the high defensive walls did I dare to take a deep breath of relief.

Stars glittered from the dark blue heavens above and the moon bathed the sleeping city around us in pale light. I motioned for my messengers to stop as we reached a dark alley.

"Go to the northeast corner of the barracks," I said. "Outside the walls. I'm going to send people to you. Take them to the Court of Trees. By that big waterfall next to the steep ledge. Then come back and do the same with the next person."

"Got it," they whispered back.

I gave them all a nod. Nicholas met my gaze briefly. Then they all worldwalked away. I did too.

The walls that boxed in the barracks and the training grounds appeared before me. Nicholas and the other messengers would be gathering right around the other corner.

I cast a quick glance up and down the length of the barrier before phasing through the wall.

A High Elf soldier stood guard a short distance away, but he wasn't looking in my direction. And if he had been, it would have been difficult to spot me in the dark shadows from the building. After making sure that he wasn't about to turn around, I hurried the short distance from the wall to the closest building and slipped inside.

Rows of beds lined the wall.

Worry fluttered its cold wings in my stomach. Waking these people was going to be even riskier than surprising the messengers in the castle.

I scanned the sleeping elves until my eyes fell on a face I recognized. Hilver. He wasn't magically gifted, but he had been one of Idra's sparring partners for years before I showed up to take over that job, which meant that he knew how to fight. So when I had freed him and all the other slaves in the Court of Fire, he had stayed to become a soldier.

Sneaking over to his bed, I sent a stray prayer to whoever might be listening that this wouldn't backfire. Then I reached out and pressed a hand over his mouth.

He flew upright, but I kept my hand firmly in place. When his pale blue eyes zeroed in on my face, he thankfully relaxed. I heaved a deep sigh of relief and took my hand from his mouth.

"Wake the others," I said before he could get a single word out.

He nodded. Raking a hand through his black hair, he climbed out of bed and moved to the next one. I snuck over to the window and peered out while Hilver woke the rest of the soldiers in the barrack.

We needed people who could fight. But we also needed

people who could get those fighters out of the city. That was why I had risked breaking into the castle to free my messengers first. They were all worldwalkers, so they would be able to get my soldiers out while I continued to free more people.

Once everyone was awake and dressed, I snuck back to the middle of the room. The elves drew closer. I slid Ellyda's sword from its sheath and walked over to Hilver. Grabbing his forearm, I moved him until his hand was above one of the beds. Then I pushed the sword through and broke the bracelet. Black shards fell to the mattress.

An excited murmur went through the room.

Hilver didn't have any magical powers, so the bracelet didn't work on him. The High Elves had put them on everyone just to be safe, since they had no way of telling who was and wasn't magically gifted. And to be honest, I didn't know either, so I would leave it up to the rest of the soldiers after this demonstration.

"Do it like that," I whispered and handed the sword to the closest elf. "Once you're free, get to the northeast corner. There are people there who can worldwalk you out. The last person gives the sword back to me."

They nodded in acknowledgement. I started back towards the window again, but Hilver grabbed my arm before I could take more than two steps. His blue eyes seared into mine as he turned me so that I faced him.

"I knew you would come for us," he said, his voice brimming with emotion.

The intensity of his gaze made a slight blush creep into my cheeks. I cleared my throat and flashed him a smile to relieve some of the heavy mood that had fallen. "Of course. This is my court, after all."

"Yes. Yes, it certainly is." A soft chuckle escaped his throat as he shook his head. "You're quite something, alright."

I gave him a warm smile. He nodded and then released my arm so that I could go back to keeping watch.

Shuffling feet and faint clinking sounded as the soldiers continued shattering their bracelets and then leaving through the back window.

When the last elf, a dark-haired female who I knew possessed the ability to shoot volcanic rocks, had broken her magic-blocking bracelet, I took the sword back and motioned for her to follow the others. She nodded her thanks before disappearing out the window.

With a firm grip on the blade, I walked through the opposite wall.

Warm night air enveloped me as I stepped into the deserted road between this barrack and the next. After a quick check up and down it, I snuck across and phased through the next wall.

Another large room filled with rows of beds met me. I once more scanned the sleeping elves to see if I could find someone I knew. A muscular elf with short brown hair was sleeping in a bed next to the wall at the far end.

Kael Sandscorcher. He had challenged Volkan in the first tournament match and lost, becoming a slave in exchange for the Prince of Fire sparing his life. When I freed him and offered him a job, he had actually teared up.

I slunk down the row of beds until I was standing next to his. Hopefully, this would go as smoothly as it had with Hilver. Blowing out a bracing breath, I leaned down and pressed a hand to his mouth.

Kael shot up from the bed and grabbed my forearm. In one fluid motion, he yanked my hand away and wrenched my arm up behind my back while kicking at the back of my legs. My knees smacked down onto the floor and I had to suppress a cry of pain as Kael forced my arm higher up my back. His other hand shot down and wrapped around the back of my neck, forcing me down on the floor. A huff ripped from my throat as my chest hit the smooth stone floor and a knee pressed down into my back.

Soft rustling and thudding sounded throughout the room, informing me that others had woken up as well.

"It's me," I croaked and yanked against the iron grip that kept me completely trapped on the ground.

For a moment, nothing happened. Then the weight pinning me down disappeared and Kael blurted out, "Lady Firesoul."

Rolling over on my back, I sucked in a deep breath to refill my lungs. Shocked brown eyes stared down at me.

"Remind me to never sneak up on you again," I said and huffed out a silent laugh.

Kael reached down and pulled me up before dusting me off. Regret blew across his face. "I'm so, so sorry. If I had known that it was you…"

"Don't worry about it." I waved him off with a tired smile. Turning, I found that the rest of the people in the barrack were on their feet as well. "Good, you're all up."

"What are you doing here?" Kael asked, his brown eyes still scanning my body for injuries that he might have accidentally inflicted.

"Isn't it obvious? I'm getting you out." I rolled my shoulder to relieve the strain in it before drawing Ellyda's blade once more. "Kael, give me your hand."

He held it out straight away. I moved it so that it was positioned over the bed before sliding the blade in and breaking his bracelet. His eyes widened. Around me, an excited rush swept through the room.

After repeating the same instructions that I had given to the other group of soldiers, I handed the blade to the closest one.

Kael stared between his now empty wrist and my face. Tears glittered at the corner of his eyes.

"Thank you," he said, his voice soft. Looking up, he held my gaze. "This is the second time you have freed me from slavery. I don't think I will ever be able to repay you, but know that you have my sword and my loyalty. Always."

"I–"

"They're gone!" a shout came from outside. "This whole barrack is empty. Check the others!"

"Shit," I swore. Drawing my blades, I ran towards the door. "Free those who can worldwalk first, we can fix the rest of you once you're out. Get to the northeast corner. Now! I'll hold them off."

The door was yanked open. A High Elf jerked back and stared in shock at the room full of scrambling soldiers. Jabbing my knife forward, I sent a spear of fire straight at him.

He dove out of the way but yelled, "They're trying to escape!"

Leaping through the wall next to the door, I whipped my head around to find High Elves barreling towards us from all sides. Adrenaline pulsed through my body, but apart from my little misunderstanding with Kael, I was feeling great. After leaving the Court of Trees, we had slept an entire night in an actual bed in the Poisonwood cabins and then taken the entire day today to rest before starting this mission. Not to mention that Rayan had healed all my injuries.

A wicked smile spread across my lips. These High Elves had no idea what they were up against.

I flicked my wrists. One after the other. Again and again. Searing arcs of fire shot through the air and sped towards the approaching soldiers.

"Get a Wielder here!" someone snapped after diving aside to escape my attacks.

Crackling flames cut through the air as I sent another volley towards them. They dodged the fire but somehow still managed to gain ground. I clicked my tongue. Right as I was about to start again, Kael barreled through the door and skidded to a halt next to me.

"How much time do we need?" I asked.

"A couple of minutes," he answered.

While I was sending scythes of fire at them, Kael began opening pits of lava in the spots where the High Elves were jumping to in order to dodge my attacks. My brows rose. He really was skilled at this.

Cries of pain ripped through the warm night air as a few of the High Elves found themselves landing in molten lava instead of on dusty stones.

"Where's the Wielder?" the voice from before screamed.

"They can't stop us all," another called. "We rush on three."

Still shooting attacks at them, I glanced over at Kael. "How large an area can you cover?"

"This whole open space," he answered, and nodded towards where the High Elves got ready to rush us.

"Wait until I tell you."

"Got it."

The High Elves sprinted towards us. They were right. There were far too many of them to hit at the same time. But I no longer needed to hit them.

Spreading my arms wide, I raised massive walls of fire that boxed in the whole empty patch.

"Now," I said.

Kael stared out at the dusty red stones. Then the whole space transformed into a field of lava. The charging High Elves screamed as the ground beneath their feet began disappearing. Whipping around, they sprinted back the way they had come only to find my flaming barriers blocking their way.

Red and orange light cast dancing shadows over our faces as Kael and I watched our enemies panic as their boots and clothes caught fire. A malicious grin spread across my lips.

A gigantic wave of water crashed down over the area, transforming our fiery battlefield into hissing steam.

"That's our cue to leave," I said as a thick blanket of white fog fell over the barracks.

Turning around, we jogged back into the building and then climbed out the back window. I locked my fingers together and crouched down, giving Kael a boost so that he could get over the wall, before I phased through it as well.

Nicholas was standing alone on the other side, holding Ellyda's sword. A moment later, Kael landed on the ground next to us.

"We're the last ones," I said. "Let's go."

Nicholas handed me the sword and then grabbed Kael. After a nod from me, they worldwalked away.

Screams and sounds of pursuit came from the other side of the wall. I had only managed to break out a fraction of the warriors in my court, and I still had to follow them to the Court of Trees to shatter the rest of their bracelets. Not to mention that it would be even harder to do something like this again now that we had almost been caught once. I really thought I would be able to free more of my people in one fell swoop. But unfortunately, the High Elves were very good at their jobs too.

Blowing out a frustrated breath, I sheathed the sword across my back. This was going to take longer than I had hoped.

I glanced up at the white mist visible over the walls as I got ready to worldwalk away.

This thing that I had sworn would be a stealth mission had turned into an all-out fight with a horde of High Elves that had almost ended with us getting caught.

Damn.

Idra was going to kill me.

CHAPTER 9

Battle cries cut through the sweet-smelling night air. I slashed my sword, sending a scythe of fire shooting into the thick mass of shadows that covered the training grounds. The sizzling of flames meeting flesh echoed from the darkness. But the battle cries drew nearer too.

A High Elf soldier barreled out of Mordren's shadow mist right as the sound of arrows whistled through the night. I raised a wall of fire in front of the darkness while Mordren poured more shadows into it to stop the other attackers. The High Elf who had made it through charged straight at us.

Idra darted forward. Moonlight gleamed in her shoulder-length white hair as she ducked under the soldier's sword. Twisting around with effortless grace, she smacked her palm into his side. He crumpled to the ground, lifeless eyes staring up into the star-dusted heavens.

"See," Idra snapped as she stalked back to us. "This also turned into a fight."

Flicking my wrists, I sent another volley of fiery attacks

into the shadows. "Yes, thank you, Idra. I heard you the first fifteen times."

"How could you think that breaking into barracks in the Court of Fire and Court of Shadows, which are heavily guarded by High Elves, would be a *stealth* mission?"

"Again, I heard you the first fifteen times."

"Well, if you weren't such a moron, I wouldn't have to keep stating the obvious all the time."

Lightning flashed through the darkness, breaking up the shadows. I cast a glance over my shoulder. We had only managed to get one barrack tonight. After my fight in the Court of Fire yesterday, the High Elves must have increased their security in the Court of Shadows too.

A wall of water rose above the shadows. I tore my gaze from the final group of elves escaping through the back window and raised another barrier of fire to meet it. White lightning tore through the shadows like vicious snakes while steam exploded over it and rolled down over the buildings.

"Though Idra certainly has a point," Mordren began as he tried to patch up his mass of shadows, "perhaps we could table this argument for another time?"

Idra shot me a pointed look. "See. Even he agrees with me."

I blew out a sigh and sent a barrage of flaming scythes into the shadows before twisting around and giving Idra a push towards the open door and the back window inside. "Just go."

She narrowed her dark eyes at me but then took off at a run. After making sure that Mordren was following too, I sprinted after her.

Only rows of empty beds watched us as we raced into the room and across the worn floorboards. I snatched up Ellyda's sword from where the last elf had left it on a side table next to the window. Behind me, the silvery light of the moon grew clearer as Mordren's shadow wall fell.

Climbing up onto the windowsill, I jumped out after Idra. A thud informed me that Mordren was right behind me. From the other side of the building, High Elves were calling out orders, and lightning and fire roared between the barracks, as if to light the way. Or maybe to fry us alive. It was a bit hard to tell.

Idra crouched down in front of the wall and locked her fingers together. Without breaking his stride, Mordren ran up to her and placed his foot in her hands while she gave him a boost upwards. He twisted around and reached his hand back.

While I did what Idra had just done, she moved back to get some speed and then ran back to get a boost from me. Mordren grabbed her wrist and helped pull her up while I walked right through the stone wall.

They landed on either side of me and rolled forwards to break the fall right as I made it through the wall.

"Let's go," Mordren said as soon as they were on their feet.

We worldwalked out.

A dark street appeared around me. A moment later, Idra and Mordren materialized too. There was one more person in the Court of Shadows we had to pay a visit to before we could return to the rest of our friends.

Candles burned inside the house before us. I peered in through one of the windows to find a person sitting by the table. Books and small pots and vials, along with what looked like herbs, littered the tabletop. Steam rose in lazy arcs above a cup of tea. I glanced back at my companions.

Mordren motioned for us to split up. While he moved towards the front door, I jogged around the other side of the building and left the window to Idra since I didn't need a window to get inside. When I reached the point I had marked in my mind, I stepped through the wooden wall and into the warm house.

The scent of flowery tea and herbs filled my lungs as I moved away from the wall and towards the staircase at the back of the room. While I walked, Idra appeared in the window. She lowered herself down on silent feet and then leaned back against the windowsill and crossed her arms. The elf in the chair had her back to us so she didn't notice us. I reached my spot, blocking the staircase, right as the front door was opened.

Wood clattered as the dark-haired elf shot up from her chair, knocking it over in the process. She was halfway around the table when Mordren became fully visible. Her body froze as he closed the door behind him.

Then she whirled around. Taking off at a run, she made as if to escape through the window, but when she saw Idra Souldrinker waiting for her there, she swung around towards the staircase instead. Panic pulsed in her dark eyes as she found me blocking the way.

Screeching to a halt in the middle of the room, she whirled around to face the Prince of Shadows again.

"Hello, Imelda," Mordren said.

The healer who had sold us out to Anron drew in a shaky breath. "My prince."

Mordren started towards her.

She edged back a little, but then stopped and straightened while sucking in another deep breath. "I assume you're here for revenge after my betrayal." Brushing her hands down over her apron, she lowered herself to her knees and bowed her head before the Prince of Shadows. "I know that it won't make much difference, but I am sorry. Do what you have to do."

Mordren raised his brows. Shifting his gaze to me, he motioned for me to approach. I drew one of the swords from my back while making my way over. Imelda flinched at the sound of ringing steel. Once I reached them, I handed the blade to Mordren.

His fingers curled around the hilt. While adjusting his grip, he reached down and grabbed Imelda's hand. She sucked in a small breath but let him raise her hand.

Still saying nothing, Mordren unceremoniously slid the sword under the black bracelet around her wrist and pulled upwards. Gleaming shards rained down on the floor and across Imelda's skirt.

She snapped her head up. Disbelief shone in her eyes as she looked between Mordren, her now empty wrist, and the broken bracelet on the floor.

"Look at me," Mordren finally said.

Confusion still flickered on her face as she hesitantly met his gaze once more.

"The next time someone threatens your family, you come to me." Power and authority rolled off Mordren's body like black waves as he spoke. "You do not sell me out. You come to me and you tell me that someone has threatened your family, so that I can help you."

Imelda's mouth dropped open, but no sound made it out.

"Do you understand?"

"Y-yes, my prince."

"Good." He twitched his fingers at her. "Stand up."

Her skirt rustled against the wooden floorboards as she climbed to her feet. A few shards from the shattered bracelet fell from her lap, clinking against the floor, as she brushed her hands down her dress. Candlelight cast dancing shadows over her face as she flicked her gaze back up to Mordren.

"Your daughter is free," he said.

A gasp ripped from her throat and she slapped a hand in front of her mouth.

"She is in the Court of Trees," Mordren went on. "I will take you there now, so gather whatever you need. We will need healers in the war to come."

"Yes, my prince." She began to turn around, but then looked back at him. "Thank you."

He gave her a firm nod.

While Imelda hurried away to grab her things, Idra stalked across the floor and took up position next to us.

"This is taking too long," she said.

"She'll be ready soon," I replied.

"Not this specifically. I mean all of it." Her sharp eyes swept around the room as if checking for enemies. "We can't keep breaking people out one person at a time. Or even one barrack at a time. It is too time-consuming and, most of all, the risk far outweighs the reward."

"I agree," Mordren said.

Idra looked back at him for a moment before turning her attention to me as well. "We need an army. A real army. We can't keep fighting dangerous battles against High Elf Wielders just to add another fifteen people to our ranks, or another healer to our troops. We need everyone. And we need them fast, and at the same time."

Blowing out a tired breath, I raked a hand through my hair and tipped my head back. "Yeah. You're right. There has to be a smarter way to do this."

Ceramic clinked as Imelda gathered up some of the small containers from the table. Tilting my head back down, I watched her hurry over to the staircase and run upstairs to get something else.

Idra was right.

We had been lucky that we had managed to get as many soldiers as we had last night and today. But they were still only a fraction of what we needed. We had also been fortunate enough to pull it off without sustaining any serious injuries or getting captured, but if we continued this dangerous game, it was only a matter of time.

Another dejected sigh escaped my chest.

We needed to figure out a smarter way to free our people.

Or we would lose this war before it had even begun.

CHAPTER 10

The morning sun stretched its pale tendrils over the horizon. Birds chirped in the trees and insects hummed inside the thick foliage around us. Exhaustion clung to my body as I slumped down on one of the logs around the cold firepit and tilted my head back before blowing out a long sigh.

"Now that doesn't look like the face of a winner," a cheerful voice said.

Huffing out a laugh, I tipped my head back down and looked towards the source of the voice.

Valerie was strolling towards us with a grin on her face. A whole cluster of those pink cloudlike animals followed behind her while Theo and Eilan were forced to hurry on ahead so as to not accidentally step on any of them.

Wood creaked faintly as Idra and Mordren shifted on their logs to look at the group approaching us as well.

"What's with the entourage?" I asked, and raised my eyebrows as I nodded towards the cluster of pink clouds.

Valerie briefly looked over her shoulder as if she hadn't

even noticed that they were following her. "I don't know. They just seem to like me."

"It's because you're feeding them all the time," Theo announced.

"It is not. It's because they like me." Letting out an indignant huff, she plopped down next to Idra while turning to Eilan. "Right?"

Eilan, who lowered himself onto the log next to Mordren, hesitated a little before replying with a very indecisive, "Uhm..."

"Ha!" Theo said as he sat down next to me. "Told you."

Valerie narrowed her eyes at Eilan from across the unlit firepit. "Traitor."

He just grinned sheepishly.

A few of the cloud animals jumped up onto Valerie's legs while another climbed up to take a seat on her shoulder. It made the rest who were still on the ground let out a sad noise, and a moment later, they leaped up too. Fluffy pink clouds squeezed together on her thighs until it was so crowded that they almost tumbled down onto the thick grass again.

Letting out an exasperated sigh, Valerie picked up a few of them and dumped them on Idra's lap.

The lethal warrior blinked at them in shock before turning to stare at Valerie, but the thief wasn't looking at her. She was petting the animals in her own lap.

One of the clouds on Idra's legs let out a lonely little squeak. It looked up at the deadly elf with hopeful blue eyes as she turned back to the fluffy pile in her lap. Blowing out a sharp breath full of reluctance, Idra moved her hand and awkwardly patted the cloud animal on its head. It let out a tiny purr and nestled deeper into her thighs.

It took all of my considerable self-control not to laugh.

Drawing a hand over my mouth, I wiped the smile from my face because I knew that Idra would have kicked my ass for it.

"So, how did the mission go in the Court of Shadows?" Theo asked.

Idra's dark eyes slid to me. "Yes, Kenna. Tell them how it went."

I grimaced at her, which made a sharp smile that promised revenge during our next training session spread across her lips, before I launched into the story. While I was filling them in on the fight by the barracks and the visit to Imelda's house, Vendir drifted over as well. Even though I had seen him like this several times now, it still made me do a double take.

Ever since the first time we met, Vendir had only ever worn his bronze armor. But after our final showdown with Anron and the Emperor and Empress of Valdanar, when Vendir had decided to return here with us, he had taken it off. Now, he wore a pair of black pants and a white shirt. Like a normal person. It was still taking me some time to get used to.

He sat down at the edge of the log and listened to the story in silence.

"So it turned into a fight?" Eilan asked once I was finished. "Again."

Idra shot me a smug I-told-you-so look.

"Yeah," I answered. Frowning, I turned to Vendir. "Why is it that all of you Wielders only use stone, water, wind, fire, and lightning? Why not shadows or any of the other elements?"

"Those are the elements best suited for battle," he replied with a shrug.

Mordren arched a dark brow at him. "I would argue that shadow magic is quite suited for battle as well."

"For you, yes. Because you have somehow transformed

that magic into something more specialized. We can only use the magic to make the area around us dark, but that isn't very helpful in a fight since we can't see inside it either. We can't make it grab people or do any of the more tangible things that you can do with it."

"Huh," I said.

"Yeah. I think it has to do with the fact that you have been using it for so long. Like I said, we and our ancestors have mostly been focusing on fire, lightning, wind, water, and stone since those are the most obvious choices for battle magic."

Leaning back on my hands, I stretched out my legs before me and heaved a sigh. "Imagine if we could wield more than one element too."

Eilan let out a soft chuckle and nodded. "Yeah. Imagine if we could have drunk a little from all the bowls in the White Tower so that we had everything."

"Then we could have gone up against Anron on our own without issue."

"Indeed."

"Too bad we can't mix magical elements," a voice said from my left.

We all turned to find Ellyda and Hadeon walking towards us. Ellyda's eyes were fixed on us, but Hadeon seemed to be watching his sister more than the path before him.

"Our bodies can only handle one magical element," Ellyda went on as she sat down in the empty spot between Vendir and Theo. "Probably because that unlimited elemental magic wasn't even meant for our species to begin with."

Since there was no more room on that log, Hadeon hesitated as he glanced between Ellyda and the log Mordren and Eilan were occupying, which still had room on it.

"Stop hovering," Ellyda snapped.

"I'm your brother," he protested and crossed his arms. "I'm allowed to be worried."

She stabbed a hand towards the spot next to Eilan. "You can be worried from over there."

"How are you feeling?" I asked before he could retort.

"I'm fine," she said, but there were dark circles under her eyes and her movements were uncharacteristically sluggish.

"She collapsed while trying to get out of bed yesterday," Hadeon said as he sank down next to Eilan.

Ellyda narrowed her eyes at him. From across the firepit, he only stared back at her with raised eyebrows, daring her to deny it. Tearing her gaze from him, she blew out a breath.

"I'm fine," she repeated. "Anyway, we can't mix magical elements because the magic was never supposed to be used by us to begin with."

"She's right," Idra said. "Prince André did some experiments on it. Trust me, the result wasn't pretty."

"You worked for the Prince of Light?" Hadeon asked, his brows raised high.

A tiny hint of panic flickered in Idra's dark eyes before it disappeared and she answered with a clipped, "Yes."

She had told the rest of them that she was from the Court of Light, but I was still the only one who knew what her life had been like there and what Prince André had done to her.

"So how…" Hadeon trailed off as his gaze dropped down to her legs for the first time. "What the actual….?" Whipping his head from side to side, he looked at us before pointing at the pile of fluffy pink clouds in Idra's lap. "Am I hallucinating?"

"Nope," I answered.

"It's her fault," Idra said with an irritated growl and jerked her chin at Valerie. "She dumped them there and now they're sleeping so I can't move them."

"Ha!" Hadeon grinned at her in challenge. "Lies."

She glared back at him. "You–"

"I never thought I would see the day."

"Don't–"

"I only wish there was a way to save this image forever. This is the cutest damn thing I've seen this decade."

Death flashed in her black eyes. "Not. Another. Word."

He gave her a quick rise and fall of his eyebrows. "Or what?"

"Or I will make you wish that you had stayed in that little cabin for the rest of your life."

"Come try it, *cuddles*."

A smile so sharp it could've drawn blood spread across Idra's lips and her dark eyes promised the coldest, sweetest revenge.

Something between a groan and a chuckle escaped my throat. Eilan massaged his forehead and shook his head in exasperation while Vendir looked genuinely worried.

"Anyway..." Theo began before the two warriors could get started on that murderous vengeance, "we need to figure out a better way to free everyone from the bracelets."

"Indeed," Mordren said. "However, we seem to be short on options for how to do that."

"I might have an idea," Ellyda cut in. Tearing her gaze from the charred remains of the fire in the pit that she had been staring at for the past few minutes, she looked at each of us in turn before continuing. "I've been thinking. Last time, I had to make a sword to break the bracelets because I was being watched."

Vendir shifted uncomfortably in his seat at the mention of it, but he said nothing.

"But now that I can work freely..." She paused. "I might be able to reverse engineer the bracelets."

Several pairs of eyebrows rose.

Theo furrowed his. "What does that mean?"

"It means that I might, *might*, be able to reverse the flow of power so that it goes from Anron and to the person wearing the bracelet instead of the other way around."

"You can do that?"

"Maybe. But I'll need an unused bracelet. Preferably a whole stack of them."

"El..." Hadeon began, and shook his head.

"What?" she snapped. When he only continued looking at her with concerned eyes, she blew out an irritated breath. "I said I'm fine."

"Have you looked at yourself in a mirror lately?"

"Have you?" She swept sharp eyes over all of us. "Have any of you? We're all tired. But our problems don't go away just because we're exhausted. I know my own limits, and I'm not there yet." Standing up abruptly, she stepped over the log and started stalking away. "Get me those bracelets and I'll see what I can do. Until then, I'll be in the forge, making more of those swords in case it doesn't work."

Vendir stood up as if to follow her, but Theo placed a hand on his arm, urging him to sit down again. His brown eyes tracked Ellyda as she disappeared between two wooden buildings, but he lowered himself down onto the log once more.

Something cold and wet brushed my hand. I looked down to find a midnight fox nudging my hand with its nose. Reaching down, I stroked its beautiful fur. The morning sun had climbed over the tree line and its bright rays made the silver in the fox's otherwise dark blue fur glitter like stars.

"She's right," Idra said into the silence. "The world doesn't stop just because we're tired or hurt. Until this war is over, we will all need to push the limits of what we think we can handle."

Looking up from the midnight fox, I met her gaze. If the others only knew the amount of awful shit Idra could actually handle. Compared to what she had already been through in her life, this must seem like nothing.

"Well alrighty then," Valerie said as she spread her arms. "She said she wanted bracelets, and we're gonna have to assume that Anron keeps a stash of them somewhere up in that castle there on the mountain. So..." She grinned. "Who's up for a little burglary?"

Laughter rippled through our group, relieving some of the somber tension that had fallen.

Pushing out the tiredness in my soul, I sat forward on the log as our sneaky group began plotting some more mayhem.

CHAPTER 11

"The last time you went to see this person, I found you on your knees, surrounded by three people with swords." Mordren locked eyes with me. "And with a bruise on your face."

"That had nothing to do with her." I reached up and gave his cheek a couple of brisk pats. "Now, wait out here like a good boy."

His hand shot up. Strong fingers curled around my wrist while he stepped in front of me. Placing his other hand against my collarbones, he pushed me back against the smooth stone wall. Golden afternoon sunlight fell across his face and set his eyes sparkling as he leaned closer to me. I watched the way the light painted gilded streaks in his dark hair.

"You are starting to enjoy bossing me around a little too much," he said as he traced his lips over my jaw.

"Oh, I think I'm enjoying it just the right amount."

His hand slid up my throat. Placing his thumb under my

chin, he forced my head back while a sly smile graced his lips. "Cocky, aren't you?"

"You're one to talk."

"You know," he whispered as he slanted his mouth over mine, "we have not had a moment to ourselves in weeks due to all this traveling."

"I know. Which is why I have to find all these other opportunities to boss you around."

"Oh, my little traitor spy, I think you have forgotten who gives the orders and who does the begging in those situations."

Lifting my free hand, I grabbed the collar of his shirt and pulled him harder against me. "Is that so? Then perhaps we need to go over that tonight."

He brushed his lips against my mouth. "I look forward to it."

I drew in a shuddering breath as he kissed his way over my jaw before he released me and took a step back. Soon. Soon we would have time for this and everything else we had been forced to put off because a power-hungry High Elf invaded our lands. Pushing myself away from the wall, I ran my fingers through my hair to smoothen it down.

"The sooner we get this done, the sooner we can go back to the cabin." I flashed him a mischievous grin. "And then we can see who's really the boss."

Mordren let out a dark laugh and jerked his chin. "Get to it then."

After checking to make sure that the next street was empty, I left Mordren in the deserted alley and snuck around the building.

The Court of Stone wasn't as busy as it usually was, but I wasn't sure if that might just be the new normal since the

High Elves had taken over and put bracelets on all the elves. It was the middle of the day so there should have been people walking around most streets, even in the shady part of town. But the area was uncharacteristically empty. As I slunk towards a door a bit farther in, I just hoped that the person I was about to see was still free and open for business.

Silk brushed against my skin as I walked straight through the door.

My heart sank. The hallway inside was deserted and the stairwell was dark. *Damn.* Had they gotten her too?

Sweeping my gaze over the room, I snuck up the stairs. The door at the top was closed. I paused on the landing for a few seconds, but nothing happened so I took another step forward.

Stone shot out from the doorway and wrapped around my throat before slamming me into the wall. I let out a strangled gasp as my back connected with it. Panic blared in my mind as my hands shot up and tried to pry the hard thing from my throat, only to find solid stone. Blinking, I tried to refocus my eyes just as something massive became visible.

An elf with silvery white hair stared down at me in confusion.

"Wait, aren't you…?" he began.

"Yes," I pressed out.

He relaxed his grip on my throat and took a step back while his stone arms returned to normal flesh and blood. Running a hand over my throat, I coughed and drew in a couple of deep breaths.

"I'm a bit short to be a High Elf, don't you think?" I said as I continued to massage my throat.

He crossed his arms. "I'm not taking any chances."

"Uh-huh." I glanced behind him to try to see in through the now open door. "Is she here?"

"Yeah, go on through."

Sidestepping the massive elf who usually guarded the door downstairs, I slunk across the threshold and into the room beyond. An elf with brown hair and eyes, and a very bland face, looked up from her gigantic marble desk.

"Kenna," she said. A slight smile tugged at her lips. "Or perhaps I should now call you Lady Firesoul."

I smiled back at her. "Hello, Liveria."

Liveria Inkweaver, the best document forger I had ever met, nodded before motioning for me to come and sit down. I slid into the chair opposite her.

"I'm glad to see that you've managed to stay undetected," I said to her while nodding at her empty wrist.

She rubbed it as if thinking about the awful bracelet that could have been locked around it. "Yes, me too. It hasn't been easy, but Ruben has been a great help."

Ah, so his name was Ruben. I had been to Liveria a couple of times, but I had never known what her guard was called. It was a bit ironic since I had gone to the trouble of blackmailing him during our very first encounter.

"Now, what can I do for you?" she asked.

"Can you forge a document that looks like it's from the High Elves? Like an order for a shipment of goods?"

She considered in silence for a few seconds before nodding. "Yes, that shouldn't be a problem."

Sliding my hand into one of my many pockets, I pulled out one of the stacks of emergency cash that I always kept inside my magic-imbued jacket. It produced a soft thud as I placed it on the table before Liveria.

She lifted it and ran a finger down the edge of the stack, as if she could count it all that way. Given her powers, she probably could. Once she got to the bottom, she gave me a nod and then pulled out a piece of paper.

While I specified what I wanted the order to say, she crafted the words in flawless script.

Once the document was done, complete with sigils and stamps and everything, she slid it over to me.

"There we are," she said.

"Thank you. It's perfect, as always."

She smiled while pocketing the cash. Tilting her head, she studied me intently for a few moments. "You have come a long way from needing forged work orders to get into the castle in the Court of Trees. Now the halls of power open at the flick of your wrist." A wistful look crossed her face as she continued to watch me. "I wonder if we will meet again."

"Of course we will. An incredible forger is always needed sooner or later."

"Hmm. Where you're heading, I'm not so sure." Shaking off her pensive mood, she offered me another smile. "Good luck, Lady Firesoul."

As I snuck down the stairs and slipped back out onto the street, I mulled over her words. Where I was heading? Where would I be heading that I wouldn't need to forge documents anymore? A sudden thought sent a cold spike of fear through my chest. Did she think I was going to die in this war?

To be honest, I was probably arrogant enough to think of myself as more or less immortal. Yes, I feared for my life in certain situations. But in the end, I always assumed that I would somehow pull through anyway because... Well, because I couldn't die. I hadn't even started living yet.

Worry fluttered its poisonous wings in my chest. What had Liveria seen in my soul that made her think I wouldn't survive? That I wouldn't come out on the other side of this war intact and ready to finally start that life I had been fighting for all this time? That my story would end here before it could truly even start?

Shaking my head, I shoved the morbid thoughts out as I rounded the corner to where Mordren was waiting for me.

His perceptive silver eyes searched my face. "What's wrong?"

"Nothing." I forced the last of the trepidation out and instead flashed him a smile while waving the document in my hand. "We have it."

He continued studying me for another few seconds before finally saying, "Good. Then we only have one more stop to make before we can return to that waiting cabin."

I chuckled and slid the document into one of my pockets. "Well, come on then."

The world twisted around me as we worldwalked away.

An empty room furnished with a pale wooden table and chairs appeared around us. Paintings of different sceneries hung on the pristine walls. I studied a painting with a yellow and orange sunset behind a black city silhouette while Mordren walked over to the table and rang the small metal bell that was waiting there. It tinkled merrily. The scent of coffee and food hung in the air, and plates clinked from somewhere downstairs.

"How did you convince him to leave this room unwarded?" I asked as I tore my gaze from the painting and turned to face Mordren.

A sly smile slid across his lips. "I financed the purchase of the building."

"Ah. Then a VIP room just for you wasn't too much to ask."

"Exactly. And I like having a place in the Court of Stone

where I can come and go as I please without anyone being the wiser."

"Of course you do." I chuckled and shook my head before my gaze drifted back to the pale chair on the other side of the table. Mordren used to sit there and drink coffee before the world became this crazy. We had met here a couple of times back when we were still enemies. "Now this brings back memories, doesn't it?"

Mordren's silver eyes glittered as he let out an amused breath and nodded towards the wall on my right. "Indeed. If I am not mistaken, you came flying through that wall over there and put a knife to my throat while I was sitting here trying to enjoy a nice cup of coffee."

I laughed. "Yeah, I did." Twisting around, I motioned towards the chair on the other side. "And that's where I sat when you summoned me to interrogate me on my progress in finding the Dagger of Orias. Did you know that I had only slept two hours that day?"

"Yes."

"And you still summoned me?"

A wicked smirk spread across his mouth as he held my gaze. "And you still came."

"Yeah, well, you threatened me a lot more back then."

"Back then? Are you saying that I have gone soft? Perhaps I need to do something to remedy that."

Footsteps sounded from the stairs. After flashing Mordren a challenging look that made him smirk even more, I turned towards the doorway right as a young man walked through.

"My prince," he began. "It's good to see you. Ever since the High Elves invaded, I haven't seen…"

He trailed off and his brown eyes widened as his gaze found me. Herman, the owner of the White Cat Coffeehouse, blinked in surprise and flicked his gaze to Mordren again before turning it to me.

"You," he blurted out.

"Hello, Herman," Mordren said smoothly before jerking his chin towards me. "I believe you remember Kenna."

"Hard to forget someone who threatened to burn my coffeehouse to the ground."

Mordren turned and arched an eyebrow at me.

"I wasn't actually going to burn it down," I protested. "It was just to make sure that you did as I said."

Herman crossed his arms, looking very unconvinced, but he didn't argue the point. Amusement tugged at Mordren's lips as he shook his head at me in disbelief, which only made me flash him a look of fake innocence. I really had blackmailed quite a lot of people in my day, hadn't I?

"Well, she is not here to threaten you today," Mordren assured Herman as he turned back to the coffeehouse owner. "We are here because I have a job for you."

His eyebrows rose. "You do? I thought, with the High Elves having taken over the Court of Shadows, you didn't need any deliveries right now."

"Correct. However, this delivery is not for me."

"Then who's it for?"

"The High Elves."

"What?" Herman shook his head, making his brown hair fall into his eyes. He drew his fingers through it to push it back. "I'm sorry, my prince, I don't understand. You want me to deliver food to the High Elves? Won't I need some kind of order request for that or something?"

Sliding my hand into my pocket, I withdrew the document I had gotten from Liveria Inkweaver. "Here."

He eyed me suspiciously for another few seconds before

moving closer and taking the paper from my outstretched hand. His brows deepened into a frown as he read the list.

"Is there an issue?" Mordren asked.

"No, my prince. It's just…" He looked up to meet Mordren's gaze. "This food… They will need to eat it straight away, otherwise it will go bad."

"They will indeed." A calculating glint appeared in his silver eyes before he turned to me again. "Kenna, darling, if you please?"

I stuck my hands into two other pockets and pulled out the items I had procured from another acquaintance in the Court of Stone before we went to see Liveria. Glass clinked faintly as I set the small bottles down on the table.

Fear flickered across Herman's face. "Please tell me it's not poison. I can't… I'm not a murderer."

"It is not lethal," Mordren assured him. "If they suddenly started dying after your delivery, they would know that it was you. I would not put you at risk like that."

Biting his lip, he studied the bottles for another minute before finally nodding. "Okay." He looked back up at Mordren. "When?"

"Tomorrow. Midday."

"And I'm delivering it to…?"

"King Aldrich's castle."

"And no one will die?"

"No one will die." Mordren cocked his head. "We just need a little distraction while we pay them a visit."

"Okay," Herman repeated. Leaning forward, he gathered up the bottles from the table. "I'll get it done." His eyes slid to me. "You know, this is the second time you have used me in order to break into a castle."

A laugh bubbled from my throat. Holding his gaze, I gave

him a small smile. "Yes, I guess it is. But this time, we really are on the same side."

He studied me for a while in silence, as if trying to decide whether he forgave me for blackmailing him last year. Then he smacked his lips and gave me a decisive nod. "Yeah, I guess we are."

After shifting the bottles so that he could hold them all, he turned to Mordren and bowed his head. "My prince." His gaze flicked back to me. "Lady Firesoul."

Then he disappeared back down the stairs. Pots clanked from the kitchen below, and the murmur of the White Cat's other patrons drifted up along with another cloud of aromatic scents.

Shadows flickered in the corner of my eye. I only had time to turn around before dark tendrils wrapped around my limbs. Raising my eyebrows, I looked up to find Mordren advancing on me. The shadows moved with me, keeping me trapped, as Mordren backed me up against the wall. Shining black hair slid across his shoulder as he cocked his head.

"I had forgotten about that," Mordren said, his breath hot against my skin as he leaned closer. "That you threatened to burn this coffeehouse down."

"I sure did."

"First, you try to boss me around, and now I am reminded that you threatened to burn down my favorite coffeehouse while you ran that scheme that ended with me drinking poisoned wine in my own home."

I flashed him a cocky grin. "So?"

"So…" He traced light fingers down my throat. "It is high time to return to our cabin." Wicked mischief glittered in his eyes as he held my gaze. "Because now, I really want to hear you beg."

CHAPTER 12

The door closed with an ominous click. Turning around, I leaned back against the wall and crossed my arms while raising my eyebrows expectantly at the elven prince across the floor. Red and golden light from the setting sun fell in through the windows of the cabin and painted shimmering highlights in Mordren's dark hair.

A smirk played over my lips as I watched him. "What was that about making me beg again?"

Taking a step forward, he matched the sly smile on my lips. "So eager."

"To prove you wrong, yes."

"I'm never wrong."

I tracked him as he moved across the floor. Wood scraped against wood as he flicked a wrist, using his shadows to push the heavy table and chairs out of the way as he advanced on me. Power rippled off him with every step. My heart fluttered. By all the gods and spirits, he really was stunning.

"Well, then..." he began as he reached me.

A wicked grin flashed across my lips as I melted through

the wall. Air smelling of pine and moss enveloped me as I appeared outside the cabin. Drawing my knife, I darted to another spot on the wooden wall and leaped through it.

Mordren had taken a couple of steps back, but he was looking in the wrong direction so I snuck up behind him without notice. With that smirk still on my face, I placed my knife against his throat from behind. He started slightly at the cold kiss of steel.

"No, see," I began, "we really need to reconfirm who gives the orders in this relationship."

He let out a dark laugh. "Oh I was so hoping you would do that."

A concentrated burst of pain shot up and down my leg. I sucked in a breath as my knee buckled and my arm dropped, shifting the knife away from Mordren's throat. The flicker of pain had stopped almost before I could even feel it, but my muscles had reacted the way Mordren wanted. With the blade gone from his throat, he spun around to face me.

"Did you really think that would work?" he teased.

Shadows slid across the floor. I had barely managed to straighten again when the cool silken tendrils wrapped around my ankles. Calling up my fire, I burned them off.

Amusement tugged at Mordren's lips, and he sent another cluster of shadows towards me while backing me across the floor. I leaped back to avoid them. The back of my thighs smacked into the table that Mordren had moved earlier, but the damn thing was so heavy that it barely even shifted.

Dark shadows curled around my legs and arms, trapping them in place right as Mordren reached me. Drawing his hands over my thighs, he grabbed my ass and lifted me onto the table. While his shadows kept my hands spread wide, he plucked the knife from my grip and twirled it in his hand before placing it lightly against my throat.

He cocked his head, making his black hair ripple. "I told you it would end like this."

"Except, do you know what the problem is?" A victorious grin slid home on my mouth. "I'm more powerful than you are now."

Fire pulsed from my body, consuming all of Mordren's shadows in a flash. He jerked back slightly in surprise and I took the opportunity to scoot back across the tabletop and then phase through it. My stomach lurched a little at the fall, but I twisted so that I landed in a better position.

With that smug victory still sparkling inside me, I rolled out from under the table.

Something cold appeared around my wrist, and I got ready to burn away more shadows as I suddenly found my movements halted right as I cleared the last table leg.

I snapped my gaze to my right wrist, but then stopped. *What the...?*

A pair of metal handcuffs locked my hand to the closest table leg. They rattled faintly as I pulled against them. Still lying on my back on the floor, I propped myself up on my other elbow and slid my gaze to the Prince of Shadows.

"Where the hell did you get these from?" I asked.

He smirked down at me. "I acquired them while you were visiting your friend the Inkweaver."

After shifting so that I sat on my knees, I narrowed my eyes at him. "Been planning this a while, have you?"

"I like to come prepared." Smug amusement shone on his face as he motioned towards the handcuffs. "You can't burn those off without getting metal all over yourself."

Steel clanked again as I yanked at them once more. "I could just burn off the table leg."

"How would you explain that to Mendar?"

Silence fell as I considered whether I really was enough of a sore loser to actually destroy someone else's table just to make sure that Mordren didn't win. In the end, I wasn't. But there was something else I could do.

Keeping the handcuffs at the bottom of the wooden leg, I let my other hand shoot upwards to push the table up so that I could slip out. My palm connected with the underside of the table, and it lifted the tiniest bit. Then it slammed down into the floor again. I snapped my head up to find Mordren leaning casually against the tabletop. His silver eyes glittered.

I let out a frustrated growl and yanked against the handcuffs again.

A smile dripping with satisfaction graced his lips as he twirled the knife in his hand and then leaned down towards me. Cold steel kissed my skin as Mordren placed the flat of the blade under my chin and used it to tilt my head farther back, exposing my throat.

"Your move, darling," he challenged, his hot breath dancing over my skin.

I glared up at him for another few seconds before finally pressing out. "Fine."

"Fine what?" he coaxed.

"You win." I narrowed my eyes at him. "But if you want to hear me beg, you're going to have to work for it."

"Oh that will not be an issue."

A surprised yelp slipped my lips as Mordren set the blade aside and instead lifted me off the floor. Twisting me around, he put me down on the tabletop in front of him. Since my right hand was still connected to the wooden leg on the other side of the smooth surface, I had to lean back and stretch my right arm above my head while propping myself up on my left elbow.

"Really?" I arched my eyebrows at him and jerked my chin towards the handcuffs. "You're going to leave these on then?"

"Of course I am." He placed one hand against the tabletop and leaned down over me. "Why do you think I went to the trouble of procuring them?"

His other hand skimmed the side of my ribs, sending a crackling bolt of desire burning through my skin. Still propped up on one elbow, I watched as he pushed my shirt higher up my stomach. My skin prickled with heat as he traced his fingers along the top of my pants.

He leaned down and kissed his way over my ribs and across my stomach while his fingers undid the fastenings on my pants with torturous slowness. I lifted my back slightly off the table as I stopped propping myself up on my elbow, and instead moved that hand down to speed up the process. My fingers barely had time to brush against the fastenings before a cool silken shadow slid around my wrist. It pulled my hand away and drew my arm towards the left side until it lay flat against the tabletop. With both my arms spread wide, I could no longer prop myself up and had to lift my head to see Mordren.

He smiled like a villain. "So impatient."

"Well, you said you were going to make me beg." I met his smirk with a challenging one of my own. "And yet here I am, still not begging."

A dark laugh filled the air between us, caressing my skin before Mordren placed a final kiss on my ribs and then straightened. His strong fingers curled around the top of my pants. I raised my hips as he slid the dark fabric over my ass and down my legs. My skin prickled at the exposure.

After removing my shoes, he pulled off both my pants and my underwear and let them flutter to the floor. He ran his hands up my calves and cupped the back of my knees as he stepped closer again. I raised my head from the tabletop again just in time to see more shadows sliding across the smooth wood.

Two dark tendrils wrapped around my thighs, one from each side. Mordren released my knees. A sly smile curled his lips. Then the shadows pulled outwards, spreading my legs wide open until I was completely exposed to him. The silken restraints tightened so that my thighs were pinned to the table in that position.

I drew in a shuddering breath and rested my head against the tabletop as Mordren's fingers began tracing circles over the inside of my thighs. Anticipation coursed through my body.

His fingers brushed against my entrance. Lightning crackled across my skin.

Mordren let out a dark chuckle. "So wet already."

He braced a hand on my thigh while his other circled closer. My breath was growing heavier. A moan slipped my lips when his fingers finally slid across my throbbing clit. I raised my head so that I could see what his clever hands were doing.

The pressure on my thigh disappeared as he removed his other hand and instead planted his palm against my chest.

"Oh I don't think so," he said with a smirk as he pushed me back down on the table.

Before I could try again, a shadow slid around my throat and locked my head to the smooth tabletop. The annoyed huff died in my mouth as Mordren rolled my clit between his fingers, and a shuddering moan escaped instead.

He continued his expert movements until my chest was heaving with the building pleasure. I squirmed against the table. The shadows tightened around my limbs and throat, keeping me firmly trapped in place.

Since my gaze was limited to the wooden ceiling above, I couldn't anticipate his moves and the thrill of it made dark desire crackle through my body with every stroke of his fingers.

A gasp ripped from my lungs and I bucked my hips as he pushed two fingers inside me. While his thumb continued caressing my clit, he began pumping his fingers. My body trembled with pleasure. Release built inside me and I heaved shuddering breaths as it drew closer.

Tiny flickers of pain shot through my body. It snapped me out of the building pleasure before the wave could crash, and I blinked up at the ceiling. Then realization dawned on me.

"Oh no," I warned, "don't you dare."

Mordren continued moving his fingers while he leaned over me so that I could see his face. Wicked satisfaction glittered in his eyes. I tried to scowl at him but his thumb hit just the right spot and I gasped instead.

"You will beg," Mordren promised.

He continued sliding his fingers in and out while his thumb worked its torturous magic. I pulled against the restraints as release built inside me once more. The shadows around my thighs tightened, keeping my legs spread wide open. Mordren curled his fingers inside me and stars almost burst behind my eyes, but another flicker of pain shot through me before it could.

A frustrated moan escaped my mouth. Mordren let out a

dark laugh and just continued his movements. I trembled against the table as another wave built inside me. He pumped his fingers faster. His thumb rolled over my clit, bringing me right to the edge. It was so close that I only needed another second to feel that sweet, sweet release coursing through me.

Mordren sent another small burst of his pain magic through my body. I let out a pitiful groan.

"Beg," Mordren commanded.

My mind was splintering until it almost fractured as he brought me to the edge again before once more ruining my orgasm.

"P-please," I pressed out.

"I said beg."

My chest heaved and I could no longer focus my eyes. "Please, Mordren."

"You call that begging?"

I could hear the smirk in his voice. His fingers curled inside me again while his thumb pushed against all the right spots. Pent-up desire coursed through me. I bucked my hips and yanked against his shadows, but it did nothing to stop his mind-shattering moves.

"Oh, fuck," I gasped out. "Please, Mordren. I'm begging you."

"Surely you can do better than that."

My mind was threatening to shut down and my whole body felt like it was going to explode.

"P-please," I begged, breathless, surrendering to him completely. "I'll do anything. I'll do whatever you want, just please... please let me come."

He brought me over the edge. My legs shook violently as the intense orgasm crashed over me. I sucked in desperate breaths as pleasure washed through my whole body and sent my vision flickering white. Mordren continued sliding his fingers over my throbbing areas, prolonging the release.

When the last tremors had left my body, I just slumped back against the table. My chest heaved. The cool silken shadows around my limbs and throat disappeared. Then metal rattled as Mordren unlocked the handcuffs and placed them on the tabletop next to me. For a moment, all I could do was lie there and try to piece my mind back together.

Gentle hands slid around my back. I drew in a deep breath as Mordren lifted me into a sitting position. Red and golden light from the sunset outside made his eyes glitter like stars.

Once he was sure that I wouldn't topple backwards again, he took his hands from my back and instead brought one up to my face. Brushing his knuckles over my cheek, he pushed a loose curl away and hooked it behind my ear.

"You're so gorgeous when you do that," he said, and stole a soft kiss from my lips. "I cannot wait to spend an eternity making you beg and tremble with pleasure underneath me."

Grabbing the front of his shirt, I pulled his face back to mine and slanted my lips over his. "I will have revenge."

His dark laugh caressed my mouth. "Yes, so you keep saying."

CHAPTER 13

Majestic mountains watched indifferently as a young man crossed his arms and raised his chin before a squad of High Elves. A winged serpent waited behind him. Dull thuds sounded as two other soldiers jumped down from the serpent while carrying wooden crates.

One of the High Elves at the front of the group twitched his fingers at Herman. "Let me see that order document again."

"I'm telling you, it checks out," said the dark-haired one who had flown up here with Herman and the crates of food. "It has the right stamps and everything."

Herman kept his spine straight, but from our position behind a boulder, I could see the tension in his rigid shoulders as he held out the document I'd had Liveria Inkweaver forge for us. The leader of the squad snatched it from his hand and flicked his gaze back and forth across the paper.

"Why would High Commander Anron order this?" he demanded as he looked back up at the human before him.

"How should I know? I just received the order. And no one

refuses the High Commander so I prepared the food and rushed it here. So can I go home now? Please."
"We still—"
"Is that the food?" a different voice interrupted. Armor clanked as the other High Elves turned to find one of their own striding down from the castle. The leader of the squad scowled at the blue-eyed soldier.
"Who are you?" he asked.
The newcomer frowned back at him and gave a little shake of his head as if the answer to that should have been obvious. "Gadrien."

I swiped a hand over my mouth to hide my smile as Gadrien, Eilan's High Elf persona, strolled right past the flabbergasted soldier and peered into one of the crates that the other two were still holding. Next to me, Valerie grinned like a fiend. Theo glanced over at her, amusement playing over his lips, before shifting his gaze back to our sneaky little shapeshifter.

"Great, it's here," Gadrien said.

"What is? Why would High Commander Anron order food from a human?" The leader looked down into the other crate again. "What even is this?"

"It's a reward, of course." Gadrien stared at him as if he was retarded. "For keeping all the courts in check while he was gone. How have you not heard about this?"

The soldier cleared his throat. "Of course I've heard about it. I just didn't expect it to turn up today."

Gadrien gave him a dubious look before grabbing the side of the crate and tilting it so that he could see better. Raising his brows, he looked up at Herman. "You."

"Yes?" Herman said, worry making his voice tremble a little since he didn't know that Gadrien was really Eilan.

"This looks perishable. Is it?"

"Well, yes. It's special delicacies from all the courts that my coffeehouse prepared fresh for you this morning. That's why I rushed it here. It needs to be eaten soon or it will go bad."

"What are you standing around here for then?" Gadrien demanded as his blue eyes snapped to the two soldiers with the crates. "Get it inside. Lunch break's coming up soon anyway."

"I wouldn't wait that long, if I were you," Herman piped up. "Like I said, this kind of food goes bad fast."

"Yeah, well, as opposed to you *humans*," Gadrien spat the word, "we actually have something called work ethic and discipline." Whirling around, he jerked his chin at another High Elf while motioning towards the waiting air serpent. "Get him out of here."

Without another word, Gadrien stalked up the slope after the two soldiers carrying the crates. I suppressed a laugh at the baffled looks on the other High Elves' faces. For a moment, they just stared after him. But then they ushered Herman up onto their winged mount and flew him back down the mountain. Valerie raised a hand to her brow and gave the coffeehouse owner a salute that he couldn't see.

I smiled at Gadrien's retreating back.

That was the thing about lying. If you just showed up and acted with unshakable certainty as if you were right, the other person would more often than not start to doubt themselves. With enough confidence, you could bluff your way through most things.

"That went well," Theo whispered.

"Yeah." I pulled back from the boulder we had been using for cover. "Let's head inside. We have about an hour and a half until they'll start eating. Ideally, we should already have a rough idea of where they're keeping the bracelets by then so that we can get in, steal them, and get out fast."

He nodded. "Let's split up. It'll be faster that way."

"You mean otherwise *I* will slow you down."

"Well, uhm... you can walk through walls so you won't–"

"Yep," Valerie interrupted and flashed me a grin. "You'd slow us down."

"Alright then." I narrowed my eyes at them, but a smile tugged at my lips. "Go do your thief things, oh masters of burglary."

Spinning her hand in a couple of circles, she gave me a theatrical bow before elbowing Theo in the ribs and jerking her chin. I chuckled and shook my head at them as they scampered up the mountainside.

After checking to make sure that I wasn't about to blunder into any High Elves who were patrolling the rocky landscape around me, I snuck around the gigantic marble castle so that I could get to the entry point I had used before. When King Aldrich had lived here, there had been almost no gaps in his security. He had built the place, after all, so he knew where the weaknesses were. But thankfully, the High Elves still hadn't found them all.

I drew a deep breath of cool mountain air, tasting snow on my tongue, before stepping through the shining white wall and into a small storage closet on the far side of the castle. Surprised mops and buckets glared at me as I disturbed their slumber. Moving them aside, I made my way towards the door.

If I had a stash of magic-siphoning bracelets that were connected only to me, I would keep them where I was sure that no one else could mess with them. I didn't understand how they worked or how Anron made sure that the magic flowed only to him, but if I was amassing power for a coup or a rise to godhood, I would make damn sure no one tampered with the source of my power.

Edging the door open, I peered out into the corridor. Walls of shining white marble stared back at me. I waited another few seconds, listening for potential footsteps, before slipping through the door and then edging it closed again.

After another quick check up and down the corridor, I started towards the wing where King Aldrich's room had been. Everything I knew about Anron told me that he had taken over the king's quarters as his own. Anything less was beneath him.

I slunk down several corridors and phased through even more walls before my luck almost ran out. Footsteps came from just around the corner. I didn't know how I had missed their approach but I only had seconds before whoever was coming would round the corner and see me. Acting on instinct, I threw myself through the nearest wall.

The footsteps fell silent and a beautiful room appeared around me instead. An elf, not a High Elf but one of us, was sitting at a carved marble desk. Bent over a pile of papers, he scribbled some notes onto a document. I stared at the back of his blond head, desperately hoping that he wouldn't turn around, while counting down the seconds in my head.

Based on my calculations, whoever had rounded the corner was still in the corridor outside.

My heart pattered in my chest.

The pen scratched against the paper. Then it stopped. Ice sluiced through my veins as the elf put down the pen.

If I phased through the wall now, the person in the corridor would see me. But if I didn't move soon, this stranger would.

Locking his fingers together, he raised his arms and stretched them above his head while letting out a soft groan.

I counted the seconds in my head. Soon. The corridor would be clear soon. I just needed another few moments.

The elf lowered his arms again. My heart was pounding so hard against my ribs that I feared he might hear it.

Please don't turn around. Please don't turn around.

Just a few more seconds.

He blew out a deep breath and placed his palms on the tabletop.

Come on!

Wood scraped against stone as he pushed his chair back and stood up. With another faint groan, he took his hands from the desk and began to turn around.

I threw myself back through the wall.

Whipping my head to the left, I saw a High Elf in bronze armor right before he turned the corner on the other side of the hall. It took all my self-control not to heave a deep sigh.

Since I didn't know if the elf in the room was about to walk out the door too, I whirled around and hurried down the corridor in the opposite direction. Taking care to stay even more alert, I made my way deeper into the castle.

While walking, I couldn't help thinking about that elf back there. Nicholas had said that only the people who served Anron willingly were left in the castle. What had made the elf in that room choose to stay? Did he truly believe that Anron would create a better world for him and everyone else? Or maybe just for him? And why was he valuable enough for Anron to keep around? As I slipped down another series of hallways, I wondered how many non-High Elves were here. Hopefully, it was a tiny minority.

Two voices stopped me in my tracks when I had almost

reached the king's quarters. It wasn't the two voices in and of themselves that made me pause. After all, I had guessed that they would be here. But rather, it was what they were saying.

I glanced towards the sound. It was coming from a waiting room to my left. The bracelets wouldn't be there, but I decided that I could afford the detour. I had to see this for myself.

Moving on silent feet, I snuck down the hall to the left until I could peer through the doorway.

Comfortable couches in white and silver stood arranged around a low marble table. Fruit and pastries were arranged neatly on gleaming silver trays, and glass goblets with some pale sparkling liquid waited next to them. A cool breeze smelling of snow and iron blew in through the window and made the long white drapes flutter.

My eyes fell on the two people seated together on one of the couches.

"I can't believe that I spied inside the Court of Trees so many times, and we never met," Monette said.

Evander leaned forward and brushed a strand of her long blond hair away from her face, his fingers lingering on her cheek. "I know. But I would certainly have remembered meeting someone as gorgeous as you."

She giggled and swatted his arm. "Oh, stop it."

Bile rose in my throat. Though, I supposed those two traitors deserved each other.

Smiling at her, Evander lowered his hand and then leaned back against the fluffy white cushion instead. His dark green eyes gleamed like emeralds in the bright sunlight. Monette picked up a strawberry and bit into it. A satisfied moan drifted from her lips as she nestled deeper into the cushions as well.

"But seriously, though," Evander began. "I'm so glad I've met you." Drawing a hand through his short brown hair, he twisted around to face her. "You're the only one who really understands. Understands that *this*..." he spread his arms to encompass the room, "is what a good life is. Wealth. Comfort. Safety. When I was with..."

"Kenna," Monette finished for him. The acid in her voice could have burned a hole through the floor.

"Yeah. When I was with Kenna and those other people, I always felt like..." He heaved a deep sigh. "Like they were always throwing themselves into these absurd situations, killing and torturing people, and almost dying themselves. And for what? I don't get it. I will happily bow before Anron if it means that I have a life like this."

"I know. Me too. What does freedom matter if it's spent running and hiding in caves and fighting awful battles?" She pursed her lips and flicked her hair behind her shoulder. "But Kenna was always like that. She never cared about what other people wanted. Only about her own plans. I always had to use my mood manipulation on her to guilt trip her into helping me because she never wanted to do it on her own. She was so selfish."

"Yeah, I'm beginning to see that now too. I thought I could change her if I just got her away from Mordren Darkbringer, but she never even gave me a real chance."

Monette let out an annoyed groan. "Ugh. Do we have to keep talking about her? I thought you wanted to be here with me. Not her."

"I do." Evander sat up straight and cupped her cheek. "You know I do."

Moving on silent feet, I made my way back to the corridor I had come from. As their voices faded behind me, I rubbed a hand over my chest. Their words shouldn't hurt me. I was too strong for that. I had survived too much for that. And most importantly, I knew what Monette and Evander were like. But for some pathetic reason, those words still hurt.

I had suspected that Monette had used her powers of mood manipulation on me, but now I knew for certain. It made me sad to hear them call me selfish for pursuing my own dreams. Especially when I had always sacrificed so much for other people. But most of all, it broke my heart to realize how much of my life I had spent letting other people walk all over me. It wasn't until last year that I had finally decided to start putting myself first. And that was far too late.

Shaking my head at the mistakes I'd made in life, I shoved the hurt and regret aside and instead focused on my mission. The king's quarters were just up ahead. Based on what I remembered of the map I'd seen in Mordren's library all those months ago, there would be a bathroom connected to the room on this side. If I was lucky, maybe I would catch Anron unawares while relieving himself. Then I could end this war right now.

Two guards stood straight-backed next to the door around the corner. I frowned. Why would Anron need people guarding his door all the way in here? Then I remembered my desire to slit his throat while he was taking a shit, and decided that maybe his caution was justified after all.

After slipping through the walls of the interconnected rooms, I did indeed end up in a spectacular bathroom. The sunken bath in the white marble floor alone was larger than my whole bedroom back in the Court of Fire. Ducking behind a pair of gigantic plants with thick green leaves, I pressed myself against the wall and peered around the doorjamb.

Confusion fluttered through me.

Seated on a white lounge chair by the open window was a well-dressed person. But it was not Anron.

I scanned the room again. Beautiful dresses in varying shades of violet and purple lay draped over pieces of expensive furniture, and jewelry worth more than most families made in a lifetime was scattered across shining tabletops.

My eyes returned to the person by the window.

This wasn't Anron's room. It was hers.

I raised my eyebrows in surprise. The arrogant High Commander hadn't taken the king's rooms for himself. He had given them to Princess Syrene. Still pressed against the cool marble wall, I studied the former Princess of Trees for a few moments.

She had her knees pulled up to her chest, her arms circling them, where she sat leaning against the cushioned backrest. Since she was turned halfway away from me, I could only see part of her face. But as she sat there in the big empty room, staring out at the snow-capped mountains outside, I couldn't help thinking that she looked a bit... lonely.

In that moment, I had to wonder if it had been worth it to her. If everything she had done to get here had been worth it. She wanted power, and I didn't blame her for that. Gods and spirits knew that I craved it too. And while I had certainly murdered and blackmailed my way onto my throne, she had betrayed *everyone* to reach hers. So as she sat there alone, in a castle surrounded by High Elves and with those foreign guards outside her door, I couldn't help wondering if she was still happy with the side she had chosen in this war.

Either way, I supposed it was too late for her to back out now. I glanced back towards where I had seen Evander and

Monette. For them too. We had all chosen our sides, and now all that was left was to finish this dangerous game.

As I snuck back through the bathroom and made my way towards the soldiers' dining room instead, I thought back to that promise I had made Evander when I left him in this castle while we escaped. I had told him that if I saw him across the battlefield, I would not be as merciful as I had been back then. Since he was still here with High Commander Anron, I took that to mean that he was helping our enemies. As was Monette.

Next time I saw them, I would show them just how selfish and cruel I could really be.

CHAPTER 14

The intoxicating scent of food hung over the whole room. Utensils clinked against plates as the High Elf soldiers dug into the food that Herman had delivered. I watched with a wicked smile on my face for another few seconds before disappearing back through the wall and into the corridor on the other side.

"How long until it starts?" Theo whispered as I joined him, Valerie, and Eilan in the deserted hallway.

"Ten minutes," I answered. "Give or take."

Eilan narrowed his eyes at me. "Is this by any chance from the same place that you used when you poisoned my brother last year?"

A grin spread across my mouth. "Maybe."

It was, in fact, precisely from that place. It had been my first stop yesterday, before we went to see Liveria, and the blond elf who ran that shop remembered me. Not because I was now the Lady of Fire, but because the first time I walked into his store, I had bought five bottles of very dangerous poison while I looked like death and heartbreak myself. I supposed an order like that made an impression.

"We should get going," Theo interrupted before Eilan could respond.

"Yeah, we're pretty sure the bracelets," Valerie began, "or at least some of the bracelets, are kept in the smithy. They're using it as a kind of armory, and I swear I could see a stack of them through the half open door to a cabinet. But it was packed with soldiers, so I don't know for sure."

"Alright." I nodded. "There's a ledge up in the ceiling of that forge. We'll meet there."

They nodded back. And then we split up again.

Valerie and Theo disappeared to sneak through the castle without either of us slowing them down, and Eilan shapeshifted back into Gadrien so that he could walk the halls normally. It was a dangerous gamble, because at any moment he could run into someone who recognized every face in the castle and who knew that Gadrien was not supposed to be there. But as long as he stayed away from the most suspicious locations, like anywhere near Anron or the other Wielders, we deemed the risk low enough to justify his presence. After all, we would never have gotten the soldiers to take the food and eat it if he hadn't tipped the scales in our favor.

Slipping through the walls, I moved towards the forge downstairs using the same route I had opted for when I snuck in to see Ellyda all those weeks ago. Since the guards were still posted in the same places, I made it to my target wall without issue. Silk brushed against my skin as I stepped through the wall and then crawled forward on my stomach.

Age-old dust and metal shavings covered the unused ledge up in the ceiling.

As I reached the edge, I found two thieves already waiting for me.

"What took you so long?" Valerie whispered with a grin on her face.

I rolled my eyes at her. "Where's Eilan?"

"In the next room. He didn't know how to get up on this ledge, so he's waiting for the signal."

"What signal?"

"I suppose we'll know it when we see it."

After frowning at her for a second, I tilted my head to the side and gave her a nod. She did have a point.

Lying on our stomachs, we watched the soldiers in the room below us. Metal dinged and wood clattered as they moved armor, swords, bows, arrows, and other equipment into neat piles while marking things down on several pieces of paper. Apprehension fluttered through my stomach. They were most likely getting ready for the war that we still had no way of winning. I flicked my gaze towards the series of cabinets at the back of the room. We had to get those bracelets.

Twenty minutes passed with no distraction in sight. I was beginning to worry that the potion I'd bought had somehow been defective, but then the door banged open.

"Finally," said one of the soldiers in the room. "It's our turn to eat? You'd better have saved some of that fancy stuff for us."

The one who had walked through the door let out a huff. "You're lucky you missed it. It went bad, just like that little human said. Gods damn it... we should have eaten it straight away."

"What do you mean it went bad?"

"It's a fucking mess up there. Half of our brothers are

throwing up their damn intestines while the other half are shitting their pants."

"What the fuck?"

"Yeah." He shook his head. "So I was sent to tell you that we're gonna have to cover the second shift too."

"Are you fucking kidding me?"

"Nope." He jerked his chin at the room full of stunned soldiers. "Let's go. Can't leave the castle unguarded."

Irritated sighs and annoyed grumbling filled the forge as the High Elves left their positions and filed out of the room. Villainous smiles shone on all of our faces as I turned to look at Valerie and Theo.

"Well, I'd say that worked out splendidly," I announced.

"I don't want to see it," Theo began, "but I kind of do want to see it too. Just out of morbid curiosity, you know?"

"Yeah, no, I think I'm going to pass."

He chuckled right as the door opened and another High Elf strode inside.

"I take it that was the signal?" Gadrien said as he looked up at us.

Valerie grinned down at him. "Yep."

"Thought so." He motioned towards the door. "I'll keep watch so that no one blunders in. Hurry up and get the bracelets."

"So bossy." She gave him a quick rise and fall of her eyebrows. "I like it."

While Theo let out a groan, Gadrien cleared his throat and then disappeared out the door without another word. However, the color in his cheeks spoke for him. Valerie cackled and then swung herself down over the edge, holding on to it for a few seconds before dropping down. Barely a thud sounded as she landed on the floor like a cat. A moment later, Theo did the same.

Raising my eyebrows, I stared down at them. I had no idea how I was going to get back up onto this ledge if I dropped down, so I stayed where I was. Valerie and Theo zigzagged around the workbenches, heading straight for the cabinets at the back. A soldier had locked them before they left, but that didn't stop the two master thieves.

They whipped out a pair of lockpicks and got to work. I watched in amazement as the lock clicked open in a matter of seconds. Valerie swung her cabinet open to reveal shelves full of smaller pieces of equipment.

"Ha!" She whirled around to grin at me while stabbing a finger towards a stack of round black things. "Told you."

"Not so loud," Theo hissed at her.

"You're loud."

"You're the one who's yelling."

"Just get the bracelets," I interrupted.

Valerie scooped up the small stack of bracelets while Theo searched his cabinet for more of them. Finding nothing, he moved on to the next one, while Valerie did the same. Only tools for forging and small pieces of what I assumed was armor stared back from the shelves. When Theo opened the final one, we were forced to accept that the stack we had found were the only bracelets there. But hopefully, it would be enough.

"Someone's coming," Gadrien snapped as he barged through the door.

Valerie whirled around to face him. "Will you be okay?"

"If I leave now, yes."

"Then go. We've got this."

He nodded and then darted out the door again. Bracelets

clinked faintly as Valerie shoved them into her pockets while Theo quickly locked all the cabinets again. When the final one had clicked shut, they turned to look at each other. Then they nodded.

Theo sprinted across the floor and then interlaced his fingers while crouching down. Moving almost at the same time, Valerie ran after him and then placed her foot in his hands. He pushed off from the floor, giving her a boost up. Her fingers gripped the ledge and she swung sideways a couple of times before hooking her leg over the edge and nimbly climbing up.

While she did that, Theo ran back across the room and jumped up on one of the workbenches.

Heavy footsteps sounded in the corridor outside.

"Hurry," Valerie hissed at him before elbowing me in the ribs. "Get ready."

We leaned over the edge and stretched our arms down while Theo raced across the workbenches until he reached the last one. Pushing off from it, he leaped into the air. My heart lurched at the sight.

Then his hand wrapped around my wrist. I gripped him tightly while Valerie did the same with his other arm.

Armor clanked right outside the door.

My pulse pounded in my ears as we hauled him up over the ledge right before a High Elf soldier stalked inside. I would have heaved a deep breath of relief if it wouldn't have given away our position.

"We'll see you outside," Valerie whispered to me.

I gave them a nod and then crawled back to the wall before phasing through it. That had been close. But at least we had what we came for. And we had also dealt out a little bitter-tasting revenge to the High Elves who occupied our late king's castle.

The sounds of people vomiting echoed through the shining white halls as I snuck back outside. That, along with the lingering smell in the air, turned my stomach, but I still couldn't help cracking a malicious grin. No matter how small the win, it was still a win.

Fresh air filled my lungs as I snuck down the mountainside. Cool winds whirled around the snow-capped peaks and tugged at my hair. I pulled up the collar of my jacket.

Eilan, Theo, and Valerie were already waiting for me when I reached our entry and exit point.

"What–" Valerie began.

"Took me so long?" I finished for her. Huffing out a laugh, I shook my head as I closed the final distance. "Yes, yes, I know. You are better than me at this."

She flashed me a satisfied smile that made the others roll their eyes.

"Ready?" Eilan asked as I came to a halt next to them.

I nodded. Theo stepped closer and I wrapped an arm around his back, while Eilan and Valerie did the same on my other side. After a quick glance down at Theo, I worldwalked us out.

A busy camp and a vibrant green forest appeared around us.

"They're back!" Hadeon's voice boomed across the clearing.

I barely had time to release my hold on Theo before Hadeon, Idra, and Mordren had closed the distance to us.

"Did you get them?" Idra demanded.

"Of course we did," Valerie replied. Grinning at the elves

around her, she brushed imaginary dirt off her shoulders. "Who do you think we are?"

"Two cocky humans with a proclivity for pulling off impossible heists?" Eilan supplied.

"Bah!" Valerie slapped his ribs with the back of her hand before she frowned in confusion. "Actually, that was a nice compliment." She tipped her head from side to side as if considering. "I'll take it."

"So you managed to retrieve the bracelets?" Mordren asked, bringing the conversation back on track.

"Yes," Theo replied. "Not a massive amount, but it's a small stack at least."

"Excellent. Ellyda is in the forge over there."

Hadeon cupped his hands around his mouth. "El!"

The elves around the camp turned to look at him, but there was no answer from Ellyda.

"She probably didn't hear it," Hadeon said.

Idra snorted. "She's probably ignoring you."

"Shut up." He gave her arm a shove before motioning for the rest of us to follow. "Come on."

The white-haired warrior narrowed her eyes at him, but said nothing as we all moved to follow him towards the forge. All the windows, along with the door, were open to let fresh air in and out. Mordren drew his hand down my arm in an affectionate gesture as he stepped aside to let me move inside before him. I gave him a small smile.

A lone figure stood by one of the workbenches. Her long brown hair was tied up in a messy bun and she had rolled up the sleeves of her loose white shirt. Shuffling boots filled the forge but Ellyda didn't even look up as we all poured across the threshold.

"Whoa," I said as I turned to stare at the massive number of weapons that now filled the entire space.

Swords and daggers and axes and a whole host of other weapons hung from the wooden walls, their sharp edges gleaming in the sunlight. Apparently, this was what Ellyda had been doing while she was recovering from the trip to Valdanar.

"What is all this?" I asked.

Ellyda, who had been staring unblinking at a massive longsword on the workbench in front of her, at last tore her gaze from the weapon and looked up. Her violet eyes went in and out of focus as she blinked a few times before they finally cleared.

"They're for a worst-case scenario," she replied. Her gaze snapped to Valerie. "Do you have the bracelets?"

"Yes." Faint clinking sounded as Valerie pulled out the black jewelry from her pockets and stacked them into a little tower in front of Ellyda. "These were all the ones we could find. I hope they're enough."

Ellyda stared at the stack in silence for a minute. Then she nodded. "Yes."

She sat down abruptly and picked up the top bracelet. Her eyes turned sharp as she shifted it in her hands, studying it from every angle. Paper rustled as she pulled a notepad closer and began writing something.

We all watched her in silence for a while before it became apparent that our presence was no longer required. After exchanging a glance, we shrugged and turned to leave again.

"Kenna," Vendir called from across the grass as I stepped outside. His long blond hair rippled down his back as he jogged up to our group. "There's a strange elf here who says that he knows you."

My eyebrows rose. "Okay. Let's go see him then."

The others followed too as Vendir led the way towards the edge of camp. A group of Poisonwood elves were standing in a circle around a person on his knees. They had their bows drawn and pointed straight at him, and a couple of blood panthers prowled before them as well.

Nervous brown eyes shot to me. "Kenna, could you please tell them that we're friends?"

A surprised laugh escaped me. "Felix."

Lifting my hand, I motioned at the scouts to stand down. They lowered their bows but kept their eyes on the half-elf who now struggled to his feet.

Felix dragged a hand through his copper-colored hair and blew out a breath. "Man, this place was not easy to find. I've never been this far out before, so I had to worldwalk to the closest point and then just keep jumping ahead as far as I could see in the direction you'd told Prince Iwdael about. Good thing I started early."

"Yeah, sorry about that," I said. "But you're really good at this, you know."

A beaming smile lit up his freckled face. "Thanks. Anyway, now that I've been here once, it'll be much easier next time."

"So what brings you here?"

"Oh right." He grinned sheepishly and slapped a hand to his forehead. "Prince Iwdael sent me. It's your turn to guard the temple."

I raised my eyebrows. "Right now?"

"No, we're doing the shift tomorrow afternoon. Like I said, I had to start early because I didn't know how long it would take to find you. So rest up and get ready, and then I'll be back tomorrow and help you worldwalk there."

"Alright." I gave him a nod. "Thanks, Felix."

He flashed us all a smile before disappearing into thin air. I turned to face the rest of my friends. Apprehension and a bit of excitement blew through our group.

None of us had ever been to the temple, so I had to admit that I did look forward to finally seeing it for myself. But at the same time, guarding the temple was our most important job right now. If Anron got a hold of those bowls, we could kiss our freedom and our lives goodbye.

Hopefully, nothing would go wrong.

CHAPTER 15

Majestic trees rose around us while a massive mountain formed a formidable backdrop as it almost blocked out the sky. Tilting my head back, I stared up at it. I had grown up in the Court of Stone, but I had never been here. I didn't even know that there was something all the way out here. But then again, I supposed that that was the point.

"Great, you're here."

I sucked in a sharp breath and whipped around while yanking out my blades. All around me, my friends did the same.

"Oh, right," the voice said. "Sorry."

Two seconds passed, and then a gorgeous male elf with long golden hair became visible in front of a tree trunk.

"Augustien?" I blurted out.

"Hello." He took a step away from the tree and then turned to Felix. "Thank you for getting them here. I'll take them the rest of the way."

Felix nodded. "I'll be going then. I need to get back to Prince Edric."

"Hold on," Hadeon said. Steel rang through the forest as he pulled out two swords and held them out to the confused worldwalker. "El made more of those swords that can break the bracelets. So now we've got one for each court."

"Oh." He blinked in surprise and then looked around for Ellyda, before presumably remembering that we had left her and Captain Vendir in the Court of Light. Giving his head a little shake, he took the offered blades. "Great! I'll get them to Prince Edric and Prince Rayan then."

"One more thing," I said as he got ready to leave. "Tell Prince Edric that…" I hesitated for a moment as I met Felix's gaze. "Tell him that Monette is staying in the castle with Anron."

Pain swirled up in his brown eyes for a few seconds, but then he raised his chin and gave me a nod. "I'll tell him."

Before anyone could say anything else, he worldwalked out. My heart hurt from watching the expression on his face as I gave him the news. I knew how madly in love Felix had been with Monette. And probably still was. It must have taken everything he had just to leave with Prince Edric while she stayed behind when we broke them out of King Aldrich's castle. To now hear that she remained living there, willingly, must hurt terribly.

"Come on," Augustien said, breaking the silence that had fallen.

I shook off the heavy emotions and turned to follow him towards the mountain. Mordren fell in beside me, along with Eilan, while Hadeon and Idra brought up the rear. Valerie and Theo strolled along next to us, taking in every detail of the beautiful forest.

"So... this is what you do?" I asked, glancing over at Augustien. "You're a lookout."

"Yes." His golden eyes glittered in the afternoon sunlight. "I can camouflage myself against trees. It's pretty handy in these kinds of situations."

"Cool!" Valerie said from my left. "I wish I could blend into the environment like that. Imagine the havoc I could wreak."

"I'd argue that you're already quite accomplished at blending into environments," I said.

"Yeah," Theo added, "and I'd argue that you're already a master at wreaking havoc."

"Oh shush," she answered and flapped her arms at us. "But seriously, imagine having magic that could camouflage you against any surface."

"I can only do it against trees," Augustien reminded her.

"Yeah, but..." She trailed off as we cleared the tree line. "Whoa."

All eight of us stopped. Tilting our heads back, we stared up at the gigantic wooden walls before us.

"The wards reach all the way out here," Augustien explained, and swept his arms to indicate where the forest began and ended. "So if you want to worldwalk, you have to go back into the trees." Raising a hand to his mouth, he blew a sharp whistle. "Apple pie!"

A surprised laugh escaped my chest. "What?"

He shrugged. "To make sure it's not enemies." As the door set into the front of the defensive walls swung open, he raised a hand and motioned for us to go inside. "Reena will meet you in there. I have to go back to my position and make sure it's clear to leave."

We nodded goodbye as the golden-haired elf disappeared back into the forest while we started towards the doorway.

Right as we reached it, a female elf with long silver hair and turquoise eyes popped her head out.

"You made it," Reena said. "Great! We're just packing up the final things. Follow me."

I looked around in confusion as we entered a relatively small space boxed in by high wooden walls. When the door behind us clicked shut, another one opened in front of us. As we filed through the doorway, I realized that another small box with walls of wood waited us on the other side. Once more, the door swung shut before the next one opened.

"This is an impressive construction," Mordren observed.

"Yeah," Hadeon said. "It forces an enemy to split their army into tiny groups."

Idra rapped her knuckles against the wood next to her. "And creates kill boxes. While they're waiting to get through the next door, someone can just pick them off from above."

"I know, right?" Reena flashed us a beaming smile. "A few people are enough to hold off a massive army with this."

"Did Iwdael make it?" Eilan asked as he shifted his gaze to her.

"Nah. It's been here for a long time. You'll see when we get through."

Silence fell as we continued through the wooden maze full of kill boxes. They were right; with this design, even Anron would have trouble getting through.

A flat stretch of grass greeted us as we at last cleared the final door. In the middle of the open area was a beautiful temple made of white stone. I studied the arches and twisting spires as they pierced the air.

Halfway between the temple and the walls, a group of elves had gathered with some gear.

"My prince," Reena called. "They're here."

Prince Iwdael looked up from where he had been securing a giant bow to a backpack. The leaves and twigs woven into his long brown hair rustled as he pushed it back over his shoulder and then started towards us. We handed Reena one of the bracelet-shattering swords that Ellyda had forged, and explained what it was, while the Prince of Trees closed the final distance.

"Excellent, excellent," he said as he reached us. Lifting a hand, he patted Reena on the shoulder. "Thanks, my love. Go make sure the others are ready, will you?"

"Of course." She nodded a goodbye before striding over to the waiting group.

Iwdael turned back to us and clapped his hands together. "Well then, let's get you up to speed. Did Reena explain the purpose of the maze?"

"Yes," Mordren answered.

"Good, good." Iwdael swept his arms towards the temple. "As you can see, it's made of stone on the outside. And the inside..." He abruptly took off towards the temple door. "Follow me."

We all scrambled to catch up with him as he crossed the grass with brisk steps. The temple loomed above us as we drew near, but it was roughly the same height as the defensive walls. Up close, I could tell that it was an old building. The stone looked like it had withstood millennia of harsh weather. And yet, it still looked strong. I frowned as I realized that there were no windows on it.

Darkness enveloped us as we stepped across the threshold. I had to blink several times to try to get my eyes to adjust after the bright sunlight and white stone outside. Squinting against the gloom, I realized that the walls were black on the inside. Torches and lanterns burned throughout the empty room we had entered, casting flickering shadows against the glossy walls. Realization crashed through me.

"Isn't this the same material that your castle is made of?" I asked as I turned to Mordren.

He studied the black glass-like material before replying, "Yes. It would appear so."

"Keen observational skills, Lady Firesoul," Iwdael said and spun around while sweeping his arms out in a dramatic gesture. "The inside of the temple is made of shadow glass."

"Shadow glass?" Theo said.

"That's the one." Iwdael turned to peer at Mordren. "Though it appears as though the art of manipulating shadow glass has been lost somewhere throughout the millennia."

A hint of regret blew across Mordren's face. "Indeed. It has been a long time since any Prince of Shadows was able to use that magic."

"Hmm. Yes, very sad. Anyway, as you could see on your way in, the defensive walls are made of wood, the outside of the temple is made of stone, and the inside is made of shadow glass."

He paused, waiting for us to fill in the blanks.

"Meaning that no single prince could ever storm this place on his own," Eilan finished.

"Correct. Only the Prince of Trees can lower the wooden walls that make up the maze, and only the Prince of Stone can lower the outer walls of the temple, and so on. They're also keyed to the specific magic in these bowls. So even though Anron can access all elemental magic, he won't be able to just lower the walls at will. He has to blast through them in that case." He spread his arms. "Like I said, impenetrable."

"But what if the Prince of Shadows, Stone, and Trees

formed an alliance and did it together?" Valerie asked, her brows raised expectantly.

"Yes, well, then these lands would have been well and truly screwed." He turned to wink at Mordren. "Good thing none of our ancestors ever got along that well."

Mordren huffed out a surprised laugh. "Indeed."

"Anyway, let's go see the magic then, shall we?" Iwdael set off at a brisk pace again. "Keep up."

Idra's dark eyes swept across the large empty room. As we continued into a corridor that took us deeper into the heart of the temple, I wondered whether she remembered a time when the Prince of Shadows could manipulate shadow glass. She had never told me exactly how old she was, but I knew that she wasn't kidding when she said that she was older than all the rest of us combined.

Firelight danced over shining black walls as we moved through the halls. Every single room we passed was completely empty. Apart from the torches on the walls and the oil lamps secured to the ceiling, there was nothing else inside the temple.

Prince Iwdael stopped as we reached yet another square room in what felt like the very middle of the building. Pausing with his hand on the handle, he looked back at us.

"And this," he began in a theatrical voice, "is where the magic is."

Theo and Valerie exchanged an excited look. Behind them, Idra and Hadeon crossed their arms with ridiculously synchronized movements. I drew in a soft breath as Iwdael pulled open the door.

The same black glass-like material covered the floor and walls inside, and firelight lit the windowless room. In the middle of the room were six pedestals. A pair of white stone bowls rested on top of five of them. One on each pedestal was empty. Magic swirled above the other. Fire. Shadows. Water. Stone. Wood. The sixth pedestal had no bowls at all on it.

"As you can see, this is where it's all kept," Iwdael said as we moved inside. He jerked his thumb over his shoulder to point back towards the door. "We all sleep in the empty rooms around it because, well, it feels a bit ominous in here, doesn't it?"

"Got it," I said.

"I also recommend staying inside the defensive walls while you guard the temple," Iwdael continued. "Unless you have someone who can camouflage themselves in the forest."

"Ha!" Valerie said and elbowed me in the ribs. "Told you being able to camouflage would be a neat power."

The Prince of Trees shot her an amused look before continuing. "Like I said, stay inside the defensive walls. It's much easier to defend them from inside. Any questions?"

"Yeah," Theo said as he frowned while pointing at the back wall. "What's in there?"

Clothes rustled as we all turned towards where he was pointing. It looked like a door. But there was no lock and no handle, so I wasn't sure how anyone would open it.

"Ah, yes, that." Iwdael scratched his jaw. "That is the reason for the sixth empty pedestal. According to what King Aldrich told Edric, the bowls from the Court of Light used to be kept out on the pedestal. But when someone wiped out that court, they moved those two bowls into that room."

That someone who had wiped out the Court of Light had been none other than Volkan Flameshield, but I refrained from saying so since it would raise questions on how I knew that. Apparently, King Aldrich had still been too ashamed that he had done nothing to stop what was happening in the Court of Light to share that part of the story with Edric.

Iwdael blew out a sigh of regret. "If we only had someone from that court, then we could open that door. Too bad they're all dead."

Everyone in our group made a very admirable effort to not look at Idra.

"What do you mean?" I asked carefully.

"It's warded, you see. With a barrier spell. It will only open for someone from the Court of Light. And once it's open, it's gone. So all we'd need is for someone from the Court of Light to stand in front of that door once, and then the barrier spell is broken." He shrugged. "Then maybe we could reinstate the Court of Light."

We all continued looking everywhere except at Idra.

"I see," I said.

Iwdael rolled back his shoulders and turned towards us again. "Any other questions?"

"When do we switch again?"

"Five days. Rayan and his people will come relieve you. The code word is purple potato."

A smile pulled at my lips. "Purple potato. Got it."

"Well, then." He touched his hand to his forehead and gave us a salute. "I wish you good day, good luck, and good fortune."

We nodded goodbye and then watched as the Prince of Trees strolled back out of the temple.

Once his footsteps had faded and only the hissing of the torches disrupted the silence, we all turned to glance at each other. Idra was the only person left from the Court of Light. She alone could break the barrier spell. But the only people who knew that, apart from Ellyda, were in this room. Prince

Iwdael had talked about reinstating the Court of Light once this was all over. I wondered how Idra felt about that.

That usual mask of complete indifference sat securely over her features as she spun around to face us. We looked back at her. Only an impassive iron wall stared back at us from behind her dark eyes.

"Let's go set up a watch schedule," she said, her tone clipped.

Without waiting for a reply, she stalked out the door.

CHAPTER 16

Sitting on the short steps in front of the temple door, I watched as Mordren and Eilan sparred on the grass. A pair of long knives gleamed in their hands and metal dinged faintly as they clashed before breaking apart again. Both of them had taken their shirts off and their lean muscles shifted as they moved across the grass with lethal grace. A smirk spread across my lips as I drank in the sight of Mordren's body. Mine. That was all mine.

"You're drooling," Idra remarked as she stalked through the doorway and sat down next to me.

I slapped her arm with the back of my hand. "Am not."

"Uh-huh."

We fell into a comfortable silence as we just sat there for a while, watching the two dark-haired brothers train in the bright sunlight. The air out here smelled of snow-covered mountains and deep forests, but the winds still clung to summer's warmth. I drew in a deep breath and stretched out my legs before me.

It had been three days since we arrived at the temple, and

so far, everything had been quiet. We always kept two people up on the walls as lookouts, so we slept in shifts to make sure we had it covered at all times.

I glanced over at Idra.

She and Hadeon had covered the previous shift before being relieved by Valerie and Theo, and as far as I could tell, it looked like she had gotten at least some sleep. There were no dark circles around her eyes, but she looked... tense. I wasn't sure if that was because of Iwdael's mention of reinstating the Court of Light, or just the situation in general. Or something else entirely.

"Have you thought about it?" I asked, keeping my eyes on the sparring session ahead. "What Iwdael said about reinstating the Court of Light?"

Idra was silent for a while. "I have."

Saying nothing, I just waited to see if she would go on. Eventually, she let out a soft exhale.

"I don't want to reinstate the Court of Light," she said. "I want the elves from Poisonwood Forest and all of their animals to make it their home instead. To make it something... different."

"Okay." I glanced over at her with a small smile on my lips. "Then it's decided."

She met my gaze briefly, and the ghost of a smile drifted over her mouth before she nodded.

"You're already up?" came a voice from behind us.

Idra shifted her gaze to the muscled warrior who had just wandered through the door, before lifting her shoulders in a shrug. "I couldn't sleep."

"Yeah." Hadeon blew out a deep sigh as he dropped down on Idra's other side. "Me neither."

Leaning forward slightly, I studied him where he sat on

the white stone steps next to Idra. He raised both of his hands and raked them through his short brown hair a couple of times. His red eyes were sharp and alert as always, but he also looked tense.

"What's wrong?" I asked.

Hadeon paused with his hands halfway through his hair. For a moment, he only sat there, watching Mordren and Eilan as they lunged at each other. Then he let his arms drop and turned to me.

"I'm worried about El," he said as he flicked his gaze between me and Idra.

My heart squeezed painfully in my chest, but I gave him a small smile. "Vendir is with her. He'll make sure she remembers to eat and drink."

"Yeah, I know. But..."

"You don't trust him?" I asked.

He was silent for a few seconds. "No, I do trust him. She's happier when he's around. Even if they're not talking or anything, just being in the same room... I can tell that she's breathing easier. I think he gets her in ways that most people don't. And the way he protected her back in Valdanar... Yeah, I trust him. And especially with keeping her safe."

"Then what is it?"

"I haven't seen her like this in a long time. Sometimes it's better and sometimes it's worse. It's always been like that. But this... I haven't seen her like this since our parents..." He trailed off. Worry crept into his eyes as he met my gaze. "I'm worried that if she continues to push herself, something in her brain is just going to snap and she'll never recover."

Tiny needles stabbed into my heart. Opening my mouth, I was just about to say something to help reassure him, but someone else beat me to it.

"She's strong," Idra said in a steady voice as she turned to lock eyes with Hadeon. "Her name is Steelsinger, but it's not just because of her talent for forging metals. I can see the steel in her eyes. But more importantly, she possesses something that most people don't. Self-awareness. She's among the most perceptive people I have ever met, and she knows and understands *herself* on a soul-deep level. She knows her own limits. And she knows that you will always be there for her, so when she reaches the point where it all gets too much, she will tell you."

Hadeon stared back at her, his mouth slightly open, while a whole tangle of emotions swirled in his red eyes. Then a wide smile spread across his lips. "Yeah, you're right. That's exactly what she's like." He glanced down before meeting Idra's gaze again. "Thanks."

Idra cleared her throat a bit self-consciously. "Yeah."

"Anyway." He slapped his knees and then stood up. "I've got this move I wanna try out." Turning back around, he looked down at Idra. "Can you help me out?"

"Oh, uhm, sure."

I ran a hand over my mouth to hide my smile as the two of them left the stone steps and walked down to a spot on the grass a short distance from Mordren and Eilan. Bright sunlight kissed their lethal bodies as they squared up against each other.

In a flash, Hadeon shot forward and flipped Idra over so that she landed back first on the grass. I raised my eyebrows. That wasn't like Idra.

With a slight frown on his face, Hadeon reached down and held out a hand to help her up. She eyed it suspiciously before locking her hand around his wrist. Wrapping his fingers around hers as well, he pulled her to her feet. Before she could back away again, he casually plucked a blade of grass from her shining white hair. She blinked at him in stunned confusion, but he was looking at the blade of grass as it fluttered to the ground. And when he met her gaze again, the expression was gone.

"Alright, I could tell that you saw that coming," Hadeon began. "And you let it go through anyway. What gave it away?"

"Your hips, and your elbow," Idra answered, and gestured towards his body. "When you shifted them like that, I knew what you were going to do."

"Ah, so if I–"

"They're coming!" Theo's voice cut through the air like a sword.

Panic flashed through my body and I shot to my feet while whipping towards the sound of his voice.

"Anron! The High Elves!" Theo bellowed from atop the front of the defensive walls. "They're coming! They're coming *now*!"

A sharp whistling sound suddenly filled the air above us.

I snapped my head up to find a cloud of arrows big enough to block out the sun speeding towards us.

Fire roared through the air as I threw up a massive wall of flames to stop the barrage. The wooden shafts were incinerated as they hit the barrier, but another cloud of projectiles quickly took their place. Mordren and Eilan yanked their shirts back on and sheathed their knives while Idra and Hadeon were already racing towards where Theo still stood.

"They're firing from inside the forest," Theo yelled from his position atop the walls.

"Kenna, keep the shield up," Idra snapped. "Everybody, get up on the walls."

Taking the steps two at a time, we sprinted up the stairs on the inside of the defensive walls so that we could see out over the wooden maze. The kill boxes were still empty but soldiers in bronze armor were pouring out of the forest to cover the ground between the walls and the tree line. At the front was High Commander Anron.

"How the hell did they find us?" I hissed to myself.

"Valerie!" Hadeon's voice boomed across the temple grounds as he turned towards the back of it. "They're coming from the front."

"It's clear back here!" Valerie's voice came from behind the white stone spires that blocked the view of the back half of the defensive walls.

"Signal if they try to circle!" he called back.

"Got it!"

We had to keep this battle contained to the front of the walls. If the High Elves surrounded the whole temple, it would be much harder to defend. But since the only door through the walls was located at the front, I hoped that they would focus on that. And if they did decide to circle the building, Valerie would spot them before they could surround us completely.

The rain of arrows stopped as the ranks of High Elves positioned themselves just outside the defensive walls. Magic hummed in the air.

"Get ready," Idra snapped.

It was too far to tell for sure, but I swore I could see a malicious grin on Anron's lips as he started rising from the ground. Six other High Elves flew up into the air alongside him.

"Shit," I cursed. "I forgot that they can levitate."

"Mordren," Hadeon said. "Kenna. Create a wall of magic.

Fire in the front. Shadows in the back. Get ready to shift it as Eilan picks them off."

We nodded. Steel rang out as Eilan drew his knives. I raised a thick barrier of flame right in front of the wooden walls. It wasn't very wide, but it was high enough to make flying over it impractical.

"Do you have their position?" Hadeon asked without turning to look at Eilan.

His eyes tracked the figures visible on the other side of the flames. "Yes."

A moment later, a mass of twisting dark shadows rose as well.

"Now!" Hadeon called.

Eilan flicked his wrists.

Lightning shot out in two long lines and sped towards our magic barrier. Right before it hit, Mordren and I created gaps in our walls to let the lightning through. It crackled as it cut through the air.

The High Elves outside dropped abruptly to avoid getting struck by it.

Waves of water slammed into my fire, making part of the wall explode into steam, but Mordren's shadows remained intact. I patched up my flaming barrier as the Wielders sent a volley of lightning back at us. The white bolts tore through my flames but were slowed down enough that they didn't do much damage to Mordren's shadows.

Eilan flicked his wrists again, sending lightning through the holes while we patched them up.

He was using the same cheating technique as me. Since he hadn't had more than a few weeks to practice wielding lightning, he had taken my advice and used his blades to focus the attacks. It worked remarkably well.

THE LAST STAND

One of the bolts struck a High Elf in the shoulder, and he dropped almost all the way back to the ground before recovering.

Coordinated blasts of water hit from all sides.

I blew out a steadying breath as I summoned more magic to patch it up while Mordren strengthened the shadows in those places.

The mass of soldiers on the ground remained firmly in place.

"Why are they just standing there?" Theo asked, fear making his voice shake slightly. "Why aren't they trying to get through the door?"

"They probably think that they can take us out with just their Wielders before they have to walk through the door," Idra answered.

Worried gray eyes shifted between the five of us. "And can they?"

We exchanged a glance.

"I'm getting reinforcements," Idra announced.

Hadeon's hand shot out and grabbed her before she could sprint away. "Wait!"

She yanked her arm out of his grip.

Lightning cut through the air and slammed into our barrier. Mordren clenched his jaw as the white bolts tore through his shadows. Stabbing his knives forward, Eilan sent attacks back through the holes.

"You are perfectly capable of directing this battle without me," Idra snapped at Hadeon. "And apart from those three, I'm the only one here who can worldwalk. And my powers aren't suited for long-distance fights anyway. I'll circle to the back and drop down from atop the wall so that I can get out of the wards and worldwalk. Hold down the fort. I'm getting the other princes."

Without waiting for a reply, she sprinted along the high defensive walls towards where Valerie was keeping watch.

A combined blast of water and lightning ripped through our shields. I snarled and threw up a second wall behind our first one to stop the attack from going all the way through. Eilan slashed his blades through the air, sending bolt after bolt of lightning back at the Wielders while Mordren and I desperately worked to repair the barrier.

"What the hell!" Idra's voice cleaved the air like a sword. "They're circling! They're closing in on the back too. Where the hell is Valerie?"

Fear exploded in my chest like a cloud of poison.

Since the temple was in the way, we couldn't see Valerie from here. Theo whipped around and stared towards the back of the grounds while terror washed over his features.

"Keep your eyes on the Wielders," Hadeon snapped at me.

"Valerie is down!" Idra bellowed as she came back into view from behind the temple spires with the unconscious thief in her arms. "She's breathing but–"

My stomach lurched.

Panic crackled through my whole body as the wood beneath my feet suddenly disappeared.

The entire wall around the temple and the maze before it shot back down into the grass.

Winds ripped through my hair as we plummeted towards the ground.

CHAPTER 17

*D*read shot up my spine as the ground got closer. I tried to roll over in the air so that I wouldn't break anything too important, but this landing was going to hurt.

A mass of twisting darkness bloomed below me. I sucked in a shocked breath as I landed in Mordren's shadows and then slid down the slope they created. The smell of grass and earth enveloped me as I rolled to a halt on the ground.

Snapping my head up, I just managed to see Idra and Valerie roll off a net of shadows on the other side. Around me, Mordren, Eilan, Hadeon, and Theo were already jumping to their feet.

Battle cries rang through the warm air.

"Kenna!" Hadeon shouted. "Push them back!"

I yanked out my blades and slashed them through the air. Great scythes of fire shot towards the ranks upon ranks of High Elves now rushing towards us on the open ground.

The walls and the maze had completely disappeared.

Steam hissed as the Wielders in the air sent waves of water to counter the fire. Anron shifted his arm towards us.

"Mordren!" Eilan called.

Lightning exploded through the air and shot straight towards us. We leaped back to escape it while Mordren threw up a shield of shadows in front of us. White light tore holes in the darkness.

Idra sprinted towards us from the other side while Valerie's unconscious form bounced in her arms.

High Elves in bronze armor swarmed in from all sides as we backed towards the door to the temple while continuing to throw magic at them to hold them back.

"How the hell did he get the walls down?" Hadeon growled as we backed across the grass. "Only the Prince of Trees is supposed to be able to affect them."

"I don't know," I answered while shooting fiery arcs at the soldiers closing in around us. "Maybe he..."

I trailed off as my gaze fell on a figure standing behind us to the left, halfway between the door and the deep ruts that marked where the walls had been.

"Kenna!" Eilan snapped as my shield faltered.

Shoving my arms forward, I sent a massive wave of fire towards the soldiers and then whirled around to face the person I had spotted.

Dark green eyes watched me from across the grass.

"You son of a bitch," I screamed while shooting more attacks at the charging soldiers over my shoulder. "You led them here?"

Evander lifted his shoulders in a nonchalant shrug. "It was actually Monette who knew the location. I just passed on the information to High Commander Anron."

A vicious snarl ripped from my throat as I slashed my sword through the air, sending a searing arc of fire straight at the traitor who had sold me out far too many times.

Wood shot up from the grass. It formed a thick wall in front of Evander and blocked the attack. My flames carved a blackened rut into it, almost all the way to the other side, but it hadn't touched Evander.

My steps faltered and I trailed to a halt on the grass.

"Move," Mordren ordered as he grabbed my arm and yanked me with them as they continued retreating towards the door.

Idra skidded to a halt on the grass behind me. "They're coming from all sides."

"He has magic," I blurted out, dumbfounded.

The others tore their gazes from the advancing soldiers to stare at Evander as he lowered the wooden shield he had raised. He let out a satisfied laugh.

"Looks like I might be the new Prince of Trees," he called, and then shook his head. "You really should have paid more attention to what was happening behind your backs."

White-hot terror burned through me. Evander had snuck inside the temple and drunk the magic from the second bowl belonging to the Court of Trees while we had been busy fighting Anron and his Wielders.

"I tried to take the other bowls too." Evander slid his hands into his pockets and stuck his fingers through the holes there. "But as you can see, it doesn't transport well." He shrugged again. "It doesn't really matter, though. High Commander Anron will get them in a few minutes anyway." A wicked smile spread across his mouth. "And besides, I got what I wanted, so…"

Anger ripped through my chest. Slashing my blades through the air, I sent wave after wave of flaming scythes at him. Wooden shields sprang up to block them.

"Kenna!" Idra snarled and yanked me back around. "Keep your eyes on the real threat."

The charging High Elves were barreling across the grass. Water and wind and lightning crackled through the air as the Wielders tried to keep us from attacking the soldiers on the ground. I shot a blast of fire at Anron, which he blocked with a shield of water.

Theo now had Valerie draped against him, while Idra moved into position next to Hadeon.

Something hard met my heels.

We had reached the steps to the temple door. After backing up them, we formed a half circle before the opening. Pain magic and lightning and fire split the warm air and filled it with embers and the smell of ozone as Mordren, Eilan, and I tried to keep the High Elves army at bay.

"Raise a shield instead," Hadeon finally ordered. "Same as before. Only around the temple instead. Attacking them won't work in the long run. We need to focus on holding them off."

"For how long?" Theo asked.

Fire roared across the ground as I raised a flaming shield around the temple. A moment later, Mordren added his shadows.

"The Court of Water is coming in two days," Hadeon replied, leaving the disheartening answer hanging in the air.

Valerie let out a gasp. "They're coming! Evander and a Wielder, they—"

"We know," Idra interrupted. "They're already here."

I couldn't take my eyes off the fire wall that I had to keep patching up, but silence fell for a few seconds before Valerie spoke up again.

"I'm sorry," she said, her voice soft. "They just flew out of the woods suddenly and the Wielder dropped Evander over the wall. I tried to warn you but he shot lightning at me, and part of it hit me before I could call out."

"It's alright," Theo reassured her. "We'll figure this out."

No one answered. I wasn't sure how we would survive this, and I had a feeling that we were all thinking the same thing.

Through the holes that we kept mending in our magic barrier, I could see Anron and his Wielders landing on the grass next to Evander. Over the noise of the battle, it was impossible to tell what they were saying, but Anron leaned down and spoke to the treacherous elf.

Shock flashed across Evander's features. He edged a step back before something Anron said froze him in his tracks. After turning to stare straight at us through one of the holes, he held out his arm.

I patched up the hole right as a blast of water tore another one open.

Through it, I was just able to catch Anron locking a black bracelet around Evander's wrist.

Smug spitefulness swirled in my chest. Evander had been desperate to gain magical powers, and now that he finally had them, Anron had taken them away just as quickly.

The smugness evaporated as realization flashed through my mind. *Shit.*

"Anron has Evander's magic now," I blurted out. "It will increase his powers."

As if the High Commander had heard me, he turned towards us slowly while a wide grin spread across his face. Then he raised his arms.

"Brace!" I screamed.

Mordren ground his teeth and called up another layer of shadows while I increased the thickness of my fire.

Lightning crackled through the air, carving a gigantic hole in our shield. Through it, Anron smirked at us. Then he raised his arms again.

"Get inside!" Hadeon commanded. "Now."

I let out a yelp as he grabbed the back of my magic-imbued jacket and hauled me inside. Mordren kept the shadow barrier up while Idra and Hadeon swung the doors shut after everyone was through. Loud bangs echoed against the shining black walls as they slammed the heavy bars into place.

Theo looked up at the massive doors before saying in a soft voice, "That's the only way out."

Idra and Hadeon exchanged a glance.

"Get to the room with the magic," Idra ordered.

I frowned at her and Hadeon, but followed them as we ran towards the room at the center of the temple, barring the other doors behind us as we went. Did they really think that these walls would be able to withstand Anron's attacks for two days? They had to have another plan up their sleeves.

Boom.

The building shook as the High Elves threw their magic straight at the door. Torches hissed and spluttered. I tried to calm my pounding heart as we sprinted through the final corridor before reaching the room with the bowls.

"Kenna," Idra said as we stopped before the pedestals. "That jacket of yours, it's imbued with magic, right?"

"Yes. Why?"

"Take the bowls and put them in your pockets," Hadeon answered in her stead. "Your jacket should be able to hold them for a short while at least."

"*Why?*" I repeated with more force.

Idra locked hard eyes on me. "Because you need to take the

magic and run through the walls until you get out past the wards where you can worldwalk."

"And leave you here?"

"Yes."

"No!"

She grabbed the front of my jacket and hauled me closer until I could see the faint scars covering her face. "Stop talking and do as I tell you."

I shoved her back and cast frantic eyes over the rest of them. "I am not leaving you here!"

"Yes, you are. Listen to me." She waited until I met her gaze again. "Anron won't kill us. He knows what we mean to you, so he will take us as hostages and try to trade us for the magic. That gives you time to find a way to get us out."

"But if we do nothing," Hadeon filled in, "Anron will take both us and the magic. And then it will be all over. This gives us a chance."

"They're right," Eilan said. Picking up the bowl of stone magic, he handed it to me. "You have to go. Right now."

Shaking my head, I turned pleading eyes to Mordren.

He brushed a hand over my cheek. "We will be fine. You will find a way to free us."

The building shook violently as attacks pounded against the walls.

"But only if you leave now," Idra snapped and shoved the other bowls towards me.

Tears burned behind my eyes, but I gently placed the bowls in separate pockets. My jacket seemed to almost tremble from the force of the magic now inside it, but the fabric held.

"No goodbyes," Theo said as I opened my mouth.

Valerie nodded. "We'll see you soon."

Swallowing against the lump in my throat, I closed my mouth again and only nodded back.

Then I turned and ran.

Silk brushed against my skin as I cleared the black wall of the magic room. Continuing towards the next one, I ran straight through the walls towards the back of the temple.

My heart shattered with every single step, but I kept going because I knew that they were right. I had to believe that they were right. Otherwise, I would never have been able to leave behind the people I loved like family while I alone escaped.

Rogue tears ripped from my eyes as I ran.

If Anron hurt them in any way, I would never forgive myself. My infuriating, insane, and incredibly brave family. I would get them out. I would save them. We would win this war. And then we would live happily ever after.

Blinding sunlight met me as I leaped through yet another wall and abruptly found myself outdoors.

"She's here!" someone called.

Whipping my head from side to side, I found an impenetrable wall of High Elf soldiers in gleaming bronze armor. Swords glinted in the sun as the soldiers took off towards me.

I threw myself back through the wall.

Darkness enveloped me again and I had to blink frantically to get my eyes to readjust as I sprinted towards another side of the building.

Boom. Boom. Boom.

The whole temple shook as magic pounded it from all sides.

My heart thumped in my chest as I leaped through a wall on the other side of the temple.

Another impenetrable ring of soldiers surrounded it as far

as the eye could see. Shouts rang out. I jumped back into the temple as calls for my capture echoed along the lines. With panic crawling its way up my throat, I raced to another side of the building. And then another.

Dread and fear seeped through my veins. Anron had anticipated this. Of course he had. I had lured him into buildings and then escaped through the walls so many times now. As soon as we slammed the door shut, he must have given the order to surround the temple so that I wouldn't be able to fool him like that again. And this time, there was no one on the outside to make the soldiers leave their posts.

The wall next to me exploded.

CHAPTER 18

*B*lack shadow glass rained down over me as I was flung back against the inner wall by the force of the blast. Sunlight streamed in through the gaping hole in the outer wall.

"Get a Wielder in here," someone called from the outside.

My ears rang, but I pushed myself to my feet and staggered through the inner wall just as soldiers poured through the hole. Throwing out a hand, I braced myself against the wall of the next room as the temple shook again.

Terror sluiced through me.

They had already gotten through the outer walls. If they kept this up, it wouldn't be long until they reached the room with the pedestals in it. And my friends. I took off back towards them.

A small flicker of relief coursed through me. At least I wouldn't have to leave them behind. Whatever happened next, we would face it together.

I immediately felt bad for thinking it.

Of course it would have been better if Anron hadn't had

the whole temple already surrounded. If I had been able to escape with the magic instead of being trapped here too. I knew that it made me a selfish person, but I was secretly relieved that I wouldn't have to face the rest of this war alone while constantly wondering what kind of torture Anron was currently inflicting on the people I loved.

Voices cut through the booms as I leaped through a wall and skidded to a halt in the room I had left earlier.

Six people whirled around to face me.

"What the hell are you doing?" Idra demanded. "I told you to run."

"I can't."

"I already told you, this is—"

"No, I mean I literally can't. The whole temple is surrounded. Anron has seen my tricks one too many times so he has a whole ring of soldiers watching every single part of the building. Oh, and they've already blasted through part of the outer wall."

The building shook as if to confirm it.

I swept serious eyes over the six of them. "They're inside the temple."

They all stared back at me in silence, dread flickering on their faces.

"Shit," Idra finally said.

My jacket trembled against my body. Jogging up to the pedestals, I yanked the bowls from my pockets and put the magic back before it burned holes in my jacket.

"We can't let him get them," Eilan said into the tense silence. "You saw how much his magic increased after he siphoned Evander's powers. If he gets all of this," he stabbed a hand towards the bowls now resting on the pedestals again, "this war will end today."

"Agreed," Mordren said.

Hadeon dragged a hand through his hair while shaking his head. "So what do we do? We can't hide it." Flinging out a muscular arm, he motioned towards the sealed door at the back of the room. "If we could get the barrier back up again, we could hide them in there. But now, if Idra goes to stand there, the barrier will just fall and we'll only have two more bowls of magic to protect."

More booms echoed through the temple. The torches on the walls spluttered as the building shook violently. It was coming from the same direction that I had returned from, meaning that the High Elves were probably just blasting their way through in a straight line instead of bothering to try to get through the barred doors.

Valerie, who had been uncharacteristically silent since she had accidentally let Evander get past her, cleared her throat. "What if you drink the magic?"

Stunned silence rang through the room as we all turned to stare at her.

"I mean," she began and tucked a loose brown curl back behind her ear, "Anron can't take the magic if the bowls are empty. It worked for Kenna back in Valdanar even though she already had fire magic. When she drank it, she only got stronger. So if you all drink the rest of the magic now, you will both make sure that the bowls are empty and you might actually become powerful enough to get us out of this."

Theo had his eyebrows raised in surprise, but he turned towards us and nodded enthusiastically. "She's right. Since Evander drank the tree one, there are only four bowls. And there are five of you. Kenna takes the fire, Mordren the shadows, and then Idra and Hadeon take the stone and water ones."

We all exchanged a glance. Crumbling shadow glass fell from the ceiling and clattered against the floor as the walls shook again.

"This is insane," Idra finally announced.

"Yeah." Hadeon shook his head. "It'll mess up the whole power structure and order of succession for every single court."

Eilan flicked a glance towards the wall as another boom echoed from outside. "Yes, but if Anron gets these bowls, there won't be any power structure or court succession left to protect."

Attacks slamming into the walls around us punctured the anxious silence that had fallen over the room.

"They're getting closer," I said as I whipped my head from left to right to see the walls vibrate on all sides. "And they've spread out."

"So, drink the magic," Theo urged.

"We can't." I threw my arms out in a desperate gesture. "Edric, Rayan, Iwdael... It would be a huge betrayal if we took the magic for ourselves."

Valerie fixed us with a stare. "Do you think they'd rather you have it or Anron?"

"But..."

"I hate to say it," Mordren interrupted, "but Valerie and Theo are right."

Turning around, I found him looking back at us with serious eyes.

"Yes, it would be unfair to the other princes," he continued. "And yes, it would upset the power balance. However, there would be no more bowls that needed protecting, so it would make sure that Anron could not get his hands on the magic unless he captured the five of us. And the people in this room are among the most capable people I have ever met. With the extra bit of magic added to that, we would also stand a significantly better chance of not only surviving today, but also winning this war in the long run."

Powerful attacks slammed into the walls around us, making them tremble.

"Spirits damn it," Hadeon groaned. "He's right. We need to do this now before they break through."

His leather armor creaked as he stood up straighter and stalked towards the pedestals. A second later, Mordren followed. Idra and I exchanged a glance before making our way over as well.

"I'll go first and make sure that this will actually work," I said as I reached the one with the bowl of fire. "If it doesn't, I guess you'll have to sweep my charred remains off the floor and come up with another plan."

Before any of them could protest, I picked up the bowl and sucked in a deep breath. Then I placed it against my lips and poured the twisting flames into my mouth.

Just like last time, it was thick like molten lava, and at the same time light like the flickering top of a candle. And it tasted like honey and spices. Warmth spread from my throat as I swallowed the magic. It swirled through my entire body, setting off sparkles like tiny fireworks as it moved.

Fire flared to life along my arms and then spread until my whole body was covered with it. Dark red flames played in my hair, lifting it up before letting it flutter down against my back once more.

My friends looked back at me, apprehension evident on their faces.

The fire on my skin died down. I blew out a deep breath in relief over the fact that adding a third dose of fire magic to my body hadn't in fact turned me into a lump of coal. The relief was quickly replaced by stunned disbelief.

Power the likes of which I had never felt before rolled through me, soaking my whole soul in dark red flames. The fire seemed to burn through my every vein and pulse with every beat of my heart. I felt as though I could burn down the world with a snap of my fingers.

"It works," I managed to press out while trying to keep in check the incredible power now crackling under my skin.

Mordren's eyes searched my face, but before he could say anything, Theo's voice cut through the room.

"Great. Hurry up then."

After tearing his gaze from me, Mordren picked up the bowl of shadows and drank the twisting mass of darkness.

Shadows materialized on his skin. They snaked down his limbs, wrapping themselves around his whole body, and continued all the way out until they flickered around his fingers. Darkness swirled in Mordren's silver eyes for a second. Then they all disappeared.

"You okay?" I asked.

He stared down at his own body for a couple of seconds before meeting my gaze. "Yes."

We all turned to Idra and Hadeon.

Hadeon, who was the only one of us, not counting Valerie and Theo, who had been born with no magical power, looked at the bowls before him as if he didn't know what to do anymore.

"Which one?" Idra asked, shifting her gaze to the warrior standing next to her.

For a moment, Hadeon only continued to stare at the bowls. More crumbling shadow glass fell from the ceiling and clinked against the floor as another attack shook the temple.

The torches trembled, casting dancing shadows over the shining black walls.

"Stone," Hadeon said at last. He spoke slowly, as if he was having trouble forming coherent thoughts. "I'll take stone."

"Okay." She handed him the bowl belonging to the Court of Stone before picking up the one with water swirling inside it. Her dark eyes searched his face for a few seconds. Then she raised the bowl before her chest and held Hadeon's gaze. "Together."

He blinked, then his red eyes snapped back to hers. Raising his own bowl, he blew out a shuddering breath. "Together."

As one, they placed the bowls against their lips and tipped them forward.

Shifting white stone fell into Hadeon's mouth while the twisting stream of water disappeared down Idra's throat. I had to remind myself to keep breathing as I waited to see what would happen. For a moment, nothing did.

Then pale stone crackled across Hadeon's skin. It kept going until his entire body was covered in the craggy material. Next to him, Idra tipped her head back as water whirled around her, lifting her white hair above her head and twisting around her limbs.

Tilting her head back down, she met Hadeon's gaze.

The magic disappeared from their bodies.

I stared at them, barely daring to breathe. Mordren brushed his hand against mine in a gesture of comfort.

Both of them blew out a deep breath and then turned towards us.

"It accepted me," Hadeon said in a baffled voice. "The magic... It actually accepted me."

"Of course it did," Mordren said.

Hadeon shook his head in disbelief as he stared down at

his hands. Closing the distance between them, Mordren stopped right in front of his friend.

"Hey," he said, giving Hadeon's cheek a couple of soft slaps until he looked up. Mordren held his gaze. "Of course it accepted you. We have always said it. With or without magic, you have always been the best of us."

Hadeon's red eyes brimmed with emotions as he stared back at Mordren.

The Prince of Shadows cracked a smile and let his hand drop. "Now, the High Elves will be coming through these walls any minute. Let's show them what our new powers can do, shall we?"

"Yeah." Hadeon blew out a shuddering breath and then bounced on his feet a couple of times while shaking out his body. "I don't know how to use these powers though."

Idra glanced at him from the corner of her eye before adding, "Me neither."

"Calling it up is easy," I said. "You just think it and it happens. Then you only need to direct it where you want it. Pointing a hand or a weapon helps with focusing it."

Steel rang through the room as Hadeon drew his sword. Idra only repositioned her hands before her.

"They're coming from all sides," Eilan said. "So spread out. When we know which wall will be breaking first, we'll all move and concentrate on that one. If we all blast them with our combined powers when they get through, we should be able to create enough of an opening to escape." He turned towards our two thieves. "Keep an eye on the walls. When we know which one we're blasting, make sure to stay behind us."

They nodded.

"And, Idra, stay as far from that wall as you can," I said.

"We don't want to risk the barrier falling. If we can't get in, neither can Anron."

After flicking a gaze towards the sealed door to the hidden room, Idra nodded and moved to cover the opposite one. I shifted to stand next to Valerie by another wall, while Hadeon moved towards the back one.

Cracks started spidering across the shining black wall before me.

Booms echoed from outside.

Firelight danced against the smooth surfaces as the torches shook throughout the room.

The High Elves would break through soon. We would have to be ready at a moment's notice to run to the wall that fell first and attack before the soldiers could swarm in and overwhelm us.

My heart thumped against my ribs.

Casting a glance over my shoulder, I watched as Eilan and Theo moved into position at the wall behind me. To their left, Hadeon closed the final distance to his spot.

"I don't think they'll be coming through this part," Hadeon said as he came to a halt before the door to the hidden room. "If it's protected by a barrier spell, they won't get through on the other side either. So we should focus on–"

A grinding sound scraped against my eardrums.

I whirled around.

Across the floor, Hadeon stumbled back several steps. I stared at him in disbelief.

The magically sealed door protecting the bowls from the Court of Light had swung open.

CHAPTER 19

Disbelief rang through the room like a gigantic bell. My mouth fell open as I stared at Hadeon, who was backing away from the now wide-open door. Two bowls were waiting on the floor inside. Bright golden light shone above them like two miniature suns.

Shock bounced across Idra's entire face as she snapped her gaze to Hadeon. "You're from the Court of Light?"

"What?" He flicked his gaze between her face and the open door. "No."

"Then why did the barrier spell fall?"

"I don't know!"

A loud crack sounded on the other side of the wall. I whirled back towards it. Broken shadow glass rained down and the wall splintered further.

"You have to be," Idra continued, her voice full of complete bafflement. "Otherwise, how could–"

"Guys!" I interrupted. "Not the time. They're coming through this wall right now."

Another boom rocked the wall and the cracks widened further.

"Gather up," Mordren ordered. "This is where we make our stand."

"What about the bowls of light magic?" Hadeon asked as he jogged over.

"We're going to have to protect them as best as we can while we fight them off," I answered. The flames inside me rolled through my body and it took all I had to stop them from bursting through my skin. "I can't keep them in my jacket. Not now. My own fire magic is far too unstable and I have a feeling that things will start to go boom if I do anything that messes with my control of it right now."

Idra and Eilan ran over to our wall as well and positioned themselves next to us.

"What about Eilan?" Theo said from behind our backs, hope filling his voice. "You didn't drink any of the bowls, so you can drink these!"

"I have lightning magic now, remember?" he answered over his shoulder.

A disappointed groan drifted through the air right before another attack exploded into the wall. Big chunks of shadow glass tumbled down and smacked into the floor.

"Valerie, Theo," Mordren began. "Take the bowls of light magic and then come stand behind us. Hold on to them and be ready to run as soon as the opportunity presents itself."

"This will never work," Idra said. Her voice was devoid of all emotion, but tension was crackling over her body. "How are we supposed to escape when they can clearly see that we are carrying bowls of magic? The closest soldiers will be knocked out by our initial attack, which means that the rest won't know that we have blasted them with a mix of all the elements. So the rest will only see us running, which means that they might think that we left the bowls behind to escape. And that's the only advantage we have. But there is no hiding those two balls of sunlight. As soon as they see it, they will know that we are carrying the bowls and they will concentrate everything on us rather than splitting it between us and figuring out where the magic is."

"If you have another plan, now would be the time to share it." When Idra said nothing, Mordren cast a glance over his shoulder at the two thieves. "Do as I said."

The soft footsteps behind me informed me that they were hurrying back to the open door. Someone blew out a steadying breath, and then the footsteps started back up again.

A blast slammed into the cracked wall before us. More chunks of shadow glass rained down over the floor. My heart thumped in my chest. Idra was right. Even with our new magical powers, this was going to be next to impossible when the High Elves could clearly see that we were escaping *with* the magic. This plan had largely hinged on the fact that the closest soldiers would be knocked out by our attack, and the rest would be forced to split their attention between catching us and figuring out what had happened to the magic bowls. When they saw us leaving with their prize, all their attention would be on us.

"If you believe in any gods or spirits," Eilan said, "it might be time to ask them for a favor right about now."

Next to me, Hadeon rolled back his shoulders and shifted his grip on his sword. The footsteps behind us fell silent.

"Do you have them?" Mordren asked without taking his eyes off the crumbling wall.

When Valerie and Theo didn't answer, I twisted to look behind me.

The two thieves were standing a couple of strides behind us, holding the bowls in cupped hands. For a moment, they only looked between the wall and the bowls. Then they exchanged a glance.

"Don't–" I called, but it was too late.

Moving without hesitation, Valerie and Theo drank the light magic from the bowls.

For a second, nothing happened.

Then their eyes rolled back in their heads and they toppled backwards. Thuds rang out as they slammed down back first on the floor. The small stone bowls clanked as they rolled off their stomachs and hit the shadow glass.

"No!" The word ripped from my throat with pure desperation as I left my place by the wall and sprinted over to the two thieves.

The others, who had been keeping their eyes on the wall, turned to stare when they heard my scream. I dropped to my knees between Valerie and Theo.

"What's…" Idra trailed off.

Looking up, I met her wide eyes. "They drank the light magic."

She closed the distance between us and dropped down on Theo's other side. A moment later, Eilan was kneeling beside Valerie as well.

"No, no, no, no," he bargained, his voice cracking at the edges. Grabbing her by the shoulders, he shook her limp frame. "Don't you dare."

"Are they alive?" Mordren snapped, worry evident in his voice as well.

"Yes." Lifting her fingers from Theo's neck, Idra looked up at me and flicked her wrist. "Move." Once we had switched so that she sat between them instead, she placed two fingers to Valerie's throat as well. "Yes, they are alive."

A shuddering breath whooshed out of Eilan's lungs.

"But their pulses are beating like crazy," she finished.

Hadeon cast a frantic glance over his shoulder while the wall before him shook once more. "Can human bodies even handle magic that was originally created for High Elves?"

"I don't know." A storm of emotions flickered in her dark eyes. "We need to get them out."

Large pieces of shadow glass crashed to the floor as another explosion rocked the wall. My heart lurched as bronze armor was suddenly visible through the holes.

"They're coming in!" Hadeon called.

"Kenna, get the empty bowls," Mordren ordered as he ran over to us and heaved Theo onto his shoulder. "Eilan–"

"I've got her," he finished for him, and lifted Valerie in his arms.

My fingers trembled as I shoved all twelve bowls into different pockets. Since there was no magic inside, my jacket accepted them without issue. The black wall shook and more pieces fell to the floor. Firelight glinted against bronze breastplates outside. I raced back to the compact line we had formed in front of the section with the largest holes.

"One more!" someone yelled from the other side of the crumbling wall.

"As soon as it falls, we attack," Mordren said.

"Shoot straight through the hole," Hadeon added. "Then we run like hell."

"Once we're past the wards, worldwalk out," Mordren finished.

Panic flashed across Hadeon's face. "I don't know what to do to make myself worldwalk."

"I'll do it," Idra said as she stepped up beside him.

He opened his mouth to respond, but an earsplitting explosion tore through the air.

"Now!" Mordren screamed.

The wall before us shattered.

I shoved my hand forward.

My instincts screamed at me that I would burn my friends too so I held back some of my power. The intensity of the flames that shot out from me still made me jerk back.

Fire, shadows, lightning, stone, and water tore through the hole in the wall like a lethal storm. Screams ripped through the air, only to be silenced completely a second later.

"Run!" Mordren snapped.

We took off.

Ducking through the hole in the wall, we sprinted into the corridor beyond. My eyes widened. The bodies of High Elf soldiers lay crushed and charred and twisted throughout the space all the way to the next opening that they had created in the wall farther down. But now there was another way out.

Sunlight shone at the end of a straight path that had cut through every wall in the building all the way to the outside. Melted shadow glass ran down the edges of the holes.

Without breaking stride, we raced down the passageway I had created.

My heart pounded wildly in my chest when I looked at the destruction that I was responsible for as it flashed past.

"What the hell, Kenna," Hadeon pressed out while we barreled towards the exit.

Not sure what to say, I just met his shocked gaze.

The clanking of armor came from outside the building as someone screamed orders to re-form the lines.

"Whatever you did, get ready to do it again," Eilan said as

THE LAST STAND

he shifted his grip on Valerie. "We need to make it past the wards."

Fire sang inside my blood, begging to be let out. Fear fluttered in my chest. I had no idea how to control this power and make it move in the direction I wanted. What if I hurt the people around me too? I might be fireproof but they weren't.

We were approaching the final wall rapidly. Bright sunlight upon green grass, and lots of people in bronze armor, became visible through the hole. Drawing in a shaky breath, I reined back some of my power and then shoved my hand forward as we cleared the last opening.

Dark red flames roared across the grass.

The soldiers screamed and threw themselves out of the way as a torrent of fire burned through the area, leaving the ground blackened in its wake. Winds ripped through my hair as we sprinted down the scorched path. The smell of burning grass and charred flesh clung to the air like thick mist.

Twangs rang out.

A cloud of arrows shot towards us from the left.

I yanked up a shield of fire to stop them. Shouts echoed through the air as the wall of flame surged up to lick the heavens.

"Get the Wielders back out here!" someone screamed from the other side of the burning barrier as the arrows were incinerated. "Where's High Commander Anron? They're escaping."

Soldiers ran towards us from our unprotected left. Mordren twisted around. Keeping one arm over Theo's back to stop him from bouncing off his shoulder, the Prince of Shadows swept his gaze along the line of charging High Elves.

They dropped to their knees and pressed hands to their temples while cries of agony tore from their throats.

Our feet pounded against the ground.

The tree line was so close now.

My lungs burned as I sucked in desperate breaths while hurtling towards the thick tree trunks.

Another mass of twangs echoed through the air. I blindly threw up a shield of fire that covered the whole sky above us.

Water slammed into it.

Hissing steam exploded over us as the wall of flames disappeared.

We had almost reached the trees.

The *zap* of lightning cut through the noise around us.

I whirled around to see a bolt of white lightning shooting straight at me. My breath got stuck in my lungs. There was no way to block it.

A crack split the air. Chips of white stone flew around me and rained down on the blackened grass. Hadeon had raised a wall of stone to stop the lightning.

Sucking in a shuddering breath, I spun around.

Idra and Hadeon were standing on the other side of the tree line.

"Go!" I yelled at them.

Grabbing his arm, Idra worldwalked them out. Eilan reached the same spot a second later. He cast a frantic look back at me and Mordren before disappearing as well.

Arrows whistled through the air.

Mordren reached the trees. Holding on to Theo, he whirled around to face me just as another storm of lightning shot towards us.

Darkness flashed out to stop it at the same time as I threw a blast of fire to block the arrows. Wind and lightning and water slammed into our magic from both sides. Hissing and crackling filled the air as embers whirled through the forest, mixing with the thick steam and strips of torn shadows.

"Go!" I snapped at Mordren as magic hummed behind me. He worldwalked out with Theo.

Crackling and whooshing of gigantic magical attacks rose behind my back.

Pushing off from the ground, I threw myself the final distance to the tree line.

White light lit up the forest.

I was out of time.

Still in mid-air, I called up my worldwalking power just as the world exploded.

CHAPTER 20

y breath was knocked out of my lungs as I slammed into the grass. I gasped and rolled over on my back while trying to get my bearings. A pale blue sky watched me curiously from above and a mass of trees was visible at the corner of my eyes.

"What happened?" a sharp voice demanded.

Pushing myself into a sitting position, I found Ellyda and Vendir stalking towards us. A couple of strides away from me, Mordren and Eilan were gently lowering Theo and Valerie to the grass.

"Mordren." Eilan's eyes were still fixed on Valerie's unconscious body. "Get Rayan."

The Prince of Shadows flicked his silver eyes to me. I nodded to indicate that I was alright. He worldwalked out.

Struggling to my feet, I staggered over to them. Idra and Hadeon were standing next to the still kneeling Eilan.

"We were attacked," Hadeon finally said in response to Ellyda's question.

"We can't leave them lying out here like this," Idra snapped before Ellyda could say anything. Bending down, she lifted Theo in her arms. "They need to be in an actual bed."

Without waiting for a reply, she stalked towards the cabin that the thieves shared. Eilan looked towards her retreating back for a second before picking up Valerie as well and following her.

I heaved a deep sigh and did the same. As did Hadeon, Ellyda, and Vendir.

Mendar jogged over and fell in beside me as we crossed the camp. Concern swirled in his brown eyes as he shifted his gaze between me and the two unconscious thieves.

"Trouble?" he asked.

"Yeah." I dragged a hand through my hair. "We might need to stay here a bit longer than we expected."

Placing a hand on my shoulder, he gave it a squeeze. "You're welcome to stay as long as you like." His observant eyes searched my face. "Anything I can do?"

"Not unless you know anything about how High Elf magic affects humans."

"I'm afraid not."

"Yeah." I turned to meet his gaze. "Thanks, though."

He nodded. "I'll spread the word among our people, and the animals, to be on the lookout for trouble." Clapping me on the shoulder again, he drifted off towards another cabin. "Let me know if you need anything."

Wood banged up ahead as Idra used her hip to shove open the door to Theo and Valerie's cabin. I waited for the rest of them to enter before following them inside.

When I stepped across the threshold, Eilan and Idra had already placed the two humans on their beds. But both of them lingered by the bedside. Bending down, Idra pressed her fingers to Theo's neck again.

"His pulse is still beating like crazy," she said, her voice fraying a little. Moving over to Valerie, she repeated the process. "Hers too."

She brushed a loose brown curl away from Valerie's forehead. Then she cleared her throat and stepped back. Eilan stared down at Valerie and Theo with pale green eyes full of worry and fear.

"What happened to–" Vendir began.

I sucked in a gasp.

Light pulsed from underneath Valerie's skin. A moment later, the same happened to Theo. It seemed to be moving almost like waves through their bodies. Bright light was flaring up on their cheeks until the skin looked almost translucent, before it died down and then moved on to their throats. Then their hands. Another pulse of light. Then it disappeared. After a while, the light shone from their faces again. And then from their throats. As if it started over and over again.

Eilan drew in a shuddering breath.

"Move aside," came a commanding voice from outside the door.

We all scrambled to get out of the way as Prince Rayan strode across the threshold. Stopping at the foot of their beds, he stared down at Valerie and Theo. Confusion flickered in his purple eyes.

"Wait outside," he said. "I need space to work."

I placed a soft hand on Eilan's shoulder. "Come on. Rayan will come and find us when he's finished."

Reluctance flashed across his handsome face. Then he slowly tore his gaze from the human he loved and turned to follow Ellyda and Vendir out the door. I was about to follow

Hadeon across the threshold when I noticed Idra still standing rooted to the floor.

"Idra," I said.

She snapped her gaze to me. Then she stalked out without another word.

Mordren, Edric, Felix, and Iwdael waited for us when we stepped back out onto the thick grass.

"Kenna," Edric Mountaincleaver said as he met my gaze.

I gave the Prince of Stone a small smile. "Hello, Edric."

Anxious silence fell over our group as we moved into one of the cabins that Mendar used for meetings. Tiredness washed over me as I collapsed into a chair. The adrenaline from the battle had drained from my body, and the fight, along with using my new powers, had taken its toll. I leaned my cheek against Mordren's shoulder as he sat down next to me. Warmth spread through my body as he wrapped his arm around my back and held me tightly.

Iwdael and Edric knew that we had a story to tell, but both of them sat across the table in silence while we waited for Rayan to finish. They probably realized that we wouldn't be able to focus until we knew that Valerie and Theo were okay. And besides, this was a tale that Rayan needed to hear too.

While Ellyda and Vendir had taken a seat at the table, along with Hadeon, the final three members of our group were still standing. Idra, with her arms crossed over her chest, was leaning against the wall on the other side of the room while Eilan was pacing back and forth across the floor. He was spinning a knife in his left hand, and his eyes darted towards the door every few seconds. Idra, on the other hand, showed nothing. Her dark eyes were devoid of all emotion and her face was impassive.

Felix stood behind Edric's shoulder, glancing nervously between his prince and the doorway.

At last, footsteps sounded outside the door.

Eilan stopped pacing and I sat up straight as we all turned to look when Rayan walked through the door.

"Are they okay?" Eilan blurted out before the Prince of Water had even fully stepped across the threshold.

"I don't know," he replied.

Several people opened their mouths to speak, but Rayan held up a hand to silence them. When they had closed their mouths again, he drew a hand through his long black hair and blew out a slow breath.

"No human has ever drunk the magic from the bowls," he explained as he let his hand drop back down again. "I have no idea what it's doing to them. They are alive and, as far as I can tell, they are not in pain. But the magic is clearly doing something to their bodies. I don't know when they will wake up or what state they will be in when they do."

"But they will wake up?" I asked, staring straight at him.

Regret blew across his face as he shifted his gaze to me. "I don't know. Right now, all we can do is wait."

Worry washed over the room like a sweeping wave. Eilan turned to stare at the wall, as if he could see through it all the way to where Valerie and Theo were still lying unconscious.

"I think you'd better start from the beginning," Prince Rayan said as he walked over to sit in the empty chair next to Hadeon. "What happened?"

Mordren and I exchanged a glance. Letting out a long breath, I motioned for him to tell the story.

Surprise, confusion, and dread blew across their faces as Mordren explained what had happened at the temple. From outside the open window, the elves from Poisonwood went about their day as usual. As if a chain reaction hadn't occurred that had shifted our whole world because Evander and Monette had sold us out to High Commander Anron. Again.

A ray of sunshine fell in through the window and warmed my cheek. I closed my eyes for a few seconds and listened to the birds singing outside in the trees and the midnight foxes that barked as they played amongst themselves. Strong winds swept through the forest, making the leaves rustle.

Silence descended on the cabin as Mordren finished.

"Evander?" Prince Iwdael said, a frown on his face. "My wife's former spy?"

"Current spy," I said. When they all turned to look at me, I shrugged. "Since Princess Syrene is working with Anron too, I guess he still works for her as well."

"But that doesn't make any sense. Syrene doesn't know the location of the temple."

"He said that Monette had told him."

Stone rumbled deep below the ground as Edric clenched his jaw. "Monette?"

Behind his shoulder, Felix flinched. Then his face drained completely of color as his mouth dropped open.

"But she doesn't know the location either," the Prince of Stone continued in a voice like grating rocks. "The only people I ever took to the temple were some of my senior advisors, but they've been dead for years."

Iwdael raised his eyebrows. "You've known the location of the temple for years?"

"Yes." Edric swept an unapologetic stare over us as he lifted his broad shoulders in a shrug. "It's in my court, after all." He ran a hand over his jaw. "But like I said, the only people who've been there are..." Trailing off, he shifted in his seat to lock shocked eyes on Felix. "Except for you. You helped me worldwalk them there."

"I..." Felix stammered as he staggered a step back.

Wood clattered against the floor as Edric Mountaincleaver shot to his feet, knocking over his chair in the process, and lunged at Felix. The rest of the table jumped to their feet as well while the Prince of Stone wrapped a hand around Felix's throat and slammed him up against the wall.

"You betrayed us?" he growled down into his face. Stone rumbled beneath our feet.

"N-no, I–"

"Edric–" Rayan began.

"Stay out of this, Rayan," Prince Edric snarled as he stabbed a hand at the Prince of Water. Anger flashed in his gray granite eyes as he turned back to Felix. "You told Monette where the temple was?"

Hesitation fluttered through my stomach. Felix and I had been friends back when I lived in the Court of Stone, and it pained me to see him at the receiving end of Edric's wrath. But at the same time, if he had indeed betrayed us for Monette, I kind of wanted to kill him myself.

"Y-yes," Felix pressed out.

Bitter disappointment crawled up my spine. So him leaving Monette in King Aldrich's castle to follow Edric had all been an act?

Prince Edric let out a growl and tightened his grip on his throat. "You–"

"But it's not what you think," Felix croaked out in a strangled voice. His hands were desperately trying to pry Edric's fingers off to give himself room to breathe. "It was years ago. Please, my prince."

"Perhaps you should let him explain," Prince Iwdael interjected. "Before you crush his windpipe?"

With a snarl, Edric released his grip on the copper-haired half-elf. Felix collapsed to his knees. Pressing his palms to the floor, he gasped in deep breaths for a few moments. After running a hand over his throat, he looked up at the Prince of Stone.

"It was years ago," Felix began. Drawing in another breath, he cleared his throat before continuing. "It was right after you took me there. I was trying to impress her because... well, I was in love with her. I didn't think... I never thought... I didn't even remember that I did that. I was just a kid back then."

"You're still just a kid." Prince Edric glared down at him. "How am I supposed to believe you? How am I supposed to know if this is true?"

"I... It is the truth. I swear. I would never willingly betray you, my prince."

"Except there is nothing to prove that."

"Yes," Iwdael interrupted. "There is."

"Don't tell me this is some of your mood-sensing mumbo jumbo," Prince Edric said as he twisted towards the Prince of Trees.

"Due to the high-tension situation, I'll choose to overlook that insult." Iwdael shot Edric a pointed look before continuing. "And yes, I can sense his mood and he's currently feeling fear, shame, and regret. But no guilt. However, that was not the proof I meant."

"Oh, of course," Rayan said as he turned towards Iwdael with raised eyebrows.

"Ah, yes, it seems that I'm not the only one who has figured this out. If Felix had indeed betrayed us, we would have been captured long ago."

For a moment, Edric only scowled back at them. Then realization lit his eyes. Tipping his head back, he drew a hand through his long blond hair and blew out a deep exhale before meeting Felix's gaze again.

"Because you are one of the few who have known everyone's location this whole time," Edric said at last. "And if you had been a traitor, the High Elves would have found our camp and captured us long ago."

"Indeed," Iwdael answered in Felix's stead.

The Prince of Stone twitched his fingers at his worldwalker. "Get up."

It wasn't exactly an apology, but Edric had never been known for them anyway. Relief washed over Felix's freckled face as he struggled to his feet again. Several chairs scraped against the floor as we all sat down again.

"I'm sorry," Felix mumbled from behind Edric's shoulder.

"Yeah," Prince Edric answered. He shifted his gaze to Mordren and me. "Well, at least you kept the magic out of Anron's hands by drinking it."

"I agree," Rayan Floodbender said. "You did the right thing. We can figure out the new power structure and how to handle court successions after Anron is dead."

Iwdael shrugged, making the leaves in his long brown hair shift. "I've never really been interested in having more power anyway."

Surprise shot through me. I had expected them to be a lot more angry about this.

"But there is one thing I don't understand," the Prince of Trees continued. "How did you get the barrier down?"

"Ask him," came a sharp voice from the back wall.

Clothes rustled as everyone turned towards Idra. She was still leaning against the wall with her arms crossed, but her dark eyes were fixed on Hadeon.

"I don't know how it happened," Hadeon said as we shifted our attention to him. "I just stood in front of the barrier and then the door swung open."

"But only someone from the Court of Light can make it do that," Rayan protested.

"I know."

"So you must be from the Court of Light."

"No! I was born in the Court of Shadows." He turned towards his sister. "Tell them, El."

Ellyda, who was still staring at Idra, at last tore her gaze from the white-haired warrior and met Hadeon's eyes. "Yes. You were. And so was I. But our mother wasn't. She was from another court."

"Yeah, but not from the Court of Light."

"Then which one?"

"Well…" A frown creased his brows as he shook his head at her. "I don't know."

"Me neither. Because she never told us. All she said was that terrible things were happening and she decided to run."

A sharp intake of breath came from the wall. "He knew."

We all turned to look at Idra. Pushing off from the wooden wall, she staggered towards the middle of the room. Her eyes were wide with shock.

"He knew," she repeated.

Eilan backed a couple of steps away to let her pass. "Who?"

"Volkan Flameshield. He knew that your mother was from the Court of Light. That was why he was always mocking your parentage." Pressing a hand to her forehead, she shook her head. "How could I not have seen it? Volkan always said things like, it's no wonder you're so uncivilized *given your parentage*. Because he knew where your mother was really from."

Prince Edric scowled at her. "How would Volkan have known that?"

"He was the one who wiped out the whole Court of Light."

"What?" He drew back a little and frowned even deeper at her. "That can't be right." Narrowing his eyes, he studied Idra. "And besides, how would you know that?"

She leveled a flat stare at him. "Because I was there when it happened."

"You worked for him all the way back then?"

"No." A sharp glint crept into her eyes as she cocked her head. "I know that because I was in Prince André's castle the day Volkan attacked and slaughtered them all."

Iwdael's eyes widened. "You're from the Court of Light?"

"Yes." A storm of emotions flashed in Idra's eyes as she slid her gaze to Hadeon. "And apparently, your mother was from there as well."

"Okay, so maybe she was." Genuine confusion swirled in Hadeon's red eyes as he looked back at her and threw his arms out in an exasperated gesture. "But why are you looking at me like that? Yeah, maybe our mother was from the Court of Light too and she fled before Anron killed everyone. Why does that matter so much?"

The thunderstorm of emotions in her eyes snapped free. She had been turning back towards the wall, but now she whirled around to face us. Her shining white hair fluttered through the air as she spun before jerking to a stop. Pain and rage flashed across her face.

"Because the Court of Light tortured me for centuries!"

she screamed at us. "Prince André strapped me to a table and cut me up and experimented on me. For *centuries*."

Everyone in the room stared at Idra with wide eyes, as if truly seeing her for the first time. As if truly seeing the scars that covered every part of her skin. Hadeon's mouth dropped open and he jerked back in his chair in shock.

Embarrassment shot across Idra's face.

With a snarl, she whirled around and stormed towards the door. Hadeon jumped to his feet, but I was closer. I leaped straight through the wall to catch her outside as she stalked out onto the grass.

This was the first time she had told anyone other than me what had happened to her, and I was pretty sure that this wasn't how she had wanted to go about it.

I grabbed her wrist as she stormed past. "Wait–"

She yanked her arm out of my grip and whipped around to face me right as Hadeon ran through the doorway. "Don't touch me. And don't fucking follow me."

Before I could get another word out, she worldwalked away.

Bright sunlight shone down from the pale blue sky and illuminated the faint footprints that Idra had left in the grass. Now, she was just gone. I stared at the spot she had been standing in, without knowing what to do, for what felt like several minutes.

"Is she... coming back?" Hadeon asked as he moved over to stand next to me.

"I don't know."

We stared at the slowly disappearing footprints in the thick grass.

"Where was she going?"

"I don't know," I repeated.

Since she could worldwalk, she could be anywhere in the world right now. For a while, we just stood there next to one another, watching the blades of grass rise again as if to confirm that Idra indeed had left us. My heart cracked as I glanced up from her no longer visible footsteps to stare at the cabin across the grass. First Valerie and Theo. And now Idra.

Boots shuffled behind us as the rest of the people in the cabin moved outside as well.

"She left," Ellyda said.

It was more of a statement than a question, but Hadeon answered anyway. "Yes."

"I didn't know that she was from the Court of Light," Rayan said gently into the silence that fell. "Or what she had suffered at the hands of its prince."

"None of us did," Hadeon answered, his eyes still locked on the spot where she had been standing.

My eyes flicked over at him for a second.

"Kenna did," Ellyda suddenly said.

I looked up to find her observant eyes studying my face. Hadeon snapped his gaze to me while the others turned towards me as well.

"Yes, I did," I admitted.

It wasn't really my place to elaborate on her story, so I left it at that. After a few seconds, Edric cleared his throat.

"Well," he began a bit awkwardly. "In any case, we should probably lay low for a while. Since there is no temple to guard, and since Anron can't take the magic right now, we should probably all spread out and hide for the time being. At least until Ellyda can figure out a way to reverse engineer the bracelets."

"Agreed," Mordren said. "Until we can do something about

those bracelets, we are in no position to engage Anron in any large-scale conflict."

"We also need to give Valerie and Theo a chance to recover," Eilan said.

"Please do let us know if there is any change," Prince Rayan said.

Mordren nodded. "Once you are in position, send a worldwalker so that we all at least know each other's locations."

The other princes nodded back.

After a somber goodbye, they all worldwalked out.

Those of us who were left exchanged serious looks.

Theo and Valerie were in a coma after drinking magic that no human had ever touched, and Idra had left and we didn't know if she was coming back.

For now, all we could do was wait and see if our friends would return to us.

And what state they would be in if they did.

CHAPTER 21

Morning winds blew through the camp. Mordren brushed a loose curl from my face and hooked it behind my ear. His fingers lingered on my jaw. After closing the door to our cabin behind us, I looked back up at him.

"They will be fine," he said. "Everything will be fine."

I wasn't sure if he was trying to convince me or himself, but I nodded despite not being entirely certain of the fact. "Yeah."

"I will see if Ellyda has made any progress. She usually gets up early when she is in the middle of her work, so she has probably been working for hours already."

Glancing towards another cabin across the grass, I nodded again. "Yeah. I'll go check on Valerie and Theo."

"Everything will be fine," he repeated.

Cupping my cheek, he leaned down and brushed a kiss over my lips. I buried my fist in his shirt, holding him there for another few seconds as I just breathed him in. He rested his forehead against mine.

Another gust of wind ripped through the camp, making my jacket flutter behind me.

After kissing Mordren one final time, I let go of his shirt and stepped back.

"Yes, everything will be fine," I said with as much conviction as I could muster. "I'll see you later."

The camp was waking up around me as I strode across the grass. Firebirds streaked past above, lighting up the overcast sky with their fiery plumage, while some of Mendar's scouts got ready to head out into the forest. They nodded to me as I passed.

Halfway to Valerie and Theo's cabin, I found a lone figure standing on the grass, staring at the sword in his hand.

"Training?" I asked.

Hadeon started slightly, apparently not having heard me approach, before turning towards me. Raking a hand through his short brown hair, he met my gaze. "Yeah. I'm trying to get the hang of how to use this stone magic."

"How's it going?"

He looked down at his sword again. "I don't know. I've been kind of distracted so I haven't really…" Trailing off, he lifted his broad shoulders in a shrug. "I'm gonna need someone's help with telling me how to worldwalk, though."

"Of course. Just let me know when you're ready."

"Yeah."

Leaves rustled around us as another strong wind swept through the forest. Hadeon shifted his gaze to where Mendar's scouts were disappearing into the trees.

"She didn't come back last night," he finally said.

I didn't need to ask who he was talking about.

"Or this morning," he finished.

"I know."

"If I had known that she... I didn't know that my mother was from the Court of Light. If I had known, I wouldn't have... I don't know." Regret swirled in his eyes as he let out a long exhale. "I shouldn't have pushed the issue. I never wanted to force her to tell us something she didn't wanna share."

"I think she wanted to tell you. I think she just never found the right time to actually do it."

"And now she hates me."

"She doesn't hate you."

He let out a disbelieving huff. "My mother was from the court that tortured her for centuries. If I were her, I would hate me." Shaking out his muscles, he spun the sword in his hand and shoved out the regret in his eyes. "Anyway, I need to get back to training."

"Sure. Just... let me know when you're ready to try worldwalking."

Without looking at me, he gave me a casual nod. "Yeah."

From what I had been able to see in his eyes before he smothered all of the emotions in them, he blamed himself for Idra's departure, and I didn't want to leave without reassuring him that it wasn't his fault. But I also wasn't sure what to say. So in the end, I only tore my gaze from the now stone-faced warrior and started towards the thieves' cabin.

Something colorful became visible against the dark brown of the wooden walls.

My heart cracked.

As realization sank in, my steps faltered and I could barely make myself walk the final distance to Valerie and Theo's door.

A big pile of pink fluffy clouds sat waiting below the steps. The small animals perked up when I approached and started jumping up and down on the thick grass while letting out excited squeaks. I tried to swallow past the lump in my throat as they looked up at me with hopeful blue eyes.

Crouching down, I stroked a hand over their soft forms. "She's still sleeping."

The multitude of big blue eyes only blinked back at me uncomprehendingly.

"They still haven't woken up," I explained even though I wasn't sure how much they understood. "They're... sick."

A heartbreakingly sad noise came from the closest cloud. It started a chain reaction and soon every single animal in the pile was letting out distressed cries. They clustered together and slumped down on the ground while opening their tiny mouths and wailing up into the gray sky as if the world itself was ending. The sound of their sadness threatened to shatter the brave front I had spent all night piecing back together, and I had to blow out a slow breath to stop the tears that burned in my eyes from spilling out.

Carefully moving past the pile of crying pink clouds, I opened the door and slipped into the cabin before my heart could break completely. Thankfully, the closed door blocked out their soul-tearing wails.

As it clicked shut, Eilan turned to face me.

He was sitting on a chair at the foot of their beds. Dark purple circles were visible below his eyes and his normally so smooth black hair was messy, as if he had been repeatedly raking his fingers through it.

As if to prove the point, he lifted a hand and dragged it through his hair. "Kenna."

"Did you sleep at all?" I asked, studying his face.

He shook his head. "No."

"How are they?"

"No change."

Wood scraped against wood as I dragged over the other chair and sat down next to Eilan. Reaching out, I squeezed his hand.

"Get some sleep. I'll watch over them."

His pale green eyes were locked on Valerie's face. For a while, he said nothing. Then he slowly shook his head. "I think I'll stay a little while longer. I don't mind the company, though."

I nodded, and we fell into a comfortable silence.

The light from the overcast sky outside cast the whole room in a dull gray light. All except the two thieves. Pulses of golden light still moved under their skin.

"They didn't have to do this," Eilan said at last. He cast a quick glance at me before looking back at Valerie. "It wasn't her fault that Evander got inside. They had nothing to prove. Nothing to make up for. *She* had nothing to make up for."

"I don't think that was why she did it."

Eilan turned to look at me in surprise.

"I mean, yes, I think she felt a bit bad that she had let Evander get through on her watch." Shifting my gaze back to the two thieves, I let a small smile spread across my lips. "But I don't think that was why they decided to drink the magic."

"Then why?"

"Because Valerie is fearless. When she wants something, she goes after it with everything she's got. No hesitation." I slapped his ribs with the back of my hand. "Which you know from firsthand experience."

Eilan chuckled.

"Theo is the same. He might pretend that he is the responsible one who reins her in, but in reality, he's just as crazy as she is." I turned back to the two thieves. "They didn't do this because of some misplaced sense of guilt. They did it because they genuinely believed that this was the best course of action, and that they would be able to handle the effects of the magic. And you know what? They might actually be crazy and stubborn enough to pull it off."

"Yeah." Eilan blew out another soft chuckle, and when he nodded, a bit of light had returned to his eyes. "Yeah, you're right."

The mood in the cabin was a lot less heavy as we once more fell silent, watching the two humans before us. I studied the way their chests rose and fell with even breaths. They would pull through. They had to.

"Ow."

Eilan and I shot to our feet.

"I think I hit my back on something," Valerie mumbled as she pushed herself into a sitting position.

"Yeah," Theo replied as he struggled to sit up as well. "I think I did too."

Shock bounced through my body as Eilan and I just stood there, staring at them with our mouths open.

The light under their skin had stopped pulsing, so they should have looked normal again. Except they didn't.

Once the light stopped pulsing, their features had changed. Their faces were still the same. And yet not.

Their features were sharper. Clearer. More beautiful. As if someone had taken their natural looks and enhanced them. And their ears were slightly pointed. Not as clearly as Eilan's, but more like... mine.

"Whoa," Theo said, still looking over at Valerie. "Do you feel that?"

"Yeah. That's so cool. It's almost as if..." She trailed off as she finally noticed us. A frown creased her brows as she shifted her gaze to us. "Uhm, you're staring. Like, a lot."

Her voice snapped Eilan out of the trance. Closing the distance in two quick strides, he braced a knee on her bed and wrapped his arms around her.

Valerie blinked at me over his shoulder. "Oh. Not that I'm not a huge fan of public displays of affection, but we've only been…" Trailing off, she frowned again. "Actually, what have we been doing?"

Eilan placed his hands on her cheeks and studied every part of her face while I filled them in on what had occurred after they drank the magic.

"Oh, right," Theo said. "The magic."

Mischief glittered in his eyes as he raised a hand, palm up. Light bloomed throughout the room, lighting it up with hues of white and gold.

"That's so cool!" Valerie blurted out. Swatting at Eilan's arm, she ducked out from underneath it. "Hold on, let me try."

Another ball of light appeared above her own palm.

Matching grins spread across their lips. Then they laughed.

The sound healed something broken in my soul and I slumped back into the chair.

"You're okay," I breathed.

"Of course we are." Valerie winked at me. "What kind of amateurs do you take us for?"

An exhausted chuckle escaped my throat. "Sorry. I'll never doubt you again."

"Good. Now, why are the two of you staring so much?"

Instead of answering, Eilan walked over to grab the mirror from the other side of the room. Twisting it around so that they both could look into it, he held it up in front of them.

"Whoa," Theo said again.

For a few moments, they just ran their hands over their

faces, as if to check that they were still the same. Or similar at least.

When Eilan at last returned the mirror to its proper place, the two thieves exchanged a long look.

"You know," Theo began. "I don't think we're entirely human anymore."

"I agree." Valerie held his gaze. "I don't know how to describe it, but it feels as though everything inside me has… slowed down."

Eilan whirled back around to stare at her.

A brilliant smile lit her face as she met the shapeshifter's gaze. "I think we're going to have a lot more than sixty years together."

Hope and gratitude and overwhelming love washed over Eilan's features as he closed the distance and pulled her into a kiss so passionate that I almost blushed.

On the bed next to them, Theo crossed his arms while trying to hide the smile tugging at his lips. "I'll be here for a lot more than sixty years now too, you know."

I laughed. Moving over to the door, I placed a hand on the handle and then paused to look back at Valerie.

"Oh, by the way," I began. "Are you up for some visitors?"

"Always." She grinned at me while Eilan took a seat at the edge of her bed. "What kind of visitors?"

Pushing down the handle, I opened the door.

Excited squeaks came from outside. Then a whole host of fluffy pink clouds poured across the threshold. Valerie let out a rippling laugh as the clouds jumped up onto her bed and swarmed into her lap. She wrapped her arms around the giant fluffy pile and cuddled them as they nestled deeper against her.

Shaking his head, Theo let out a chuckle. "Again, I'm here too."

I sat down next to him on the bed. Grabbing his hand, I gave it a squeeze while holding his gaze. "And I'm damn glad for it. You had me really worried there for a while. All of us, in fact."

He squeezed my hand back. "I know. I'm sorry."

A midnight fox slunk in through the open door. Surprise blew across Theo's face as it jumped up onto his bed and walked in circles a couple of times. Then it curled up against Theo's legs and yawned. He reached out and ran a hand over its dark blue and silver-dusted fur, while a small smile lit up his face.

After glancing up at me, he slid his gaze to Valerie. "But like she said, I think we will be here with you for quite some time now."

Following his line of sight, I watched as Valerie picked up one of the pink clouds and put it on her shoulder before reaching down to pat the others still in her lap. I flicked my gaze back to Theo. The love of family, not by blood but forged in years of always looking after each other and choosing each other first and always, shone in his gray eyes as he looked at her.

My heart warmed inside my chest.

Yes, we would indeed spend a very long and bright future together now.

All of us.

CHAPTER 22

Power burned through my veins. I held most of it back as I threw a fireball at my opponent. Stone shot up from the ground and blocked it, making dark red flames lick the pale surface while embers swirled in the air. A deep rumbling sound echoed through the clearing as the block of stone disappeared back into the thick grass. Red eyes looked back at me from behind it.

"It's getting easier to time it correctly," Hadeon said as he shifted his gaze to look at the spot where his stone shield had disappeared. "But I still don't know how I'm supposed to use this effectively in a fight."

"Maybe just to shield against other magical attacks," I suggested. "And then fight the way you normally do otherwise."

"Yeah." Worry blew across his face as he cast a glance towards the camp. "But I'd need… another sparring partner for that."

It had been a week since Theo and Valerie had woken up with their new magical powers, but Idra still hadn't returned.

I had wanted to look for her but the harsh truth was that I could've spent my entire life worldwalking back and forth across our lands and still never found her. So I had stayed in the camp. *We* had stayed in the camp. While Ellyda was still trying to find a way to reverse engineer the bracelets, the rest of us had been training to get used to our new powers. But we all still hoped that Idra would return soon.

"Not to sound ungrateful or anything," Valerie said as she looked up from her hand. "But this power is kind of underwhelming."

Light bloomed from her palm, lighting up the area around her a bit. Cool winds chased thick white clouds over the heavens, but it was still a relatively bright afternoon so her magic only made the grass around her a little bit brighter.

"There has to be a smarter way to use this power." She turned to Mordren. "You can, like, grab things with your shadows. And make walls and nets and stuff. So we should be able to do something other than just light things up too."

Theo lit up the grass around himself as well while nodding. "I agree. There has to be more to wielding light than this."

"Well alrighty then." Valerie grinned and rubbed her hands together. "Let the scheming commence. I have rules to break and loopholes to find."

I chuckled. If there was one person who would be able to find a creative way to use light magic, it was certainly Valerie. Mordren and Eilan shook their heads at the two thieves, but smiles played over their lips. I turned back towards Hadeon while the light wielders started grabbing their gear to return to camp.

"You're alive."

We all whipped around.

Idra was standing in the middle of the loose circle that our three pairs formed, and she was staring straight at Valerie and Theo.

"Idra," I began.

"So you're okay?" she said, her eyes still locked on the thieves.

"Yeah, we woke up like a week ago," Theo answered. "But you were already gone." Confusion and worry danced in his gray eyes. "Where have you been?"

"Away." Without even looking at the rest of us, she started towards the camp.

"Wait." Hadeon hurried across the grass and stopped right in front of her, blocking her path. "Can we talk about what happened?"

She looked back at him with completely expressionless eyes. "There is nothing to talk about."

"Yes, there is!"

There was nothing, not even a flicker of emotion, on her face. Even I, who had learned to read the micro expressions on her features during our time together, could detect nothing that gave away how she was feeling. It was as if she had pulled down an iron curtain over herself, hiding everything that was underneath.

"Move aside," she said, looking back at Hadeon with blank eyes.

He shook his head. "Don't do this."

When he still didn't step aside, she moved to walk around him instead. Hadeon's hand shot out. Grabbing her arm, he whirled her back around to face him.

"No!" he snarled, still holding on to her forearm with a firm grip. "Don't do that. Don't shut me out again."

"I suggest you take that hand off me."

"If you stop acting as if nothing's wrong. I get that you hate me but—"

She slammed the heel of her hand into his stomach. Air exploded from his lungs as he staggered backwards from the force of the hit. Idra started towards the camp.

Sucking in a desperate breath to refill his lungs, Hadeon whirled around and grabbed her arm again. Idra let out a snarl as she whipped around and swung her closed fist at his head. He ducked.

Winds ripped at their clothes as they twisted and then lunged again. Idra aimed a kick at the side of Hadeon's ribs, but he slammed his forearm down to block it. Her foot smacked into his arm with a force that would've made an ordinary person stagger sideways, but Hadeon only shifted his stance and swung a fist towards her side. While leaping back, she hit his wrist with the palm of her hand, making the strike change direction.

"Uhm," Theo began as he and Valerie slunk over to stand next to me. "Should we... do something?"

I cast a glance down at him before shifting my attention back to the warriors battling each other. "I'm pretty sure either or both of them would kill us if we got involved now."

Idra slammed her palm against his chest and growled, "I could kill you with a single touch."

At first, Hadeon rammed his forearm down into the crook of her elbow, making her arm shoot downwards. But then as she twisted and swung at him again, he just stood there, letting it go through. Her hand wrapped around his throat a second later.

"Then do it!" He spread his arms wide. "Do it."

Her chest heaved, probably more from anger than

exertion, as she kept her hand firmly against his throat while rage now flashed openly on her face.

"Look, I'm sorry that our mother was from the Court of Light," Hadeon began as he looked down at her with eyes full of compassion. "I had no idea that you—"

"This has nothing to do with that!"

Hadeon blinked at her in shock.

Taking her hand from his throat, she instead put them against his muscled chest and shoved him back. "I don't care that your mother was from the Court of Light. She wasn't the one who hurt me, and even if she was, I wouldn't blame you for that."

While staggering back a step, probably more from surprise than the force of her shove, he looked back at her with confusion blowing across his face. "Then what is it?"

"I blame you." She stabbed a hand at him before spinning around to point at Theo and Valerie. "And I blame you." Her dark eyes flashed as she shifted her accusing hand to me. "And most of all, I blame *you*."

I stared back at her in shock. Rage rolled off her like lightning as she turned in a half circle to sweep her arms out to indicate every one of us.

"I am older than all the rest of you combined. I have watched countless people live and die and I have never had to care. But now I... *feel* things."

Her white hair fluttered in the wind as she stalked over to me. Shock was still bouncing around inside me so I just stood there as she grabbed the front of my jacket and hauled me closer.

"And it's all your fault," she growled in my face. "If you hadn't come to the Court of Fire and started acting as if we were friends, talking to me like a normal person, touching my hand and not flinching... If you hadn't done that, I would never have let my walls down for you. And I would never have met all these people," she spat the words as she stabbed a hand towards the others, "and started to care about them too."

I stumbled a step back as she shoved me away and instead stalked over to the two thieves. Anger and pain and desperation crackled across her face like a storm.

"You. You who just casually sit down next to me and hand me cake and put fluffy animals in my lap as if I haven't slaughtered *thousands* of people with my scarred blood-soaked hands." Her voice cracked and she forced out the words as if they cut their way up her throat like broken glass. Tears welled up in her eyes as she grabbed Theo's collar and shook him violently. "And now you've made me care about you."

Releasing her grip on him, she staggered back a couple of steps while shaking her head. Pure desperation shone on her face.

"And now it feels like my heart is breaking *all the time*. Because I'm worried about you!" Idra screamed the words at them. "And you might have survived drinking the magic this time, but I will still have to watch you die. In sixty years. And my heart is shattering into a million tiny pieces just thinking about it." Her knees buckled and she crashed down onto the grass. Bending down over her knees, she slammed her hand into the ground over and over again. "Why did you make me care about you?"

Theo and Valerie approached her and crouched down in front of her.

Reaching out, Theo placed his hand over Idra's. "We're not going to die."

"Yeah." Valerie lifted a hand and pushed Idra's hair out of

her face, hooking it behind her ear. "You kind of missed that, but we're pretty sure that we're not entirely human anymore."

"So we're pretty certain that we'll be here for a lot longer than sixty years."

Idra's head snapped up. "You will?"

They smiled at her. "Yes."

Hope sparkled in her eyes for a few seconds. Then she snuffed it out and shot to her feet while drawing the anger back around her like armor. Backing away, she dragged her hands through her hair and shook her head at all of us.

"But I still don't understand." She swept desperate eyes over the six of us. "I don't understand you at all! Everyone else flinches when I so much as look at them. Why don't you? Instead, you pat me on the shoulder and..." Twisting, she stared straight at Hadeon. "And argue with me and fight me."

"Because we're your friends," I said.

"But I've never had any friends!" She threw her arms out in a helpless gesture. "I don't know what to do. My whole life, people have looked at me with fear in their eyes. And then you come along. You complete and utter morons who just treat me like a normal person. And it's making me *feel* things. And I've never felt anything. Ever. All my life, I have shut out all of my feelings so that it wouldn't hurt so much when I see the way people look at me. And so that I couldn't feel any pain." Her eyes were wild and her voice rose to a broken scream. "But now you've made me feel things and I don't know how to stop!"

"You don't have to stop."

"But I have to! My heart almost shattered when you collapsed after drinking the magic." She shook her head at the two thieves before sweeping her gaze over all of us again. "I never used to feel anything, and now my heart won't be able to handle it if something happens to you." A broken sob tore from her throat as tears spilled down her cheeks. "I hate you all for tearing down my walls like this."

"Feeling things for your friends is not a bad thing," Hadeon said gently.

"And you." She whipped around to face him. Emotions flashed across her face as she stalked up to Hadeon and gave his chest a shove. "You bastard. I hate you most of all."

He made no move to stop her as she forced him back again.

"I hate you most of all. I hate you so much because you've made me want to let you in. I hate you because you've made me lo–" Her voice broke. Shoving him back once more, she screamed at him, "Because you've made me love you!"

Shock lit his red eyes. It was followed by glittering, all-consuming happiness. A wide smile spread across his lips as he reached up and grabbed her hand before she could push him back again.

"I love you too, you stubborn, violent, absolutely brilliant warrior soul."

Idra's mouth dropped open. Frozen in her movements, she just stared up at him for a few seconds. Then she shook her head.

"I don't know how to do this."

Hadeon released her wrist and brushed a hand over her cheek. "We can take it slow."

Her shining white hair skimmed the top of her shoulders as she shook her head once more. Then her hands shot out. In a matter of seconds, she had grabbed the front of Hadeon's leather armor.

"I don't want to take it fucking slow." She yanked his face down to hers.

With her hands still buried in his collar, she kissed him savagely. While returning the kiss with ferocious passion, Hadeon reached down and grabbed her ass, lifting her off the ground. Idra wrapped her legs around his waist as he braced one muscular arm underneath her while his other hand slid to the back of her neck.

Next to me, Valerie and Theo whooped and whistled at them.

Taking one hand from Hadeon's collar, Idra rested her forearm against his shoulder and flashed the two thieves a rude gesture.

I laughed.

Across the grass, Mordren and Eilan exchanged a smug smirk.

Leaves fluttered in the wind as the two warriors lost themselves in each other and a moment that had been a long time coming. A bright smile lit my lips.

Theo and Valerie were okay.

And Idra was back.

Truly back.

The world might have gone to hell around us, but at least we had each other.

CHAPTER 23

"If you narrow it into a whip, you can increase the strength of the hit without having to increase the power behind it."

Idra slid her gaze to Vendir. "I know. I can change the shape, but I can't make it snap like a whip."

"Pretend that you're holding a real one," he answered. "And then use your mind to fill in the space where the whip would be if it had been real."

A scowl appeared on Idra's brows but she positioned her hand as if she was gripping an invisible handle. "This feels ridiculous."

"I know." Vendir chuckled and drew a hand through his long blond hair. "But in the beginning, it's easier to use visual cues."

She nodded. Shifting her gaze back to the empty field in front of her, she raised her hand and flicked her wrist as if she was holding a whip. A thin stream of water flashed through the air, shooting mostly forwards. After blowing out an irritated sigh, she tried again.

On the other side of the flat stretch of grass that we used as a training field, Mordren had raised a massive wall of shadows that he tried to keep steady while Eilan sent a volley of lightning magic into it. The white bolts crackled through the darkness. Changing position, Eilan shot another, even more controlled, blast at his brother.

Valerie and Theo stood facing each other at the edge of the tree line. They weren't moving, but their skin glowed as if sunlight was trying to break through from within.

In the middle of it all, Hadeon appeared and disappeared in various locations on the now flattened grass. It had been a week since Idra returned. Once she was back, it was as if Hadeon could finally focus fully on his training, and he had improved greatly since then. Especially when it came to worldwalking. He only wobbled a few times now as he landed, and it looked like he ended up where he wanted to be.

"Vendir," I said as I turned back to the High Elf. "Can you raise another wall of water?"

Nodding, he moved into position in front of me. "Of course."

Water rose up from the ground until a gigantic wall separated the two of us. I shifted my grip on my blades. Since drinking the third bowl of fire magic, my control had decreased rather drastically. I could still direct it where I wanted it to go with the help of my blades, but the attack always ended up much bigger than I had planned. And if we were going to be fighting Anron on a crowded battlefield, I needed to make sure that my attacks only hit our enemies and not our own ranks as well.

Blowing out a breath, I slashed my sword through the air.

A sweeping arc of flames shot out. It cleaved Vendir's

whole shield in half, sending steam blowing towards the forest. I frowned.

"Still not the size you wanted?" Vendir asked.

Since Vendir could already wield all the elements, he had been a tremendous help in assisting with our training. He had shared some really useful tricks for how to use fire magic. I just needed a bit more time to practice it.

"No," I answered. "I hold back as much as I can, because while I want it smaller, I don't want the attack to be weaker."

He ran a hand over his jaw. "Try to... How should I describe it? Try to imagine the fire the size that you want it, but also make it... more compact." Letting the water wall drop, he instead lifted a hand and let a ball of fire bloom in his palm. "Like this. Keep the ball the same size, but pour more flames into it so that it fills up all the spaces between all the different fires."

Cool winds blew across the training field and tugged at my clothes. I adjusted the collar of my jacket before raising a hand and summoning a ball of fire in my palm as well. Following Vendir's instructions, I tried to add more flames to the ball without making it bigger. The ball expanded in a flash, making me flinch in surprise.

"I don't get it," I said as I continued frowning at my now empty palm for another few seconds before looking up to meet Vendir's gaze. "What do you mean by filling up the spaces between the different fires?"

"Okay, let's put it like this. Imagine that you have ten candles and they're all burning where they're standing in a circle. Then you tip one of the candles so that it's lying on its side, with the wick in the middle and the flame still burning. Then you tip another candle. It's also lying on its side with the wick in the middle, in the exact same space as the first one.

Then you tip another one. And another one. And so on, until all the candles are lying down with the wick in the exact same space in the middle." His brown eyes locked on me as he looked up after demonstrating the tipping of the candles. "The strength of each individual candle is still the same, which means that the fire on the wick is still the same size. But since there are now ten candles taking up the same space, the fire is thicker."

I blinked at him. "Oh. That makes so much sense." Cocking my head, I studied him intently. "Thank you. You really are good at this."

"I, uhm…" He cleared his throat and rubbed the back of his neck. "Anytime. I'm glad there's something I can do to help."

"Something? I think you're selling yourself a bit short. You do a lot more than–"

A frustrated yell echoed through the camp. Colorful birds flapped away in fear and the two midnight foxes that had been trotting between the buildings slunk in through an open doorway to escape the unknown threat. Vendir snapped his gaze towards the sound. Magic blinked out of existence across the whole training field as we all turned to find Ellyda stalking towards us.

We all hurried to meet her. For a moment, it looked like she was going to plow us all down, but then she stopped in front of the small semi-circle we had formed.

"What's wrong?" Hadeon asked, searching his sister's face.

"I can't do this," she snapped. Her violet eyes were flashing with anger and they flicked back and forth across us and the training field as if she couldn't quite get them to focus on what she wanted to look at. "I *cannot* do this."

Hadeon gave her a reassuring smile. "It's alright. We'll just come up with another plan."

"No. I mean..."

Raking her fingers through her messy brown hair, she blew out a slow breath and closed her eyes. For a moment, she just stood like that. We all only waited for her to finish pulling herself back from wherever her mind had taken her. Cool winds that spoke of the fast-approaching fall stroked the trees around the field and made the leaves flutter.

At last, Ellyda let her arms drop and opened her eyes again. After blinking several times, her eyes became clear and sharp as she turned to meet Hadeon's gaze.

"I *can* do this," she said. Sweeping her gaze over the rest of us, she clenched and unclenched her hands. "But I can't do this like this. I need the right tools. I need *my* tools."

"You mean the ones that are still back home?"

"Yes."

"When you say *back home*," Theo began, "you don't by any chance mean the castle in the Court of Shadows that's currently occupied by an entire army of High Elves, do you?"

"Yes. And they're not in my forge out on the grounds. They're in my room inside the castle."

He blew out a resigned breath. "Fantastic."

"Is there any way to get them without any of the High Elves noticing?" Idra asked.

Mordren slid his gaze to her. "You remember what it looked like when we were trying to free my soldiers."

"I could probably get in and out of there," I said. "With the walking through walls thing, and all that."

Hope fluttered through our group.

"No," Ellyda announced, stamping it out like a fragile butterfly. "Your knowledge about these kinds of tools is practically nonexistent."

"Ouch." I huffed out a laugh. "But you're right. I have no idea what's what, but can't I just grab everything and run?"

Amusement tugged at Hadeon's lips as he raised his eyebrows at me. "You've never seen her room, have you? You'd need a horse-drawn cart or two to transport all the junk she's got in there."

"It's not junk." Ellyda cut a sharp glance at Hadeon, which had him raising his hands in surrender. "The point is, I have to be the one to go inside and get what I need."

"What if we create a distraction?" Eilan said.

Several pairs of eyebrows rose.

"We could split into two teams," he continued. "One that goes home with Ellyda to get her tools, and one that goes to another court to stir up trouble."

"It would have to be trouble big enough for the High Elves to pull soldiers from the Court of Shadows and instead send them to wherever we are," Idra said.

"That shouldn't be a problem," I said. "I could go to the Court of Fire and attack my own castle. That would give them something to worry about."

Mordren leveled a stare dripping with authority on me. "Except you are not going alone."

"Fine." I waved my hand towards Mordren, Eilan, Ellyda, and Hadeon. "What if you four go and take care of business in the Court of Shadows, since you know it better than anyone, and then we," I motioned at myself, Idra, and Vendir, "go to the Court of Fire to create the distraction."

"Hey," Valerie protested. "What about us?"

"Exactly," Theo chimed in.

"You are not fighters," Idra said, her dark eyes hard as she turned to look at them.

"Well, duh." Valerie rolled her eyes as if that was the most obvious thing she'd ever heard. Then a wide grin spread across her face. "But we're great at creating trouble."

"I agree with Idra," I said, and spread my hands in a helpless gesture. "Yes, you're good at creating mischief, but you need to focus on getting full control of your magic. That's the most important thing in the long run if we're going to win this war."

The two thieves exchanged a look. Then they blew out a synchronized sigh and answered, "Fine."

"Yeah, you're still gonna need more people," Hadeon said as he looked between me, Idra, and Vendir. "You three are strong, but you're not strong enough to take on an entire castle full of High Elves."

"Agreed," Mordren said. "We will get in touch with Edric and Iwdael so that they can back you up as well."

Idra and I glanced over at each other for a second before shrugging.

"Alright, sounds reasonable," I said. "You'll get the tools and we'll make the High Elves regret the day they decided to take over my castle."

Anticipation bubbled around us. After two weeks of just training and waiting, we would finally be taking the fight to the High Elves. Not that we would be able to actually take back my castle with this attack, but just the thought of showing Anron that we were still a threat made the power in my blood sing.

If all went well, we would also be one step closer to getting those bracelets off our people.

And then, we could really bring the fight to them.

CHAPTER 24

Warm air that smelled of sand and hot stone filled my lungs as I drew in a deep breath. Hidden in an alley, I watched the High Elves that stood guard before the wrought metal gates set into the tall red walls. A massive castle made of red stone was visible beyond them.

My gates.

My walls.

My castle.

Narrowing my eyes, I glared at the High Elves who now occupied it. I would get it back.

"This is going to do some damage to your castle," Prince Iwdael said as he followed my gaze.

"I know," I replied. "But buildings can be repaired. So don't hold back your powers on that account. What's important is that we turn Anron's gaze to us so that Ellyda has a chance to get her tools. And that all of us make it back out again. So don't worry about destroying things."

Edric Mountaincleaver tore his gaze from the defensive walls and turned to look down at me. The ghost of a smile drifted over his lips as he gave me an approving nod. "Well said."

"So how do we get inside?" Reena asked from her place next to Iwdael. Her turquoise eyes flicked back and forth across the castle. "The gate is closed and guarded."

The others shifted their attention to me. We were a small but quite formidable group. In addition to me and Idra from the Court of Fire, we had Prince Edric and Ymas from the Court of Stone, Prince Iwdael and Reena from the Court of Trees, and of course also Vendir. Between the seven of us, there was a wide range of magical abilities that would come in handy.

A smile stretched my lips as I met their gazes. "Leave that to me."

After running a hand over the hilt of my blades, I pulled up the hood of my jacket and slunk out of the alley. Once my back was to the others, I also reached up and slid out the black mask that was sewn into the top of the hood. If this was going to work, I needed to get closer without the guards recognizing me.

There were no other people crossing the empty space between the walls and the rest of the city. Only the wind kicking up small clouds of dust from the stones. It was as if no one wanted to venture outside their homes unless they absolutely had to, and most certainly not anywhere close to the High Elf infected castle.

Resentment raked its spiteful fingers up my spine. A lot of elves had willingly put on the bracelets and worshipped the High Elves as gods when they first arrived on our shores. I hoped that all of them bitterly regretted that decision now that their magic and their lives were being held hostage by the ones they had celebrated earlier.

"Hey," one of the soldiers called from the gate. "Where do you think you're going?"

Trailing to a halt a short distance in front of the gate, I raised my hands as if to show that I meant them no harm.

Then I slammed my palm forward.

Dark red fire shot out. The guards screamed in panic and fear as the flames hurtled towards them, but they were standing too close and the attack was moving too fast for them to dodge. Strangled cries were quickly cut off as the fire consumed everything in its path.

Keeping my hand stretched forward, I continued sending a torrent of dark red flames towards the wrought metal gates until they began twisting under the heat. A few moments later, large drops of dark metal began dripping from them. Fire covered my entire arm and a few flames played in my hair as I watched the gates to my castle melt underneath my power.

When the doorway was at last clear, I pulled back the fire and rolled my shoulder.

Footsteps sounded behind me as the rest of my group joined me in front of the now open path inside.

"Uhm." Prince Iwdael looked over at me with raised eyebrows while pointing towards the melted remains of the gates. "I was under the impression that those were fireproof."

I shrugged. "Fire-resistant. Everything burns if you try hard enough."

Shouts came from atop the defensive walls as the soldiers stationed there raised the alarm.

"Enough talking," Prince Edric muttered. "Let's do this."

We ran through the open gate right as a mass of High Elves poured out of the tall doors leading into the castle proper. Steel rang into the warm air as they drew their swords.

"I'll hit them from behind," I said as I sprinted towards the side of the castle.

The hum of magic filled the courtyard behind me as a High Elf Wielder appeared and shot a blast of air. Casting a glance over my shoulder, I just had time to see Edric raise a wall of stone to block it while Vendir shot lightning back at the Wielder. Red stones appeared in front of me. I leaped through the castle wall and drew my blades as I reappeared in my grand throne room.

Clamoring came from the open doors as the High Elves tried to get through while also battling the rest of my friends outside. I cast a quick look at my empty throne before slashing my blades through the air. A searing arc of flame shot towards the soldiers from behind.

Screams erupted as the back row was hit without warning.

The middle part of the squad whirled around to face the new threat while the ones in front still tried to keep my allies at bay. I sent more fire flying towards them from behind at the same time as a block of stone slammed into them from the other side.

Steam exploded into the throne room as one of the Wielders at last got into position to block my attacks. I sprinted through the white cloud right as lightning tore through the room. It cracked into the wall where I had been standing only seconds before, making the noise echo through the high-ceilinged hall.

Since I couldn't tell where my friends were, I didn't send any more fire towards the door. Instead, I ran towards the hallway to the right of the throne. If I could get some of the soldiers to chase after me, it would make it easier for the others to get in through the door.

Boots pounded against the stone floor behind me.

A wicked grin slid home on my face. *Perfect.*

Making sure that they would just barely see me round each corner, I raced through the halls that I knew far better than them. I had the perfect location in mind. Somewhere I could fight them without having to worry about accidentally hitting one of my friends with the fire as well.

"Lady Firesoul," a frightened voice blurted out as I rounded yet another corner.

I swerved to avoid mowing down the blond elf who had worked as one of my administrators in the castle before she'd had a black bracelet forced on her. She leaped back and stared at me with big blue eyes as I continued sprinting.

"Get to the kitchen," I called at her over my shoulder. "Or somewhere far from the front doors. Tell the others. There's going to be a lot of fighting in here."

Before she could answer, I had already disappeared around the next wall. A terrified squeak came from where she had been, informing me that the High Elves were right on my heels.

Grabbing the edge of the doorjamb, I swung myself into the opening I had been aiming for. A twisting stairwell made of red stone appeared before me. I darted into it.

Boots thudded against the floor from the corridor below while I ran up the stairs, taking the steps two at a time.

"She's in the stairwell," someone yelled from below.

A moment later, the pounding feet were coming from the steps behind me instead. I quickened my pace.

Red walls watched me impassively as I continued around and around, hurtling up the stairs. My lungs burned with every breath and my legs were screaming at me but I kept going.

The footsteps had gotten dangerously close when I finally reached the top of the stairs and threw open the door. It banged against the wall. Sucking in desperate breaths of warm air, I weaved through the lounge chairs and plants that were positioned on the rooftop terrace, and then sprinted towards the flat empty roof on the other side.

Just as I whirled back towards the small square structure that held the opening to the stairwell, the group of High Elves who had been chasing me barreled through the door and poured out onto the red stone roof.

I slashed my blades through the air. Scythes of flame shot towards them while they were still trying to reorganize themselves again. Bronze armor gleamed in the bright sunlight as they dove aside while the Wielder threw up a shield of stone.

Dark red flames slammed into the stone shield and embers whirled in the warm air. A moment later, the block of stone shot towards me. Alarm flashed through me instinctively, but I smothered it and instead positioned myself right in its path. It was coming at me with incredible speed, and if it hit, it would've pushed me clean off the edge of the roof.

Holding my position, I drew in a deep breath.

Right before the block of stone hit me, I phased through it.

It passed harmlessly as it raced across the flat roof and then flew out into the air on the other side.

"That doesn't work," someone snapped from the group of soldiers. "She can just walk through it."

"And be careful," someone else added. "High Commander Anron wants her alive."

Not wanting to give them time to get organized, I sent

another volley of flaming attacks at them. The Wielder shot a blast of water to counter it while the rest of the soldiers started fanning out across the roof. I flicked my gaze over them while throwing more fire at the Wielder. I couldn't let them box me in.

Fire roared to life as I raised a gigantic wave and sent it rolling towards them. Screams ripped through the air as they were forced to jump out of the way while the Wielder tried desperately to block it.

White mist filled the air as he managed to turn part of it to steam. The rest of the flaming wave rolled over the stairwell and washed down the side of the building. Power thrummed in my veins. I got ready to finish them all when something else caught my eye.

While throwing up a shield of fire, I whirled around to see a mass of air serpents speeding towards us from the direction of the closest courts.

Shit. That was a lot faster than I had predicted. I had to get off this roof.

Lightning crackled through the warm air. I barely managed to leap away as a bolt of white lightning tore through my fire shield and struck the stones where I had been standing. Rolling across the roof, I stabbed my knife forward. A concentrated line of fire shot towards the Wielder. It was much thicker than I had wanted, so the High Elf saw it coming and managed to dodge before it could hit. But at least his moment of inattention bought me the time I needed.

Sweeping my arm wide, I sent another massive wall of fire rolling towards them while I sprinted straight for the back of the stairwell. It would have been impossible to get back in through the door since they were blocking that side. Thankfully, I didn't need doors.

Winged serpents in different colors were landing right outside the defensive walls as I pushed off the ground and leaped through the back of the building that housed the stairwell. Silk whispered against my skin. Then I slammed into the wall on the inside and fell down a few steps. Struggling to my feet, I readjusted my grip on my blade right as the door was yanked open above me.

I phased through the floor.

My stomach lurched as I fell through the air and then landed in a crouch on the steps below. It sent a jolt through my legs but it was much faster than following the twisting path of the stairs. My feet had barely touched the steps when I phased through them again.

Only pausing enough to break my fall a little, I dropped down through the stairwell at record pace while the soldiers behind me were forced to run down and around it all.

When I at last reached the final part, I sprinted down the last steps and skidded into the hallway. The sounds of battle came from down the corridor. I ran towards it.

Chaos met me as I came charging through the doorway and back into the throne room. A mass of bodies lay around Idra's feet. She dodged and struck like a viper at the soldiers around her, relying on her mastery of hand-to-hand combat rather than her new water magic. Blocks of stone lay shattered across the floor from where Edric had presumably thrown them at people, and leaves covered the red stones as well.

Reena shoved her hand forward, sending a flurry of leaves towards the High Elves who were trying to back her up against the wall. The cluster of green, yellow, and red leaves cut bloody streaks in their faces.

"Reinforcements are here," I yelled at the top of my lungs as I barreled towards them. "Time to leave."

A crash echoed through the red throne room as Vendir came flying in through one of the other doorways. He smacked into an empty pot and rolled across the floor while the Wielder who had hit him stalked in after him. I stabbed my knife in the enemy's direction. A lance of fire shot towards him, forcing him to abort his next attack.

Vendir leaped to his feet and sent a blast of wind to follow my fire.

"We need to go!" I repeated.

"Iwdael," Edric snapped from halfway down the room. "Create an opening."

The Prince of Trees was standing next to the throne, sending a twisting tangle of vines at a pair of soldiers. They cut the thick green vines with impressive speed, but another cluster only took their place and ensnared them again.

"Alright," he called back. "Brace yourselves. I'll try to keep it away from you but you might get hit with some of it too."

"Just do it!" Idra yelled as she ducked under two swords while trying to get her palm into position.

I was still running towards them when Prince Iwdael stopped his vine attacks and spun around as if to look at the whole room.

Fear shot up my spine.

It was so intense that I gasped and my steps faltered.

But it was nothing compared to how the High Elves reacted.

Bloodcurdling screams echoed throughout the throne room as all of the soldiers jerked back, their eyes wide and filled with terror. They appeared to be moving only by sheer survival instinct as they turned and bolted.

I stared in open-mouthed shock as the fierce High Elf warriors ran for their lives. Tearing my gaze from them, I shifted my attention to Iwdael. So this was what his power of mood manipulation could really do. Instill fear so intense that it made battle-hardened soldiers run from their posts.

"Now!" Prince Edric ordered as the path to the front doors was suddenly clear.

I whirled in that direction right as shimmering powder shot through the air and slammed into all of us. Panic flashed through my mind. But nothing happened. I was just about to open my mouth to tell everyone to get moving again when a heart-tearing cry ripped from Iwdael's throat.

His knees hit the stone floor with dull thuds as he collapsed onto the ground. Pressing his hands to his temples, he squeezed his eyes shut while rocking back and forth.

"No, no, no," he begged. "Please. Not again. Make it stop. Make it stop. Please."

"You should have stayed in your precious forest, Iwdael," a voice cut through the room.

I snapped my gaze to the front doors.

Princess Syrene strode into the throne room, her majestic violet gown rustling against the sandy floor. A host of High Elves followed behind her.

Boots pounded against stone from the corridor to the right of the throne as well. The soldiers I had left on the roof had made it down again.

"Shit," I swore. Taking off towards the nearest wall, I called over my shoulder. "Don't stand in the path from the door. And get ready to run."

Hoping that my friends would understand what I was about to do, and that the High Elves wouldn't, I leaped through the wall right as the battle started back up.

Iwdael's agonizing cries and the rumble of Edric's stone magic were abruptly cut off as I skidded to a halt outside the castle.

Riderless air serpents snapped at me as I darted around the castle and positioned myself in the doorway. My chest heaved and I was pretty sure I could hear the boom of gigantic wings as more air serpents approached from the other side of the defensive walls, but I shoved the fear and panic aside. Blowing out a steadying breath, I sheathed my blades and instead raised both hands in front of me. And then I shoved forward.

A storm of fire roared through the open doors.

Screams rose from inside, but they were quickly cut off.

Terror bloomed inside my chest as I couldn't help thinking that my friends hadn't understood what I was going to do and had gotten caught in the blast.

Feet thudded against the ground.

Relief washed over me as Idra and Vendir came barreling through the door.

"Run, you moron!" she screamed at me.

I fell in beside Prince Edric as he appeared with a half-delirious Iwdael braced against him. Draping Iwdael's other arm over my shoulder, I helped drag the Prince of Trees towards the gates.

Air serpents crested the defensive walls. Their massive forms blocked out the sky as they poured over the edge so that their riders could catch us. I cast a glance over my shoulder to see Reena sprinting out the doors after us. Then my attention was pulled back to the threats descending from above.

Raising a hand, I sent a blast of fire towards the sky. It created a flaming dome above the courtyard and forced the air serpents to shoot back up into the sky. Dark red fire cast dancing light against the stone ground.

In front of us, Idra and Vendir had made it out the gate and therefore out from the wards.

"Go!" I snapped at Idra.

Her dark eyes flicked between me and the courtyard behind as if to ascertain that there was no risk of me not making it out. Apparently satisfied, she grabbed Vendir and worldwalked them away.

My muscles screamed at me as Edric and I hauled Iwdael the final bit out the gate. A moment later, Reena skidded to a halt next to us. I whipped around. The courtyard behind us was empty apart from the dome of fire.

Dread sluiced through my veins.

"Where's Ymas?" I demanded.

"Maybe he's already left," Reena said.

"He can't worldwalk."

Prince Edric stared back towards the doors. "Last I saw, he was fighting some High Elves in the room where Vendir was too."

"He's still in there?"

The look on Edric's face was answer enough.

High Elves in bronze armor poured out through the front doors and ran towards us. Edric threw up a shield to block their magic while Iwdael's head lolled to the side like a broken doll.

"We need to get Prince Iwdael out of here," Reena pleaded.

Edric looked from the charging soldiers to the Prince of Trees. Indecision and impossible choices swirled in his gray eyes. Then he wiped all traces of emotion off his face and nodded. "Yes. Ymas is a skilled warrior. He'll be alright. We'll come back for him later." He turned to me. "Kenna. Take Reena. We need to leave now."

Battle cries echoed between the walls as the soldiers drew closer and the booming of massive wings filled the air above.

"No," I said. "Reena. Run into the city. Edric will come back and worldwalk you out after he's dropped off Iwdael."

"What are you going to do?" she asked, worry coloring her voice.

I stared at the High Elves barreling towards us while I let the dome of flames fall.

"I'm getting Ymas."

CHAPTER 25

*A*ir serpents slammed down onto the courtyard behind me as I sprinted the final distance to the castle wall and leaped through it. Prince Edric had said that Ymas had been fighting in the same room that Vendir had come from. There was a large reception room to the left of the throne room. So instead of going back into the actual throne room where no doubt a whole host of pissed-off soldiers waited for me, I aimed straight for that reception room.

The clanking of metal assaulted my ears as I skidded in through the wall and found myself in the middle of a battle.

Ymas grabbed a High Elf by the front of his bronze armor and threw him into the opposite wall as if he weighed nothing while at the same time leaping almost all the way up to the ceiling to avoid a sword coming for his chest. The desks and chairs around the room shook in terror as he slammed down into the floor again. More soldiers kept flooding in through the door.

Yanking out my blades, I stabbed the closest one through the back of the neck while ramming my sword through another's, also from behind his back. Strangled gurgling ripped from their mouths as I pulled out the blades. It made the other High Elves whirl around. Their eyes widened as they found me having appeared seemingly out of nowhere.

"Didn't you hear me?" I called to Ymas. "We need to leave."

"I heard you." He rammed his closed fist into a soldier's breastplate, making the whole thing buckle underneath the force of his strike. "But I'm a little busy at the moment."

Two High Elves lunged at him from behind. Grabbing the arm of the one on the left, he used him as a bat to whack the other one. Metal dinged as their armor clashed.

Half of the soldiers had now turned around to face me and I had to dodge a sword coming for my throat as I tried to get into a better position. Steel cleaved the air next to me. I stabbed my knife into the High Elf's armpit as his swing went wide. A scream shattered from his throat. Ripping out the blade again, I threw it up to block another strike from a different direction while drawing my sword in a wide arc to force the other back. More soldiers welled in through the doorway.

Ymas threw a roundhouse kick into the side of the closest attacker, sending him flying across the room and crashing right into his companions. I rammed my knife into a soldier's throat. Blood spurted from the wound and splattered across my face.

"Get ready!" I screamed.

As soon as I had seen Ymas nod, I kicked at the hip of the soldier charging me. The move bought me a two-second window and I swung my sword out to the side.

"Now!" I yelled.

Using the power of his magically enhanced physique, Ymas leaped so far up into the air that he reached the wide oil lamp hanging from the ceiling. A moment later, a searing scythe of fire cut through the room. It cleaved the High Elf soldiers in half as it burned through their bodies before they could duck, and left black scorch marks along the red walls. The smell of burning flesh filled the room.

"Let's go!" I sprinted towards the other doorway at the back of the room while the loud thud from behind informed me that Ymas had dropped down from the ceiling. "This way."

His boots pounded against the floor and he quickly caught up with me as we sprinted down the next corridor.

"There's a flight of stairs coming up on our right." I flicked my wrist in that direction while continuing forwards. "Run up them and then jump out the first window you see. I'll meet you outside."

Shouts rose behind us. It was followed moments later by the sound of pursuing soldiers. A stairwell opened up on our right.

I gave Ymas a shove towards it. "Go!"

He leaped up the first four steps and then disappeared from view. With his magical abilities, he would be able to make a jump from an upstairs window without getting hurt. I, on the other hand, would've broken my ankles, so I skidded to a halt and then ran straight through the outer wall instead.

Warm air enveloped me as I appeared outside the castle. From around the corner, the noise of soldiers hurrying across the courtyard echoed between the red stones.

I almost leaped out of my skin as Ymas suddenly slammed down into the ground right next to me.

"They're over here!" someone called from our left.

"Shit." I pulled Ymas with me as we ran towards the right instead. "Come on."

My throat burned as I heaved in deep breaths while sprinting with everything I had. Ymas wasn't even winded, and I knew that he was slowing his pace so that I could keep up, but he didn't try to make me go faster.

Twangs rang out behind us. Casting a frantic look over my shoulder, I found a cloud of arrows speeding towards us. I stumbled a step as I raised a massive wall of fire while still trying to run in the other direction at the same time. Ymas threw out a hand and steadied me.

Flames roared up towards the heavens, incinerating the arrows.

"Get a Wielder!" someone shouted from the other side of the flaming barrier.

Magic hummed from behind us as I let the flame shield drop. I cast another desperate look behind me right as lightning cleaved the air. Panic flashed through me as I realized that I wouldn't be able to dodge because my body was already twisted in two different directions with my head looking backwards and my body going forwards.

A palm slammed into my upper arm.

I flew through the air and crashed into the side of the tall defensive walls that we had just reached. Pain flared up my shoulder. A fraction of a second later, a white bolt of lightning split the air where I had just been running.

"Sorry," Ymas said. "I didn't have time for anything else."

"Thank you," I replied instead and pushed away from the wall.

Winds whirled behind us. I raised a wall of dark red fire to block it as the gusts roared between the castle and the barrier on our other side. Rogue flames and smoldering embers swirled in the air as the winds hit the fire shield. I gave Ymas a push on the shoulder to signal that we needed to keep going, before I took off in a sprint again.

His brown eyes slid to me as he followed. "The front gate is in the other direction."

"I know. But the whole area in front of it is full of High Elves and air serpents now."

"So how do we get out?"

Stairs that had been cut into the tall defensive wall suddenly appeared on our left. I shoved Ymas towards them right as another series of twangs rang out.

Arrows rained towards us as we sprinted up the steps. It was a very vulnerable position, but we needed to get to the top of the walls and this was the only way. My chest heaved as I raised yet another wall of fire to destroy the barrage of arrows while also sprinting up the stairs.

The arrows hit the dark red flames and disappeared without a trace. I was just about to open my mouth to answer Ymas when wings boomed from the other side of the wall.

Terror washed over me as a brown air serpent rose before us.

"Get down!" I screamed since Ymas was running in front of me.

He dropped to his stomach on the steps. Leaping over him, I slashed my blades through the air and sent arcs of flame hurtling towards the air serpent. The riders on top of it yelled in frustration as their mount veered left to avoid my fire, which took their own attacks out of position as well.

Sharp teeth set into a massive maw closed in on us from the side. Since we were still on the steps, there was nowhere to go to escape them so I flattened myself against the wall on my right while shoving my blades back into their sheaths. Then I pushed both hands forwards.

A storm of fire shot out and rolled across the grounds until it hit the side of the castle and washed up over the roof like a flaming red wave. The air serpent flashed up into the sky to avoid it, and the other ones that had been on the way as well sped back around the building.

"Come on," I said to Ymas as I took off up the stairs once more.

He leaped to his feet and sprinted after me. "Kenna. We can't make it back to the front gate or any of the side ones from here."

"I know."

"You should leave me. You can walk out through the walls at any time. I'll be alright. I'll find a way."

"I'm not leaving you." I had to press out the words between heavy breaths as we finally reached the top of the walls. "And there is a way."

Three air serpents were speeding back towards us. Another set of twangs echoed through the warm air as the High Elves sent a volley of arrows towards us. I threw a massive fireball at them before looking back at Ymas.

Winds ripped through my hair as I ran straight for the other side of the wall. Ymas followed.

"Do you trust me?" I asked.

"Yes," he answered without hesitation.

I grabbed his hand while we continued running. He glanced down at me curiously but said nothing as he followed my lead while holding on to my hand.

"When I say jump," I began, "jump."

The low barrier on the far side of the walkway was rapidly getting closer.

Wings boomed through the air. Then the twang of multiple bowstrings rang out again, followed by the whistling of arrows shooting towards us.

We reached the edge.

"Jump!" I screamed.

Leaping up onto the short barrier, we pushed off the red stones and jumped right off the tall defensive walls. The ground stared up at us in shock as we cleared the wall and continued out into the empty air.

Pain shot through my body.

I sucked in a gasp as something grazed the inside of my thigh at the same time as something else pierced my shoulder.

Winds tore at our clothes as we free-fell down towards the ground outside the walls for a second. I scrambled to push out the panic and pain that flared up inside me.

The sandstone street below sped towards us.

I worldwalked us out.

Blinding pain crackled through my body as I slammed into the grass. Losing my grip on Ymas, I crashed down on the ground and let out a raw cry of pain as both my ankles snapped from the force of the landing. Another wave of agony rolled through me as the arrow lodged in my shoulder was pushed farther through my body before the shaft broke when I tumbled to a halt on my back. Something warm and wet spread fast down the inside of my leg.

I felt lightheaded.

Ignoring the pain in my shoulder and ankles, I pressed a hand against the inside of my thigh. When I pulled it back, it was covered in blood.

Fear seeped into my bones like cold death.

The arrow had severed my femoral artery.

I was bleeding out.

Worried brown eyes appeared in front of my face as Ymas came into view. He appeared to be standing unharmed, which meant that I had gambled correctly. His magical powers allowed him to handle that kind of landing. I knew that I would most likely break my ankles, but there was no other way out of the castle and I had figured that Rayan could fix that later.

The severed artery was a surprise, though.

"Get Rayan," I croaked. "Hurry."

His face drained completely of color when he saw the blood pooling on the grass below my leg. Without another word, he shot upright and sprinted away so fast that the flowers on the ground took cover from the draft he created.

Shouts rang out all around me as the elves from Poisonwood realized that something terrible had happened. I sucked in a deep breath while the world around me started growing fuzzy. If this stream of blood kept up, I would bleed out in about five minutes. Tops.

The air around me tasted like copper.

My fingers fumbled as I shifted my other hand to my neck and pulled at the gold chain that hung around it. Relief flooded my veins, or maybe it was the delirium from the blood loss, when I finally managed to get the necklace out from underneath my shirt.

Boots thudded against the ground around me and I swore I could hear Mendar barking orders, but everything sounded muffled and very far away.

Pain shot through my shoulder as I moved my arm to grip the pendant. The red gem in the form of a teardrop was warm against my palm as I squeezed it. Magic shot out and wrapped around me like a cocoon.

Mendar's face, and then Endira's too, became visible in the

corner of my blurry vision. Their mouths were moving so I assumed that they were speaking to me. Or maybe to each other about me.

But all I could do was lie there on the grass and watch the two firebirds that soared high above me in the sky.

CHAPTER 26

"I was right."

Opening my eyes, I found Prince Rayan looking down at me with raised eyebrows. Pain pulsed through my shoulder as I moved my head a little so that I could meet his gaze properly.

"About what?" I pressed out.

His purple eyes glittered with both amusement and exasperation. "I do spend a disproportionate amount of time repairing holes in your body."

I laughed. It sent another wave of pain rolling through me. Sucking in a breath, I tried to keep completely still.

"Is she going to make it?" a worried voice asked from my other side.

Rayan flicked his gaze to Ymas. "Yes."

"And her ankles, you can fix them too?"

"I can indeed."

Ymas blew out a shaky breath and slumped into the chair next to my bed. Raking a large hand through his short black hair, he rested his head against the wall behind him for a moment. A small smile played over Rayan's lips.

But when the Prince of Water returned his attention to me, his eyes were serious. "However, it was a close call. A *very* close call."

"Yeah, well," I huffed. "It's not like I ask people to try to kill me."

"Why did you do it?" Ymas asked, his brown eyes locked on my face, before Rayan could retort.

"Why did I jump from the wall with you? Because it was the only way to get you outside the wards so that we could worldwalk without having to first fight our way through half a legion of High Elves as well as their air serpents."

"That's not what I meant. You almost died because of this. Why did you risk everything just to go back for me? We're not friends." There was nothing unkind about his words. Just a simple statement of fact.

It was true. When we had lived together in the Court of Stone and worked for Prince Edric as spies, we had always been more or less friendly. But we had never been friends.

"Because I owed you a huge debt," I answered. "And it was high time to repay it."

His dark brows creased. "A debt? For what?"

"Do you remember when I was on the run and Prince Edric sent you to capture me?"

"Yeah."

"And you did. You chased me into that building and I lost the fight. You had me completely at your mercy and you began dragging me back to the castle. Then I begged you for more time. You gave me one more day."

"So? It was just one more day."

I smiled at him. "If it hadn't been for that one day you gave me, I would never have gotten to where I am today. Because of that one day, I managed to secure enough money to buy my freedom from Prince Edric. Which then led to everything after that, ending with me becoming the Lady of Fire. If you had taken me in straight away, I would have stayed a slave forever. So this was all possible because of that one more day." I held his gaze. "When you let me go that day, I told you that I would never forget it. And I never have. This was me paying back that debt."

Shaking his head, he smiled back at me. "You really are something else, you know that?"

"If by that you mean reckless and too clever for her own good," Prince Rayan added as he moved from my thigh towards my ankles, "then I concur."

I laughed again, which immediately made me wince.

Warmth spread through my ankles as Rayan healed the broken bones.

Once he was done, Ymas helped me to sit up so that the Prince of Water could more easily reach the wound in my back and shoulder. The arrow was already gone, but blood still trickled down my skin.

The door to the cabin I shared with Mordren was thrown open. It banged against the wooden wall. A moment later, a furious Prince of Shadows stalked across the threshold. His silver eyes flashed like lightning storms as he locked them on me.

"What the hell were you thinking?" he demanded as he advanced on me.

"Hey, at least the blood ruby worked." I flashed him an innocent grin while gesturing towards the necklace lying on the nightstand next to me.

When Mordren had given it to me on my birthday, it had

been dark red. Now that the magic had been used up, it was clear like glass.

"Of course it worked," he growled down at me. "That was why I gave it to you."

"Exactly." I spread my arms. Or at least the one that Rayan wasn't patching up a hole in right now. "It temporarily kept all the blood inside my body until a healer could arrive. Which is precisely what happened."

Bracing a knee against the bed, Mordren leaned down and grabbed the front of my shirt.

"Careful," Prince Rayan said from behind my shoulder.

Mordren flicked a gaze at the Prince of Water, but he kept his fist buried in my shirt as he brought his face closer to mine. "And why did you need to use the blood ruby? Oh, that's right. Because you jumped off the fucking walls of your castle!"

"You make it sound a lot more dramatic than it really was," I protested.

Ymas cleared his throat. "Actually, that's exactly what you did. And it's not even half of all the dangerous things you did before that."

"Hey." I twisted as best as I could with Mordren's hand still gripping my shirt, and raised my eyebrows at Ymas. "I thought you were supposed to be on my side."

"Oh." He blinked at me before flicking his eyes towards the furious elf glaring at me. "Right. Sorry."

The Prince of Shadows slid his gaze to him. Power rolled off Mordren's body as he locked eyes with Ymas. "And you. We are going to have words later."

Ymas blanched.

I swatted at Mordren's wrist. "Stop it. Don't come after

him for this. I owed him a huge debt. This was me repaying it."

Before either of them could say anything else, Edric and Iwdael crossed the threshold. Mordren shifted his gaze to me and held it for a few seconds, as if promising that we would have words about this later too, before he finally released my shirt and stepped back.

"How are you feeling?" I asked Iwdael as he slumped down into the chair next to Ymas.

The dark-haired spy scrambled to his feet and bowed to Prince Edric, who moved farther into the room as well. After a nod from his prince, Ymas gave my arm a gentle squeeze and then disappeared out the door.

"I feel like I should be the one asking you that," the Prince of Trees replied.

"She will be as good as new in a few minutes," Rayan said from behind me.

Before anyone else could say anything, Idra, Hadeon, and Ellyda strode into the cabin as well.

Idra's dark eyes snapped straight to me. "You bloody idiot. Why—"

"Don't you start too," I interrupted, and then flapped a hand in Mordren's direction. "He has already yelled at me for this."

"Good." A lethal smile spread across her lips. "And when you're up again, I will show you exactly what I do to morons who almost get themselves killed."

Rolling my eyes, I heaved an exasperated sigh.

"How did your mission go?" Prince Rayan thankfully asked before Idra could begin making good on her promise.

"Good, I think," Hadeon answered while glancing over at his sister. "Right, El?"

"Yes." Ellyda was staring at a spot somewhere above Rayan's shoulder, but her voice was confident. "I got all the tools I needed. With this, I should be able to figure out a way to reverse the bracelets."

"That's good," Prince Edric said. After giving the blacksmith an appreciative nod, he turned to sweep serious eyes over the rest of us. "And we have freed all the worldwalkers we could find these past few weeks, so when the time comes, we should be able to quickly get our army where we want them."

"Indeed," Idra said. Her gaze slid to the Prince of Trees. "However, there is one more problem we need to solve first."

"There," Rayan interrupted. Patting my shoulder, he smiled down at me. "Good as new."

I reached up and squeezed his hand while holding his gaze. "Thank you."

He let out an amused chuckle. "You can thank me by not getting yourself this badly injured again."

"I'll try." After giving his hand one final squeeze I turned and instead looked between Idra and Iwdael. "Idra is right, though."

"Of course I am," she shot back before shifting her attention to the Prince of Trees again. "You're incredibly powerful when you use your mood manipulation, and it would help us greatly in a battle. But we need to find a way to neutralize that powder that Princess Syrene has, otherwise you won't even make it one minute on the battlefield."

Iwdael heaved an endless sigh and reached up to rake his fingers through his long brown hair. The leaves woven into it shifted as if adapting to his movements. "I know. I'm not sure what's in it, but the smell of it somehow makes all of my senses go crazy and I'm bombarded with how everyone and everything is feeling. From how hungry the worm in the ground below my feet is to how terrified the soldier across the room is, and it all feels as if the emotions are my own. It's too much. It makes it feel like my brain is going to melt."

"And it's the smell that does it?" I asked.

"Yes. I wasn't sure the first time, but now I am. I don't even need to breathe it in for it to work. As soon as that shimmering powder gets close enough that I can smell it in the air, things start going to hell."

Prince Edric crossed his arms and drew his eyebrows down. "So can we block your sense of smell in some way then?"

"How? And it also needs to last through an entire day of fighting."

Several more people around the room crossed their arms and frowned as they tried to come up with some sort of miraculous solution.

An idea crept into my mind.

"Oh, I don't think so, Kenna," Hadeon said as he caught the look. "You need to rest up before you do anything else."

"Rayan has already healed all of my injuries," I protested.

"But you still need to rest," the Prince of Water added very unhelpfully. "The rest of the day, and an entire night of sleep at least, before you're fit to get out of bed."

Mordren leveled a stare dripping with authority on me. "I will make sure she does."

"Fine." Rolling my eyes, I raised my hands in surrender. "But tomorrow morning…"

Prince Iwdael shifted his yellow eyes to me and raised his eyebrows. "Tomorrow what?"

A triumphant grin spread across my lips as I swept my gaze over all of them.

"I think I know someone who can help."

CHAPTER 27

Perfume hit me like a brick in the face. It smelled as if someone had smashed a couple of hundred bottles of it and then left it to blend into one thick cloud. Even from behind the protection of my mask, I had to draw shallow breaths to prevent it from soaking my lungs completely. I inhaled one final dose of clean air before stepping into the small cabin and closing the door behind me.

Beads rattled from the doorway at the back of the combined kitchen and living room.

A moment later, an elderly human woman with a wrinkled face and graying hair appeared through the curtain of multicolored beads. She blinked at me from behind her thick glasses.

"The Black Mask," she said. Her blue eyes twinkled as she smiled. "It has been a while."

I smiled back even though she couldn't see it underneath my mask. "Hello, Stella."

Raising an arm, she motioned for us to sit down at the table. I swept my gaze over the cluttered kitchen counters while I moved towards the table. Everything in here looked exactly the same. From the stacks of paper, to the small potted plants, and to the multitude of colorful decorations.

There were only two chairs at the table, so I slid into the one opposite Stella after she had taken a seat in the one closest to the curtain of beads.

"I haven't seen you for many months," Stella said as she leaned back in her chair and rested her hands on her stomach.

"I know," I replied. "I've been... very busy."

"I bet you have." She chuckled before her face turned serious. "So, what kind of information are you after today?"

"It's actually not information I'm after."

She raised her eyebrows at me. "Oh?"

"I need to buy something that can block a person's sense of smell completely, and for at least an entire day at a time. And I have a feeling that you might be able to help me with something like that."

Silence fell inside the cabin as Stella only studied me from across the table without replying. This whole meeting was just based on a hunch, and I had no idea how it would play out. But at this point, all I could do was to see it through.

Wind chimes tinkled from outside the window.

Stella kept studying me.

Then a grin slowly spread across her face and she huffed out a laugh. "Well, I always knew that you were too smart for your own good."

Relief and hope fluttered their sparkling wings in my chest.

Wood creaked as Stella rose from her seat and pushed her chair back. "Wait here."

I watched as she disappeared back behind the curtain of beads that separated the living room and kitchen from the rest of the cabin. Since I had only ever been inside this room, I had no idea what was behind it. But if I had to guess, I would say her bedroom. And a workplace.

Glass clinked from somewhere on the other side of the sparkly divider.

Sliding my hands into one of my pockets, I ran my fingers along the edge of the stack of bills in there. They flapped faintly from inside the dark fabric. Not for the first time, I was incredibly thankful for my magic-imbued jacket and its mass of shifting pockets. And the stacks of emergency cash I always kept in there.

The curtain rippled again as Stella's plump figure became visible. Moving with confident steps, she returned to the table but she didn't sit down. Instead, she stopped right next to me.

There was a small bottle in her hands. It had a flat bottom, but the rest of it was shaped like a teardrop and ended with a gem-decorated stopper. The glass it was made of was clear. And so was the liquid inside.

A small pop sounded as Stella uncorked it. In a fluid motion, she drew the now open bottle right under the edge of my mask.

"Here," she said. "Smell this."

The bottle swept past my face. Scrunching up my eyebrows, I concentrated on the smell while Stella walked back to her chair and dropped into it. My frown deepened.

"It doesn't smell of anything," I said at last.

Satisfaction shone on her wrinkled face. "Exactly. I call this my shield perfume."

"Shield perfume?"

"Yes. It blocks all other smells and tastes so that the wearer doesn't get affected by... other things."

The small bottle produced a soft thud as Stella leaned

forward and placed it on the table in front of me. I eyed it for a second before picking it up and studying it curiously. Light from the morning sun shone in through the window and was refracted in the glass as I carefully turned it.

A smile spread across my lips as I looked back up at Stella. "So this is how you do it."

"Yes, it is." Mischief glittered in her eyes as she matched the smile on my face. "…Kenna."

I let out a short laugh as I pushed the mask up into the top of my hood. After lowering the hood as well, I shook out my long red hair and met Stella's gaze without a mask between us for the first time ever. "How long have you known?"

She gave me an innocent shrug. "A while. Information is my trade, after all." Raising her eyebrows, she nodded towards the bottle in my hand. "And you, how long have you known?"

"I've suspected it, but I've never known for certain." I rolled the bottle between my fingers and studied it for a few seconds before meeting Stella's eyes again. "Is it magic?"

"No. Maybe. I don't know. I can create perfumes that make people… more open to suggestions. More willing to share. Or to make them feel calm and at ease."

I raised the bottle a little. "And this is a kind of antidote to make sure that you don't get affected by it too?"

"Indeed. It wouldn't do to start spilling my own secrets too."

"True. So people really just… tell you their secrets because you wear a certain perfume to the meeting?"

She gestured at the perfume-drenched cottage around us. "I'm very good at what I do." Her blue eyes sparkled as a secretive smile spread across her lips. "Or maybe people just really do like talking to harmless little old ladies."

I laughed. "Yes, perhaps they do."

Putting the bottle back on the table, I stuck my hand into my pocket again and withdrew the stack of bills from it. Paper rustled faintly as I slid it across the table.

Stella looked at the rather significant pile of money. Then she pushed it back towards me. "Keep it. This one's on the house."

Surprise flickered through me as I raised my eyebrows at her. Stella wasn't the type to refuse a payment. Based on everything I knew about her, she loved money.

When she noticed my silent question, she shrugged. "The High Elves are bad for business. High Commander Anron doesn't seem to like humans very much because most places where I go to… *gather* information have become restricted to me. So you can pay me by taking our lands back."

Holding her gaze, I gave her a sincere nod. "I will."

"Good. I will do what I can from my end." Wicked mischief glinted in her eyes again. "Spreading misinformation, and all."

My fingers wrapped around the stack of bills. After making sure that she wasn't going to change her mind, I put it back in one of my pockets. Then I placed the small glass bottle in another one. Looking up, I met Stella's eyes again. I held out my hand.

"Thank you," I said, and truly meant it. "I knew that I could always count on you."

A hint of surprise flickered across her face. Then she reached across the table as well, making her bracelets jingle. Her wrinkled hand was warm in mine as I shook it.

The wind chimes outside tinkled as another early fall wind blew through the forest.

I gave Stella's hand one final squeeze and then stood up. After taking a step to the side, I pushed the chair back against the table and then started towards the door.

"Kenna," Stella said right before I could place my hand on the handle.

When I turned back around, I found her watching me with a wistful smile on her kind face. "Yes?"

"It has been wonderful watching you grow into the strong and independent person you have become." Tears gleamed at the corner of her eyes. "You will come and visit an old lady from time to time, won't you?"

Warmth spread through my whole soul. I smiled back at her.

"Always, Stella."

CHAPTER 28

The lake glittered like diamonds in the afternoon sunlight. Placing my boots on the ground, I rolled up my pants and stepped into the water. It rippled around my ankles as I turned to face the Prince of Shadows.

"It's really not that cold," I said.

"Says the Lady of Fire." Mordren placed a couple of towels on the grass before looking up at me and raising an unimpressed eyebrow. "Forgive me if I don't trust your assessment of temperatures."

I rolled my eyes at him. "You got in last time."

"Yes. However, both the air and the water are much colder than last time."

"Then I guess you'll have to wait until Mendar and his people figure out a way to install real showers and baths in their cabins."

Mordren leveled a flat look at me. I grinned.

Water sloshed around my ankles as I stepped back onto the grass. Turning so that I stood facing the scowling Prince of Shadows, I grabbed the hem of my shirt and started sliding it up my stomach.

Mordren, who had been glaring at the lake as if he could force it to increase its temperature by the ferocity of his wrath alone, flicked a glance in my direction. When he noticed what I was doing, he slowly turned towards me.

Black fabric brushed my skin as I drew my shirt up over my breasts. Keeping eye contact with Mordren, I took my time tracing my fingers over them.

He clenched his jaw.

A sly smile spread over my lips. Putting him out of his misery, I finished pulling the shirt over my head and dropped it on top of my boots. Then I began tracing my fingers along the top of my pants.

"Kenna," Mordren began.

"Yes?"

Holding his gaze, I undid the fastenings on my pants while continuing to stroke my hands back and forth across my skin. He opened his mouth again, but before he could get a single word out, I turned around.

His eyes burned holes in my back as I remained motionless for a moment. When I had calculated that he was just about to intervene, I pushed my pants down my legs and stepped out of them. Casting a glance over my shoulder, I found Mordren watching me intently. I smirked at him.

After twisting so that my back was fully to him again, I bent over and stripped out of my underwear.

A chilly wind blew through the thick forest, making the leaves flutter on the trees around the lake. My hair rippled where it hung over my shoulder. Bending all the way over so that my fingers skimmed the grass, I stepped out of the final garments.

"Kenna," Mordren said again, his voice like midnight thunder.

With slow and calculated movements, I drew my hands up my legs as I straightened again. That wicked smirk was back on my lips as I turned to face him. "What?"

His eyes raked over my naked body.

"Well, you can stand there if you want." I shot him a challenging look. "I'm going for a swim."

Keeping my eyes on him, I walked backwards out into the lake. The cool water wrapped around my legs like silk. Mordren tracked my every movement.

When I reached waist level, I stopped and arched an eyebrow at him. "Coming?"

He narrowed his eyes at me. Then he reached up and began unbuttoning his suit jacket.

Smug victory sparkled through me. He was so easy to manipulate.

Shining dark hair slid across his shoulder and fluttered in the wind as Mordren stripped out of his clothes with precise and efficient moves. I watched the way his muscles shifted as he twisted to place the dark garments on the grass next to mine. As soon as they were resting on the ground, he started towards me.

Small waves rippled out as he stalked through the water.

I dipped my hands in the cool water and then drew them across my exposed breasts as if I was washing myself.

Mordren's eyes darkened.

Biting my lips, I kneaded my skin while my gaze slipped to over his abs and down the V that was visible below them. A triumphant smirk slid across my lips at what I found there.

"So hard already?" I teased.

"How am I supposed to stay on the shore when your body

is over here looking like this?" He came to a halt before me, water lapping around his hips. Reaching out, he traced his thumb over my mouth. "And when you are biting your lip like that?"

"You're not. You're supposed to surrender to my will. Just like you did."

"I don't surrender."

I stepped closer and wrapped my hand around his hard length. With my fire magic running through my veins, my hand was warm against his skin.

A moan ripped from Mordren's throat as I started slowly sliding my hand up and down.

"Oh, but you will," I promised, a villainous smile on my lips.

He blew out a controlled breath as I continued the movements of my hand. I drew my thumb over his tip. A tremor passed through his body and he tilted his head back forcing out another breath.

Readjusting my grip, I started moving faster.

Mordren pressed forward, forcing me back a step. I changed up my rhythm. Another shuddering breath made it past his lips as he advanced again. The water reached up to cover my breasts as Mordren backed me up again while I tightened my grip and started up a steady beat. I drew my thumb over his tip once more.

His hand shot out. Strong fingers wrapped around my throat as Mordren forced me back another step. The water reached the base of my throat.

I was not going to let him win. This time, he would surrender to me before I ever yielded to him.

With a firm grip on his hard length, I pumped my hand up and down. It pulsed against my warm palm.

Mordren shifted his hand around my throat. Placing his thumb under my chin, he forced my head back as he moved us deeper into the lake. Water lapped against my jaw. If it weren't for his fingers forcing me to tilt my head back, it would've covered my mouth. I drew careful shallow breaths to avoid inhaling any of the water.

Shadows flickered erratically around Mordren's entire forearm. His eyes seemed to lose focus several times and his body trembled underneath my touch as I carried on mercilessly.

His muscles tensed as if getting ready to force me to back up another step.

I pushed him over the edge.

A loud moan ripped from his throat as he came. I continued stroking my hand up and down his skin while release pulsed through him. His grip on my jaw tightened as he held my head up above the water through it all.

When the final tremors had passed over him, he staggered a couple of steps back, bringing the water level down to my chest. The snapping shadows around his body disappeared and he heaved a deep sigh. With his hand still around my throat, he blinked a few times before his silver eyes locked on me.

"Told you you'd surrender to me," I taunted and gave him a quick rise and fall of my eyebrows.

He leaned down and stole a savage kiss from my lips. "You infuriating little blackmailer."

I chuckled. "You know you love me."

"Yes, I do." Drawing back, he cupped my cheeks with both hands and held my gaze. "I really do."

Sliding a hand over his muscled chest, I placed it against the back of his neck and pulled his lips back to mine. He drew his hands down my sides and then lifted me up. I wrapped my legs around his waist while he gripped my ass as he started walking us back towards the shore.

Water sloshed around our bodies.

Another early fall wind whirled through the forest, sending our wet hair fluttering to the side. Goosebumps prickled Mordren's skin. I called up more of the magic inside me, making my whole body hot. Mordren moaned a sigh into my mouth and wrapped his arms tighter around me.

His muscles hardened against my body as he knelt and put me down on top of the towel. I raked my fingers over his back and down his arms as he leaned down to kiss me while moving his knees into position. Straddling me, he braced one hand on the ground while tracing the other over the side of my ribs. A sigh escaped my throat as he tore his lips from mine and started kissing his way down my throat. He reached up and wrapped his hand around my wrist. With an iron grip, he moved it away from his back and towards the ground.

Knitting his fingers through mine, he pushed the back of my hand against the warm towel and kept it there while his lips brushed my chest. I shifted my free hand to his side and dragged my fingers over his ribs and towards his abs.

I sucked in a gasp and arched my back as Mordren's tongue flicked my nipple. His fingers tightened around mine.

Pleasure coursed through my body as Mordren kissed my skin all the way down towards my hips. While keeping his grip on my hand, he moved our arms downwards and then adjusted his position between my legs. A moment later, silken shadows snaked around my thighs.

While blowing out a shuddering sigh, I raked a hand through my own hair to push the wet strands out of my face.

My whole core throbbed as Mordren used his shadows to

spread my legs while his lips continued brushing over my skin. His fingers traced my entrance, making me suck in a breath. Fire surged inside my veins as he teased my clit. He continued with his agonizing torture even though I was more than ready already. I had been ready ever since I watched him come in the water.

A desperate moan tore from my throat. Mordren answered with a dark chuckle.

Leaning down over me, he braced his forearm against the ground while moving our joined hands back up next to my head. With his shadows still keeping my legs spread, he pushed inside me.

I let out another shuddering moan.

After drawing out slowly, he slid in once more. Farther this time. I tightened my grip on his fingers as he started moving in and out at a slow pace.

Golden light from the afternoon sun warmed our naked skin and set Mordren's eyes glittering.

He started moving faster. I gasped with dark desire as he drove into me harder. My hand shot out and wrapped around the back of his neck. He leaned down and kissed me roughly while he continued pounding into me. Letting out a loud moan, I arched my back and shifted my hips. My legs trembled against the shadows as Mordren slammed into me all the way to the hilt. His teeth grazed my nipple.

I sucked in a shuddering breath as release built inside me.

Threading my fingers through his silky black hair, I gripped it tightly while he drove into me over and over. A wave of pleasure rose up inside me as his tongue teased my hard nipple at the same time as he continued his merciless pace.

Dark moans erupted from my throat as release crashed

over me. My fingers dug into his neck, and my inner walls trembled and tightened around him. He continued sliding in and out of me, riding the wave with me as he came as well while also prolonging my orgasm.

My legs shook with the force of it.

When the last trembling pulses of pleasure had rolled off our bodies, he collapsed down onto the towel next to me.

For a while, we just lay there next to each other, our chests heaving in sync. The pale blue sky visible above the lake paid us no mind as we stared up at it while trying to piece our minds back together. A gentle breeze played in the leaves and a pair of starlings danced past above us. Closing my eyes, I blew out a slow breath.

"You really are extraordinary."

I opened my eyes to find Mordren studying me. He had rolled over on his side and propped himself up on one elbow. A smile played over his mouth.

A matching one slid across my lips as I met his gaze. "Likewise."

Adjusting his position, he slid his arm underneath my shoulder blades and took a firm grip on my arm on the other side. With a decisive pull, he rolled me over onto his towel until I was pressed against his side. Using his other hand, he lifted my towel and draped it over the both of us. I sent a controlled wave of fire magic up and down my body, drying both him, me, and the two towels.

He settled down onto his back again while keeping his arm tightly wrapped around me. Nestling deeper under the towel, I pressed myself harder against his honed body and rested my hand on his warm chest.

"What are we going to do when this is all over?" I asked softly into the silence.

"When this is all over, we are going to live."

My chest shook against his side as I huffed out a laugh. "Well, I know that. But where?"

"Wherever we want."

"Except that I have a castle in the Court of Fire, and you live in the Court of Shadows."

Tilting his head, he looked down at me with eyes full of worry. "What's wrong?"

"Nothing." I blew out a sigh. "It's just... I don't know where home is."

Silence fell. Avoiding his gaze, I started tracing circles on his muscled chest.

"What do you mean?" he asked at last.

"Well, I... At first, I lived in the Beaufort mansion. But that never felt like home. Then I was sold to Prince Edric and went to live in his castle. But that wasn't home either. Then, I lived with Valerie and Theo for a while. And then after I bought my freedom, I also lived in your castle in the Court of Shadows. Then I became Volkan's slave and moved to the Court of Fire. And now that castle is mine..." I blew out an annoyed sigh. "Or at least it was until the High Elves stole it from me. But anyway, that's not the point. The point is that I don't feel like that castle in the Court of Fire is my home either. Nothing really feels like home, and I'm not sure what to do about it."

"We could build a new home."

My head jerked up as I snapped my gaze to him.

Endless love swirled in his beautiful eyes as he looked at me. It made my heart swell and emotions well up inside my chest.

"A home for both of us," he continued. A smile drifted over

his lips. "We could put it on the border between our courts so that it will belong as much to me as to you."

Holding his gaze, I smiled back at him. "I would like that."

"Then it is settled."

I slid my arm over his chest and pulled him closer to me. His warm breath ruffled my hair as he leaned down and kissed the top of my head.

For a long while, we stayed like that. Our chests rising and falling in tandem. Breathing each other in. Sharing the warmth in our bodies and the hopeful future in our hearts.

Only when the sun began slanting across the trees and its light painted a golden path across the glittering lake did we force ourselves to return to reality and get dressed. I slid my hand into his and held him tightly as we walked back to the camp.

As the trees thinned out and the cabins became visible, we found Mendar sitting on a stone, whittling something, while a couple of blood panthers rested around his feet. Amusement tugged at his lips as he gave us a nod, as if he knew exactly what we had been up to. I flashed him a grin.

On the training field up ahead, Hadeon and Idra were sparring with both blades and magic while Vendir looked to be helping Eilan to focus his shots of lightning. I flicked my gaze to Theo and Valerie, who were standing at the edge of the open area. A frown creased my brows. However, I couldn't stop the amusement sparkling inside me at the same time.

They looked like a pair of human-shaped, gold-glittering gems. Light shone from underneath their skin as if it was reflecting against a mass of mirrors. As I watched them, I couldn't help wondering if they would really be able to make their powers work before this war started.

"I might not have gotten you to surrender in the water,'

Mordren said as he released my hand and turned towards me. "But I can certainly do it on the sparring field."

Raising my eyebrows, I looked back at him. "I think you're forgetting that time I beat you in a sword fight."

"I seem to recall it ending with you back first on the ground with me straddling your chest and my knife at your throat."

"That's because you cheated."

"Well…" He raised an arm to motion towards the open stretch of grass. "Here is your chance to prove it."

Flicking my hair back behind my shoulder, I brushed past him and strode out onto the training field. I had only just squared up against Mordren and called up my fire magic when something moved in the corner of my eye. Letting the ball of flames die out, I turned in the direction of the figure hurrying towards us.

Magic flickered out all across the grass as we exchanged a look. Then we jogged towards the edge of the field.

Ellyda almost barreled into us as we all screeched to a halt on the grass. Her violet eyes were clear and sharp as she swept her gaze over all of us, and triumph shone on her face.

"I did it," she announced. "I found a way to reverse the flow of power in the bracelets."

Valerie let out a whoop and pumped her fist in the air.

"The ones in your workshop?" Eilan asked while trying to curb the hope glittering in his pale green eyes.

She shook her head. "No. All of them."

"I knew it!" Hadeon called as he wrapped his arms around his sister and pulled her into a massive hug. "I knew you could do it."

Ellyda blinked in surprise at the sudden embrace. Clearing

her throat, she patted him awkwardly on the back a couple of times.

From across Hadeon's shoulder, Mordren met her gaze and gave her a nod while a smile lit his face. "Well done."

She nodded back while Hadeon released her and clapped her on the shoulder once before withdrawing to his place next to Idra.

Then we all exchanged a look.

The joy at her success drained from the air and disappeared like spilled wine through gaping floorboards. In its place, a sense of dread descended on our group.

This was it.

We could neutralize the magic-siphoning bracelets that the High Elves had put on all of our people. And that meant one thing.

It was time to take the war to them.

CHAPTER 29

King Aldrich's mountain rose up from the ground and stretched its peak so high up towards the heavens that it was impossible to make out the white marble castle at its top. I stared at the large open field that separated us from the foot of the mountain. Somewhere on the other side was a forest and the entrance to the prison. But here, there was only swaying grass on the flat empty ground.

My heart thrummed in my chest.

This was it.

This was our battlefield.

Here we would make our last stand.

Leather groaned and armor clanked as all of our worldwalkers flashed back and forth between this field and our different courts, bringing everyone who could contribute to a battle. Almost all of them still wore magic-siphoning bracelets. But we would change that soon.

We had prepared everything that could be prepared. We had cheated what could be cheated. We had stacked the deck as much in our favor as we could. And we had a plan. Now, all that was left was to see it through.

Two armies would meet on this battlefield.

Either Anron would die.

Or we would.

Blowing out a steadying breath, I adjusted my black armor and ran a hand over the hilt of my blades. This would work.

"This will work," Mordren said as if he could read my mind. Stepping up beside me, he gazed out at the swaying grass. "Once we start reversing the bracelets, we will have the advantage. This will be over in a day."

"I hope so."

Wings boomed through the air.

A nervous ripple went through our ranks as the soldiers and magic-users whipped their heads around, looking for the source of the sound.

"Hold your positions," Idra snapped at them.

They stopped moving and stood up straighter as her dark gaze cut across their faces. An approving smirk played at the corner of Hadeon's lips as he watched her, but it was wiped off his face a second later as the source of the booming wings came into view.

Air serpents shot down from the mountain while others sped towards it from the other courts. I wasn't sure what they had spotted first: that we were worldwalking people from our courts in droves, or that a great army was gathering right on Anron's doorstep. Perhaps a bit of both. Regardless, the effect was the same. High Commander Anron was on his way.

"How much longer?" I asked, turning to meet Prince Edric's gray eyes as he strode through the ranks towards us.

He cast another glance over his shoulder. "They're

bringing in Rayan and his healer corps now, so it's almost done."

I nodded.

This had gone surprisingly well. With a few perfectly timed distractions, courtesy of the Hands, the rest of our people had managed to create enough chaos to let our fighters and magic-users slip away long enough for our worldwalkers to get them out. That we had done it in every court simultaneously had probably helped too.

The ground trembled as a mass of air serpents slammed into the grass right in front of the mountain. Bronze armor gleamed in the bright morning sunlight that fell across the plains. I swept my gaze across the forming ranks of High Elves.

Anron had been right about one thing. His legion outnumbered our army. And his Wielders were a lot stronger than most of the magically gifted elves among our soldiers. But thanks to Ellyda, that wouldn't matter. We would end this war in one fell swoop.

A majestic white air serpent swept down from the mountain. Atop it was High Commander Anron, along with three smaller figures.

Surprise, anger, and a hint of dread swirled in my chest as I watched the four of them dismount. The High Commander strode forward a couple of steps so that he was standing in front of his legion while the other three remained with the High Elves.

Princess Syrene, wearing a beautiful suit of armor that shifted in silver and violet, stood with her chin raised as she stared at us from across the grass.

Next to me, Prince Iwdael rolled his shoulders.

"Did you use the perfume?" I asked.

"Yes." His yellow eyes were locked on his wife on the other side of the battlefield. "It had better work."

"It will."

When he only nodded, I slid my gaze back to the two figures standing on either side of her. Despite the black bracelet around his wrist, Evander stood with his spine straight while a smug sense of superiority seemed to pulse from him. I resisted the urge to roll my eyes. He had no idea what true power really was.

On Syrene's other side stood another traitor. Monette. Her long blond hair tumbled down her back, but as opposed to the other two, she was hunching her shoulders. I couldn't tell from this distance, but I imagined that her turquoise eyes were flicking nervously back and forth over our ranks. It looked like she would rather be anywhere but here.

The air vibrated next to Prince Edric. A moment later, Felix appeared out of thin air.

"Everyone is here," he announced while bowing his head to the Prince of Stone. "We will start worldwalking all the supplies in now."

"Good," Edric Mountaincleaver answered.

"There are..." Trailing off, he stared across the grass while his brown eyes widened. "Is that...?"

"Monette. Yes."

"She's... She's actually going to fight... for *them*?" Shock and heartbreak blew across his face as he turned to look up at Prince Edric. "She's going to fight against us?"

"Yes. Hurry up and get started on the supplies."

After one last look at the half-elf spy that he had been madly in love with for years, Felix pulled himself together and stood up straighter before bowing his head again. "Yes, my prince."

Sadness swirled inside me as I watched him patch up his broken heart and put on a determined face before worldwalking out. I recognized that look in his eyes. It was the look of someone who had been hoping that there was a way back to how things used to be, but who had now accepted that some bonds were shattered forever.

The final air serpents landed on the ground and dropped off the waiting soldiers before flying back up towards the mountain with empty saddles. I drew in a shaky breath.

"This is it, huh?" Theo said.

"Yes," Eilan answered. He shifted his gaze between Theo and Valerie. "Try to blind them as best as you can during the first strike, and this might be over sooner than we think."

Valerie nodded, and then she and Theo moved to stand a short distance to the side and in front of the rest of us.

Across the plains, High Commander Anron took a step forward.

"Are you ready for this?" I asked without taking my eyes off the High Commander. "These are your people. Your former friends and brothers-in-arms."

On Hadeon's other side, Vendir blew out a sigh. He was wearing a set of leather armor instead of the bronze one that would have marked him as an enemy. I flicked a glance at him and found him looking down at Ellyda for a few seconds before he raised his chin again.

"They are not the ones we need to take out," he answered. "High Commander Anron is."

"How good of you," Anron called across the windswept grass before I could reply. "How very good of you to bring all of your magically gifted elves here so that I can draw from their power more efficiently."

"Say when," Ellyda spoke quietly into the silence that fell.

"You really have no idea who you're playing against," I called back to Anron.

"Is that the Princess of Fire?" A mocking laugh echoed through the air. "It's almost as if you're begging to lose. How could you possibly–"

"Now!" I said to Ellyda.

Her fingers shifted and a second later she hissed, "Go."

Idra shot a thin stream of water straight up into the air.

And then all hell broke loose.

Fire, lightning, shadows, stones, and trees sharpened into spears shot across the swaying grass while a brilliant white light pulsed towards the High Elves at the same time. Vines and flowers and glass and sharp splinters followed them while pits of lava and mud and seaweed bloomed from the ground as the rest of our magic-users attacked as well.

The High Elf soldiers twisted their heads and yanked up a forearm to shield their eyes from the blinding pulse of light that Valerie and Theo had sent their way while the Wielders threw up shields. But we weren't aiming for them.

Caught by surprise in the middle of his sentence, Anron raised a massive wall of stone to block our storm of magic. It shot up from the ground. Our attacks barreled straight for it while it sped higher.

Then it stopped.

The cloud of glass doubled in size. As did the cluster of spinning flowers and the mud pools on the ground, along with several other attacks.

Shock rippled through the High Elves' ranks as Anron's shield shrank back into the ground while our barrage grew larger. Anron stumbled a step back, suddenly unable to shield.

A villainous grin slid across my mouth as I shoved my flames the final bit.

THE LAST STAND

Screams of panic echoed across the plains as the other Wielders threw their own shields towards Anron right as our massive blast hit him. Magic exploded across the grass.

Not all of the shields made it in time and High Commander Anron caught part of the attacks. His brown hair whipped around him as he was flung off his feet and crashed into the ranks of soldiers behind him.

"Again!" Idra called, and shot another thin stream of water straight up into the air to signal to the ones farther back.

Dark red flames roared across the field as I hurled another attack at Anron. Lightning split the air and massive boulders joined as Eilan and Prince Edric threw more magic at them as well. Another cluster of glass sped through the cool air. Pits of lava opened up beneath the High Elves' feet, forcing them to leap out of the way while their Wielders tried to smoothen earth back over the holes.

Anron struggled to his feet right before our next attack reached him. He yanked up his arm as if trying to raise another wall of stone, but nothing happened. Only the quick thinking of another Wielder saved him from taking Eilan's lightning and my fire to the chest, and Edric's boulder to the head.

A crack echoed across the plains as the boulders smacked into a stone wall at the same time as Eilan's lightning bolt hit it too. My flames washed over the stone, melting its sides. Screams and bellowed orders came from the other side as High Commander Anron was forced to dive out from behind it in order to escape the fire.

Glass clattered against the barrier a second later.

Anron shot to his feet and leaped backwards as Mordren's shadows chased him across the ground. He rammed a hand towards them, but again nothing happened.

From a few strides away, Evander struggled to his feet after having been one of the people to break Anron's untimely flight. He stared between his hands and the High Commander as wood suddenly rose from his own palms. Anron snapped his head towards him.

Fire from one of the Wielders roared across the ground to burn away Mordren's shadows. A hail of stone and glass sped towards Anron instead. I sent another wave of flames at him too while Eilan aimed a third lightning strike.

Diving away from the blast, Anron rolled across the ground while trying to look both at us and Evander at the same time. He shot to his feet. His gaze snapped between Evander, us, and himself.

"Hurry!" I screamed.

In a coordinated blast, we threw every single piece of long-distance battle magic we had at Anron all at the same time.

Lethal power shot across the grass in a storm of light and darkness.

Anron slammed a hand to his wrist, then his heart, and then he smacked his hands together in front of his chest before drawing them apart in a violent gesture.

Our deadly attack crashed into him.

CHAPTER 30

The sound of shattering glass rippled through our ranks. I whirled around to face our army. Surprise flashed across their faces as they stared down at their wrists.

Shards like black glass tumbled down and clinked as they hit the grass.

My eyebrows shot up.

All of the magic-siphoning bracelets had shattered completely.

"It didn't work," Prince Edric ground out.

I whipped back around towards the legion of High Elves. A tall figure became visible through the smoke and the steam and the cracked bits of stone falling to the ground.

Rage pulsed from High Commander Anron's whole body.

"Did you think you could use my own magic against me?" he bellowed at us in a voice that sounded uncharacteristically unhinged. "That you weak and unworthy cowards could draw the Great Current out of me and use it for yourself? You will pay for this insolence."

"I didn't know he could shatter the bracelets remotely," Ellyda said from somewhere on my left.

"It's alright," Hadeon answered. "We might not be able to draw power from him anymore, but at least all of our people are now free."

He was right. Our plan had been to kill Anron in a surprise attack while he couldn't use any magic to protect himself, but unfortunately his Wielders had been too skilled for that to go as smoothly as we had hoped. When he broke the bracelets, that chance disappeared completely. While it destroyed one opportunity, it created another one.

With all the bracelets gone, we could finally fight more evenly.

"Form up," High Commander Anron snapped at his legion.

Armor clanked as the ranks began reorganizing themselves.

"Get to the back," Hadeon said to his sister.

I shifted my gaze to the two thieves. "You too. We're changing to the backup plan."

"What backup plan?" Valerie threw her arms out and shook her head at me. "We haven't even finished it yet."

"We're going to have to figure it out as we go."

Idra leveled an authoritative stared at them. "And you're not skilled enough in combat to survive on a battlefield. Until you can fully control your magic, you will only be in the way out here. So follow Ellyda to the back and work on your sneaky shit from there."

"She's right." Theo put a hand on Valerie's arm. "Let's go, Val."

Glaring, she stabbed a finger at us. "You'd better not die."

"That's the plan," I said, and huffed out a tired laugh.

After meeting each of our gazes, she grabbed a fistful of

Eilan's shirt and pulled his face down to hers. Holding him firmly there, she kissed him before turning around and stalking after Theo without another word.

"Kenna," Idra said, her voice full of command. "Keep the arrows from us."

"Got it."

Without turning to look, she nodded. "Prince Edric. We need a shield against magical attacks."

"I'm on it."

"The rest of you, long-distance attacks only." She shot a couple of blasts into the air to relay the order to the ones farther back as well. "Don't charge until I tell you to."

The ranks of High Elves had formed up into orderly lines again and they moved in unison as they produced large bows from their backs.

"Prince Iwdael," Idra continued. "Get your archers ready. Fire as soon as Kenna's shield goes up."

Iwdael gave her a nod and disappeared towards his newly trained archers.

"Mordren?" she said.

He shook his head. "It is out of reach."

"Then focus on your shadows."

Dread crawled up my spine as High Elves began rising from the ranks to hover in the air. Fire and stone and water spun around them as they spread their arms wide while winds continued carrying them upwards. There were a lot more Wielders in Anron's legion than I had estimated. The High Commander himself was positioned in the middle of the long row that they formed in the air.

"All of you, focus on surviving first," Idra finished. "Then you focus on trying to take out Anron. We're already outnumbered so don't go dying on us needlessly."

A ripple of grim laughter went through the soldiers behind us.

"We–"

Arrows shot towards us.

I raised a massive wall of flames halfway down the plains.

Twangs rang out from somewhere behind me.

The High Elves' arrows were incinerated by the flaming barrier while more arrows sped through the air from the other side. I dropped the shield right as Iwdael's volley shot across the sky and descended on Anron's legion.

Fire roared to life from their side as well, blocking the barrage. It was too far to tell, but I swore I could see Anron fuming that Low Elves were using bows against them too.

Before our arrows had even finish striking the fire shield, lightning and wind and stones shot towards us. Mordren raised a wall of shadows that stopped some of it, but the rest barreled straight for us.

"Hold!" Hadeon snapped as our ranks flinched behind us.

The mass of magic hurtled across the field.

And slammed right into an invisible barrier.

Prince Edric clenched his jaw as he held his magical shield steady.

From across the swaying grass, High Commander Anron moved his hands in what looked like signals.

"Where's the lava guy?" Idra said, not taking her eyes off the enemies.

"Kael!" I called over my shoulder.

A moment later, a muscled elf with short brown hair jogged up to us. Kael Sandscorcher gave me a nod before turning to Idra.

"On my signal," she said. Her dark eyes flicked to the right. "Hadeon?"

"I'll call it," he answered.

Another volley of arrows shot towards us. It was followed moments later by a storm of magic that tore across the landscape. I threw up a wall of dark red flames while Mordren layered a shadow shield behind it.

Battle cries echoed through the air.

The arrows disappeared into the inferno, but lightning and water and wind and stone ripped through it at terrible speed. They tore through Mordren's shadows, leaving strips of darkness fluttering in the air. Through them, a sea of bronze-clad soldiers charged towards us.

Edric shifted and planted his feet firmly on the ground as the magic slammed into his shield.

"Hold!" Hadeon called again.

The High Elves sprinted towards us across the grass.

"Now," Idra commanded.

Lava bubbled up from the ground and spread into a wide field right in front of the hurtling soldiers.

"Charge!" Hadeon ordered.

The High Elves skidded to a halt and some of them careened right into the bubbling pits of lava as the ranks behind weren't able to stop in time.

I darted forward.

While our enemies were forced to an abrupt halt that threw their whole formation into disarray, we charged straight at them while screaming into the pale blue sky.

Wielders tried desperately to cover the ground with soil again while the High Elves on the front lines tried to get their companions out of the lava. Winds ripped through my hair as I dashed across the plains.

Some of the High Elves in the back rows shot a desperate volley of arrows at us. I slashed my sword through the air, creating a wave of fire that swept the projectiles aside.

The moat of lava drew closer.

We kept sprinting.

None of our soldiers hesitated as we barreled straight for the bubbling lava before us, and no one slowed down. The High Elves shouted orders amongst themselves. Magic flashed from above. It struck Edric's shield that he was still keeping above us to protect us from the Wielders.

I reached the edge of the lava field and pushed off from the ground.

"Now!" Idra yelled.

Kael pulled every drop of lava back into the ground.

My boots landed on solid grass as I kept going.

The High Elves scrambled to get their momentum back.

We slammed into them.

Chaos erupted all around me as our army barreled into their legion. I slashed my sword through the air, sending a flaming scythe that cut straight through the closest soldier. A scream tore from his throat before it was abruptly silenced as he toppled backwards. Raising my knife, I stabbed towards the closest Wielder flying above me.

He dropped rapidly to avoid the spear of fire and then shot a bolt of lightning at me. It struck Edric's shield and disappeared. Where the Prince of Stone had ended up, I didn't know. But I knew that he would keep shielding us for as long as he could.

Cries of agony ripped from the throats of several Wielders as Mordren sent a pulse of pain magic at them. From his place at the back, High Commander Anron snapped orders to get around the magic shield.

Several of the High Elves flew back to the ground while

the others started up a merciless barrage on Edric's shield, no doubt in an effort to drain his energy quicker. I ducked under a sword that tried to take my head off before twisting around and flicking my wrists. A cloud of flaming scythes shot towards the Wielders that were pounding Edric's shield. They shifted towards it and yanked up walls of water and stone, but right before the attacks hit, Mordren sent another pulse of pain magic.

Their defenses faltered slightly and two of the Wielders were partially hit by my flames. I raised my arms to send another attack at them while they were vulnerable, but steel flashed in the corner of my eye.

My heart leaped into my throat and I barely made it as I threw myself backwards to escape the blades coming for me. Three High Elves surrounded me. Panic shot up my spine as they all attacked at the same time.

I ducked the first blade and blocked the second, but there was no way to avoid the third one.

The third soldier shot through the air as a blast of wind took him straight in the chest. Stunned surprise pulsed through me as the blade I had been bracing for never struck. While throwing a fireball at the closest soldier, I cast a quick glance over my shoulder.

Vendir nodded at me before returning his attention to High Commander Anron. With his eyes fixed on his former leader, he sent lightning strike after lightning strike at him. I rammed my sword into the second soldier's armpit and started to turn back around when something flashed in the corner of my eye.

Whirling back around, I screamed a warning, "Vendir! Behind you."

He dropped his next attack and spun to face the soldier

who had leaped out from behind him, but it was too late. Shock slammed onto his face as a sword slashed across his chest, carving through part of his leather armor.

"Vendir!" I screamed as he toppled backwards.

The High Elf who had cut him snapped his head towards me and charged right as steel whooshed through the air behind me as well. Diving to the side, I managed to evade the sword coming for my back. Dirt and crushed grass clung to my body as I rolled forward before jumping to my feet and shooting a spear of fire at Vendir's attacker.

He was thrown backwards as it burned right through his chest. Spinning around, I yanked my sword up to block the other soldier's attack. Metal clanked as our blades collided. He was much stronger than me so he forced my sword downwards as he leaned forward. I slammed my fist into his chest.

Since he was wearing armor, and I hadn't aimed with the tip of my knife, he didn't bother to dodge it. Instead, he pushed again with his sword, which made my blade wobble precariously close to my neck. With my fist against his chest, I sent out a burst of fire.

Screams tore from his throat as his breastplate melted underneath my hand. He yanked his sword back and leaped away as the metal continued melting. Stabbing forward with my knife, I sent a spear of fire right through the hole and ended him before he could recover.

With the closest enemies finally gone, I whirled back towards Vendir.

Intense relief washed over me.

Prince Rayan was crouching next to Vendir, who lay on his back on the ground. The pain disappeared from Vendir's face as the wound began to knit itself back together with the help of Rayan's healing magic. Watching over them was a third figure.

Princess Lilane, wearing sleek leather armor, stood with one knee slightly bent and the other leg stretched to the side, keeping her balance low and steady. Her arms were spread wide at her sides.

Two High Elves charged at them, intending to kill the healer prince and his wounded patient. Spinning her arms with graceful flowing moves, Lilane shot lethal shards of ice straight at their throats.

Blood spurted into the air.

More soldiers ran towards them from another direction. Drawing her arms through the air, she sent another rain of ice blades at them. I raised my eyebrows. The Princess of Water was kind and gentle, and apparently also an incredibly formidable fighter.

I spun around and shot a spear of fire at the soldiers who had been charging me from behind. They dove aside to escape it. Rolling to their feet, they continued their sprint while archers from the back loosened a barrage towards the far end of our army. Raising my arms above my head, I sent a blanket of fire over our troops to stop the arrows before they could strike.

The two soldiers closed in. Pulling up the fire shield had cost me precious seconds. Alarm crackled through me as I realized that I wouldn't be able to dodge both of them anymore.

A skinny figure with blond hair ran past us like a bat out of hell. His arms flapped in the air as he weaved and jumped and ducked on his way through a sea of High Elf soldiers. He crashed straight into the two soldiers who had been about to attack me, but he was so light that it made no difference. They only paused briefly to stare at the flailing elf as he disappeared towards the other side. Turning back to me, the two soldiers raised their swords while I called up my magic to try to kill them both at the same time while also not hurting any of my allies behind them.

A Wielder shot a block of stone towards Edric's magic shield right above us.

I tried to calculate the path of the fire right as the soldiers swung at me.

Shock pulsed through me.

The block of stone from above shot through the shield and crashed down right on top of the two soldiers. Only an arm was visible of the now flattened High Elves. But the strangest part was that the block of stone had landed on its narrow side, striking only the two High Elves and no one from the mass of allies around me.

Arms flapped through the air as the blond elf came sprinting back in this direction. Fear shone on his face but he stumbled into a High Elf and then kept going. A moment later, that High Elf was struck by a bolt of lightning from one of his own comrades, which allowed Hadeon to ram a sword through his throat.

I stared after the blond elf.

Oturion Fortunebender ran back and forth across the battlefield, leaping over boulders and ducking under swords and flapping his arms like a crazy bat, bumping into High Elves as he went. And every time he did, some kind of misfortune struck the enemy soldiers that he had touched.

An astounded smile spread across my lips as I shook my head at him. Oturion Fortunebender, indeed.

Steel sang in the air to my left. I whirled around to block the attack as another High Elf swung at me. Metallic clanking assaulted my ears. I rammed my knife towards his exposed armpit, but he saw the move coming and slammed his fist down onto my wrist.

Pain pulsed through my wrist as my arm shot downwards.

With this many allies around me, I had to be careful with my fire attacks, so I yanked my fist up to do the same trick as before.

A blast of wind slammed into me from the side.

My body shot through the air before crashing into two soldiers from the Court of Shadows. Sucking in a desperate breath, I tried to clear my head enough to figure out where all the enemies were while I untangled myself from them.

A High Elf appeared above me.

Panic screamed inside me as I tried to get my hands into position to shoot fire at him while he drove his swords straight towards me.

He stopped.

Shock bloomed in his eyes as he staggered back a step with a rapier sticking out of his throat. It disappeared right before he toppled over. I blinked at the elf that became visible behind the falling corpse.

"Lady Firesoul," Edus Quickfeet said, and bowed his head at me before he flashed away again.

With flames flickering under his feet, he flew across the ground like a loosed arrow. His body was a blur of brown and green clothes as he flashed back and forth across the battlefield, sticking his rapier into unguarded necks.

Only a few months ago, he had challenged me for my crown on Anron's say-so. And now here he was, fighting *against* Anron. Fighting for us. For me.

A small smile drifted over my lips.

I was glad that he was here. That all of them were here. We

would need all the help that we could get if we were going to survive this.

Straightening from the ground, I turned around and helped the two soldiers from the Court of Shadows to their feet as well, right as a High Elf strode towards us. The other bronze-clad soldiers moved out of his way as he walked. Lightning crackled along his arms. A Wielder.

While calling up my own magic, I spun the blades in my hands.

This was going to be a long day.

I settled into a rhythm of just trying to survive the next minute as the hours wore on. High Commander Anron stayed up in the air, far behind the fighting, the entire time which left us with little opportunity to take him out. Edric's magic shield and Rayan's healing, along with Idra and Hadeon's skillful organization of the troops, were what got us through the day in more or less one piece. The fact that we had eight people with access to unlimited elemental magic, as well as a High Elf Wielder on our side, helped quite a lot too. However, the battle was taking its toll.

When sunset was finally approaching, I was so exhausted that I could barely stand straight.

A cloud of arrows shot towards our retreating ranks. I pulled up a fire shield in front of us to stop them. Dark red flames roared up and licked the purple-streaked heavens. My legs wobbled.

Mordren reached out and grabbed my arm, keeping me steady as we continued backing towards the temporary camp that our worldwalkers had set up at the edge of the battlefield.

For the first time since the initial attack, High Commander Anron flew from his position at the back of the legion and moved until he was hovering in the air above the now empty and flattened grasslands.

"Go ahead and run," he called at us, his voice booming across the landscape. "But I would advise against sleeping."

Idra and Hadeon continued issuing orders for the retreat so as to keep our troops from focusing too much on Anron's words.

"You forget," the High Commander continued. "I know what your weakness is. Each other. If I just manage to get my hands on one of you, the rest will surrender. And I can just as easily abduct someone in the middle of the night as I can capture them on the battlefield."

Worry rippled through our ranks.

Hadeon bellowed another couple of orders to keep moving, but he and Idra exchanged a discreet glance. As much as I hated to admit it, Anron was right.

The love and friendship that had formed between us was our strength. It was what we were fighting for. But it was also our weakness. If High Commander Anron managed to capture Mordren, or any of the people I now called family, and threatened to kill them if I didn't surrender, I would do it without hesitation.

Even from across the plains, I swore I could see a vicious grin on Anron's face as he opened his mouth again.

"So you'd better sleep with one eye open."

CHAPTER 31

Weapons covered every single part of the tent walls. But none of them had been touched. Only the blades from the open chests that covered the ground looked to have been used. I swept my eyes over the mass of gleaming swords and daggers and axes on the walls as I slumped into one of the chairs.

Ellyda's work tent was at the very front of our temporary camp so that she could see the battle and send out replacement weapons as needed. It wasn't exactly the safest place to be, but we hadn't been able to make it farther than that after our retreat. Utterly spent, we just staggered into the closest available tent to have our meeting. Which was this one.

Outside the tent, Ymas crossed his arms while keeping watchful eyes on the empty battlefield beyond. A moment later, Reena closed the tent flap while taking up position next to him outside it.

Dark fabric fluttered briefly as it fell closed, separating us from the rest of the world.

"We can't keep fighting like this," Prince Edric announced. He also had his arms crossed where he was standing by one of the walls. "We will run out of energy before they do."

"Agreed," Mordren said as he slid his eyes to the Prince of Stone. "For how long will you be able to keep the shield up?"

"As long as I have Ymas and Idra watching my back, I should be able to keep going for a while. But if I have to start fighting off people on the ground too, it'll drop fast."

Idra nodded. "We will keep the other soldiers away from you. But the rest of you need to figure out a way to take out the Wielders."

"Yeah," Hadeon agreed. Leaning against one of the work tables, he rubbed a hand over his muscular arm. "We need to draw Anron out. As long as he keeps floating there at the back, we won't be able to kill him. But if we start taking out his Wielders, he might be forced to step up."

"So how do we do that?" Prince Iwdael asked. Out of all of us, he looked the least exhausted and worried. But maybe that was just due to years of controlling the moods around him. He raised his eyebrows. "I mean, isn't that what we've been trying to do all day? Well, that and kill my dear wife."

"And Monette," Edric grumbled.

"And Evander," I added.

"Indeed." The Prince of Trees spread his hands in a casual gesture. "Too bad they also stayed at the very rear this whole time."

From his spot atop one of the other tables, Theo looked over at Iwdael with a curious expression on his face. "Will you really be able to kill your wife?"

"Theo!" Valerie slapped him on the arm. "That's not something people ask."

He turned to scowl at her. "You're one to talk. You blurt

out inappropriate things all the time."

"I do not."

"Just this morning, you—"

I cleared my throat. Sheepish grins spread across their faces as they turned back to find the rest of the room staring at them. Prince Rayan let out a soft laugh and shook his head.

"Yes, my dear boy, I will indeed," Iwdael answered his original question. "I gave up my court for Syrene. And she repaid me by helping invaders murder our king." Rage the likes of which I had rarely seen from the Prince of Trees flashed in his yellow eyes for a second, and a sharp smile spread across his lips. "The next time I see my wife, I will rip her heart out. Just like she did mine."

Edric raised his eyebrows at him. "I never knew you had such an angry and vengeful side, Iwdael."

"Well..." The smile on his face turned more mysterious than sharp as he cocked his head and met Edric's gaze. "I guess you don't know me very well."

Surprise, and the ghost of a smile, drifted across Edric's face as he nodded. "No, I guess I don't."

"Let's circle back to the problem with the Wielders," Prince Rayan said, to help take some of the suddenly very curious attention off Iwdael. "With the help of the worldwalkers, my team of healers can patch you up on the battlefield. But I can't fix someone who has been turned into a piece of charcoal. So how do we stop the Wielders from wiping us all out the minute Edric's shield falters?"

"It won't falter," the Prince of Stone grumbled.

"*If* it falters," Rayan amended. "Regardless, you said it yourselves, we need to lure Anron out by targeting his Wielders. But how do we do that?"

"Edric's shield is already doing it for us," Eilan answered

His pale green eyes swept across the crowded tent. "You saw it yourselves, they had to come back to the ground to fight us since they couldn't get through from above."

"Fair point," I said. "So how do we kill them on the ground without hurting our own allies in the blast too?"

Silence descended on the tent.

The thick fabric walls fluttered slightly as an early fall wind whirled through our camp. I brushed my hand down the side of it to smoothen it down again. A faint clanking sound filled the space as Ellyda started tinkering with a dagger by her worktable in the back.

"We must have something that they don't," Rayan said into the stillness when no one offered up an immediate answer.

"Worldwalking."

We all turned to look at Vendir. He was standing a bit awkwardly at the edge of the tent, watching us all with observant brown eyes.

"You can worldwalk," he repeated. "That's something none of us can do."

"Yeah, but how–"

"Oh!" Hadeon blurted out. Raking both hands through his short brown hair, he tipped his head back and let out a disbelieving laugh. "Why didn't I think of that sooner?"

"Think of what?" Eilan asked.

Hadeon turned towards the High Elf. "Vendir, that's brilliant."

"What is?" Valerie demanded impatiently.

"Here, let me show you." Straightening from the table, he walked over to me and placed his hands on my arms before moving me slightly. "Kenna, can I borrow you?"

"Sure."

"Alright, check this out."

Several pairs of eyebrows rose as Hadeon demonstrated his plan.

"That's brilliant," I said as he stepped back again.

"Right?"

Mordren nodded as well. "It will definitely give us an advantage."

"Right?" Hadeon repeated. Turning around, he looked towards his sister. "How are things looking on your end, El?"

For almost half a minute, she only continued tinkering with the dagger. Then she replied without even looking up, "Good."

"Alright, I'll say that's a win." He shifted his gaze to the two thieves. "And you?"

Valerie grinned back at him. "Operation sneaky sneak is on track."

"Good." Hadeon met each of our gazes in turn. "Then get some sleep. We have another long day ahead tomorrow."

We all nodded back to him. Clothes rustled and leather creaked as Edric, Iwdael, and Rayan filed out of the tent. The rest of us lingered.

"I have another idea as well," Eilan said once their footsteps had gone silent from outside.

"Absolutely not," Mordren declared.

"You don't even know what I'm going to propose."

"Of course I do. I know you quite well, brother."

"It's still a good plan."

Valerie threw her arms out. "What plan?"

"He intends to shapeshift into a High Elf and sneak into their camp to kill some of the Wielders." Mordren raised his eyebrows in challenge. "Am I right?"

"Yes."

"Absolutely not!" I, along with most of the people in the

tent, blurted out.

"It's a smart plan," Eilan defended while crossing his arms.

"It's an incredibly risky one," Idra announced, her dark eyes locked on his face.

"This is what I do. And I am very good at my job. I won't try to go near Anron, but slitting the throat of even one Wielder while they're sleeping would give us a huge advantage tomorrow."

"No," Mordren said.

"Are you–"

Stalking across the floor, he grabbed the front of Eilan's shirt and hauled him closer. His voice pulsed with power and command as he spoke. "You are my brother, but I am still your prince. And the answer is no."

Eilan glared back at him while clenching his jaw. Then he clicked his tongue and looked away. "Fine."

Mordren continued staring him down for another few seconds before releasing him. From behind their backs, Hadeon blew out a deep breath.

"Alright, all the stupid ideas are out of the way," he said. "Now can we go sleep?"

Murmurs of agreement rippled through the tent. Boots shuffled against the ground and leather groaned once more as we all started towards the exit. Right before I pushed open the tent flap, I paused and looked back at the others.

"I hate to say it but," I began, "Anron is right about our weakness."

Serious looks passed through our group.

Pushing open the tent flap, I stepped out onto the flattened grass and drew in a deep breath of cool evening air before meeting my friends' gazes again.

"So make sure to watch each other's backs."

CHAPTER 32

Pink and golden streaks lined the heavens. My throat was raw and every breath felt like I was inhaling shards of glass. Twisting aside, I dodged a sword coming for my chest and rammed my knife into the side of my opponent's throat while magical attacks pounded the shield above our heads. The coppery smell of blood hung over the trampled grass like mist.

Bowstrings twanged from somewhere on the other side of the hostile legion.

I wanted to scream in exhaustion.

While jumping back to avoid another High Elf charging towards me, I threw up a fire shield to block the arrows that once again sped towards the back half of our army.

We had to do something about their archers. And soon. Because I didn't know how long I could keep fighting both soldiers on the ground and burning arrows out of the sky at the same time. But Valerie had said that she and Theo were working on some kind of sneaky plan to deal with that, so I would just have to make it until they could set that in motion.

The wooden shafts were incinerated as they hit my shield. I let it drop the moment it was done and whirled around to face yet another soldier swinging his sword at me. Metal clanked as I blocked it with my own. Keeping his blade trapped against mine, I stabbed my knife forward. It wasn't far enough to reach his body, but the spear of fire it released did the trick. The attack also hit one of the High Elves behind him who had been fighting Reena.

While the first one collapsed, the second let out a scream of pain as the flaming spear took him in the shoulder. Reena used the moment of inattention to draw her arms through the air. An angry horde of leaves shot right at the wounded soldier. They whirled around him like a tornado, cutting into his skin until blood ran down from the slashes in his face.

I flicked my wrist, sending another scythe of dark red flame towards our enemies. It struck two of them but also veered dangerously close to some of my allies. My control still wasn't entirely back to what it had been before I drank the third bowl of magic, and when I was this exhausted, it was slipping even further.

Calling up my worldwalking powers, I switched to the strategy that Hadeon had showed us last night.

Two soldiers advanced on me in a coordinated attack. I let them come a little closer. Then I worldwalked to a spot behind the one on the left. They started in surprise as I disappeared in front of them only to materialize a step behind and ram a knife into one of their throats. The one on the right whipped around as the soldier next to him let out a strangled gasp. Ripping the knife from his throat, I blinked out of existence again.

Dull thuds sounded as the first High Elf crashed to the ground, blood spurting from his throat, right as I worldwalked to a space behind the other one. He didn't even have time to twist his head before I shoved my blade through his neck.

Before my latest victim had even hit the ground, I worldwalked a few steps away and ended up behind another High Elf who was currently trying to cut Kael's head off. My sword disappeared into his neck from behind, abruptly stopping his movements. Kael gave me a nod before swinging around and opening up a pit of lava underneath another cluster of soldiers.

I yanked out my knife and worldwalked again.

It was a brilliant strategy because there was almost nothing the High Elves could do about it. Short of grabbing us so that we couldn't worldwalk, they couldn't stop us from just disappearing and appearing wherever we pleased. Granted, that part of the battlefield had to be a bit less crowded for it to work. Otherwise, the other people moving would interfere too much with the landing. But as long as there was enough space to land undisturbed, those of us who possessed the worldwalking power could wreak some real havoc.

Unfortunately, though, we couldn't worldwalk up into the air where Anron was still hiding.

Waves of fatigue rolled over my body as I worldwalked again and again, striking at High Elves while their backs were turned. After yet another one had fallen to my backstabbing blade, I stumbled to the side and had to throw my arm out to keep from toppling over.

Casting a glance over my shoulder, I watched the way the sun dipped lower towards the horizon. Red and purple had started joining the pink and golden streaks in the sky, meaning that sunset was close. We had survived yet another day of fighting. It had to be only minutes left until Idra and Hadeon gave the signal to retreat.

My muscles trembled.

High Commander Anron should be giving the signal to pull back as well soon.

I sucked in a desperate breath as the soldiers before me drew back a little. Relief washed over me. Finally.

Battle cries split the air.

Jerking back a step, I tried to smother the panic that flashed through me as the ranks of High Elves suddenly charged with all their might.

From his place where he was hovering in the air at the back of the legion, High Commander Anron looked down at the battlefield with a smirk on his face. Dread sluiced through my veins. He had been trying to wear us down and now he planned to finish it with one massive push when we were at our most vulnerable and exhausted.

Boots thudded against the ground as our enemies rushed us. Slashing my blades, I tried to stop their momentum with arcs of fire, but water sped through the air to neutralize it. They had pulled another Wielder from the team trying to wear Edric out and placed him somewhere in the mass of soldiers.

I whipped my head from side to side, trying to figure out which one he was, while I raised a wall of fire. Winds ripped through the battlefield and forced my flames up into the sky.

The High Elves slammed into our ranks.

Magic crashed into Edric's shield above us like a vicious storm, the boom of fire and stone and lightning drowning out the battle cries of the soldiers barreling across the ground.

Bronze-clad arms and legs appeared all around as a mass of enemies swarmed me. Alarm crackled through me as I felt their hands trying to grab me from every side. My sword was too long to wield in such close quarters so I stabbed frantically with my knife at everything I could find while also sending small bursts of fire to keep them from getting me from behind.

"HADEON!" Mordren's voice tore through the whole battlefield with enough desperation that my hair stood on end.

Fighting desperately against the mass of hands yanking at me from all sides, I tried to get eyes on Hadeon or Mordren.

"Hadeon!" Mordren screamed again. His voice broke on the final syllable.

Flames pulsed around me, sending a couple of the High Elves jerking back enough to allow me a small gap to see through.

My heart lurched.

Mordren was in the same position as me, desperately battling a swarm of High Elves who were trying to grab him from every side. And Hadeon…

Fear froze my blood.

Hadeon was being dragged away. His head lolled back and forth across his chest as four High Elves hauled his unconscious body back towards their own ranks.

High Commander Anron had made good on his threat.

If the High Elves got Hadeon, then Ellyda, Mordren, Eilan, Idra…

Slamming my fist onto the nearest breastplate, I sent a pulse of fire that melted right through it. Someone grabbed my other arm, yanking me around. I rammed my knife at the attacker but it only carved a deep rut in his armor without hitting anything. Hands appeared on my shoulders and the back of my neck. Panic screamed inside me.

Lightning crashed into Mordren's shadows across the field.

Fire shot from my back, searing the soldiers there, but more of them lunged from the front. Leaping back, I caught sight of Eilan desperately trying to dodge as more soldiers attacked him while Prince Edric had raised both arms towards the sky to keep the shield intact as magic hammered it mercilessly. Idra and Ymas fought like demons around him to keep the High Elves from reaching him.

Full-blown terror surged up inside me as I tried to hold back the tide around me while Hadeon was dragged farther and farther away.

This couldn't happen.

They couldn't take him.

A cry of desperation ripped from my lips as I fought to get the soldiers off me for long enough to worldwalk. Hands snatched at my body from every side.

Steel glinted in the setting sun from across the battlefield.

Burning through another breastplate, I rammed my knife into the next soldier's unprotected armpit while casting a quick glance over my shoulder.

Our ranks were parting like the sea before a massive cliff. Worry shot through me before I realized that it was parting from the back and towards the front, not the other way around.

I ducked under two arms and stabbed at a soldier's groin while slamming the back of my hand into someone else's side to melt his armor.

The widening gap in our ranks was heading straight towards where Hadeon was still being dragged off.

A fist took me in the side of the ribs. Air exploded from my lungs and I staggered to the side. Hands shot out to grab my arms and twist them up behind my back. I sent a wave of fire rolling over my body and the hands disappeared long enough for me to suck in another breath and get my balance back.

Straightening once more, I took in the scene across the grass.

Shock slammed into me like a brick to the face.

High Elves in gleaming bronze armor were falling like severed stalks of wheat before the figure advancing towards Hadeon.

Ellyda Steelsinger.

Swords, knives, and axes fanned out around her to form a gigantic cloud of sharp metal. The blades shot back and forth through the air as she walked, cutting down every High Elf within reach. Blood sprayed and hung in the air like red mist. And Ellyda was covered in it.

Red splattered her face and clothes, and her arms all the way from her hands up to her shoulders were soaked with blood. She looked like a demon from hell as she spread her blood-drenched arms wide and unleashed another terrible storm of blades on her enemies.

Stepping over dying bodies, she stalked down the red path she carved through the High Elves' ranks while weapons flashed through the air around her.

I swore the whole battlefield stopped to stare at her.

It was the most terrifying thing I had ever seen.

"GIVE. ME. BACK. MY. BROTHER!" she screamed with such force that the mountains almost cowered before her.

The ranks of High Elves who were still standing between her and Hadeon darted out of her way. For a moment, only the four soldiers who were dragging Hadeon remained.

Ellyda slammed her arms forward.

THE LAST STAND

Steel whizzed through the air as the whole cloud of weapons shot straight towards them.

Hadeon crashed down onto the ground as they dropped him and dove aside. Panic rippled through their ranks as everyone tried to get out of her way. Then Anron sounded the retreat.

The attackers around me swiftly withdrew while their archers made sure that we wouldn't follow. Even if I had wanted to press the advantage, I could barely make my legs obey me anymore. And besides, we needed to get Hadeon back to our camp.

As the other attackers left as well, Mordren and Eilan were finally free to move too. They worldwalked to Hadeon across the flattened grass right as Ellyda reached him. I did the same.

Crouching down beside him, she pressed two fingers against his neck.

"He's alive," she said. Her voice sounded very hollow.

Relief washed over me.

"We have to get him to Rayan," Mordren said.

Eilan nodded. "I'll find him. Bring him back."

Before Mordren could reply, Eilan worldwalked away to find the Prince of Water.

Ellyda, who was still crouching beside her brother, reached out and brushed a lock of hair from his forehead. Her fingers left red streaks on his skin. She jerked back. Shooting to her feet, she staggered a step back and looked down at her hands. The cloud of weapons still hung in the air above her like a gray mirror.

Her gaze snapped between the blades and her hands. Then she slashed an arm through the air, sending the weapons shooting across the field and disappearing from view somewhere far to the side.

Mordren slid an arm under Hadeon's back and hoisted him up before meeting my gaze. "Take her."

I nodded.

Mordren and Hadeon disappeared from view. Placing an arm around Ellyda's back, I worldwalked us away as well.

The area around us was empty when the four of us appeared on the grass in front of Ellyda's work tent. From down the plains, Idra was shouting orders of retreat. My heart bled for her. Even though the one she loved was wounded, she still forced herself to first make sure that our army withdrew without being attacked on the way.

Next to me, Ellyda was staring unseeing at Hadeon while Mordren gently placed him down on the grass.

A moment later, Eilan and Rayan materialized.

The Prince of Water sank down to his knees straight away and moved his hands over Hadeon's body. I held my breath.

"He's fine," Prince Rayan declared. "It's nothing I can't fix." Looking up, he met Mordren and Eilan's eyes. "Get him back to his tent. I'll treat him in there. Then he needs rest."

"He's fine," Ellyda repeated.

"Yes," Rayan answered while Mordren and Eilan draped Hadeon's arms over their shoulders.

"He's fine," she said again.

It sounded more like she was talking to herself than the others, so Mordren just gave me a look that told me to stay with her as they disappeared with Hadeon and Rayan.

"He's fine," Ellyda said a third time.

I glanced into her work tent. All the weapons that had been covering the tent walls were gone. *So this was what she had meant when she said that they were for a worst-case scenario.*

Turning back to her, I nodded while replying, "Yes, he is. Thanks to you."

Her violet eyes flashed back into focus and snapped to my face. For a few seconds, she only stared at me. Then she looked down at her hands again. Blood coated her like a second skin.

She crashed down to her knees before I could react.

Boots pounded against the ground from my left as Vendir sprinted up to us. His eyes shot between me and Ellyda and the flattened grass where Hadeon had been lying a minute before.

"He's okay," I said in response to Vendir's silent question. "Rayan is healing him now and he's going to be fine."

Sitting on the ground, Ellyda held out her blood-soaked hands in front of her. They shook forcefully. She gasped in a breath and ran her hands over her forearms. It only served to smear out the blood even more.

A sob tore from her throat.

"I didn't want to do this," she said, her voice trembling.

Vendir crouched down next to her right as Idra materialized on the grass too.

"Tell me he's alive," Idra demanded.

"He's alive," I said. "Rayan is with him in his tent."

Idra's dark eyes shifted to Ellyda. Her brows creased as she looked back up at me. I shook my head.

"Go," I said instead, and jerked my chin towards where Hadeon was.

She held my gaze for another second before giving me a slow nod and taking off towards Hadeon's tent. Lowering myself to the grass on Ellyda's other side, I met Vendir's gaze briefly. I had no idea how to handle this. How to pull her back from the chasm she was approaching and assure her that she had done the right thing.

"I didn't want to do this," Ellyda pleaded again as she stared at her red hands.

Kneeling beside her, I placed a gentle hand on her arm. "It's okay."

"Don't touch me!" The words tore from her throat as she jerked away from me while guilt and pain shone in her eyes. "I'm covered in blood."

"I know." My hand hovered in the air above her shoulder. "I know, but it's okay."

Ellyda put her hands to her forearms and started scrubbing up and down. "I'm covered in blood."

Her palms only smeared the red across her skin and clothes.

"I'm covered in blood. I'm covered in..."

She frantically tried to scrub the blood from her hands and arms but everything she did only made it worse. Her eyes widened as she stared at the red mess that was only getting bigger. Sucking in shallow breaths, she increased the pace. Her chest heaved and she started hyperventilating as she scrubbed and scrubbed.

"Get it off me. Get it off me. Get it off me!"

"Hey." Vendir took her chin in a firm grip and forced her face towards him instead. His other hand shot out and wrapped around her wrists, stopping her jerky movements. "It's okay."

"Don't touch me! I'm covered in blood."

Vendir kept his grip on her even as she tried to pull away. "It's okay. Listen to me. It's okay."

She tried to yank her chin out of his grip and her eyes darted back and forth like erratic birds. "I can't... I can't do this. I didn't want to do this."

"Ellyda. Listen to me." When she only continued rambling,

he shifted his hand from her wrists to her shoulder and spun her fully towards him. "El! Listen to me."

Silence fell as she stopped struggling and instead blinked at him.

He held her gaze with steady eyes for a few seconds until her chest was no longer heaving.

"It's okay," he said again in a slow and stable voice. "We know that you didn't want to do this. We know that this isn't who you are. You are still the person who looks at the world and sees colorful new solutions that will make things better. You are still the person who sees everyone and accepts them for who they are without judgement. You are still the person who is always there for the ones you love. You did what you had to do to save your brother. And that's okay. It doesn't change who you really are inside."

"I didn't want to do this." Tears welled up in her eyes as she blew out a long shaky breath. "I want to create things. I don't want to destroy them."

Releasing her chin, Vendir drew his hands down her arms. "I know."

"I want to make things." She choked out a sob and tears spilled freely down her cheeks. "I didn't want to... *kill* people."

As her voice broke on the final two words, Vendir drew her into his arms. Her whole body shook as she cried into his shoulder while he held her tightly.

"I don't want to be in a war," she sobbed. Her cracked voice trembled as she grabbed fistfuls of Vendir's leather armor and clung to it like it was the only thing keeping her sane. "I want to go home. I want to read books and watch the way metal heats up in a forge and listen to the steel sing and forget to drink my tea and... *make* things."

Vendir stroked a hand down her back. "You will. I

promise, this will all be over soon. And then we will never have to go anywhere near a battle ever again. Soon we will have all the time in the world to just watch the way the sunset makes the leaves gleam and paint with beautiful colors and just... make things."

My heart cracked as I sat there uselessly on the grass, watching the two of them hold on to each other and trying to convince each other that everything would be okay.

I couldn't do anything to help Ellyda through this.

But there was something else I could do.

I could make sure Vendir's promise came true. I could make sure that we finished this war soon so that neither of them would ever have to feel the sticky wetness of blood on their skin again.

Turning my head, I gazed towards the horizon.

Yes, I would make it so.

Even if I had to get down on my knees before people who had told me that they didn't want to get involved in more wars, and beg them to come and help us anyway.

So that we could all go home.

CHAPTER 33

Our tent flap was thrown open. I leaped up from the mattress that Mordren and I shared, and raised a ball of fire above my palm while shadows shot out from Mordren as well.

"Kenna," Felix said as he met our surprised gazes. "Prince Mordren. You need to come to the back of camp. An army approaches."

"What?" I said.

"Hurry," Felix only replied before he disappeared again.

Mordren pulled on his boots while casting a glance at me. "I thought you said that they would not be arriving until tomorrow."

After Ellyda's breakdown earlier that evening, I had worldwalked away from our camp to selfishly beg for help from people who had already seen too much hardship. To both my relief and shame, they had agreed to come. However, they would not be able to get ready and make it here before midday tomorrow.

"They won't," I answered while lacing up my own boots.

"So why is an army approaching us now? In the middle of the night?"

"I don't know."

As soon as our shoes were on, we worldwalked to the scouts' location at the back of our camp. Prince Edric and Rayan were already there. A moment later, Iwdael appeared next to us as well.

The moon was only a sliver in the dark sky, and thick clouds drifted across the heavens, making it even harder to see across the field. But there was definitely something huge moving towards us. I squinted against the darkness.

Felix materialized in front of us.

"Who is it?" Prince Edric demanded as soon as he came into view.

"You're not going to believe this," the copper-haired spy replied.

My eyebrows shot far up into my hair as he explained what he had seen when he worldwalked out there.

"Are you sure they're on our side?" the Prince of Stone grumbled.

"I... I think so."

Shaking my head, I huffed out a tired chuckle. "Well, I guess we're about to find out."

Idra appeared on the damp grass right as I finished speaking.

"Hadeon is still sleeping," she said as she crossed her arms.

"Good. And I'm glad no one woke Eilan or Valerie and Theo either. They need the rest too."

"They weren't there."

I turned towards Idra. "What?"

"I went to their tents. None of them were there."

Next to me, Mordren clenched his fist. "I swear, I..."

"One problem at a time," Idra said.

Silence fell as we watched the army draw closer. Here at the back, far from the battlefield, the tang of blood was harder to detect. I drew in a few deep breaths of night air that still smelled like damp soil and mountains and fallen leaves.

Once the army had reached a spot a short distance away, it stopped. Then a lone figure started towards us. This was not something I'd ever thought I'd see.

"Lady Firesoul," the leader of the army said as he stopped before us and inclined his head. "Prince Edric."

I stared back at him. "Elvin."

My half-brother met my gaze again before nodding to the other princes.

"What is this?" I asked.

"I have brought an army," Elvin Beaufort replied.

"We can see that," Prince Edric said in a rumbling voice as he crossed his arms. "But why have you done that?"

Elvin's blue eyes shifted to the Prince of Stone. "To help you fight this war, of course."

"You..." My mouth dropped open as I trailed off for a second while trying to gather my scattered wits. "You *willingly* mustered an army of humans from what looks like at least three courts? To go into battle against the High Elves?"

"Yes." He nodded as if that wasn't the most surprising thing I had seen in a long time. "It was the most logical course of action."

A laugh bubbled from my throat as I shook my head at him. It wasn't exactly a declaration of love, but feelings had never been his thing anyway. Facts, odds, and statistics had.

"This is our home too," Elvin continued as he raised his chin. "We humans don't want new gods any more than you do. We already have gods. And we want peace and stability.

Not for some jumped-up High Commander who sneers at humans to come here and dictate what we are allowed to do or where we are allowed to go." Dragging a hand through his red hair, that was the exact same shade as mine, he flicked his gaze briefly to me again. "And besides, my family owes Lady Firesoul quite a large debt. So I figured this was one way to repay it."

Taking a step forward, I held out my hand. "You and your army are more than welcome here."

A small smile played over his lips as he reached out and shook my hand.

"Felix," Prince Edric said. "Help get them organized."

"Yes, my prince," the freckled half-elf replied.

Idra blew out a deep breath. "I'll stay and go over the battle formation with you as well. Then you need to make sure both you and your people get some sleep. Marching through the night and then fighting the next day is a bad move."

Letting go of my hand, Elvin turned to bow his head at Idra. I clapped her on the shoulder before starting back towards our tent. Mordren fell in beside me.

I could barely believe it. My half-brother had actually gathered an army to come and help us. Maybe there was hope for some parts of the Beaufort family after all.

"I'm glad that your brother turned out to have at least half a spine," Mordren commented as we weaved through the mass of dark tents. "Now, if mine has done what I believe he has, then I am going to beat him within an inch of his life."

"You can try."

We both whirled around. A smug smirk graced Eilan's lips as he strode out of the shadows to our left. Cocking his head, he lifted one shoulder in a nonchalant shrug as if to drive the statement home.

Anger flashed in Mordren's silver eyes. "Tell me you did not disobey my orders."

"Well, technically, I didn't sneak into their camp. I just shapeshifted into Gadrien and snuck around their camp. It wasn't my fault that one of their Wielders just happened to go out there to relieve himself just as my knife occupied the same space as his neck."

Mordren's shadows shot forward. Wrapping themselves around Eilan, they yanked him closer until he and Mordren were practically sharing a breath.

"You could have been killed," Mordren growled into his face. "Or captured."

Eilan just arched a dark eyebrow. "But I wasn't."

"That does not–"

"They almost got Hadeon today," Eilan interrupted. Glaring back at Mordren, he raised his chin. "We needed to do something to even the playing field."

"Uhm, is there a threesome happening that I don't know about?" came a voice from behind our backs.

Mordren's shadows disappeared. While letting out an exasperated laugh, Eilan brushed his hand down his shirt to smoothen it again before we all turned towards the voice.

Two grinning faces met us when we did.

And then two more. And four more. And six more. Until a mass of humans became visible like silent spirits on the darkened grass.

"What's going on?" I said as I raised my eyebrows at them.

Theo and Valerie exchanged a glance. Then they raised their arms. Behind them, every single member of the Hands raised their arms into the air as well.

My mouth dropped open. "You did not…"

Valerie cackled. "Of course we did."

Next to her, Theo winked at us. "Come on, we're called the Hands for a reason."

"Exactly." She wiggled her eyebrows. "It's gonna be real difficult for the High Elf archers to shoot their arrows at you... when we've stolen all of them."

I stared in stunned disbelief at the mass of quivers and arrows that the thieving gang hoisted into the air. Gratitude and relief washed over me. With this, I wouldn't have to spend half of my time burning arrows out of the sky while also trying to fight a battle on the ground.

A chuckle escaped my throat. "So this was your sneaky plan, huh?"

"Working on our powers, plotting burglaries, stealing stuff." There was a wide grin on her face as she shrugged. "We can multitask."

"Indeed," Mordren said as he gave them an approving nod. "Well done."

After drawing a hand through my hair, I let it drop back down by my side. My fingers brushed an empty knife holster. Alarm shot through me.

"Wait," I said as I whipped my head down and stared at the spot where my knife had been only a minute before. "Where's...?"

"Looking for this?"

I whirled around at the sound of that familiar yet totally unexpected voice.

A thin elf with hair so dark it was more blue than black, and eyes the color of storm-swept seas, looked back at me. Amusement tugged at her lips as she handed me my knife back.

"Hello, Kenna," she said.

"Viviane," I blurted out.

She nodded towards Valerie and Theo. "So these were the two thieves you told me about before."

"What are you doing here?" was the only thing I could think to answer as my mind spun to try to make sense of this.

Viviane was originally from the Court of Water, but she had become one of Volkan Flameshield's slaves after she stole from Rayan's palace. She was a skilled thief who could use her magic to touch people without them feeling anything, and she had helped me in my scheme to kill the Prince of Fire. I had freed her from the slave collar afterwards. But after that, Viviane had left, and I had never seen her again. Until now.

"We put out word that we were looking for thieves to help with an important heist," Theo answered as Viviane slid over to stand between them. His gray eyes darted to her for a second. "And Viviane showed up."

Valerie slung her arm over the elf's shoulder, even though she had to rise up onto her toes to accomplish it. "You know, she's really good at this."

"Exactly," Theo filled in.

"I can't believe you kept her from us."

I rolled my eyes. "I didn't keep her from you."

Theo flashed me a mischievous grin before looking back up at Viviane. "Well, at least you're here now. I have a feeling that you're going to fit right in with us."

Surprise flickered in her blue eyes. Then a smile spread across her lips as she looked between the two excited thieves. "You know, I think I'd like that."

"Now who's planning a threesome?" Eilan shot Valerie a sly look and gave her a quick rise and fall of his eyebrows.

She winked at him. "You wish."

Shaking his head, Theo looked back at us again. "So,

Mordren was yelling at Eilan for something. What else did we miss?"

We exchanged a glance. A cool night wind smelling of damp grass blew through the camp and made the tent walls around us flutter. The sounds of lots of people moving about drifted towards us from the back of the camp.

Elvin had showed up with an entire army of humans to help us.

The Hands had stolen all of the High Elves' arrows.

And Eilan had assassinated one of their Wielders.

I smiled at the waiting thieves.

The scales of this war might just have tipped in our favor.

CHAPTER 34

Storms of magic hammered against the shield above us. The explosions echoed across the bloodstained fields and Prince Edric's knees almost buckled. But the shield held. And more than that, we were pushing the High Elves back.

With the loss of their arrows, they had to focus on close combat on the ground while trying to get through Edric's shield. And with the human army bolstering our ranks, we had managed to turn the tide of this battle.

I shot arcs of fire at the soldiers before me in an effort to get to where Evander, Monette, and Princess Syrene had finally joined the fight. Vines shot out from around Syrene, snatching at our troops and pulling them off balance so that the High Elves in the front ranks could cut them down. At the same time, Evander shot what I think was supposed to be sharpened spears of wood at them as well. And Monette was most likely doing one of two things. Either using her mood-influencing magic to bolster the morale of the High Elves around her or to sow fear in our ranks.

Water shot out from a Wielder somewhere behind the rows of common soldiers, and turned my flames into steam. It billowed like white mist over the heads of the fighters before me. I shot more fire at them, trying to get through.

In the grand scheme of things, I knew that it was petty and not very strategic. Anron was still hovering in the air far behind the army, so we still couldn't reach him, but Evander, Monette, and Syrene were so close to the front lines now. And after everything that they had done, I just really wanted to kill them.

An earsplitting screech cleaved the afternoon air.

I snapped my gaze up.

Dread surged through my stomach.

We had been steadily pushing the High Elves back all day, forcing Anron to send out everyone he had. But apparently, that hadn't been everyone.

Air serpents shot down from the mountain and sped straight for us.

"Take cover!" I screamed.

Panic tore through our army as the winged beasts crashed into our ranks. Gigantic maws crushed elves and humans between gleaming teeth, and lethal claws slashed at the survivors. I threw up a wall of fire that barely did anything to slow them down.

Wings boomed as the serpents swooped down again and again, leaving gaping holes in our formation as they snatched up our soldiers. I dove to the side and rolled across the muddy grass as a massive red beast shot down. Its jaws snapped in the air right next to me as I desperately scrambled away.

"Fall back!" Hadeon boomed across the plains. "Long-range users to the front."

Leaping to my feet, I blindly threw a barrage of flaming

scythes into the air while I sprinted across the ground. In this chaos, I couldn't risk worldwalking. Screams came from our panicked soldiers as the air serpents continued their onslaught. My chest heaved. Skidding to a halt, I narrowly managed to stop before being skewered by a long claw. I threw myself to the side just in time.

The air serpent let out a screech and shot up into the air again.

Dull thuds filled the afternoon as broken bodies fell from the sky and slammed down into the grass after having been caught in the winged serpents' attacks. I leaped aside to avoid being hit by one, and sadness washed over me like a tidal wave when I saw the lifeless blue eyes of an elf staring up into the heavens as his corpse landed next to me.

Elves and humans lay scattered across the blood-soaked grass, dead or dying, as our army scrambled to fall back while the winged serpents shot down from the sky. The dead bodies seemed to stare accusingly at me as I sprinted towards the front where Mordren, Hadeon, and the others were gathering. Staring at me as if wanting to know if this had really been worth it. If we had just let Anron and Syrene rule, none of these people would have died.

People who would never go home to their loved ones again, who would never watch another beautiful sunrise, who would never taste the sweetness of summer's first strawberries again, stared unseeing at me, waiting for me to give them an answer, as I ran between their broken and torn bodies.

Was this all worth it?

Guilt welled up inside my chest.

I didn't have an answer for them.

Skidding to a halt on the muddy ground, I threw up a fire shield behind Mordren's shadow one.

"I thought you said that Anron wouldn't send in the air serpents," I said to Vendir while Idra, Edric, and Ymas reached us as well.

Vendir shot a blast of wind towards the attacking beasts. They veered off course and roared at us, but it saved the final ranks of soldiers who were still trying to retreat to a position behind us.

"He shouldn't have," the High Elf replied as he sent another blast of air at them. "Breeding air serpents is slow and difficult, and training them is even harder, so sending them into a battle where they risk getting hurt or killed is something that High Commanders usually avoid at all costs."

Idra shot a wave of water at a brown serpent speeding towards us from the left. It swerved out of the way before shooting back to its pack to try again. Stone flew through the air as Hadeon slammed his hands forward. Iwdael followed that up with a mass of twisting tree branches that sought to ensnare the serpents' limbs while Eilan aimed lightning strikes at them.

"We were doing too well," Idra said as she continued making sure the area around Edric was clear. "Anron couldn't risk letting us get the upper hand, so he sent in the air serpents because we have no way of countering them."

"Fire!" Prince Iwdael called over his shoulder.

Bowstrings twanged.

A moment later, a cloud of arrows shot towards the winged serpents.

They flashed back and forth through the air, trying to get past our walls of magic to lunge at Iwdael's archers.

Lightning and wind and stone crashed into the shield

above our heads as the Wielders renewed their barrage. I frantically tried to keep both the air serpents and the Wielders at bay, but there were too many of them and too few of us. Prince Edric clenched his jaw and braced one leg behind him while raising his arms into the air.

Magic exploded above us.

Teeth and claws sliced the air.

Wielders steadily flew closer while the soldiers on the ground had re-formed their ranks and started advancing on us instead of steadily retreating.

My heart pounded in my chest.

We wouldn't be able to hold them off.

The pulsing moan of whales echoed across the landscape.

I whipped around.

Coming from the direction of the Court of Light was a mass of sky whales and firebirds.

Relief, so intense that I actually gasped, coursed through me.

The elves of Poisonwood had come.

"By all the spirits," Prince Iwdael said as he craned his neck to watch the gigantic sky-colored whales that soared high in the heavens. "That is not something I thought I'd ever see."

"You got them here?" Prince Edric asked, his gaze flicking to me.

"Yes."

I knew that asking them had been selfish, because they had already been through a war with the High Elves that had ended with them banished into a forest full of hallucinogenic plants. But we really needed their help.

"Don't just stand there," Mendar called as he and Endira swooped past us on a couple of firebirds. "Get on."

The sky whales plowed into the cluster of air serpents,

sending them scattering to avoid a full crash. Speeding across the sky like flaming streaks, the firebirds attacked the fleeing air serpents. Their talons clawed at their wings. Screeches of fear and pain rose from the serpents as they tried to escape.

A firebird landed next to me. Its orange and red plumage rippled as it turned its head to look over at me expectantly.

Not hesitating a second, I rammed my blades back into their sheaths and leaped onto the massive bird's back. A moment later, a sky whale touched down on our other side. Mordren and Eilan jumped up on it.

"Keep the shield up," I said.

"Protect the rest of our army," Mordren filled in.

"And what are you going to do?" Iwdael asked.

Wicked smirks spread across our faces.

"We're going to take the fight to them."

My stomach lurched as the firebird sped up into the pink and golden sky. Pressing my knees into the bird's body, I leaned forward as it shot towards the High Elves ahead.

Whales and birds and air serpents clashed around us, led by Mendar and Endira. The two elves expertly attacked our enemies while the rest of their people arrived to join the fight and rain down arrows on the High Elves as well.

Wielders rose higher into the sky, forming a long line above their soldiers.

Magic hummed in the air.

I braced myself for their joint attack as the firebird continued speeding straight towards them.

Screams tore from their throats.

There was a villainous smile on my lips as I watched the row of Wielders suddenly drop halfway to the ground. Lightning split the air at the same time, striking two of the High Elves before they could stabilize themselves.

Standing atop a sky whale, Mordren and Eilan smirked at me before the Prince of Shadows jerked his chin, telling me to get going.

While Mordren, who was now finally in range, sent wave after wave of pain magic at the Wielders, Eilan shot lightning at them to take them down before they could recover. Their combined attacks created a small opening in their ranks. Leaning down against the firebird's flaming neck, I urged it forward.

Red and orange streaks of fire fluttered behind us as we sped through the gap and flew straight towards Anron.

Surprise flashed on the High Commander's face. Blowing a series of whistling sounds, he flew through the air until a giant white serpent appeared and allowed him to land on its back. I drew my knife and shot scythes of fire at Anron while we continued speeding through the air towards him and his mount.

While the air serpent veered out of the way, he sent a wave of water towards me. Lightning crackled through the sky as he also shot a white bolt straight at my chest while the water made my fire explode into steam. The firebird beneath me dodged it in a flash and then repositioned itself slightly behind Anron.

Shoving my knife forward, I sent a concentrated spear of flames hot enough to burn through his whole body. The flames tore through the air towards his heart.

At the last second, he leaned to the side, escaping the attack, while also hurling a block of stone at me. Panic flashed through me. I pressed myself flat against the bird's neck and squeezed my knees into its sides with everything I had as it rolled over, spinning in the air, to avoid getting hit.

Wind slammed into us from the side while we were still

trying to get back upright, and I had to grip the flaming feathers tightly to avoid being thrown off as we tumbled away. Blood pounded in my ears. Righting itself, the bird shot back up to Anron's altitude while the High Commander let out a derisive laugh.

"Oh, you will never be able to compete with me," he mocked. "*Princess* of Fire."

Flames fluttered in the air as the firebird I rode flapped its magnificent wings. Spreading my arms, I raised a wall of fire behind me. Dark red flames spread across my black armor until it covered my whole body and lifted my hair up into a fiery inferno. A lethal smile curled my lips as I stared back at the High Commander while flames billowed around me.

"I am not a princess. I am the fire."

Red flames tore through the sky as I slammed my arms forward, shooting the whole burning wall straight at Anron.

He threw a blast of water at it, but it didn't stop the full attack and he was forced to swerve away with his air serpent. I aimed my palms at him. Torrents of dark flames shot towards them. The air serpent twisted through the air to evade it while Anron threw up stone shields to block the fire. Molten stone dripped down onto the ground below as my flames melted his shield from the edges.

The half-melted block of stone barreled towards me as Anron tried to force me back. As the firebird dodged, I cast a glance over my shoulder.

Behind me, Wielders screamed as Mordren and Eilan attacked them with pain magic and crackling lightning. And even farther behind, the other air serpents screeched as sky whales, firebirds, and Poisonwood elves attacked with everything they had. The soldiers on the ground were once more being pushed back by our army, led by Hadeon, Idra,

Ymas, and Iwdael, while Prince Edric kept the shield firmly in place. Rayan and his healer corps, assisted by a team of worldwalkers and protected by Princess Lilane, appeared and disappeared all over the grass, saving those who could still be saved.

Flicking my knife through the air, I shot another volley of flaming scythes at Anron with one hand while another thick torrent tore through the sky from my other palm.

Fire exploded into the red and orange sky as Anron blocked it with a blast of wind.

My firebird weaved around it while I raised my hands for another attack.

A shrill whistle echoed across the blood-soaked battlefield.

In an instant, every single High Elf sprinted towards the air serpents that suddenly shot down towards their own ranks. I barely had time to grab the flaming feathers before me as my firebird shot away to escape the mass of Wielders, soldiers, and air serpents suddenly speeding towards us.

Panic clawed its way up my throat before I realized that they weren't chasing us.

As the firebird slowed down and flapped around so that we faced our old position, I found Anron and his whole army disappearing up towards the castle atop the mountain.

Indecision flitted through me.

"Kenna," Mordren called from somewhere behind me. "Do not follow. You will be flying into an ambush."

I clicked my tongue and an annoyed snarl ripped from my throat. But he was right. Following Anron and his whole army up the mountain when we had no idea what they intended to do was a really bad idea.

Narrowing my eyes, I was forced to watch as Evander,

Monette, and Princess Syrene followed High Commander Anron up the massive mountainside on another air serpent.

They couldn't possibly plan on hiding up there. If they were, I had no idea how we were supposed to fight them effectively.

Blowing out an irritated sigh, I nudged the firebird with a knee, urging it to return to the ground.

What in the world was Anron plotting?

CHAPTER 35

Clouds drifted lazily across the sky. The golden afternoon sun was painting the heavens with streaks of red and orange as it dipped lower towards the horizon. I stared out across the empty plains.

It had been a full day since Anron had disappeared up the mountain with all his people. We had kept our soldiers ready from the early morning hours, but now as evening was fast approaching, we were forced to admit that the High Elves would not be coming down from the mountain to resume the battle.

Clanking pots and flapping fabric sounded behind us as our army got ready for the evening. Even though I wanted to finish this war as soon as possible, I had to admit that this day of relative rest had been a gift for our exhausted army.

"Still nothing, huh?" Valerie said as she and Theo came to join us.

Mordren glanced down at them before sliding his gaze back to the mountain in the distance. "No."

Prince Edric crossed his arms and drew his eyebrows

down. "We need a plan for what to do if they decide to stay up there. We can't have our army camped here indefinitely."

"Yeah, I know. But we can't bring all of our soldiers up there either." Turning to my other side, I looked over at Mendar and Endira. "Can we?"

The two Poisonwood elves exchanged a glance. A soft breeze ruffled Mendar's long black hair and the afternoon sun heightened the contrast between it and the crown of spiky red branches that circled his head.

"We could probably get enough sky whales to transport everyone up there," Mendar began.

"But the problem would be how to fight," Endira finished. Her white hair rippled as she shrugged. "Everyone who can't engage in any kind of long-range battle would just be sitting ducks while standing up there, stuck on the sky whale's back."

"Exactly. Unless we can..." Mendar trailed off. His dark brows creased as he frowned towards the closest tent behind us. "Where did you come from?"

Following his gaze, I turned around to see who he was talking to.

Big blue eyes blinked up at us from where they were peeking out underneath the cloth wall. To my left, Valerie let out a surprised laugh.

Excited squeaks came from the pink cloud animals as they squeezed out from underneath the tent wall and rushed over to Valerie. There were at least ten of them and they jumped up and down around her legs once they reached her. Crouching down, she patted all ten of them on the head, one at a time.

"Hi," she said as she smiled down at them while shaking her head. "What in the world are you doing here?"

Still standing next to her, Theo let out an amused huff. "You have got to stop feeding them."

"I'm not feeding them. They just like me."

"Uh-huh."

Massaging his brows, Mendar blew out a deep sigh. "They must have snuck onto one of the sky whales when we left."

"Sneaky, sneaky, huh?" Valerie ran her hand over their fluffy forms again. "But you can't be here. We're in the middle of a war."

They only answered with a few lonely squeaks as they burrowed up into her palm. I turned back to Mordren.

"We need to gather everyone for a meeting," I said.

"Agreed." Mordren shifted his attention to our camp. "We need to get Eilan, Hadeon, and Idra."

"And Iwdael and Rayan," Prince Edric added. His gray granite eyes slid to me. "Probably that half-brother of yours too. If I remember correctly, he's good at calculating odds and stuff."

"Yeah, he is. Let's–"

"Incoming!" Endira snapped.

I whipped back towards the plains. My heart dropped. High Commander Anron, atop his white air serpent, was speeding across the empty grasslands with four Wielders flanking him on their own winged mounts.

"Get ready for battle!" Prince Edric boomed across the camp behind us before he turned and raised his hands while saying to us in a quieter voice, "The shield is up."

"If they're coming together, they'll be attacking all at the same time too," I said. Fire flickered in my hair as I raised my arms as well. "We'll try to counter some of them."

Shadows twisted around Mordren's forearms as he did the same.

The High Elves were closing the distance rapidly.

"Go on," Valerie said as she pushed the small pile of pink

clouds towards the tent they had come from. "Go hide in there."

"You should probably go too," I said.

"Not a chance." Theo squared his shoulders. "We can help."

Valerie straightened while the cloud animals scrambled towards the closest tent. "What he said."

"Fine." I turned to Mendar and Endira. "Get some sky whales and firebirds ready. We'll hold off the initial attacks."

"On it," Mendar said.

Turning around, they sprinted back into our camp. Clanking and bustling came from behind us as the rest of our army hurried to get ready as well. My heart pattered against my ribs. But between the five of us, and especially with Edric here, we should be able to hold them off until we could get our flying units back up into the sky.

"Get ready," Mordren said as they closed in.

Brilliant white light pulsed out from Theo and Valerie.

The air serpents swerved slightly and two of the Wielders raised their arms to shield their eyes from the blinding light.

As soon as they righted themselves, Mordren flung a mass of twisting shadows straight at them.

Lightning crackled across the sky, tearing his darkness to shreds as three High Elves shot simultaneous lightning attacks at it. I raised a massive wall of fire behind. The white bolts of lightning struck the barrier, but since Mordren's shadows had weakened them, they didn't make it through the thick shield of flames. Water rose.

"Steam incoming," I said. "Brace for low visibility. Edric, how's the shield?"

"Intact." He kept his eyes on the sky as he spoke. "Whatever they throw, I'll be able to handle it."

Waves of water crashed into my flaming shield right as the

five air serpents flew through it. Hissing filled the air as my fire exploded into steam. It washed over us on billowing winds and turned the world into a hazy white mist.

Booming came from both above and in front of us as Anron and his Wielders peppered Edric's shield with both fire and wind magic. Yellow flames licked the edge of the shield and the wind blew away most of the steam.

Lightning cut through the air from the High Elves on Anron's left while water whooshed towards us from the ones on his right. Theo and Valerie sent a blinding pulse of light at them. The attacks faltered slightly, allowing me and Mordren to raise another shield each which took the brunt of the attacks. White bolts shredded through Mordren's shadows while another massive cloud of steam billowed over our camp after the water hit my fire.

A whistling sound came from the front.

Sharpened stones the size of long daggers shot out of the mist as Anron snapped his arm forwards in a throwing motion. The lethal rain of stone shot towards us while Anron and his Wielders veered away from our camp before they could crash into us.

The projectiles sped towards us from far too close.

Prince Edric ground his teeth and shifted his hands to presumably strengthen his shield.

Sharp thuds echoed across the grass as the first row of sharpened stones hit his shield.

Something metallic flashed at the corner of my eye.

A grunt sounded.

I snapped my head towards Edric right as he toppled backwards.

The Dagger of Orias was buried in his chest.

My body jerked sideways as someone crashed into me.

Stones pounded into the grass all around me as the rain of lethal projectiles descended on us with no shield to hold them off. I slammed into the ground with Mordren on top of me. Thudding filled the air as the sharpened stones bombarded the area.

Then it stopped.

A soul-shattering cry split the air.

"THEO!" Valerie screamed. "No. No. No. No."

Mordren coughed above me and then rolled off me, landing on his back in the grass beside me. I shot up into a sitting position and whipped around. Anron and the High Elves were disappearing back to the mountain. My gaze snapped to Mordren.

Ice spread through my veins and my heart shattered like brittle glass.

Sharpened stones pierced Mordren's whole body and pain clouded his eyes as he sucked in a wet rattling breath. It made his body spasm and he coughed. A cloud of red mist appeared above his mouth. Blood ran down from his mouth and welled up from the wounds in his chest and arms.

"No. No," I pressed out. Shaking my head, I refused to believe what I was seeing as I shifted around to lean down over him.

"Theo!" Valerie screamed again.

My gaze snapped to her.

A few strides away, Theo was also lying on the ground. Sharpened stones were lodged in his chest, and pain flashed in his eyes as he struggled to draw in a breath. Valerie, with stones only piercing her upper arm, knelt beside him with a desperate look on her face. Next to them, Prince Edric also lay. The Dagger of Orias shook in his chest as he forced air into his lungs.

"RAYAN!" I screamed into the sky over and over again until my voice broke. "Rayan! They're dying!"

Mordren coughed again. I snapped my gaze back to him as he winced and coughed once more. Blood trickled down his chin.

"Hey," I said, placing gentle fingers on his jaw to steady him. "Just hold on. Rayan is coming."

"Don't do this," Valerie begged next to me. Tears streamed down her cheeks as she bent over Theo's body. "Don't leave me. Please." Her voice cracked. "You can't leave me."

"I d-don't think..." Theo drew in a gurgling breath, "... choice."

Mordren's body spasmed as he tried to shift his position.

"Don't move," I said. Tears welled up in my eyes too as I looked down into his beautiful bloodstained face. "Rayan will be here soon."

"Theo, please," Valerie pleaded through strangled sobs. "I can't make it if you're not here with me. I can't face this world without you by my side. You're my family. We're each other's family. You can't leave me here alone."

Only a rattling breath answered her.

A wheezing noise came from Mordren's throat.

Placing my palm against his cheek, I held his head steady as he coughed more blood into the air. It ran down from his mouth and onto his throat. His eyes were glassy and unfocused.

Chaos came from the camp behind us where the rest of our people had gotten hit by the stones as well.

"K-kenna," Mordren pressed out.

"Don't speak," I said. "Just keep breathing until Rayan gets here."

"You... hurt?"

"No, I'm not hurt." While still holding my palm to his cheek, I used my other hand to brush a strand of hair from his face. Guilt and regret rose like a monster in my chest. "You protected me."

He let out a shaky breath and another tremor coursed through his body. "G-good."

"RAYAN!" I screamed at the sky again.

"I think..." he sucked in a breath that made him choke, "it might..." his chest convulsed, "b-be too late."

"Theo," Valerie cried beside me. "Hold on. Please, just hold on."

"No." I shook my head at Mordren. "It's not too late. You hear me? You are going to live. We are all going to live. Together."

Mordren's eyes rolled back into his head. Panic surged through me and I gave his cheek a slap. His eyes snapped open and he blinked several times while coughing again. The coppery tang of blood hung over the whole area as red streaks ran down from the holes in his body.

"I think..." Mordren sucked in a shuddering breath and more blood welled up from his wounds, "you will have to... live for both of us."

Tears poured down my cheeks. With one hand on his jaw and the other holding on to his shaking hand, I choked out broken sobs. "No. You have to make it. You have to..."

Mordren raised his other hand. It wobbled in the air for a moment as he drew in a wheezing breath. Then his fingers bumped into my cheek.

"I really do..." his fingers smeared blood across my cheek as his hand dropped back down again, "... love you."

"No. No!" Tears dripped down onto his face as I leaned over him and placed my hands on his shoulders. Desperation filled my cracked voice as I screamed down at him. "You have to make it! Because I'm calling in that favor now. You owe me a debt and you can't refuse it when I collect it. This is me collecting the debt. I don't care how much pain you're in. You have to hold on."

"My little... traitor spy." His beautiful silver eyes focused on me for a second and his lips turned up into a blood-soaked smile. "Trying to... blackmail death."

"Stop it!" Valerie screamed. "Theo, look at me. You need to keep your eyes open. Okay?" Strangled sobs bubbled from her throat. "No going to sleep. You have to stay with me."

I flicked a quick glance over at them.

Theo was staring up into the sky while his chest barely rose and fell, and Valerie was crying her eyes out over his bloodied body while pleading with the gods not to take her family from her. All ten pink clouds were nestled against his body, their tiny mouths open as they wailed heartbreaking cries into the sky. One of them nudged Theo's bloodstained hand and crawled underneath it. Red streaks coated its pink fluff as its face appeared on the other side while Theo's limp hand rested on top of it. A few strides away, Prince Edric was still fighting to draw breath. All alone. With no one by his side but the Dagger of Orias watching as he desperately tried to cling to life. Mordren sucked in another death rattle.

"NO!" The word ripped from my throat which such desperation and unending sorrow that it almost tore the veil between the living and the dead. Looking at my dying friends, I screamed at the whole world. "What's the fucking point!"

My voice shattered and I cried uncontrollably as I met Mordren's pained silver eyes. The eyes of the one I loved. My family. The one person who loved me with the blazing passion of a million stars. And he loved *me*. All of me. And I loved all of him. And we were going to start a life together. A happy life. And we were going to live. All of us.

"What is the point of anything, of everything we've been through, if not all of us are going to make it!" I screamed at the red-streaked sky. "We have been through enough! *I* have been through enough!"

I had been beaten and captured and tortured. I had been used and discarded. I had been betrayed over and over again by people who pretended to care about me. I had been a slave for most of my life and when I finally clawed my way to freedom and power, it was stolen from me. I had watched the people I loved endure far too much pain and heartache. We had fought and schemed and gone through hell for far too long. What was the point of us going through all of that if we didn't get to live happily ever after together at the end of it all? We deserved a happy ending. We had been through enough. I had been through enough.

Valerie sucked in a broken gasp next to me.

"Kenna."

I whipped my head around.

Prince Rayan Floodbender dropped to his knees next to me. Healers were materializing all across the grass, and two of them were already bent over Theo and Edric. My hands shook and I tried to move aside, but my body was stuck where it was. The Prince of Water didn't care. He just placed his hands over Mordren's body.

Tears still streamed down my cheeks. "Is he...?"

"Yes," Rayan answered. "If I hurry." His purple eyes snapped up to someone above my shoulder. "Imelda. Get over here and remove the stones when I tell you to."

Imelda knelt on Mordren's other side.

I couldn't stop crying, but I smiled through the tears and squeezed Mordren's hand. "You're going to make it."

A choked breath was the only thing that answered me as Mordren tried to refocus his eyes. I cast a glance at Theo and Valerie. Before I could get any sound out, the second healer in charge of removing the stones from Theo's chest nodded at me in answer to my unspoken question. I slid my gaze to Edric.

The Dagger of Orias, that had cut through his magical shield and pierced his chest, now lay on the grass. Its wavy blade was slick with blood, but Edric's chest rose and fell steadily as another healer poured her magic into his body.

Relief crashed over me and a sob ripped from my throat. We were all going to make it.

"What are they doing?" Imelda suddenly asked, her eyes drifting towards the mountain while Rayan was healing one of the holes left by the stones.

I followed her gaze.

High Commander Anron, astride his massive white air serpent, was hovering next to the side of the mountain. The rest of what had to be his Wielders were spread out around it as well so that they circled it. I frowned at them.

"What–"

The mountain exploded.

CHAPTER 36

Bone-deep terror pulsed through my whole body as the king's mountain exploded and started tumbling down. An enormous wave of broken boulders fell down the mountainside.

More explosions sounded.

The rest of the mountain shattered as well and the mass of stone rolled down like a gigantic landslide.

Towards the battlefield.

Towards us.

"It's going to crush us," Imelda cried. "We're all going to get buried underneath it if we don't worldwalk away right now."

"We can't move them," Prince Rayan said, his voice surprisingly calm. "If we move them now, they will bleed out."

"How would we even get the whole army out in time?" said the blond elf who was healing Prince Edric.

"We can't," I breathed, disbelief clanging through me.

High Commander Anron and his Wielders sped away across the darkening sky as King Aldrich's mountain crashed down and rolled towards us.

This was how they were going to win the war.

They would bury us all.

My eyes darted to Rayan.

He held my gaze while continuing to pour magic into Mordren's bleeding body. "I'm not going anywhere."

I drew in a shaky breath. After giving him a nod, I pushed to my feet.

And then I worldwalked.

A tidal wave of rock barreled towards me as I reappeared in the middle of the battlefield. It was so tall that I had to crane my neck to see the top of the lethal mass that swallowed the landscape before it.

As I stared up at the impending death, I expected to feel fear. Panic. Regret.

But all I felt was anger.

Rage, rage so hot that it burned through my blood, coursed through my whole body, leaving a deadly calm in its wake. Raising my arms, I held my palms out towards the oncoming avalanche of stone.

Ever since I drank that third bowl of fire magic, I had kept a tight hold of my power. I had locked most of it behind doors of steel and dampened it to a manageable level because I didn't know how to control it without the risk of hurting the people around me too.

Now, I removed those dampers.

Every single one.

Fire surged down my body and dark red flames flickered in my hair.

The waves of shattered stone sped towards me.

This was not the end. We would not die here. Because we had been through enough. *I* had been through enough. And I was no longer a little girl who was desperate to please her family and friends so that they would love her. I was no longer a bound servant. I was no longer trapped and weak. No.

I was the fire.

Dark red flames tore across the grass.

They were so tall that they licked the purple-streaked heavens, and they spanned all the way across the massive landslide hurtling for us.

The first stones slammed into the fire shield.

A boom echoed across the landscape as they hit. I poured more power into my flaming barrier. The stones melted underneath the heat of my fire while more of them crashed into it.

Holding my palms out in front of me, I continued feeding the flames with more power.

The cracked mountain melted against them.

It built upwards as more stone pushed at it from behind.

I pulled more power from the seemingly endless well inside me.

Heat washed over the grasslands, charring them black all the way to the slowly building wall of stone before me. My hair rose up around me to form a flaming crown as I poured more and more and more and more fire at the waves of crushed rock still tumbling towards us.

Dark red flames coated every part of my skin.

The melting mountain crested like a wave high up in the air.

Bracing one leg behind me, I pushed forward.

Searing flames tore from my hands to feed the thickening shield of fire and stop the wave of stone from fully breaking to fall down over me.

My heart swelled in my chest and a lightness spread

through my limbs while sparkling fireworks seemed to go off in every part of my body. I had never felt power like this in my entire life. And my whole soul sang with the intoxicating feeling of it.

Stone built up beyond the fire.

I dug deeper into my well of magic.

Heat rolled over the entire battlefield as more flames surged up.

I kept drawing more power.

The massive avalanche slowed and only a few more chunks of the mountain and King Aldrich's white marble castle hit the back of the gigantic wave that had formed over the grass.

My fire flickered.

Surprise slammed into me as the power I had drawn from suddenly dried up. Scraping the bottom of the well, I forced myself to keep the fire shield up while the final pieces of stone rolled up against it.

Abruptly, the flames cut out.

Every single piece of the fire shield vanished.

I stared up at the impossible stone wave that had almost crested above me. Melted rock still ran down the front of it, but the back part had cooled enough for it to remain in the same shape.

Disbelief pulsed through me.

That was me. I had done that. I had melted half a mountain's worth of stone.

I staggered to the side. My body felt completely drained. Empty. And I couldn't for the life of me make any of my limbs obey me.

The smell of charred grass enveloped me as I collapsed and slammed face first into the ground.

CHAPTER 37

My body shook as aftershock tremors racked it. Mordren's arms tightened around me. I drew in shaky breaths and closed my eyes while trying to only focus on Mordren's warm and steady body against mine. But as soon as I closed my eyes, the image of him dying on the bloodstained grass flashed through my mind. My eyes snapped open.

"You should try to rest," Mordren said as his worried gaze met mine.

Wrapping an arm over his firm chest, I pulled him harder against me on the mattress. "I can't get the image of you dying out of my head."

"And I can't get the image of you alone before that mountain of crashing stone out of my head." He reached up and brushed a loose red curl out of my face. His fingers lingered on my jaw. "You know, I begged Rayan to let me go to you. To help you. But Iwdael arrived and held me down and used his mood manipulation magic to make me feel calm and confident that you would succeed. So all I could do was watch as you melted an entire mountain on your own."

"You would've died if you had moved before Rayan could finish healing you."

"I know. And you would have died if you had not been able to call up such an impossible amount of power."

"I know."

The magic inside me still hadn't recovered completely. I could feel the well filling back up, but it was taking time. I would probably need an entire week of rest before I was back to full power. Melting that avalanche of stone had taken everything I had, and then some.

"I'm sorry," I whispered against his skin.

"For what?"

"You almost died because you shielded me from the sharpened stones Anron shot at us."

His hand slid under my chin. Tipping my head back, he forced me to meet his gaze. "Do not apologize. I will never regret anything I do that keeps you safe."

"Just... don't ever do that to me again." I held his gaze. "Don't ever say goodbye and tell me to live for the both of us."

"I promise." A soft laugh escaped his lips and he leaned down to brush a kiss against my mouth. "My infuriating little blackmailer who calls in debts on me while I'm dying."

"Well, it worked, didn't it?"

"Yes, it did." He laughed again and pulled me closer before kissing the top of my head. "I always hold up my end of the bargain."

The tent walls flapped as a night wind blew through our camp.

For quite a while, we just lay there in each other's arms, breathing each other in and trying to convince ourselves that everything would be okay. The sounds of people walking past came from outside the tent. It was still far too early to be up and about, especially after the kind of day we'd had, but my mind was still too full of panic and fear to sleep.

When we realized that neither one of us would be falling asleep anytime soon, we climbed up from the mattress we shared and put our boots back on.

Cool winds whirled through my clothes as we stepped out of the tent and into the still dark morning. I drew in a deep breath but the air smelled like blood and ash.

Two figures moved towards us through the rows of silent tents.

"Rayan," Mordren said as they came into view. "Lilane."

Lilane Frostsinger had her husband's arm draped over her shoulders while her other arm was wrapped around his waist to lend even more support. Exhaustion swam in the Prince of Water's purple eyes.

"You should be resting," he said as they came to a halt before us.

"So should you, by the looks of it," Mordren answered.

Lilane looked over at her husband. "Yes, I've been trying to tell him that for the past three hours."

"There was work to be done." He shrugged awkwardly with one shoulder while still leaning against his wife. A serious look blew across his face as he met our gazes. "A quarter of our army was hit by that volley of sharpened stones. We've been working through the night trying to heal as many of them as we can."

"And now the whole healer corps is on the brink of complete exhaustion," Lilane added.

"I'm sorry," I said.

"It's not your fault." She gave me a tired smile. "If anything, it's because of you that we're all still alive."

"What of Edric?" Mordren asked.

Prince Rayan flicked a glance towards Edric's tent. "Physically, he's okay. But he... He blames himself for letting the attack go through."

"It's not his fault that Anron hurled the Dagger of Orias through his shield and into his chest," I protested.

"I know. But he still thinks that."

Lilane adjusted her grip on Rayan. "Come on, my love. We need to get you to bed now."

An exhausted smile blew across his lips, but his eyes sparkled with love as he looked over at her. "Yes, my dear."

As they staggered away into the darkness again, I slipped my hand into Mordren's. His warm fingers intertwined with mine and he held my hand in a firm grip as we continued towards Ellyda's work tent.

Torchlight flickered from inside it, informing us that Ellyda was indeed awake as well.

When we stepped into the tent, we were met by not only the blacksmith, but also six other people. Eilan's eyes locked straight on Mordren. Then he strode across the tent and drew his brother into a crushing hug.

I let go of Mordren's hand and moved over to the two thieves sitting atop one of the counters. Drawing Theo down from it, I pulled him into a tight embrace. His skinny arms wrapped around my back.

"I'm so glad you're okay," I said.

"Me too," he said into my shoulder. There was a smile on his face as he drew back and hiked a thumb towards Valerie. "I couldn't very well leave that weirdo on her own, now could I?

Can you imagine the havoc she would wreak upon the world if left unattended?"

Valerie let out a huff in mock affront and gave his shoulder a shove, but there was intense relief still swirling in her brown eyes as she looked back at him.

With that smile still on his lips, he held her gaze for another second before sweeping his eyes over all of us. "I've never understood what the big deal is with getting girlfriends and boyfriends. I don't need to find love. Because I already have it. The love of family. And it's going to take a hell of a lot more than a few sharpened stones to tear me away from that."

A squeak came from the counter. Looking over his shoulder, I found a pile of pink fluffy clouds jumping up and down on the wooden tabletop. Their big blue eyes sparkled with happiness, informing me that they were also very glad that Theo was okay.

"Alright, brother," Mordren said while the rest of us smiled at Theo. "If those stones didn't cause me to asphyxiate, your hug just might."

Eilan let out a breathy chuckle and stepped back as well. While Mordren was trying to smoothen down his leather armor again, Hadeon came over and clapped him on the shoulder. Reaching up, Mordren squeezed his hand and gave him a smile. From across the room, Vendir gave the Prince of Shadows a slow nod as well.

"Mordren," Ellyda's sharp voice cut through the tent. Looking up from where she was sitting behind a workbench at the back, she leveled hard eyes on the Prince of Shadows. "Don't ever do something like that again."

Boots thudded against the ground as Idra stalked over and grabbed my shoulder, yanking me around to face her. "That goes for you too. We worldwalk in to find those two dying," she gestured at Theo and Mordren before stabbing a hand towards my chest, "and you standing alone right in the path of a shattered mountain. What the hell were you thinking?"

"Good to see you too, Idra," I answered with a smile.

She hissed out an annoyed breath. "Bloody insane moron." Staring at me, she shook her head. "Don't you ever go dying on me. Because if you do, I will drag you back from the dead just to kill you myself."

I let out a tired laugh. "Got it."

Silence descended on the tent. For a moment, we all only looked at one another. The tent walls fluttered faintly before falling still again. Torches in metal holders sat on the tables, crackling into the quiet space and casting flickering shadows on the walls.

"So…" I began, drawing out the word. "Anron blew up King Aldrich's mountain."

"Yep," Valerie said.

"So what do we do now?"

Idra and Hadeon exchanged a glance.

"Well," Hadeon began. "First, we need to–"

Wings boomed through the air outside. Shouts rang out from the elves stationed around the camp and clanking steel echoed as others scrambled around.

"The High Elves are here!" someone bellowed. "The High Elves are attacking!"

Dread surged up inside me.

Anron was attacking before the sun had even risen. A quarter of our army had been wounded. Our healers were exhausted. My magic still wasn't back to full power. And Prince Edric, who kept our shield up, hadn't fully recovered either.

But battle was still here. Again

CHAPTER 38

Blood and bodies covered the battlefield before me. My head swam as I desperately slashed and stabbed with my blades to keep the rising tide of High Elves at bay. Sky whales and firebirds fought the air serpents above our heads, their roars and screeches echoing across the noise of clashing steel and whooshing magic. The rest of our army fought valiantly on the ground, but Anron was steadily pushing us backwards across the field.

His surprise attack had come from the back of our camp, forcing us to scramble out onto the grass and abandon our tents before the High Elves mowed them down. With a quarter of our army wounded, and most of the magic-users drained to the bones, it was taking everything we had just to stop them from breaking through our buckling ranks.

Steel glinted in the corner of my eye.

I worldwalked two steps away and rammed my sword through the soldier's neck while he was still following through on the strike that would've cleaved me in half if I hadn't moved. A wet sliding noise sounded as I yanked out the blade and spun around right before a blast of wind slammed into me. Screams ripped through the air as I, along with several others around me, were flung through the air.

My breath exploded from my lungs as I crashed into something hard.

Bronze-clad limbs flapped around me as the High Elf I had hit went down with me. Struggling to get my blades into position, I pushed at his body with my knees and elbows. He rolled over, his weight pinning me to the ground. Panic shot up my spine.

With one arm keeping my shoulder trapped against the scorched grass, he shifted the sword in his hand and positioned the tip in the air above my throat. I thrashed underneath him. He rammed the blade down.

I jerked my head to the side.

Steel sank into the ground a hair's breadth from my neck.

An irritated growl tore from his throat. I finally managed to yank my arm out from underneath my body as he eased some of his weight off me to pull out his sword. Spinning the knife in my hand, I drove it straight up through his chin. His dark eyes widened.

The sword he had just pulled out of the grass tumbled from his fingers as I shoved him back and ripped my knife out before slashing my sword across his throat to make sure he truly died. Blood sprayed across my face. His body hit the ground a moment later.

Clashing steel and battle cries rang out around me.

Sucking in a deep breath of air that smelled of metal and blood and burnt grass, I struggled to my feet before someone else could get into position to run a sword through my throat.

Lightning split the air.

I dove aside as the white bolt barreled towards me.

Pain crackled through my leg.

Rolling with the motion, I jumped to my feet to face the Wielder hiding somewhere in the chaos.

My knee buckled.

Terror and panic washed over me as I tried to make my left leg obey me, but I couldn't even feel it anymore. Part of the lightning strike must have hit me while I was trying to dodge.

A sword sped towards me.

Still on one knee, I threw up both my blades to block the attack. Metal clanged as the sword crashed into my intersected blades. A High Elf with long white hair loomed above me, pushing his sword down harder. I ground my teeth as I tried to hold him back. My leg still tingled and the muscles refused to work, leaving me kneeling on the ground without being able to get to my feet.

The soldier drove his boot into the side of my ribs. I was flung sideways, landing on the grass, while our blades slid free from each other. My instincts screamed at me and I swung my sword out blindly. The High Elf jumped to avoid it cutting through his ankles, but raised his own blade at the same time.

Scrambling to get out of the way, I desperately tried to escape the sword he swung straight at me, but I was too close and my leg still didn't work.

"Kenna!" someone screamed.

The sword sped towards my face.

Then it flashed off course and struck the ground beside me instead. I stared in shock at the pit of lava that had opened up right underneath my attacker, swallowing him to the waist. Flipping the knife in my hand, I dragged it across his throat while he sank into the bubbling pit. His scream cut off abruptly.

Whipping my head to the side, I found Kael Sandscorcher watching us from a few strides away. His hand was still stretched out towards the pit of lava that he now rapidly closed again.

His eyes glittered and a smile shone on his face as he met my gaze. "At least I could pay back–"

A sword shot out of his throat.

"NO!" I screamed.

Surprise flashed across his face for a few seconds. Then his body crumpled to the ground, revealing the High Elf soldier who had rammed a blade through his neck from behind. Kael's body spasmed on the ground while the High Elf stalked towards me.

I was exhausted and my magic level was running dangerously low, but I stabbed my knife forward, sending a spear of fire towards him. He dodged it easily.

Terror pulsed across his face.

His steps faltered and he let out a bloodcurdling scream. A moment later, a tree branch snaked around his throat and snapped his neck. I stared in shock as Prince Iwdael appeared through the gap left by the High Elves fleeing in fear caused by his mood manipulation magic.

"Are you okay?" the Prince of Trees asked as he cast a glance down at me while continuing to send waves of terror over the High Elves around us.

"Yes," I managed to press out between heavy breaths.

Some of Iwdael's powers were hitting me as well and I had to brace myself against the feeling of fear while I crawled over to Kael.

His body had stopped spasming and his brown eyes stared unseeing at the overcast heavens above. Blood and mud caked half of his face and body.

Guilt, sorrow, and regret crashed over me like a wave, threatening to drown me. Kael had died for me. He had taken his eyes off his own battle to save me from my attacker, and because of that, he had missed the sword that came for his own throat.

Was it worth it?

The thought swirled unbidden through my mind again. All across the bloodstained battlefield, the dead and dying were still waiting for my answer. And I still didn't know.

Swallowing back the lump in my throat, I closed Kael's kind brown eyes and then kissed my fingers before pressing them to his forehead. Kael Sandscorcher. Loyal to the end.

Leaves fluttered through the air above me. Cries of pain followed as their sharp edges sliced through the skin of the closest High Elves. I poked at my leg while Reena fell in beside the Prince of Trees.

My leg had finally stopped tingling and my muscles at last obeyed me as I staggered to my feet. Reena's beautiful silver hair had streaks of red in it, but she looked otherwise unharmed as she sent another horde of angry leaves towards the soldiers who were trying to push through Iwdael's wall of terror.

"So, you replaced me, huh?" came a sharp voice.

I tightened the grip on my blades as three people strode out unhindered from the ranks of struggling High Elves. While the others were trying to fight off Iwdael's manipulation, these three walked as if they couldn't feel it at all. As my eyes fell on the blond elf to the left, I realized that it was because they probably didn't.

Princess Syrene cocked her head at Iwdael, waiting for an answer, while Monette and Evander stopped on her left. Monette, who also possessed the ability to influence people's feelings, was probably holding the worst parts of Iwdael's magic at bay.

"Oh, I should have replaced you a long time ago," Prince Iwdael answered, his yellow eyes cold.

Sticking a hand into one of her pouches, Syrene pulled up a handful of shimmering dust and threw it straight at the Prince of Trees. "Too bad I know your weakness."

The powder hit him right in the face.

A sharp smile spread across Iwdael's mouth as he simply brushed it off his clothes as if it were nothing but dust. "Too bad I have friends who are a lot more resourceful than you."

Shock slammed home on her features.

Iwdael attacked.

Sharpened spears shot towards Princess Syrene. Evander raised a wall of wood to block them. Ramming my knife into its sheath, I slammed my palm forward, sending a blast of fire at it. Dark red flames washed over Evander's wall, setting it on fire.

It shot down into the ground again, but it had still stopped Iwdael's spears.

As soon as the shield dropped, Syrene sent a mass of twisting vines towards Iwdael.

Fear pulsed inside me.

I threw a fireball at Monette while she continued with her onslaught. Reena flinched and her attack fell short. Leaves fluttered to the ground before she could recover enough to shoot more of them towards the blond elf. While Evander raised another wall of wood to protect Monette from my fire, I poured more power into my attack. Wood popped and crackled as the tree shield was incinerated.

To my right, Iwdael sent a volley of sharp branches at his wife while she redirected them with her vine shield. Green vines stretched across the blackened grass, snatching at Iwdael's legs while he continued to bombard her with both trees and fear.

Monette scrunched up her pale brows as she no doubt tried to lessen the impact while also sending fear back at us.

I slashed my sword through the air, sending arcs of fire at them all. Another shield of wood shot up to catch it.

"Is that all you can do?" I mocked as I shot more flaming scythes at them. "Shield?"

"At least I finally have power now," Evander answered while raising and lowering the walls.

"Yes, you finally have your magic and your castle and your comfort-loving girlfriend. I hope you're happy."

He shoved one of the walls towards me. "I am! I finally have what I've always wanted."

"Bliss at last, huh?" After incinerating his flying wall, I hurled a fireball at him. "I can't wait to burn it all to the ground."

Flames exploded against another wall of wood. Before he had even lowered it, I aimed another blast straight at Monette.

Evander dropped the burning shield.

Right as it fell, my fireball sped through the air where it had just been.

Turquoise eyes went wide as the flames shot towards Monette's face with incredible speed. Her hand flashed out and she yanked at the closest thing in front of her.

Shock and incredulity pulsed across Evander's face as the fireball struck him right in the chest instead. Dark red flames burned through his clothes and skin until only a black hole was left in his chest. Smoke rose from it.

With that stunned surprise still on his face, he toppled backwards.

Monette jumped out of the way as the boyfriend she had used as a shield to save herself hit the ground with a loud thud.

Evander's dark green eyes glassed over, the biggest shock of his life still twisting his features as the final bits of life drained from his body. The traitor spy. Betrayed by his own in the end. There was some really fine poetic justice in that.

"You're fighting so hard against High Commander Anron now," Princess Syrene snapped while she sent snatching vines at Iwdael. "Why couldn't you have fought this hard to become the next King of Elves?"

Iwdael hurled a cloud of spears at her. "Because I don't want it! Why could you never accept that I'm *happy* with my life the way it is? I want to make love and dance and drink and eat good food and watch the sunrise over the trees. I don't want more power!"

Vines and leaves and wood clashed in the air between them. Fear smacked into me like a stone to the face. Before Evander's charred body had even stopped smoking, Monette renewed her attacks on me with a ferocity I hadn't expected. My body screamed at me to run in the other direction, and I had to use every bit of my strength to stop it from doing just that.

"And that's why you will never win," Syrene screamed back while sending a massive ball of vines at Iwdael while effortlessly blocking Reena's leaves. "Even though there are two of you, you can't beat me. Because you never bothered to learn how to use your magic efficiently in battles."

"Because I don't want to be in a battle!"

I shot a spear of fire at Monette. Jumping aside, she dodged it just in time. Terror slammed into me a second later. My next attack faltered as I tried to separate my own emotions from the ones Monette was forcing onto me. I had never known just how good she really was at manipulating people's feelings. Being able to both protect Princess Syrene from Iwdael's magic, while at the same time finding the small flicker of fear in my chest and blowing it into a raging wildfire, took an incredible amount of control. She must have spent every day of her whole life manipulating people's feelings for her to become this good at it.

"But now you're in one anyway," Syrene sniped back at Iwdael while shoving Reena's leaf attack aside. "You had every chance to just go back and hide in your forest, and yet you still came out to fight."

"And you had a life in our court. Friends. People who loved you." Sharpened branches smacked against her vine shield as Iwdael hurled them at her. "You had *me*. But then you betrayed everyone just to get more power, and now you're all alone."

Emotions flashed across Princess Syrene's face.

I sucked in a gasp of horror that had nothing to do with Monette's magic, and staggered a step back as Reena's throat burst open.

Syrene slid her cold gaze from the vine she had shoved down Reena's throat and to the stunned elven prince next to her. She scoffed, "Well, now you are too."

An animalistic cry of pain tore through the air and raked its claws over my skin. Terror the likes of which I had never felt before crashed into me like a tidal wave. Collapsing to my knees, I pressed my hands to my head.

While trying to blink the pain away, I tried to keep Monette in sight. But the fear wasn't coming from her. From across the grass, Monette was staring at Iwdael with wide turquoise eyes. Terror pulsed on her face as well. She flicked her gaze to Syrene, who wore a similar expression, and then she staggered a step back.

The fear on Syrene's face expanded exponentially, as if Monette had pulled the protection from the princess to use all of it for herself instead. Crouching down on the ground, Monette pressed her palms to her head as well and closed her eyes. I doubled over as another wave of crippling terror hit me.

In a wide circle around us, every soldier, enemy and ally, had also dropped to the ground while cradling their head. Pressing my palms against the scorched grass, I threw up as another pulse of fear racked my body. While gasping in a breath, I looked up at Iwdael. But his eyes were locked on Princess Syrene.

Her face was twisted in utter horror and world-ending fear as she rocked back and forth on her knees on the ground.

We were only being hit by the edge of Iwdael's power, while she was receiving the full force of it. As I threw up from fear again, I couldn't even imagine the intensity of what she was feeling.

Broken screams tore from her throat as she clawed at her own face before bending over to pound her forehead against the ground. When that didn't work, she thrashed her head from side to side.

Standing on the blackened grass before her, Iwdael only watched her with eyes so cold they could have frozen the stars.

Princess Syrene screamed until her voice broke, and raked her nails down her own face, leaving bloody cuts.

I threw up again and squeezed my hands into fists before I could force my head up and look up at them again.

Blood ran down Syrene's skin from the wounds she had

inflicted on herself while trying to get the feeling of maddening terror from her mind. Her eyes almost bulged out of her head while her mouth was open in a silent scream.

Then something snapped.

Yanking out a knife, Princess Syrene slit her own throat.

A red line appeared on her skin. Blood welled up from it a second later. Terror still pulsed on her face, but I swore that I could see a hint of relief in her violet eyes as she slumped down on the ground. Her body jerked as the life drained from her.

Just as fast as it had appeared, the crippling sense of fear disappeared. I sucked in a gasp.

Boots pounded against the grass as Prince Iwdael ran back to Reena. I wiped my mouth with the back of my hand and blew out a long breath in order to scrape together my scattered mind while Iwdael dropped to his knees next to the silver-haired elf.

Wrapping his arms around her, he cradled her limp body in his lap.

"Reena, darling," Iwdael said in a soft voice. "It's going to be okay. Rayan is going to fix you."

But Reena's head only lolled to the side like a broken doll, because she had been dead before she even hit the grass.

"This is all your fault!" Monette screamed.

I snapped my gaze towards her. Staggering to her feet, she raised her hands in front of her chest. Fear hit me again while I tried to rise as well. I threw a small fireball at her, which missed by a wide margin, but it bought me enough time to get to my feet.

All around us, the other soldiers were resuming the battle as well. Prince Iwdael continued to rock Reena's lifeless body in his arms while Syrene lay dead and forgotten on the blackened grass.

"If you hadn't been so adamant about getting your freedom, none of this would have happened," Monette continued yelling at me. "And I could have kept my good life!"

Staggering back a step from the force of her powers, I tried to concentrate enough to shoot more fire at her. "The High Elves would still have invaded."

"Yes, but you're the one who convinced everyone to fight them. We could've just left it alone. So what if they had ruled us? We would've been safe."

"I didn't convince anyone to do anything. All the elves that are here, and all the humans too, decided to fight on their own because they didn't want to be ruled by someone who stole their magic, restricted their freedom, and treated them like shit."

"Liar! You're just a power-hungry bitch who would kill everyone if that meant you could rule them. The world would have been so much better off if you'd never been born."

My emotions were raw after being hit by parts of Iwdael's magic, and Monette's power just kept making it worse. As she latched her claws into the feelings of fear and guilt and panic inside my chest and blew them into wildfires, all I wanted to do was curl into a ball on the ground and bawl my eyes out. I crashed down on one knee as the force of it became too much.

Monette took a step forward. Steel sang as she drew a short knife and gripped it tightly in her hand.

"Kenna, we…" The voice trailed off.

Forcing my head up, I looked at the source of the new voice. Felix stood halfway between me and Monette. His brown eyes widened as he looked from the dead bodies of

Princess Syrene, Evander, and Reena, to Iwdael crying over his lover's chest, and then finally to me and Monette.

Pain and indecision flashed across his face as he took in my kneeling form and the knife Monette gripped as she moved another step closer. She flicked her gaze to Felix and opened her mouth, but he had already worldwalked out.

"You always thought that you were stronger than me," Monette said. "But look at you now."

If you had melted an entire mountain yesterday after fighting nonstop for four days, and then battled an overwhelming army the entire day today before also being hit with Iwdael's powers without the ability to shield against them, and then been hit with your own emotion manipulation, then you would've been exhausted too and your magic would've been completely drained long ago.

The thought flashed through my head with acidic rage. I opened my mouth to tell her as much.

A gurgling gasp came from Monette's mouth.

I jerked back and blinked at the scene before me.

Felix had worldwalked to the spot right in front of Monette, and for a moment, all I could see was his back and his copper-colored hair. Then he drew his arm back.

Shock crackled through me as Felix pulled out the knife he had rammed into Monette's heart. She looked just as shocked as me. For a moment, only the noise of battle around us broke the stillness. Then Monette coughed. Blood splattered across Felix's freckled face. He only remained standing there, watching her, as she slumped down onto the grass while the life disappeared from her beautiful turquoise eyes.

"Felix," I pressed out, and struggled to my feet now that Monette's magic was gone.

He turned around. Blood still dripped from the knife that he had used to kill the person he had been in love with for years, but he had wiped every single emotion off his face when he met my gaze.

"Kenna," he said, and then his eyes flicked to Iwdael for a second. "Prince Iwdael. We're losing too much ground and too many people. You need to come with me."

Tears streamed down Iwdael's face as he looked up from where he was still cradling Reena's limp body. "I can't leave her."

"She's already dead," Felix said, his voice completely emotionless. "And so are a lot of other people. The rest of your court is going to follow them soon too if you don't come with me."

I studied the hard lines on Felix's face. Monette's blood was still splattered across it, mingling with the freckles, and his brown eyes were tired and distant.

Another wave of guilt washed over me.

This war had made us all grow up hard and fast.

Was it worth it?

Who was even supposed to answer that for everyone?

CHAPTER 39

"We won't be able to hold them off for much longer," Prince Edric said. "They keep pushing us towards the wall of molten stone, and once we're trapped against it with no chance to retreat, it's over."

"I agree," Prince Rayan said while sweeping worried eyes over all of us. "We need to save our people before that happens."

Clashing steel and wounded cries and screams of fury echoed through the air all around us. Edric was still keeping the shield up above our ranks while we conducted our emergency meeting in the middle of our soldiers.

"If we–" I began.

Theo and Valerie suddenly materialized on the grass next to Idra and Hadeon. A couple of strides away, Mordren and Eilan blinked at the two thieves while Prince Iwdael was still just staring unseeing towards the spot where Reena's body had been left. Ellyda had also retreated far into herself, but Vendir's eyes were sharp as he tracked the movements of the air serpents in the sky.

"What are you doing here?" Idra snapped. "I told you that—"

"We can help," Valerie interrupted. She swallowed before she and Theo raised their chins in unison. "We have full control of our powers now."

We all exchanged a look.

"Okay," Idra said with a slow nod.

"Alright, so what's the plan?" Edric grumbled as magical attacks pounded against his shield above our heads.

Hadeon blew out a long sigh and then straightened his spine. "We need to keep Anron focused on the twelve of us and buy the rest of our army time to escape."

"He's right," Mordren said. "Out of everyone on the battlefield, the twelve of us are the strongest."

"Anron also hates us the most," I added.

"That too. If we cluster together and provide him with a clear target, we should be able to draw him close to us while the rest of our army can escape."

"Our magic is mostly drained, though," Rayan said. "And we will need quite a lot of fighting power to hold the rest of his army back in the meantime."

"I have a way to get that for us," Prince Edric ground out between gritted teeth as lightning and fire slammed into his shield.

"Okay." Idra turned towards Felix, who had been standing by a short distance from us. "Get the worldwalkers ready. We're sounding the final retreat. Get organized in a long row at the back and worldwalk everyone out as fast as you can."

He nodded. "Got it."

While he worldwalked away, Mordren turned to meet each of our gazes in turn. "Everyone knows what to do?"

"Yes," we all replied.

"Then let's do it."

Idra and Hadeon began calling out orders for the rest of our army to retreat while I sucked in a deep breath and worldwalked to the front lines.

Rows upon rows of High Elves pushed closer across the grass.

"Mendar," I yelled up as a firebird shot past. "Cover the retreat and then get the hell out!"

The leader of the Poisonwood elves raised his hand in a salute. While his people reorganized their formation, I turned back to the battle ahead and called up a long wall of fire. The short meeting we'd been engaged in had allowed me to refill some of my draining power levels. It still wasn't nearly as full as I needed it to be, but it would have to do.

A wall of shadows appeared next to mine as Mordren materialized on the grass. And then one of water, signaling that Rayan and Idra had arrived. Then stone from Hadeon while Edric kept the magic shield up above us. Finally, a wall of wood rose from the ground as Iwdael channeled his grief into power. Lightning crackled along the arms of Eilan and Vendir as they got ready to target the Wielders who were gathering their forces on the other side. Valerie and Theo raised their hands as well, and brilliant light bloomed from their palms.

"El," Hadeon said, not taking his eyes off the enemies ahead. "Call it."

Ellyda nodded. Her sharp violet eyes swept across the battlefield, taking in every detail and processing it all faster than anyone should be able to.

Behind us, our army scrambled to hold the ranks steady while the worldwalkers got them out of there one row at a time, starting from the back. Only when the line behind them was gone were they supposed to take a step back so that the next row could take their places and be worldwalked out. Otherwise, Anron would back us too far against the wall of molten stone.

"Use everything you have left, because this is it," I said as all the Wielders formed up on a long line with Anron hovering behind them. "Every drop of magic. Every sneaky move. Because this is all that's left now. This is the last stand, the last fight, for our lands, our freedom, and for everyone we love."

Magic exploded against our shields. I gritted my teeth as water slammed into my fire, turning it into steam, before I raised another wall a second later. Crackling lightning tore through Mordren's shadows and fire surged up over Iwdael's tree barricade while more of it hit Rayan and Idra's water shields.

"Eilan, one o'clock," Ellyda said. "Theo, eleven."

Lightning shot from Eilan's arm and slammed into a Wielder that appeared above Hadeon's stone wall. At the same time, Theo shot a flash of blinding light at another High Elf who was trying to fly above Iwdael's shield. Yanking up an arm to cover his eyes, he dropped back down and out of sight. My chest heaved as I poured more power into my flames.

The ranks of soldiers behind us took a step back. We followed.

From his place in the air behind his Wielders, Anron watched us all with a wide grin on his face. He probably didn't even care that row after row of our soldiers were being worldwalked out. As long as he killed the twelve of us holding the front line, the soldiers who escaped today wouldn't be a problem because there would be no one left to lead them and challenge his godhood.

I staggered another step back as wind and water crashed into my fiery shield, sending steam and swirling embers through the air. Drawing in a ragged breath, I raised another wall of fire before the High Elves on the ground could sprint through.

Lightning and shadows rippled around me as Mordren and Eilan worked in tandem to stop the soldiers until the shadow shield could be patched up. Ellyda called out shots for Vendir, Valerie, and Theo while Edric blew out long breaths as he tried to hold off the barrage from above.

My whole soul trembled with exhaustion as I poured everything I had into keeping the fire shield up while we slowly retreated across the grass. The majority of our army was still here. I tried to blink my eyes back into focus as I raised my dark red flames over and over again. This would never work. We wouldn't be able to hold them off for much longer.

Hadeon's stone shield dropped at the same time as Idra's half of the water wall. A few seconds later, Prince Rayan's wave of water disappeared as well.

"Brace!" Ellyda snapped behind us.

Scraping the bottom of my magic well, I extended my wall to cover the area that Hadeon had left open. On my other side, Vendir heaved a bone-tired breath and threw up a shield that plugged the part where Idra and Rayan's walls had been. Sweat ran down Hadeon's face while Idra had to throw out an arm to steady Rayan as he almost fell over.

"Edric," Mordren pressed out. "If you have a way to increase our fighting power, now would be the time."

The Prince of Stone clenched his jaw as winds slammed into his magic shield. "How much of our army is still here?"

"A little less than a third," Ellyda answered immediately.

"Alright, then this should buy us just enough time." While continuing to hold up the shield, he flicked his gaze over us. "Channel part of your magic into your words."

"Our words?" Iwdael asked as he raised another wall of wood.

"Yes. Pour your power into your voice as you speak, and do what I do."

Broken bits of wood flew through the air as Iwdael's shield shattered. I tried to plug it up with my fire, but I couldn't muster enough strength to fill the whole thing. High Elves sprinted through the gap. Panic swirled in my chest as they thundered towards us.

"Edric," Mordren urged.

"Do what I do," he instructed. "Now!"

More soldiers poured through the gap. My heart pounded in my chest but I diverted some of my remaining power to my voice. The dark red flames thinned out and the shield shrank.

"I am Edric Mountaincleaver," the Prince of Stone began in a voice booming with power. "Son of Edran Stoneheart, son of Fedric Spellbreaker, son of Stenic Ironleg, son of Redran Mountainsinger…"

Magic pulsed around us and the air shimmered as Prince Edric continued reciting his lineage. After a quick glance at each other, the rest of us did the same.

I wasn't really anyone's daughter, but I poured power into my voice and spoke the name of my War Dancer father, and as much as I knew of his fathers.

My skin prickled and my hair stood on end as we called the names of our ancestors while the High Elves barreled towards us. The air shimmered and the whole area around us pulsed with magic.

The High Elves were so close that I could see the sweat

running down their necks. I kept chanting. Steel gleamed as they raised their swords. My heart slammed against my ribs as I braced for the strike.

Translucent people whooshed out from behind us and charged straight at the High Elves. I jerked back in shock, and the remnants of my fire shield fell completely as I stared in disbelief at the scene before me.

Elves flew across the grass, their feet barely touching the ground, as they blocked the strikes that had been coming for us while others continued towards the other High Elves and attacking them. Some of the elves wore armor. Some wore normal clothes. But all of them had a fluid form that was mostly see-through.

My mouth dropped open as my elven father in his War Dancer armor charged into the ranks of High Elves and cut them down with his twin swords.

These were… the spirits of our ancestors.

A figure with long white hair and brown eyes came to hover next to Prince Edric. Tears gleamed in Edric's eyes as he turned to look straight at the spirit beside him.

"My king," he said.

King Aldrich Spiritsinger smiled. "Edric."

"I'm sorry to disturb the resting dead, but we need to borrow your power this one time."

"Then you shall have it." King Aldrich moved to stand in front of Edric. Raising a translucent hand, he placed it against the prince's cheek. "You know, I don't think I ever got around to telling you this. I never had any sons by blood." His eyes glittered as he held Edric's gaze. "But I always thought of you as my son."

Prince Edric choked back a sob.

"I'm proud of you," Aldrich said. "Now rest a moment while we buy you some time."

Taking his hand from Edric's cheek, the late King of Elves drew a sword from his back and charged the ranks of High Elves.

I stared in utter disbelief as the spirits of our dead ancestors fought the High Elves on the blood-soaked grass.

"How is this possible?" I stammered.

"Our ancestors are always there, listening for our prayers on the other side," Prince Edric answered in a voice full of emotion. "But they can't cross over to this side. They don't have the power to speak to both worlds. All except one."

"Aldrich Spiritsinger," Rayan said, his voice brimming with awe and understanding.

"Exactly. King Aldrich has always been able to communicate with the spirits on the other side. Before he... died, he told me about this. With him acting as a conduit, the spirits of our ancestors can temporarily visit our side in times of great need."

Translucent elves disappeared into the air as they were struck by the High Elves' swords and magic.

"What happens to them when they get hit?" I asked.

"They just return to the land of the dead."

We all watched in wonder as the army of spirits slowed the High Elves down. They were still backing us towards the wall of molten stone, but with our ancestors fighting on our behalf, our troops received the time they needed to escape.

A hint of sadness blew through me as I watched a High Elf run a sword through the spirit of my father. His fluid form disappeared a moment later.

"My prince," a voice said from behind.

I turned to find Felix there.

"This is the last row," he said, his eyes flicking between the Prince of Stone and the army of the dead.

"Good," Edric answered. "Take them and get out. We can all worldwalk out on our own."

Bowing his head, the copper-haired spy turned and disappeared towards the final rank of soldiers. We had done it. We had gotten our people out.

"Mendar," I yelled up into the overcast sky. "Get out!"

Flames fluttered in the air as a mass of firebirds shot across the gray heavens, followed shortly by the sky whales. A small pile of pink clouds was briefly visible on top of one of the whales before it disappeared towards the horizon with the rest of its friends.

The army of spirits grew thinner as the High Elves coordinated their efforts and pushed us the final bit back towards the wall of melted stone. It cast a long shadow across the grass. Smaller stones that must have rained down from the curved top of it lay in a neat line across the grass.

I gasped as a sword slashed straight through King Aldrich. His form wobbled, and then he disappeared. The other spirits across the battlefield turned towards us.

A male and a female elf, both with dark hair, locked eyes with Mordren and Eilan. Another couple stared straight at Hadeon and Ellyda. Smiles shone on all of their faces as they inclined their heads.

Then they disappeared, as did all the other spirits.

With Aldrich gone, the link was severed.

We backed up farther as the High Elves closed ranks once more and advanced. Above them, Anron and his Wielders flew closer. The only ones who stayed rooted on the grass were Valerie and Theo. Light pulsed from their hands as they held them up in front of their chests.

"Well, it looks like everyone else has abandoned you," High Commander Anron said as he flew closer to the two thieves.

"Valerie," Eilan snapped. "Theo."

I turned and looked around us to make sure that all of our people truly had made it out. Then I called up my worldwalking powers. Nothing answered.

"Finding it difficult to worldwalk?" Anron said. A wicked smirk stretched his lips. "That's because I had someone ward the area right before that wall against worldwalking."

Shock clanged through me as the random blond elf I had seen in the king's castle when we broke in earlier stepped out from the ranks of advancing soldiers. So that was why Anron had kept him around.

My eyes shot to the neat row of stones. *Oh.*

"The stones, that's what marks the end of the wards," I snapped.

Anron and his Wielders surged forward.

"Valerie! Theo!" I called as we sprinted towards the row of stones.

Since they had refused to back up, they were the only ones still outside the wards. Worry pulsed on their faces as they swung around to face us.

"Go!" I screamed. "Now!"

Magic shot through the air. Theo and Valerie dove aside as lightning crackled through the space they had previously been occupying. At the same time, a torrent of wind slammed into us, blasting us back from the row of stones. Pain shot through my shoulder as I hit the grass. Pushing myself up on my elbows, I barely had time to see our two thieves roll to their feet and jump back as another lightning bolt zapped the grass next to them.

They looked back at us for a second.

Then they exchanged a glance and disappeared into thin air.

Sucking in a deep breath, I struggled to my feet and swept my gaze over the others. Rayan looked like he was about to pass out from exhaustion, and Iwdael and Vendir were no better. Eilan staggered a step to the side and Mordren had to throw out a hand to keep him from falling over.

"Edric," I said. "Can you still shield?"

"Myself? Maybe," he answered between heavy breaths. "All of you as well? No."

"Do what you can." I slid my gaze to the Prince of Shadows. "Mordren, you and I have the most power. We need to force their hand."

Mordren nodded at me. Exhaustion seemed to roll off our bodies as we moved to stand next to each other. Anron was still hovering in the air with his Wielders. I had no idea if this would work, but it was our only chance.

Raising our arms in front of us, we aimed straight at the flying High Elves.

Then we fired.

I forced out every drop of power I still had and shot roaring flames at Anron while Mordren did the same with his magic. Dark red flames mixed with sleek black tendrils, creating a storm of shadow fire that tore across the landscape.

Anron and his Wielders dropped down to the ground and raised layered walls of stone to block the attack. I poured more fire into it.

The stones melted underneath the heat of my flames while Mordren's shadows ripped through the holes. My heart pounded and my head swam but I kept adding more power. Stones continued melting.

Then Mordren's shadows disappeared in a flash and he crashed down on the grass next to me.

My flames burned through another layer of stone.

And then my well ran dry too.

I barely had time to catch myself as I collapsed to my knees next to Mordren, utterly spent. Eilan, Idra, Hadeon, Ellyda, Vendir, and the other princes stepped up beside us.

At last, the stone walls before us fell.

A malicious laugh echoed across the landscape.

"I don't understand how you suddenly became this powerful," High Commander Anron said as he strode forward unharmed. "Too bad it still isn't enough to compete with a Wielder of the Great Current."

"You are a disgrace to High Elves everywhere," Vendir snarled at his former High Commander.

"And you are still the weak little worm who almost drowned in White Water Bay."

The mass of bronze-clad soldiers swarmed in around us, sealing off our escape in every direction, while Anron and his Wielders stalked closer. I wanted to be standing up as I faced this, but I couldn't muster enough energy to move.

An arm appeared underneath mine. I looked over in surprise as Idra hoisted me to my feet and draped my arm over her shoulders to keep me steady. Next to me, Eilan did the same for Mordren.

A victorious grin slid across Anron's face as he came to a halt a short distance away. His Wielders fanned out on either side of him. Blood pounded in my ears.

"Look at you," the High Commander mocked. "Your army is scattered and everyone who poses a real threat is here, surrounded and outnumbered." Malice crept into his sharp blue eyes. "I gave you a chance to surrender. You refused. Now, you will die instead."

My heart pounded in my chest but I sucked in a rattling breath and summoned the last of my strength to raise my voice.

"Do you know what your problem is, Anron?" I called across the blackened grass. "You think that you're so high and mighty. That *Low* Elves are beneath you. That humans are beneath you. And that's why you were always doomed to lose this war."

"Lose?" High Commander Anron scoffed while spreading his arms to indicate the massive army that surrounded us. "I don't think you–"

A thin red line appeared across his throat.

CHAPTER 40

High Commander Anron stared at us in complete and utter shock as blood welled up from the gaping wound in his throat and ran down his skin. The Wielders around him jerked back and then whipped from side to side, trying to locate the threat while Anron crashed down on his knees. Outside the wards, the rest of his army shifted in confusion.

"When I told you that we had humans on our side," I called while Anron pressed a desperate hand to his throat in an effort to stop the blood, "you said something like, what are you going to do? Have them stand on each other's shoulders so that they can reach our throats to swing their tiny swords at us?"

Wet gurgling bubbled from his throat in response.

"That's exactly what we did," I finished.

The other Wielders had pulled back several steps, uncertainty swirling in their eyes as they looked between us and their dying commander. Apparently, they didn't love him enough to risk getting their own throats slashed as well. At least not when he was already beyond saving.

Anron coughed blood onto his chest.

A few steps in front of him, the air shimmered slightly.

Then a very tall figure became visible.

I couldn't stop the laugh that bubbled from my throat.

Valerie was standing on Theo's shoulders as their bodies came into view. Blood dripped from the dagger in Valerie's hand as she lowered her arm. She spun it once in her hand before jumping down from Theo's shoulders and landing gracefully on the ground.

Magic swirled around the Wielders' forearms as they yanked them up and pointed straight at the two thieves while confusion flashed on their faces. We were all still inside the wards. No one should have been able to just worldwalk in front of Anron like that.

And that was because no one had.

"Stand down!" Vendir bellowed across the battlefield.

Drawing himself up to his full height, he pulled authority around himself like a cloak and strode towards the Wielders.

Anron choked on his own blood. His spotless bronze armor clanked as he toppled to the side and hit the scorched grass.

A sharp smile spread across my lips as I watched the final shred of life leave his cruel blue eyes. "Checkmate."

"I used to be your captain," Vendir boomed across the stunned army. "That makes me the highest-ranking Wielder here. And I say, *stand down!*"

One of the Wielders let his magic disappear. The others flicked their eyes towards him. Then they followed. One after the other. Steel rang out as the soldiers outside the wards sheathed their swords as well.

"This mission is done," Vendir yelled. "Get your air serpents and fly back home to Valdanar."

When no one moved, he drew in a deep breath.

"Now!" A dark laugh escaped his throat. "Tell Emperor Lanseyo that Captain Vendir sends his regards. And his resignation."

Shrill whistles echoed across the landscape. A moment later, the air serpents who had retreated to the back once our army was gone reappeared and slammed down into the ground. Armor clanked and orders were called as the High Elves scrambled to get back up on their mounts.

While the High Elves hurried to leave our lands once and for all, Valerie and Theo strolled over with wide grins on their faces.

"Told you camouflage would be a really handy power to have," Valerie announced as they stopped before us.

Eilan raised his eyebrows. "You did a little more than camouflage yourselves. You turned completely invisible."

"Bah." She flapped her hand in the air and then elbowed Theo in the ribs. "We just bent the light around our bodies so that no one could see us."

"Yeah I'm pretty sure that's what turning invisible means, Val," Theo said while slapping her side in turn.

"Regardless," I said before she could counter. A tired smile played over my lips as I looked at the beaming thieves. "Well done, you two. I don't know what we would've done if you hadn't come up with this brilliant plan."

Valerie wiggled her eyebrows and then winked at me. "Told you I'm the boss. And the boss always has a plan."

I laughed. Yes, the boss always had a plan indeed. And Valerie seemed to never run out of them. When they had first gotten their light powers, neither Theo nor Valerie had been particularly impressed with what they could do. So their sneaky minds had started to turn the problem over in their heads. That's when Valerie had remembered how convenient Augustien's powers of camouflaging himself against trees had been, and that had birthed the idea that it might be possible to bend the light around their own bodies. They had practiced it every single day since then, and it wasn't until today, when we had that last desperate meeting, that they had finally been able to control it completely.

Amazement washed over me as I studied the two incredible humans, or maybe not-exactly-humans-anymore, who had just outsmarted a High Commander of a Flying Legion and Wielder of the Great Current.

And because they were humans, he had never seen it coming.

Idra suddenly eased out from underneath my arm, making me collapse to the ground again. She sent an apologetic look in my direction while sprinting across the grass.

The blond elf who had warded the area against worldwalking had been left behind by the High Elves, who now started disappearing up into the sky. He saw her coming, but he still didn't make it in time.

His lifeless body slumped to the ground a moment after Idra Souldrinker's palm had touched his fleeing back.

While Valerie and Theo continued to regale Prince Edric and Rayan with the tale of how exactly they had come up with the brilliant idea that had won this war, I just sat there on the grass and stared out at the bodies littering the battlefield.

As soon as Anron was dead, Iwdael had run out from the wards and worldwalked back to Reena's body. Even from this distance, I could hear his wails of pain as he cradled her in his lap and rocked back and forth.

Somewhere on the other side lay the body of Kael Sandscorcher, who had died saving my life.

And between them, far too many humans and elves.

Had it been worth it?

I guessed only each person could answer that for themselves.

I hadn't forced any of them to come. To fight. Every single person on this battlefield had willingly joined our army for a multitude of reasons. Some wanted their magic back. Some wanted the false gods gone. Some wanted to protect their loved ones. Some wanted to fight for the glory of their court and their prince. And others just wanted freedom.

So, had it been worth it?

They would all have to make that decision for themselves.

And for me?

Yes.

Protecting the people I loved, reclaiming the power I had fought and schemed for all my life, and making sure that I didn't become a slave once more under Anron's godlike rule.

Yes, it had all been worth it to me.

CHAPTER 41

A bright sun shone down on the landscape before us. It had been weeks since our last stand against Anron, and fall had drawn its colorful blanket over the fields and forests. My eyebrows rose as I stared at the changed view before us.

The broken remnants of the king's mountain, along with the melted wall I had created on one side of it, were gone. In their place were now only sweeping grasslands with a lush forest behind. And a castle.

Twisting spires and proud towers reached towards the heavens, and the whole structure gleamed like a pale jewel in the sunlight. What looked like beautiful gardens complete with trees and bushes colored yellow, orange, and red by the fall spread out around it. As I squinted, I swore I could see a glittering brook running through them as well.

"What is this place?" I asked.

Prince Iwdael answered with a mischievous smile. "Wait until you see the inside."

We worldwalked down to the edge of the gardens and then

walked the final bit towards the castle. Mordren and I studied the scenery as we strode along while Iwdael, Rayan, and Edric led the way.

Leaves rustled faintly around us in the gentle breeze, and birds chirped up on the branches as we followed the path set into the grass. The soft rippling of water filled the air when we passed the brook while moving towards the shining steps leading up to a pair of massive doors.

Prince Edric placed his palms on the doors and pushed them open.

Wonder and awe flowed through me as I crossed into the light and airy castle. Sunlight fell in through the tall windows and illuminated the high-ceilinged hallway we traversed.

"What happened to all the rubble that used to cover this whole area?" Mordren asked while his gaze glided over the shining hall.

The ghost of a smile drifted over Prince Edric's lips. "I'm not called Mountaincleaver for nothing, Mordren."

"This is beautiful," I said as the five of us came to a halt outside another set of closed doors. "Is it going to be the castle for the new King of Elves?"

"Yes," Prince Rayan answered. His purple eyes glittered like amethysts in the sunlight. "And no."

A frown creased my brows.

Edric, Rayan, and Iwdael exchanged a look before they all turned to face us.

"We've been discussing," the Prince of Stone said.

"And since there is no more shadow magic or fire magic until you die," Rayan picked up, "you will have to continue to rule your courts."

Mordren and I shared a brief glance.

"That was what we were planning to do," Mordren answered carefully.

Confusion swirled inside me. Where were they going with this?

"Yes, well..." Edric crossed his arms. "We still need someone to shoulder the responsibility of looking out for all our courts as a whole too. And like I said, we've been discussing."

Prince Rayan hooked his shining black hair behind his ear before giving us a small smile. "And because of the enormous sacrifices that you have made to protect our lands..."

"Freeing us from Anron," Iwdael added. "Going to Valdanar and almost dying at the hands of their emperor and empress just to make them forsake Anron. Acquiring allies from that Poisonwood place. Not to mention that no one in their right mind would ever want to go up against Kenna after watching her melt half a mountain with her powers."

"Yes alright, Iwdael, I think they get it." Prince Edric drew himself up to his full height and held our gazes. "Because of all that, we have decided that the two people we trust most with the safety and prosperity of our lands... are you."

My mouth dropped open. Next to me, Mordren was staring at them with raised eyebrows as well.

"You want us to...?" I began.

Before I could finish, Prince Edric turned around and pushed open the beautifully carved doors behind him.

A deafening cheer rose.

All I could do was stare at the majestic throne room beyond the doors. And the mass of people that filled it.

Rayan Floodbender placed a gentle hand on my back and pushed me towards it while Iwdael did the same to Mordren.

Stunned amazement still clanged inside me when

Mordren and I started down the path between the crowds of cheering elves and humans. Edric, Rayan, and Iwdael followed behind us.

It was like walking through a sea of glittering colors as the people in well-tailored clothes of every color and design shifted to watch us as we passed. Bright sunlight streamed in through the windows and cast glittering shapes on the tall walls. I swept my gaze over the gathered audience.

Edus Quickfeet inclined his head while Oturion Fortunebender waved enthusiastically from a short distance behind him. Brown eyes set into a bland face met me from the middle of the crowd. Liveria Inkweaver winked at me as if saying, *I told you that you wouldn't be needing a forger where you were heading.* I smiled and gave her a nod.

Standing close to the wall was a plump woman with graying hair. But the eyes behind her thick glasses were sharp and observant. A mysterious smile spread across Stella's mouth as she looked straight at me. I touched a hand to my forehead in salute.

The path ended before a raised dais with two equally grand thrones positioned atop it.

My heart fluttered in my chest. Trailing to a halt, I just stared up at them for a few seconds.

"You should see your faces right now."

Mordren and I whipped around to face the row at the very front of the crowd. Eilan flashed us a sly smile. Next to him were a whole group of people. Idra and Hadeon stood side by side with matching smirks on their faces while Valerie and Theo grinned from ear to ear. Ellyda, her eyes sharp and clear, watched us intently from next to Vendir. Standing proudly beside them were Mendar and Endira and some of the other elves from Poisonwood Forest.

And behind them were even more people I knew. Ymas and Viviane and Felix. Imelda and her daughter Rose. Herman from the White Cat Coffeehouse. Hilver and Nicholas from my own court. Even the Beaufort family was in attendance farther towards the back. They looked more nervous than anything, but Elvin gave me a nod in acknowledgement.

"You knew about this?" Mordren asked as he stared at his brother.

"Of course we did," he answered with a satisfied smirk.

Valerie wiggled her eyebrows. "Who do you think we are?"

On our other side, Rayan had sidled up next to Princess Lilane and wrapped an arm around her back. Her warm brown eyes sparkled as she leaned into him while smiling at me and Mordren. Iwdael smiled too as he entwined his fingers with Augustien's and pulled the golden-haired beauty closer.

Standing beside them, Prince Edric crossed his arms and nodded towards the two thrones. "Go on then."

Mordren and I turned to look at each other. Then a sly smile spread across his lips as he held out an arm, motioning for me to start walking. Blowing out a deep breath, I took the first step.

My heart hammered in my chest as Mordren and I walked side by side up the steps towards the thrones. A hush fell over the high-ceilinged hall.

"Are you ready for this?" Mordren whispered.

I paused briefly as we reached the top. With my back still towards the crowd, I stared at the magnificent thrones before us. Giddiness sparkled in my soul.

"Yes," I answered. "I think I've been ready for this my whole life."

As one, we turned around.

For a moment, the gathered elves and humans only looked up at us in silence. Jewelry glittered in the sunlight from the windows, and colorful dresses and suits rustled faintly as every person in the room bowed before us.

I almost gasped at the sight of it. Absolute power, and a sense of rightness, pulsed through my whole body as I drank in this incredible moment that I never in my wildest dreams would have thought could be possible.

"Long live Kenna Firesoul, the Queen of Elves!" Prince Edric Mountaincleaver called as they all straightened again. "Long live Mordren Darkbringer, the King of Elves!"

The words echoed throughout the whole throne room as the elves and humans before us called them out as well.

Mordren laced his fingers through mine. Standing side by side, we gazed out across the throne room and then hoisted our joined hands into the air.

A deafening cheer rang through the whole castle.

I smiled at them.

Yes, I was definitely ready for this.

CHAPTER 42

Fire crackled in the hearth. The scent of garlic and fried mushrooms, along with grilled meat and thyme, hung over the cozy dining room. Outside, golden light from the afternoon sun painted gilded highlights across the orange and red trees. It fell in through the tall windows and mingled with the light from the fireplace to fill the whole room with a warm glow.

Raising the glass to my lips, I leaned back against the comfortable couch and drank a sip of rich red wine. Mordren draped his arm over my shoulders and pulled me closer to him. For a long while, we just sat there next to each other in silence, sharing each other's warmth and savoring this moment.

On the couch opposite us, Valerie was leaning her back against the armrest while her legs rested across Eilan's lap where he sat beside her. Valerie's own lap was already taken. A big pile of fluffy pink clouds nestled deeper against her as she ran her hand over their soft forms. She laughed as one of the clouds started jumping up and down on her legs while letting out excited squeaks.

Raising a hand, she brushed her fingers over Eilan's cheek before hooking his long black hair behind his ear. His pale green eyes were brimming with love as he watched her pick up the excited pink cloud and place it on his shoulder. It snuggled up against his neck and let out a satisfied purr.

From his place at the other end of the couch, Theo chuckled and shook his head at them. The midnight fox that had curled up next to him woke up from the sound and turned its head to nudge Theo's hand with its nose. A contented smile spread across Theo's lips as he stroked a hand over its dark blue and silver-glittering fur.

A pair of firebirds flew past the window, adding even more orange and red light to the sunset. Orma, Vendir's air serpent, followed after them. Vendir's kind brown eyes tracked them across the sky before he shifted his gaze back to the bowls of paint before him. Dipping his brush into one of them, he added more color to the forest scene that was slowly coming to life on his canvas. I smiled as Ellyda drifted over to him with some kind of device in her hands. Turning it over, she showed Vendir the strange contraption that would help him hold the containers of paint in a better position so that they were easier to reach. His eyes lit up as he watched her explain the mechanics behind it.

Across the room, on the other side of the dining room table now full of empty plates, were Idra and Hadeon. There was a smirk on Idra's face as she demonstrated some kind of acrobatic move that Hadeon still wasn't able to replicate. He tried again, but only succeeded in sending a bowl of pears bouncing across the floor. Amusement tugged at Idra's lips as she raised her eyebrows in smug challenge. Throwing his arms out, Hadeon started up a lengthy explanation of all the moves that he could do that she still hadn't mastered.

A surprised laugh bubbled from my throat as she silenced him by pushing him up against the wall and kissing him senseless.

Yellow, orange, and red leaves fluttered slightly, glimmering like gems in the light from the sunset, as a gentle breeze blew through the gardens of the castle. The castle that we now all shared together. Our home.

Mordren pulled me closer to him. His firm body was warm and steady against mine as I leaned into his embrace and rested my cheek on his shoulder. Glancing up, I found him smiling down at me. In the warm glow from the fire, his silver eyes glittered like liquid starlight. Love and gratitude and sparkling joy filled my soul as he leaned down and brushed a gentle kiss on my lips.

While leaning against him, I swept my gaze over the rest of our family.

At last, we had the life that we had fought so desperately for.

We were here. Safe. Together.

I let out a long breath.

A smile spread across my lips.

Now there was only one thing left to do.

Live.

ACKNOWLEDGMENTS

Well, here we are at the end of another long series. When I finished my last series, I told you that saying goodbye has always been hard for me. So, was it easier this time around? No. Kenna and Mordren and all the others have seen me through a lot this past year while I wrote this series, and I will miss them terribly. But just like I said at the end of *A Storm of Light and Darkness*, what comforts me when I have to say goodbye to characters that I love with all my heart, is that they will continue to live on. Even though I'm not writing about it, their lives continue. Just off page. And that makes me really happy.

As always, I would like to start by saying a huge thank you to my family and loved ones. Mom, Dad, Mark, thank you for the enthusiasm, love, and encouragement. I truly don't know what I would do without you. It means the world to know that I always have you in my corner.

Lasse, Ann, Karolina, Axel, Martina, thank you for continuing to take such an interest in my books. It truly warms my heart.

To Oskar Fransson. Thank you for keeping me sane when things around us get too crazy. And thank you for keeping me crazy when I run the risk of becoming too boring. I look forward to all our adventures to come.

Another group of people I would like to once again express my gratitude to is my wonderful team of beta readers who have been with me throughout this whole series: Alethea Graham, Deshaun Hershel, Luna Lucia Lawson, and Orsika Péter. Thank you for the time and effort you put into reading the book and providing helpful feedback. Your suggestions and encouragement truly make the book better.

To Faye Ostryzniuk, Laura Bartlett, and Jayse Smith. Thank you so much for your continued support and for being the amazingly kind people that you are. Chatting with you always makes me happy.

To Lotte Hoes. Thank you for everything you do for me and my books. You are a true creative soul and I can't believe how lucky I am that we've connected.

To Jennifer Davis. Thank you for your always so incredibly kind words. Receiving your emails and hearing your thoughts on each new book makes my day every time, and your amazing encouragement has gotten me through many moments of doubt.

To Rachel Sullivan. Thank you for your incredible support throughout this whole series and for everything you have done to help spread the word about my books. It truly means the world.

To Mandie Sagen. Thank you for always being there to cheer me on and for everything you do to support me and help me. It always warms my heart.

To Catherine Bowser. Thank you for still being here after all fourteen of my books. You have truly been with me from the beginning and I'm so grateful for all your support.

And of course, to my amazing copy editor and proofreader Julia Gibbs, thank you for all the hard work you always put into making my books shine. Your language expertise and attention to detail is fantastic and makes me feel confident that I'm publishing the very best version of my books.

I am also very fortunate to have friends both close by and from all around the world. My friends, thank you for everything you've shared with me. Thank you for the laughs, the tears, the deep discussions, and the unforgettable memories. My life is a lot richer with you in it.

And lastly, thank you, all of you amazing readers who have followed me on yet another adventure. I hope that you enjoyed Kenna's journey and that you are happy with how it ended. I know I am. And I hope that you will join me on many more adventures to come!

As always, if you have any questions or comments about the book, I would love to hear from you. You can find all the different ways of contacting me on my website, www.marionblackwood.com. There you can also sign up for my newsletter to receive updates about coming books. Lastly, if you liked this book and want to help me out so that I can continue writing, please consider leaving a review. It really does help tremendously. I hope you enjoyed the adventure!

Printed in Dunstable, United Kingdom